Winds of the Day

Winds of the Day

a novel by

HOWARD SPRING

Harper & Row, Publishers
New York and Evanston

For Flo Fallas

Chapter I

The first real day of my life was when I banged the front door. That was when I made a decision for myself. Until then, all the decisions for me had been made by other people. I shall always remember the bang. It was then that I threw myself upon the winds of the day, to let them bear me where they liked. This book is the story of how they bore me.

I was born in Manchester and my name was Alice Openshaw. That is a common enough name in the North, and it happened that the place I was born in was Openshaw, too. If you don't know Openshaw, which is a suburb of Manchester, you are none the worse off. It isn't—or wasn't then—a place to know. It may now be a paradise. Then it was hell. It was to me, anyhow. One mean street after another, and most of them like the rest. Two up and two down, with a scullery thrown in. There may have been better houses in Openshaw, but I never knew them.

My mother was a country-woman, and I don't know how she put up with the place. I suppose she had to, and that was all about it. She was born in Cheshire, which has plenty of small meres and fields and trees and birds. It was among such things that her life began. She was an orphan, illegitimate probably, and she was brought up in a workhouse school. She used to talk to me without reserve of those days, and on the whole her life was happy. She was red-headed, as I am. She had not been taught much except to read, write and do a bit of addition. As soon as she was old enough, they put her out to service. She was lucky in her place, with a Cheshire farmer who had recently been married to an illiterate girl. He was a good-natured man and his wife took a great fancy to my mother. The small child used to read to her in the evenings, such things as pleased her, which were mainly the stories—" to be continued in our next "—that

5

appeared in her weekly religious paper. My mother also wrote letters for her occasionally, and altogether was soon one of the family rather than a maid-servant.

Growing up in the country air and fed on country food, the child developed into a startlingly good-looking young woman, one moreover who could imagine no existence but this, which was of happiness and kindliness. She had reached the age of twenty when her mistress met a sudden death, gored by a bull that had just been bought. That was the end of all happiness for Mother.

It was at the beginning of winter, and in the spring-time the farmer married again. He had taken, like his dead wife, to treating my mother as one of the family, but this didn't suit the woman he had married now. For one thing, she was literate. She could read her own papers and write her own letters, and my mother was nothing but a servant in the household. As if this were not enough, the woman was intensely jealous, and resented the presence in the house of a growing girl who was better-looking than she was herself. Consequently, there was row upon row, and as the summer wore on the situation became impossible, and my mother handed in her notice.

It happened that, for some years past, the farmer had lent one of his fields for the annual jamboree of an Openshaw firm of engineers, and my mother gave a hand at making the outing a success. The men brought their wives and children, and mother helped with the tea and even took part in the races and things of that sort. It was thus that she met my father. The day was gloriously fine, just as May was merging into June, and the hedgerows were brimming over with blossom. Hawthorn bloomed on the bushes and the ditches were full of bluebells and campion and foxgloves. The sky was blue, and young John Openshaw, who was a packer for the firm, must have felt on top of the world. So did my mother, who was about his own age. She was looking forward to her release, for things with the new mistress had reached an impossible pass.

John Openshaw was not bad-looking, and he had put on his best clothes and his best manners. I don't know what a packer earned, but it was enough, in those days, to allow Father to spread himself a bit, for he had no relations to think of. He spent what he earned. They were tied, ankle to ankle, in a three-legged-race for men and women, and I suppose that was the beginning of it. They were tied ankle to ankle for the rest of his life.

I need not go into all that. Before the summer was ended they were married, and the green fields, the trees and flowers of Cheshire were exchanged for the two-up and two-down of Openshaw. What was enough for one barely sufficed for two, and when I was added to the household it was a tight pinch indeed.

For my father was a man utterly without ambition or even a common urge to see those dependent on him provided for decently. He remained an underling and had no wish to be anything else. Or no will, or no whatever it is that takes men to the top, or at any rate a bit farther from the bottom.

The first thing I remember about him is a row that he and my mother had about, of all things, a black tie. The Queen had died. The works closed on the day of the funeral, and my father wore the black tie. I had just begun to go to a board school, so I suppose I was five years old. I wore boots, not shoes. I had worn them for some time and they had become nothing to write home about. You could buy a pair of boots of a sort, in those days, for half-a-crown, and my mother asked, calmly enough, why father had bought the tie. He said : " To show respect for the Queen," and my mother then wanted to know why he should respect a Queen who was dead rather than his daughter who was alive and kicking. That started her off, and she could go once she was started. Her red hair and her grey-green eyes—and I have inherited both her hair and her eyes—flashed with fury. My father could not stand up to her. He fell back on his usual tactics. He sulked. And presently he went out of the house and, the works being closed for the day, he walked the streets till evening.

What I chiefly remember about him is that he was dull, dull, dull. Every night he would come home dutifully from the works, wash himself, and eat his meal. Then he would take himself off to the public house that was not far away, and he would make a pint of beer last him all the evening. He never came home drunk or the worse for liquor. There was not even that excitement. He would come home duller than he had set out, remain seated, without a word, dully in his chair in the kitchen, and then announce that he was tired and must go to bed. He never read, he never talked. He was just a cloud over our lives. He never broke and stormed.

I was ten when he died. I remember how he came home one bitter winter night, ate his meal as usual, and then said that he would not be going to the pub. He sat close to the kitchen fire, smoking his pipe and, now and then, coughing. Presently, he announced that he would go to bed. Mother could see that he was ill and did everything possible for him. I was instructed to warm a brick and wrap it in a piece of old blanket, which was, in those days, a substitute for a hot-water-bottle. When I took it up to the bedroom she was rubbing his chest with camphorated oil. The wrapped brick was placed at his feet, and soon he was in an uneasy doze. He remained like that, not uttering a word, during the next day, and it was not till the evening of the second day that I was sent for the doctor. It was then too late for anything to be done about him, even if there had been a chance from the start, for nothing was known about the drugs we have for pneumonia in these days. Needless to say, he left not a penny, and there we were, subsisting as best we could in a world not noticeably kind to the poor.

2

There appeared in our window two printed cards. One announced:
Washing, Mangling
and Ironing done
here,
and the other said simply :
Lodgings
No one wanted lodging with us. There wasn't a lodger in all my time in the small house, but we got on somehow with the washing and mangling. " Somehow " became the dominant word in our lives. I don't know how my mother managed, but manage she did. She just kept us alive. The odd thing is that we were happier now. Mother, as I have said, was literate, and many an evening we spent sitting by the kitchen fire with her

reading to me and talking about her old days on the farm. We had no recreations. Going to a theatre was out of the question, and the homes of the poor had not yet been invaded by radio or television. We just sat and talked and read, and we were happy with one another. We had nothing to do with our neighbours. I had a job. In a street not far from ours, where the houses were a little better, and even had " front gardens " where a few wilted plants threw up their leaves, there was a place where the "Lodgings" notice had been more successful than with us. The widow who lived here had three lodgers—a father and two sons—who had some sort of job in the central post office of Manchester. They had to be off early, and I had to see that their boots were cleaned and their breakfast prepared. I liked the three of them. They were jovial people who called me Carrots, and I didn't mind, and, because I liked them, I polished their boots to within an inch of their lives. When they had set off for the City I was given my breakfast and then ran off to school. The breakfast was my only pay, but no one had any objection to that, least of all I, for it was a better breakfast than I would have got at home—fried eggs and bacon as a rule.

On Saturdays, in the summer when our street became unbearably hot, my mother would occasionally—very occasionally for the money didn't run to it—take me off into Cheshire and show me something of the parts she had been brought up in. They remain in my memory, those days : the coots on the meres, the buttercups and daisies, the wide sweep of a place without walls, the sunshine, the trees. One day my mother stopped for a long time leaning over a gate, looking at a field that was not yet mown; and suddenly she said to me : " That is the field where I first met your father." I looked at the field, full of butterflies, and at the cosy red house beyond it to which she had gone as a girl, and at the blue arching over all, and I thought of our street where never a flower grew or a butterfly was seen, and where the very sky, so hot it could become, was a menace, and I began to cry. To do so was so unlike me, for I was a young stoic, bred by her to be one, that she threw her arms around me and cried, too ; and there we stood, leaning on a five-barred gate, crying our hearts out. We had plenty to cry about, but we hadn't done so till then. I suppose the unusualness of the occasion set us off.

However, we soon recovered, and I remember how we arrived home that day, hot, sun-burned, with a bundle of wilting blue-bells and campion in our hands.

3

My mother died soon after I had finished at school. I was twelve years old, and I had no friend save the good Mrs. Morrison for whom I was still working in my morning hours. I suppose she took pity on me. In any case she suggested that I should become her general servant. I did so chiefly because I had no option, but also because I knew she liked me. So I shifted my few possessions and took my place in her household. It was more cheerful than my own home had been in my father's time. Mr. Montgomery of the post office and his two sons were still there, and, when they were all about the house, they were full of quips and light-hearted conversation. Mrs. Morrison was a Cardiff woman who had married a Manchester man. He had died leaving her with no children but with this house which he had bought outright. Her own resourcefulness did the rest. She would have returned to Cardiff, but she was, as she put it, " comfortable enough ". In the time that followed, she never tired of talking to me about Cardiff, so that it became to me an enchanted city, seen through her eyes, with the cock-horse who was always ready to help the bus up the hill by Llandaff Fields, and the peacocks that screamed from the Marquis of Bute's castle, right in the middle of the town, and the sun going down behind the Garth mountain that you could see from the bridge over the Taff. And you didn't have to wash your curtains every week, as you did in Manchester. So she would run on, but she was " comfortable enough ", so that I lived in one city but always in my imagination was a citizen of another.

I stayed with Mrs. Morrison till I was fifteen years old. Then things changed with a startling suddenness. Both the sons of Mr. Montgomery married and went to live elsewhere. Instead of taking them off to the theatre or some other diversion at night, or simply staying to talk to them in their own rooms, the old man—he seemed old to me, though, I believe, he was only in his fifties—began to share our evenings in the kitchen, where Mrs.

Morrison had always treated me as one of the family. It didn't take me long to guess what was in the wind, and I think I was the least surprised of the three when Mr. Montgomery told me that he and Mrs. Morrison were to be married. " It needn't make any difference to you, Carrots," he explained. " You can stay with us as long as you like."

But I didn't like it at all. I knew that henceforth the kitchen would be a lonely place for me, while Mr. and Mrs. Montgomery would, in every sense of the word, move into the parlour. During the next few days I thought more and more of my dream city, where the curtains needn't be washed every week, and privily I took steps to get there.

Mrs. Morrison had kept a tenuous hold on Cardiff by having a Cardiff newspaper sent to her regularly ; and it was in those columns that I read of the " place " in Cathedral Road. I had heard of Cathedral Road from Mrs. Morrison. It was one of the most desirable streets in the town and ran straight to the Llandaff Fields, with the Llandaff Cathedral beyond them. My dreams came alight. I wrote for the place, and received an answer from a Mrs. Lilywhite, who told me that they were five in family, that there was a " housekeeper kept ", and that my position would be that of " general ". Ready now to jump into any breach, I asked Mrs. Morrison to write me a " reference ", which she sorrowfully but faithfully did. I think she was truly reluctant to part with me, but part with me she must. I was all agog for adventure, bought a tin trunk, stowed my few goods, and left her. I never saw her again, and hope that in her second marriage she was " comfortable enough ". But other thoughts, beside that of comfort, were beginning to stir in me, and I set off for Cardiff with a high expectant heart.

4

I took a cab from Cardiff station and arrived in the dim of a winter evening. Boldly I walked up the fairly long path that led to the front door, and boldly rang the bell. Mrs. Gregson, the housekeeper, opened the door and had me and my tin trunk weighed up in a moment. " Oh, it's You," she said. " I thought it was Callers. Take your trunk round the side of the house.

You'll find the kitchen door there." And she shut the front door in my face.

It was my first lesson in " keeping my place ". From that earliest moment I learned to hate the front door and all that it meant of social distinction. Not once in the time that I spent with the Lilywhites did I enter the house through the front door, but, as you will learn, I left by the door in the long run.

However, that was for the future. Now, though with a seething heart, I took up my trunk and lugged it round the side of the house. I found the door reserved for servants and trades-men, and Mrs. Gregson was there waiting for me. " You'd better bring that up to your room," she said. " Mrs. Lilywhite will see you later."

A word about Mrs. Gregson, who, in all the time that I was in the house, never called me anything but You. She considered herself born to stand between me and the Family. The Family was always her word for the Lilywhites. She had joined the Family soon after Mr. and Mrs. Lilywhite were married, and had been nursemaid to the three children. She had been every-thing in her time, and was now, officially, the Housekeeper. She was an old withered thing, with a great sense of her grandeur where servants were concerned and with a great sense of reverence where any member of the Family was concerned. This was especially so with Mrs. Lilywhite, for she was a peer's daughter, and though the peer was only an old dodderer, a baron who had been rewarded with the title for " political services ", she liked all her letters to be addressed to the Honourable Mrs. Lilywhite. Mr. Lilywhite was a ship-owner and colliery-owner, and his son Ronald was a not bad-looking youth, about a year older than I was. There were also in the Family Miss Betty and Miss Hetty, twins about twenty years old, who never did a hand's turn—their mother would have been horrified if they had sug-gested it, and they were far from suggesting it—and who seemed to spend most of their time in the drawing-room, playing the piano. As I got to know the Family better, it was Mr. Lilywhite that I liked best of all. He had begun with nothing, he still worked hard, and he despised Mrs. Lilywhite's father, Lord Llanelly, whom he could have bought out several times without noticing it. But I fear that the ability to " buy out " was his standard of judgment in everything. You had to watch your step with Mr. Lilywhite.

This, then, was the Family into which old Mrs. Gregson had wormed her way and on which she doted after her fashion. She was called the Housekeeper, I suppose, because the Hon. Mrs. Lilywhite thought that her household should be presided over by a Housekeeper, but she was, in fact, the cook who prepared all the meals. I did just about everything else. To her, as I have said, I was always You; to all other members of the Family I was Openshaw. There was no other servant in the house.

On that first night Mrs. Gregson led me to an attic and told me to dump my trunk there. " This is your bedroom," she said, and left me to unpack. " Come down to the kitchen when you are ready."

It was a small room with a sloping ceiling in which was a fanlight. When I was alone, I pulled out the only chair in the room, a cane-bottomed thing, with the cane already sprouting hairs, and pushed up the window. The prospect was not bad. I could see a tree or two, a thing I had never seen in Openshaw, and that, in itself, gave my heart a rise. When I descended from the chair, the room seemed not so good. It was floored with cold linoleum and the bed was of the truckle sort. I had had a better one with Mrs. Morrison. There was a varnished dressing-table on which stood a swinging mirror that was kept steady by a wad of brown paper. There was a hook or two behind the door, and that was all. For the first time in my life I felt lonely. Always till then I had had someone to talk to, someone to cry or laugh with, my mother or Mrs. Morrison, or Mr. Montgomery or one of his sons. Perhaps the loneliness was the worst thing of all. I was miles from what I knew, among strangers, and I had not been kindly received. But I could stick it. I slowly transferred my few things to the drawers of the dressing-table, and went down to meet Mrs. Gregson in the kitchen.

In these days, when you can't get a servant without all sorts of concessions, it is hard to believe that such conditions existed so short a time ago. But those were the conditions in many a house in the years just before the first World War. They were my conditions anyway. Employers were cutting their own throats right and left. I worked from morning to night. I was up at seven and was lucky to be in bed at ten or eleven. I got one evening a week to myself, with five shillings a week for wages. And there was the cap.

"Have you brought your own cap?" asked Mrs. Gregson as soon as I rejoined her in the kitchen. I hadn't. I had not thought of a cap. I had never worn one. Mrs. Gregson was horrified. "But you'll be *expected* to wear a cap!" she exclaimed. And the next day I was given time off to buy a cap. Indeed I bought two, so that I always had one to wear when the other was "in the wash". And very pretty they looked, with their ribbon and goffering; but I hated them all the same. As with many another in a position like mine, they were a badge of servitude.

5

I detested the Honourable Mrs. Lilywhite from the first. For one thing, she wore slung round her neck a lorgnette, a thing I had never seen before, and through this she used to regard me as though I were a small insect. She had little to say, leaving all to "the Housekeeper". The Young Ladies I can pass over in a word. They were for ever on my tail to do things for them that they could well do for themselves, and were a perfect nuisance by day and night simply because their Honourable mother thought it was "beneath them" to do any sort of work whatever.

Mr. Lilywhite I saw rarely, for he was away to his business early in the morning and was apt to shut himself up in a room called his "office" at nights. But Mr. Ronald I saw a great deal.

I was taking my first "night off" in Cardiff, and wondered where to go. I had seen nothing of the city, and walked down Cathedral Road asking what to do with myself when, just where the road met the one which runs right through the town, I saw Mr. Ronald. He had now and then given me a smile and a cheerful word and I felt better disposed to him than to any other member of the Family. I stopped, pleased to see someone I knew, and I said "Hallo!" just as if he had not been one of the Family, and my heart bounded with delight when he said "Hallo, Ginger, where're you off to?"

I replied by asking him the same question, and he answered :
" I thought of looking in at the first house of the Empire. What
about you going too ? "

We went to the Empire together, and very wonderful it was
to me who had not been in a place of entertainment in my life.
I remember that Marie Lloyd was on the bill, and I blushed at
some of her sallies and songs, but I blushed still more when
I was aware that Mr. Ronald was making an effort to hold my
hand and was pressing his foot close against mine. I avoided
his hand and shifted my foot, and what with the excitement of
the usual entertainment and Mr. Ronald's restiveness through it
all, I was in a dither when the " first house " ended and we
went out into Queen Street. There I made my excuses and said
I must get back quickly, and, without any further words to Mr.
Ronald, I left him standing and returned to the house in Cathedral
Road. There, although it was my " night off ", I found that
I had all the dinner things to wash up before I could go to bed.
It was a task beneath the dignity of a Housekeeper.

In the months that followed, I learned a lot about Mr. Ronald.
He was his mother's darling and his father's despair. Chief
among their many matters of dispute was that Ronald had not
been to a public school. This, at the least, Mrs. Lilywhite
thought, was due to the grandson of a peer and the son of an
Honourable. She knew that Ronald was turning into a regular
little rascal, and that he was denied a public school now, with
Oxford or Cambridge to follow, was, in her opinion, what was
wrong with him. Mr. Lilywhite was of another opinion. He had
picked up his education, such as it was, as he made his way
through life, and thought Ronald was lucky to have been at a day
secondary school and to be now attending classes at the Technical
School in the evenings. After all, a man with an education like
his own could buy out Lord Llanelly any day ; and Lord Llanelly,
come to that, had never himself been either to a public school or to
a university. When the boy had finished with his evening classes
he could come into his father's office, and what more education
anyone wanted than that Mr. Lilywhite was damned if he
knew.

So their conversation would go when I was clearing away
breakfast or dinner, for I was a cipher, a nothing, who didn't

know what they were talking about. I was the "general" with my cap perched on the side of my head.

But I knew more about Ronald than either of them. I didn't for a moment doubt that he was a young rascal, but he had a friendliness that no one else in that house had. I alone knew that Ronald looked into his evening classes when he felt like it, and that, for the rest, the Empire and the Cardiff swimming baths were his favourite places of resort. We had taken to strolling the streets together as that winter passed over, and many a time I had to avoid his hands, or even slap his face, when he tried to be too free with me. But he remained good-tempered, and he was friendly and called me Ginger, which was a change after being to everyone else Openshaw or You. It at least recognised that I was a human being with characteristics of my own.

Winter was beginning when I went to the Lilywhites' house and ended when I left it. A daffodil or two had appeared in the front garden and there were snowdrops under the front hedge. I suppose it was this that had me humming at seven in the morning. My earliest duty was to polish the brasswork on the sacred front door. It was the only time I was allowed to pass through it. But I had to pull back the chain, unfasten the lock, and take my basket of metal-polish and rags through it and give it my ministrations. When this was done, I had to go to the kitchen, wash my hands at the sink, and then lay the breakfast-things. I was outside the door, polishing as lustily as a groom ever polished a race-horse, hissing through my teeth. Suddenly the daffodils, the snowdrops, and the sky's promise of a good day were too much for me, and I began humming. I suppose I hummed loudly, and certainly that day there was something to hum about, for you could smell the spring in the air, you could forget the Lilywhites, and you could let yourself go. I was humming a hymn, too, a thing I had learned as a child in Sunday school—" for the beauty of the skies ".

Suddenly, the best bedroom window, right over my head, was thrown up. Mrs. Lilywhite stuck her head through and cried: " Openshaw, don't hum," and the window banged shut again.

I had been so happy. Perhaps it was the happiest morning I had known in Cardiff, with the sun rising and the spring flowers beginning to bloom. And that odious woman brought it all crashing about me. I packed my polishing rags, left the brass unfinished, and went into the house. Well, I was furiously thinking, if a girl can't even hum! Furiously, too, I washed my hands at the kitchen sink, stuck my cap on to my head, and began to lay the breakfast things. It was while I was doing this that I thought: " Well, why on earth do you put up with it? Bigger fool you. Walk out on the lot of them." And I resolved to do so that very night. By the front door, too.

6

It was the night of the conversazione. At least that is what Mrs. Lilywhite called it. A week before this, Mr. Lilywhite had said : " It's about time we asked a few people in for a smoke and a talk," to which Mrs. Lilywhite replied : " I suppose you mean a conversazione ? " But it didn't turn out to be anything so grand or gay. Mrs. Lilywhite, as the daughter of a peer, was a very haughty woman, to her neighbours as to everyone else. No one liked her much ; there were all sorts of reasons for turning her invitation down ; and old Gregson told me, as the night drew near, that there was to be, after all, a simple dinner party and that those present would be the Rev. Mr. Conybeare with his wife and his son Melvill, who was always called Mr. Mell.

A few words will have to be said here about Mr. Conybeare and his family. He was the superintendent minister of the Wesleyan circuit which included the church the Lilywhites attended. Although his house could be reached by a five-minutes' walk from the Lilywhites', there was no to-and-froing between the families, but Mr. Conybeare kept on reasonably good terms, for, like a sane man, he was aware of the value of a wealthy member of the congregation. I suppose that roughly describes the relationship in which the two families stood. They occasionally dined together. Mr. and Mrs. Conybeare were there soon after I arrived in Cardiff, but Mr. Mell was not with them because he was at Oxford, an undergraduate. However, he was at home now because he had been ill and was recovering after a long rest with his parents.

The only other thing I need say about Mr. Conybeare is that he had two sisters who were much younger than himself. When he was ten years old, and there had been no sign of further children for so long as to persuade his parents that they had been more lucky than most, these two girls were born, twins. These aunts of Mr. Mell were now in their middle thirties, while his father was heading for fifty. One of them was married to Bryan Graves, a Member of Parliament, and the other to Frank Melvill, the novelist. It was after him that Mr. Mell was named. So what the conversazione boiled down to in the long run was that Mell was coming to dinner, with his father and rather negligible mother.

7

It was a hard-driven day, for Mrs. Gregson was cooking this and that from soon after breakfast, and I had to be instructed, too, in my duties as waiter-on at table. Normally, the Lilywhites just helped themselves, but this day I was to do the job. Mrs. Lilywhite insisted that it was necessary to her grand evening. So I was to wear a coffee-brown frock as well as my cap, and to learn which side to serve from, how to pour out wine, and goodness knows what. I learned it in no time at all : there was nothing to it ; but Mrs. Gregson and Mrs. Lilywhite were very keen, and I had to do everything again and again.

I knew a good deal by this time about the wonderful evening. After the meal, there would be an interval during which the gentlemen " sat over their port " while the ladies withdrew, and then all would gather in the drawing-room and the Young Ladies would sing. If things turned out as well as expected Mr. Mell would sing too. I even knew the songs the Young Ladies would sing because, goodness knows, they had practised enough. There was one that Miss Betty would delight us with, ending upon a high quavering note. I had made up my mind that this should be my signal for departing through the front door. Theoretically, I should be in the kitchen then, washing up the pile of dinner things. My instructions were clear enough. I was to whip off my nice waiting-at-table dress, change into my old things, and get on with the job.

All this made me hot under the collar. If the Lilywhites wanted a parlour-maid why didn't they employ one? Why should I do the job? Why couldn't they carry on as they did on any other day of the week? My determination to go became firmer, and there was no difficulty at all in packing my tin trunk and hiding it in the hedge near the front gate. That once done, I was ready for my grand exit, but I had no idea where I was to run. However, there had already been chops and changes enough in my short life, and I had no doubt that I would surmount that difficulty, too. I was sick of being told to do this and do that, to put on this cap, to wear that dress, to be a parlour-maid one minute and a general skivvy the next. I had had enough of it.

The evening came. I was pleased to see that though Mr. Lilywhite and Ronald had changed into dress clothes, Mr. Mell had not, and a parson, I suppose, can wear the same clothes any time. Also, as I got through the service, I noticed that Mr. Mell had little to say. He was a tall young man, dark and grave-looking, and he seemed only now and then to be aware of Miss Hetty on his right and Miss Betty on his left. He had a strange way of making some remark to one or the other of them suddenly, as though he had just come up from thoughts of his own. No one can say that he contributed notably to the gaiety of the feast. When I made to refill his wine-glass, he merely shook his head and placed his hand over the glass. Mr. Ronald, who was sitting opposite him, flashed me a wink and indicated his wine which was running low.

I can't say that I increased my store of knowledge or amusement by listening to the conversation at my first dinner-party. Soon enough it was over, my waiting-at-table dress had been exchanged for the one I normally wore, and I was back in the kitchen, confronted by a higher pile of washing-up than I had faced in my life.

All I had to do now was to choose my moment to make the grand dramatic exit. But I had overlooked one factor. There was Mrs. Gregson to be dealt with. I hadn't thought that the use of the Swansea dinner service would make any difference, but it did. Mrs. Gregson told me, when I appeared in the kitchen, that this was used only on special occasions, because it had been given to Mrs. Lilywhite by her father, Lord Llanelly, on her wedding. And she was going to supervise my washing-up, to see that the precious china was treated with the respect due to a lord's offering.

But I was as nice as I knew how to be, and when, for the first time since I had been in that house, she said a word of praise, I was ready for her. " You haven't done so bad," she said. " We'll make something of you yet."

" It's nothing," I said, " to what you've done, Mrs. Gregson. What with cooking and everything you've been on your feet all day. Why don't you have a little rest now and leave this all to me ? "

" But what about the Swansea dinner service ? I'd never forgive myself if anything happened to that. I was there when Lord Llanelly unpacked it with his own hands."

I appealed to my record. I had never smashed anything yet. And I would be especially careful with Lord Llanelly's gift.

She eyed the Swansea china with some apprehension, then capitulated. " Well, just for half-an-hour, then. Mind you call me. I'll be sitting down in my own room."

And, indeed, the poor old thing looked worn out. However, she went.

I gave her a moment to become settled in her chair, sure that she would fall asleep as soon as she was in it, and listened for a while to Miss Betty's voice ringing out above the piano which Miss Hetty was punishing for all she was worth. Then, pulling on an old hat and wrapping a cloak round my shoulders, I made my way on tip-toe along the passage and opened the sacred front door. For a moment I stood there, breathing in the sweet air. It was rather cold, but a few stars were shining in the sky. I remember in that moment asking myself why I was not behaving sensibly like any other girl, why I did not give a week's notice and then walk out of the house as anyone else would do. But I was inflamed by the need to make a protest, to show all the Mrs. Lilywhites in the world what I thought of them ; and before my resolution could cool I gave the door an almighty bang, heard the glass that was in its upper framework tinkle on the path, and began to run towards my tin trunk hidden in the hedge. And that was the last I knew of my flight from the Lilywhites' house.

A blackness overcame me, and it didn't lift till I came-to in a strange bed, and Mr. Mell was leaning over me, asking, " Do you feel better now ? "

8

I learned later what had happened. That almighty bang sounded through the house, silencing Miss Betty's song and Miss Hetty's work at the piano. Everybody was thrown into confusion, and the first to recover was Mr. Ronald who ran out into the hall to see what was the matter. He found the shattered glass and half-way along the path he found me, too, lying on the ground as still as if I were dead. The pathway was made of tiles, and the toe of my shoe had met one which was adrift, and down I had come. Mr. Ronald leaned over me, touched my hair, and started back in afright. His hand was covered with blood. He ran into the house, shouting : " It's Openshaw ! She's bleeding to death on the path ! "

While the ladies, from whom horrors were to be concealed, stayed in the drawing-room, Mr. Mell and Mr. Lilywhite came out then, and it was while Mr. Lilywhite was tut-tutting over the broken glass that Mr. Mell observed : " I expect it's nothing but concussion. All this blood is caused by a deep cut in the head. I suppose it's a bit of glass. Anyway, a doctor ought to see her at once."

Mr. Lilywhite who had stepped out into the roadway said : " Well, this looks like Campbell's brougham. Better stop him and get him to have a look at her."

Dr. Campbell was returning from attendance upon a patient. Mr. Lilywhite's shirt-front in the gleam of the lanterns brought the outfit to a standstill and the doctor got out. He had been attending on Mr. Mell, and his first question was : " What are you doing out at this time of night, young man ? You ought to be in bed."

Then they called his attention to me, and he knelt upon the path, and once he had given me a look-over he asked : " Who is she ? She ought to be put to bed where I can look at her properly."

Mr. Lilywhite hummed and hawed. The thought of an

invalid on Mrs. Lilywhite's hands, or even on the hands of Miss Hetty or Miss Betty, evidently didn't please him. " Can't you take her to hospital ? " he asked.

Mr. Mell was becoming impatient. " Put her in your brougham and ask the man to drive to my father's house," he said.

" Well, with your warrant I'll risk an abduction," Dr. Campbell agreed.

And that is how, when I came to myself the next day, I was in a strange bed with Mr. Mell leaning over me. He looked pleased when I said I was feeling better, and went on tip-toe out of the room. " Sleep now," he said at the door. " Plenty of sleep is what you need."

You must understand how things were in that household. " Mell can do no wrong," about sums it up. His mother perhaps viewed some of his doings with anxiety, but his father was always on his side. He was an only child, and if they had a fault to find in him it was his disposition to work too hard. A breakdown in health at Oxford had been responsible for his long recuperative spell with them.

So when Mr. Lilywhite had gone back into the house last night with his news, it was all right by Mr. Conybeare, but his wife arrived at home like a flustered chicken. Meantime, I had been put into a bed in the spare room, with an ancient maid-servant to look after me. Dr. Campbell had confirmed that there wasn't much the matter that a few days' rest wouldn't put right. He had promised to look in the next day, and indeed I rapidly recovered. What I didn't realise was that Mr. Mell would have done as much for an injured cat. He was one of those men who are as soft as putty where any living thing is concerned, but as hard as iron when his " career " was in question. However, as I say, I didn't realise that then.

Indeed, I realised for a time little beyond my need to sleep, and it was not till the third day that I opened my eyes with the blessed knowledge that I could keep them open. However, I didn't tell that to Mr. Mell. He and Mrs. Conybeare had looked in now and then, laid their hands on my forehead, and gone quietly out of the room, and there was a coming and going, too, of old Ada, the maid-servant whose vast nightgown I was wearing. It was when I was aware of this thing, feeling like a heavily over-canvased ship, that I knew I was all right, pulled a hand-mirror towards me, and saw the large splodge of sticking-plaster just over my left ear. It was while I was gazing into this mirror that Mr. Mell came quietly into the room and asked me how I was.

I said that I was feeling much better, and he replied : " Still, you'd better stay where you are till Dr. Campbell says you can get up. What is your name ? "

I said that it was Openshaw, and he answered : " Yes. I know that. But I can't call you Openshaw, can I ? "

This was news to me, after I had been for so long Openshaw or You. I told him that my name was Alice.

" Well, Alice, you'd better rest now. You're probably not so good as you feel. Still, you do seem better, and I suppose the worst thing now will be boredom. I'll come and read to you in an hour's time."

This was like Mr. Mell, too, although I didn't know it. His day was divided into a time for everything—a time for walking, a time for studying, a time for this and that. An hour hence he would be free to read to me.

I didn't sleep during that hour. I lay there with my red hair spread on the pillow and gloated. That is the only word I can think of. I gloated. For the first time in my life I was being looked after, and it was a change coming upon so many years of looking after other people. Mr. Montgomery and his sons had been all right, and so had Mrs. Morrison who employed me in Manchester. But I had always been a bit of a joke— Ginger or Carrots—and so I had been to Mr. Ronald. I knew what *he* wanted all right. And in his father's house I had been nothing at all—just Openshaw who mustn't even hum as she polished the brass. To be looked after was heaven, and when most of the looking after was being done by Mr. Mell—!

So I lay there and waited and wondered what he would read to me, for books had not notably come my way. The only books I was acquainted with had been the weekly religious ones that my mother read to me. We could hardly wait to see what would happen next in the serial story, which was usually written by Silas K. Hocking. At the board school we had books, too, but they were never books that you read for themselves, but only to learn about wars and kings and queens.

So I lay there and turned all these things over in my mind, and stretched, and felt well, and wondered what Mr. Mell would read. He came promptly in an hour with a fat green-covered book in his hand. But after all he didn't read. He talked instead in his low melodious voice. He told me that he and his mother had called on Mrs. Lilywhite and that all was well in that quarter. There had been some question, he said, of the cost of the glass that I had shattered in the door, but all that had been smoothed out, and so had the matter of my paying a week's wages for leaving without notice. " It wasn't much," he added with a smile. Mrs. Lilywhite, poking about, had found my trunk, too, hidden in the hedge, and Mr. Mell had brought this home.

" Tell me," he asked suddenly. " What were you running away from ? You *were* running away, weren't you ? "

So then I poured out all my story, from Manchester days onward, and ended with the fierce declaration : " I was running away from being nobody, as much as anything."

" But where were you running *to* ? " he persisted. " We must do our best to get you there."

" I have no idea. I was just running away."

He looked at me sadly and said : " That was rather foolish of you, you know. You should always have your goal in sight before you act."

That, although it was another of those things about which I knew nothing, was Mr. Mell to a T.

Now, seeing that he had tired me by a long inquisition, he picked up his book and went. " Have a good rest," he said. " I've rather exhausted you. But I had to know where I stood."

The next day he mentioned his aunt for the first time. "You've never heard of Mrs. Bryan Graves, have you ? " he asked.

I shook my head, and he went on : " My father has two sisters. They're a good deal younger than he is. One of them is Mrs. Bryan Graves. She's married to a Member of Parliament and lives in a cottage called the Rowans not far from Harpenden. I was down there having a long holiday before I came on here to be with my parents, and I know that her maid-servant is leaving to get married. Would you like to go there ? "

I would have liked nothing better than to stay in bed with Mr. Mell talking to me now and then as though I were a human being. But I couldn't tell him that. I merely nodded my head, and said : " I'll have to go somewhere. You and your parents have been very good to me, but I'll have to shift as soon as I'm fit to travel."

" Well, that's settled," he said. " I'll write to my aunt at once. In a week's time I'll be going back to Oxford and I'll travel as far as the Rowans with you and see you installed. Now, what about getting up this afternoon ? I had a word with Dr. Campbell after he saw you this morning, and he says a little walk in Llandaff Fields won't hurt you."

So we walked in the Llandaff Fields, and all the time I was thinking how different this walk was from those I had been used to taking with Mr. Ronald. I was ashamed of my old clothes, though most of them were hidden by a cloak that had belonged to Mrs. Conybeare. It was a fine day. While I had been in bed the daffodils in the front gardens had all rushed out, and here and there were snowdrops and little yellow aconites wearing their frills like choirboys round their necks. The early spring sun was shining.

We were in the fields and had got so far that we could see the spire of the cathedral rising before us, when Mr. Mell said : " You seem tired. You had better take my arm for a while." I did so, shivering at the contact, and saying nothing. Indeed, I left all the talking to him, and only answered when a question was asked me. Sometimes I forgot to do even that, so entrancing was it to be walking with a young gentleman, to be treated as if I were someone. Mr. Mell's questions were all about my past, and there was little that he didn't know when the brief walk was ended.

" Now," he said, when we were back at his father's house, " you had better go and climb into bed. I'll come and read to you for a while in half-an-hour."

So I climbed into bed and lay there shivering with happiness. Oh, it was good to have ceased being Openshaw or You, to be lying in a warm bed, and to be waiting for a young man who was coming to read !

Mr. Mell came promptly in half-an-hour and he brought

with him the green-covered book that I had seen in his hands before. He sat near the window and said : " Now, if you don't like this, just tell me, and I'll read something else. This is one of Tennyson's *Idylls of the King*."

I had never heard the name of Tennyson, never heard of the *Idylls of the King*. It would not have mattered to me if the book had been *Holy Living and Dying* or one of Mr. Silas Hocking's novels. It was enough that Mr. Mell was reading to me. He read "The Coming of Arthur," and I, with my night-dress drawn carefully to my chin, as my mother had taught me—" for you never know with men, even the best of them ", my mother had said—lay with my hair spread on the pillow and watched him. A shaft of late sunshine came through the window and fell on his face and his book. He never once looked at me, and I was able to watch him all the time. I had never heard anything of that sort read before, but as Mr. Mell's rather monotonous voice went on and on I felt that I could listen and look at him for ever.

And Arthur said, " Behold thy doom is mine,
Let chance what will, I love thee to the death ! "
To whom the Queen replied with drooping eyes,
" King and my lord, I love thee to the deatl. ! "

He finished soon after, and then for the first time he looked at me. "Did you like that ? " he asked. And truthfully I could reply : " Oh, so much ! "

" Then I will leave you the book," he said. " Perhaps you would like to read it here and there for your pleasure. But go to sleep now," he said as he so often did. " Our walk this afternoon must have tired you."

He laid the book on a table at my bedside, and, before going, shut the evening sunlight out of the room. As soon as he was gone I picked up the book and clasped it in both arms. Still clutching it beneath the warm bed-clothes, I slept. I was so happy.

Chapter II

About a week after this I went to Bryan Graves's house, the Rowans, at Harpenden, with the book packed into my trunk. I became eighteen years old during my stay at Mr. Conybeare's house, and when Mr. Mell heard of it he said : " Well, you can keep that book of Tennyson's poems. It will be my birthday present. You seem to want it more than I do." I have it still, inscribed on the fly-leaf in his plain no-nonsense hand : "Melvill Conybeare. Balliol College, Oxford."

It is true that I seemed to want the book more than he did. Whenever he came into my room I was reading it, and not only now because of Mr. Mell. I hadn't known that there were such books in the world, and I hadn't known that I was a born reader. There were lots of bits in " The Coming of Arthur " that I felt referred to Mell and me. But, as I grew stronger, I got over that nonsense, and I was soon reading the book for itself. I read it through, the whole 894 pages of it, from the poem to the Queen to " Crossing the Bar ", and I knew a lot of the verses by heart. I was so innocent that I asked Mr. Mell whether Lord Tennyson hadn't written any more books. He laughed at that, the first laugh that I had seen on his face. Usually, a faint ironic smile was all that he permitted himself. But it was no laughing matter to me. I thought that Lord Tennyson sat down and wrote a book of poems just as Mr. Hocking sat down and wrote a tale. But " No," said Mr. Mell. " I think he's written enough to be going on with."

Mr. Conybeare didn't see much of me, but Mrs. Conybeare saw more now that I was going away. She ran some sort of organisation for giving clothes to the poor, things that she collected from the cast-off garments of her husband's congregation. Many of these came my way, and when I left I was fitted out as I had

27

never before been in my life. My old tin trunk was stuffed : it didn't rattle now.

It was a sweet morning when we left. The daffodils by now had reached their full glory. The gardens were alight with them, and that morning, I remember, I saw, too, the first swift flying over Cathedral Road. I craned my head to look from the cab window for the last time at Mrs. Lilywhite's house, and I wished better luck to the girl who succeeded me, but with no hope. The house was gone in a flicker, and I never, save once, saw one of the Lilywhites again. I trust that their next conversazione was more successful than the one to which I had provided so dramatic a climax.

But it was only a beginning, not a climax, for me. I sat in the cab at Mr. Mell's side and watched the landmarks slide by— Canton Bridge whence you saw the Garth mountain rising far to the west out of the River Taff, the long dreariness of Westgate Street, and then the station whence we were to embark. And all the time it was in my head that this was only a beginning, that, till now, I hadn't lived at all ; and I found, with a little wonderment I must say, that I needn't think of Mr. Mell all the time, even though he was here beside me. I was thinking far more of what sort of a house the Rowans might turn out to be, and what sort of woman was this aunt, Mrs. Bryan Graves, who was his father's sister Judith.

2

We reached London that afternoon. I passed the time in looking out of the window and Mell Conybeare in reading *The Times* and books he had in a small handbag. I think this was one of the main differences between us. I was content to look at cows and fields and villages, but he must be for ever scrutinising something that might be to his advantage. There was many a time when I wanted to say " Oh, look ! ", but one glance at him froze the words in my mouth, and I would fall again to my solitary looking. So I suppressed my exclamations about gambolling lambs and even about the dreary purlieus of London which I had expected to be gay. As we were running through this acid scenery, he merely put his book down on the seat and began to pull the trunks from the luggage-rack. I gave one glance at what he had been reading and found that I could not make head or tail of it. I could not resist asking, taking up the book : " What is this ? "

" Oh," he said, pocketing the small volume, " that won't make any sense to you. That's Greek."

But he was all attention once we were on the platform, and called a porter to put the trunks on a truck and take them to a cab at the station entrance. And that was another thing I noted about him : he could give an order without being offensive, and he was obeyed at once.

Well, there I was for the first time in my life in a London station, with bookstalls gleaming about me, and crowds hurrying, and great bursts of steam coughing up to the glass roof, though the streets outside were anything but paved in gold. They were as dreary as the approaches to the station, but this was London, and I was accordingly uplifted.

We went to a little hotel in a street that ran down hill from the Strand, and there for a moment Mr. Mell left me. " Miss Openshaw is rather exhausted by her journey, and will sleep till dinner-time," he explained to the chamber-maid. And to me he said, as he had said so often : " Sleep now. You are more tired than you think. Join me downstairs at dinner-time." Then he went off on his own affairs.

And sleep I did, though I had not expected to. I got into the bed, with my precious Tennyson, and " Now sleeps the crimson petal, now the white " soon lulled me, and I laid down the book and slept. I slept soundly, and the chamber-maid awakened me by switching on the electric light, a phenomenon that was new to me. " Mr. Conybeare's compliments, ma'am. He's waiting in the lounge."

Oh, blessed words ! Oh the change from " Here, You ! What d'you mean by sleeping at this time of day ? "

But it was with some sense of sin, all the same, that I sprang from my bed. Would the chamber-maid expect me to make it up ? But I decided to chance it, and put on a dress that Mrs. Conybeare had provided out of her bounty. It was ghastly : a thing of purple with a lot of little glass beads on it. It was the best I could do, and shyly I went downstairs to join Mr. Mell.

He was not in the lounge, but was waiting at the bottom of the stairs. He did not say a word about my dress—merely took my arm and led me into the dining-room.

I had expected a dining-room in a London hotel to be full of gentlemen wearing white starched shirt-fronts like the ones that Mr. Lilywhite and Mr. Ronald had worn at the famous conversazione. But all save a few were wearing the clothes they had worn in the day-time—all except the waiters who were wearing evening-dress to a man, a strange reversal, I thought, of normal procedure. I found at breakfast next day that the waiters wore their evening clothes all day, which seemed to me stranger still.

But here I was in my purple dress, and Mr. Mell had little to say. He enquired if I had slept well, chose my dinner for me, and for the rest was rather quiet. It was not till dinner was over, filling me with awe at being waited on for the first time in my life, it was not till the night was come and we were walking along the Embankment, that he came fully alive. But then it was I who wanted to be silent. This, now, was London, and who wouldn't be struck dumb by a first sight and smell of it ? The river was sliding by, nearing the full, and dark barges were silently upon it. The lamps were lit and their lights, from the great walk we were upon and from the bridges, fell upon the water and squiggled there like golden eels. The plane trees were in their earliest leafage ; from the Embankment Gardens the spring flowers, folding for the night, were pouring their last fragrance, and upon the sky, light-dazzled from the west, stood the tall towers of the House.

It was the House, above all, that fascinated me, and it was about the House of Commons that Mr. Mell now began to speak. " I expect," he said, " that Bryan Graves is in there now. You'll be meeting his wife, my aunt, to-morrow. I'd better tell you something about him."

We sat on a seat and he told me about Mr. Bryan Graves. He was Mr. Mell all the time, and he therefore found excuse after excuse, but it was clear that in Mr. Graves's character there was a lot that he didn't like. " He's very much given to running after every chimera that seems to have something to commend it," he told me.

" I want to learn about words," I said. " What is a chimera? "

So with his great patience he explained what a chimera was, and ended by saying : " I'm very glad you want to know about words. Always try to get to the bottom of them. That's the beginning of education, and that's what's the matter with Mr. Graves. He's rather attracted by words, even though a little investigation would show him that there's not much in them. I hope, though, that I haven't given you the impression that Graves is a bad fellow."

I learned that Mrs. Graves, Aunt Judith, had no children and that for the most part she lived alone at the Rowans. Mr. Graves lived in rooms in London, so as to be near the House of Commons, and was at the cottage in Harpenden only during the week-ends. " You'll get on well enough, I think, with Aunt Judith—just the two of you. And now I'm going to put you into a cab which will take you back to your hotel. Sleep well, and we'll make our little journey to-morrow. I'm going on to the House now, and I'll drag Bryan out to say good-bye. Don't worry about me. I'll walk back."

I found my bed all made up anew, and I slept well enough, though troubled by dreams in which Bryan Graves was chasing a flock of vivid chimeras all over the place.

3

I woke in the morning with a sense of fright. The sun was shining, and it was as good a spring day as yesterday had been, but suddenly it came over me that to-day was the end of my holiday. Since I had so dramatically left the Lilywhites I had been coddled and cosseted day after day, but on this day I should become a domestic servant again, with new people to give me my orders, and no Mr. Mell to see that everyone treated me as, I was now convinced, I had every right to be treated. And, having delivered me as the new domestic servant, Mr. Mell would go. Probably I should never see him again. But the first words Aunt Judith spoke to me were " So you're Alice ! " Well, better than Openshaw. A lot better than You.

It was a short but pleasant journey to Harpenden, and the cottage called the Rowans was, I found, a good mile from the station. We could have walked it easily, but there was my trunk to be considered, and Mrs. Graves was waiting for us with a cab. " There's a train back to London in a few minutes," Mr. Mell said, " and I'm going to catch it. So now I must leave you with Aunt Judith. I'm over-due at Oxford. Be a good girl, now. I think you'll get on well together. This will help you to understand something about words." He handed me a dictionary, and went back on to the platform.

Mrs. Graves was ten years younger than her brother, Mr. Conybeare, which means that she was in her middle thirties. She was a woman of medium size, very fair, but faded. Everything about her was faded : her blue eyes, her " Liberty " clothes, everything. I don't know why it was, unless it was this faded look, but from the first I treated her as I had noted that Mr. Mell did : and that was with a gentle consideration. She had sent my trunk on in the cab. " Just dump it outside the front door," she said. " You know where the place is."

So there we stood on the road outside the station, and I felt that everything was reversed, that whereas I had been the one who hitherto had been given the orders and did as I was told, now it was up to me to give a lead. Clutching my dictionary under my arm, for nothing would have persuaded me to send it on with the trunk, I said : " What do we do, ma'am ? Do we walk home ? "

She said that we did, and soon we found ourselves outside the little town and trudging along a by-road. Mrs. Graves seemed in no hurry, and neither was I. It was a spring morning. The hedges all about us were bursting into green leaf, and there was a swallow or two overhead. Suddenly Mrs. Graves said : " That is one thing you'll have to get out of."

I looked at her, surprised, for I was not aware of having done wrong. I merely put a question into my eyes, and she said : " This calling me ' ma'am.' I am Judith to you, and you are Alice to me. When Mr. Graves comes home at the week-end, you will be Alice to him, too, and he will be Bryan."

" But I have always called my employers Sir," I protested. " Even Mr. Montgomery and his sons," I added, though aware that she knew nothing about Mr. Montgomery.

" Mr. Graves," she explained with her faded patience, " is not like most men. He thinks a household, including the servants, should be one happy family, all calling one another by their Christian names. Indeed, there are no servants. We are all just one of another."

The by-road was not " made-up ". Few roads were then. I sloshed through the dust at her side, feeling unhappy. The cab, homing to Harpenden, passed us, and the driver raised his whip in greeting. We didn't see another soul on the road. It was a very lonely place. So we went along, without speaking, until we came to what was little more than a foot-track. We followed this for another hundred yards or so, and there at the end of it was the Rowans.

" All tiled, you see, and snug against the winter storms," said Judith. " Leave your trunk here and come round to the back."

So I left my trunk on the doorstep and went with her round the side of the house and came out upon a bit of grass at the back. Altogether, I don't suppose the place came to more than half an acre, and the little lawn was dreadfully neglected, all rough tussocks. But the view was superb. We sat down, Mrs. Graves very wearily, upon an old bench and looked about us. The land ran down to a valley, all vibrant that morning with spring-time sights and sounds, then rose again in a hillside that was wooded and overhung with busy rooks.

" Well, let me get you a cup of coffee now," said Mrs. Graves. " We'll bring it out here and drink it."

But this was too much for me. " If you'll show me the kitchen, ma'am," I said, " I'll make it and bring it out. I can be putting my things away while you rest yourself."

We went into the kitchen, and I prepared a tray while she made the coffee. " You mustn't call me ma'am," she said gently ; and it was she who carried out the tray and set it on a little table before the seat. We drank ; and she relaxed in the sunshine ; but was soon up again and said : " Now there's a thing or two I must type for Bryan."

I carried the tray in, and watched her as she went into a room that she called the study and there sat down and started hammering away at a heavy old Empire typewriter. " Your room is right over this," she explained. " Take your things up and unpack them now."

I did so, and found a neat but severe room which gave on to the view we had looked at from the garden. I could be comfortable here. As I put away my few things in a wardrobe, with my Tennyson and my dictionary on the dressing-table, I thought of Mr. Mell and his remark that Bryan Graves was too fond of chasing after chimeras. I looked up the word again in the dictionary, and only then found that Mr. Mell had inscribed the title page: " To Alice Openshaw from Melvill Conybeare." I was very pleased to see his writing there, and a strange thought came to me—that he had brought me there to look after his aunt, and that she might indeed need my care. The stutter of the typewriter came up the stairs, and I said to myself " Poor woman ! "

4

I learned a good deal about Judith in the course of time. Bryan's father, like her so much older brother, Mr. Conybeare, had been a Wesleyan parson, and so they had met. They had been married for ten years or so, and he was already a Member of Parliament when they did so. He was an up-and-coming man in the Liberal Party, and he had remained an up-and-coming man ever since. He had never really come. He was, as Mell had shrewdly remarked, too much given to chimeras. All that he advocated was slightly off-beat, and any cause would gain his adherence if it was eccentric and not likely to give his party any votes.

In the next couple of days Judith and I got to know one another. She always called me Alice, and I learned, quite naturally, to call her Judith. There was little to do in the house because it was small and because, set as it was in the open country, there was not much dirt. She wanted at first to do all the cooking, but, though I had not cooked for the Lilywhites, I was a good cook and soon took this off her hands. But really there was not work for two women in that place, and when she had finished the typing for Mr. Graves we spent a lot of time sitting in the garden and watching the day go by. The stuff to be typed used to come by post. Mr. Graves had an abominable hand. I looked at his writing now and then and had difficulty in making head or tail of it, but Judith was used to it and would hammer away, for he was a great writer of letters to the press and of articles about this and that.

It was while we sat in the garden watching the swallows flying high that she said to me : " I would have preferred to keep the thatch."

I looked at her in some surprise, wondering what this was all about, and she went on : " Of course, Bryan was quite right. Don't think I am saying a word against him." And she told me of how, years ago, they had found the cottage. They hadn't been married long then, and it was their custom to walk in the country at week-ends, looking for a place to live in. They were in a small house in Embankment Terrace which was near the House of Commons and very convenient for Bryan. But he wanted a place in the country to go to at week-ends and where Judith could live permanently, while he remained, for most of his time, near the House. They casually came upon the Rowans, and, while Judith sat in the hedge opposite, Bryan went in to have a look at the cottage, which was dilapidated and had a door swinging open.

It was a lovely spring day, and while Judith sat there she watched the early swallows, flying in and out of the thatch. They decided the matter for her, and when Bryan came out she cried : " I think this is it. Look at the swallows ! "

It seemed to her the most desirable thing in the world to live in a cottage and to have swallows nesting in the roof. " Do you know," she cried, " that some of them come all the way from Africa ? Think how tired they must be ! And to have them, year after year, coming to rest here ! Besides, it's lucky, they say, to have swallows in one's house."

Bryan looked at her and said : " They say ! Who says ? "

" Why everybody. Everybody says."

" Everybody means no one in particularly," Bryan assured her. " There's no such thing as luck. Do you know why these swallows go to Africa, or wherever they go ? Simply because winter has come over here. When winter comes, no more midges, so they go where their food is. There's no luck about it with them, believe me. They're after their grub, and they come back here when the grub arrives."

I can well imagine now the smile he gave her as he made this rational explanation. He went on : " Still, it is just what we're looking for. Yes, a bit spent on it, and it'll be ideal. I'll see the agent as soon as I get a chance."

Judith did not see the cottage again till all Bryan's schemes for it had been carried out. The thatch had not been renewed. It had been stripped off, and good utilitarian tiles had taken its place. The swallows went and never came back.

5

At the week-end Bryan came down to the Rowans. He was older than I expected him to be, a small man with lots of sandy hair disposed like a monk's all round his head but not on top. He was as bald, there, as a coot. He wore boots, not shoes, and these were lifted by an extra inch or so of leather, so that, short though he was, he appeared a little taller. As they also threw him forward on to his toes, he seemed always to be peering, and this impression was heightened by the spectacles he wore. He had blue eyes that were for ever smiling, and I didn't like his smile because it was self-satisfied—a smirk rather than a smile— and it deepened whenever he made one of his pronouncements. He did not so much speak as make pronouncements, and these, you were to understand, were always right. For example, he was a great believer in " rights for women ". So was I, though not in his political fashion, for I had never given politics a thought, but I soon learned that my function was to hear his opinions on the matter, not to express my own, unless my own happened to be an echo of his. Then he would turn with his smile to Judith and say : " We'll make something of Alice yet."

I disliked him from the first, disliked everything about him, from his appearance to his manners. He arrived early on that Saturday morning. Judith had been to the station to meet him, and it happened that when he came at about ten o'clock I was still washing up the breakfast things. He was as full of energy as of smiles, and he came straight through to the scullery where I stood over the sink with my sleeves rolled up. He said : " Ah, so this is Alice ! "

" Yes, sir," I said.

He was carrying a despatch-case, which he threw on to a table. " Why ' sir ' ? " he asked buoyantly. " One thing you soon learn here is that we are servants one of another. As you are Alice to me, I am Bryan to you."

This was something new after Mrs. Lilywhite, who had scarcely addressed a word to me. I had been to some extent prepared by Judith for her husband's ways, but I was rather taken aback. I made no answer, but stood there, I fear, looking a little sulky, when Judith came in and hooked an arm through his and took him away. As he went he was exclaiming to her : " Alice is new to our ways but we'll make something of her yet." I was to learn that Mr. Graves could never meet a new person without this desire to " make something ", and the something was always very much in his own ugly image.

6

I don't want to suggest that Bryan Graves was a bad man, but he was an ugly one. Not ugly in any physical way, though he never attracted me ; but ugly in all the things he wanted to do. In wanting everybody to be like himself, he was aiming, without knowing it, at the ugliness of uniformity. I believe in everybody being his own queer self. So it was that Bryan and I never got on. Though he continued to call me Alice in a sturdy brotherly sort of way, I never called him anything but " Sir " and I even took to calling Judith " Ma'am " if he was about. He was for ever under the delusion that he was in some way creating a community, giving a hand with making the beds and peeling the potatoes and blacking the boots, but Judith and I were unfalteringly glad when Monday morning saw him catching a train to town, always dashing for it as though the House of Commons could not spare him for a moment, always shouting as he went : " Well, good-bye, Judith. Good-bye, Alice ! " Then, if the weather permitted it, we would sigh with relief in unison, leave the washing up, and make for the bench in the garden.

7

One day, when we had said good-bye to Bryan, I went in to wash up the breakfast things and make the beds before joining Judith on the bench. She was always low-spirited, and this morning she was almost in tears. I put an arm about her, for we were on those terms now, and asked her what was the matter. " I don't love Bryan," she said, sobbing now freely. Although I was so much younger than she was, I thought I knew more of the world, and I said : " You needn't cry about that. How many married people do you think are in love with one another ? "

I thought of my mother and of my wretched feckless father. I thought of Mrs. Morrison and Mr. Montgomery, marrying for comfort and convenience. I thought of Mr. and Mrs. Lilywhite, and I felt quite wise. But Judith was not to be comforted by a few words spoken merely for the sake of cheering her up. She went on crying, and presently, drying her eyes, she told me of a strange thing—or at least she thought it strange—that had happened to her in the springtime a year ago. She had left the Rowans one Saturday morning to walk to Harpenden where she would meet Bryan. It was her custom to do so, but this morning her thoughts were not on him. It was an exceptional day. The hedges were budding. The birds were singing, and everything seemed to be rushing out to meet the spring. So was she. She sat down and listened to a stream flowing under the hedge that faced her, and watched the young clouds gambolling in the sky above her, and heard the lambs calling in a neighbour's field. She wondered what had happened to her, and suddenly realised that she was happy. " And I knew," she said to me, " that this was something strange and odd in my life, that I hadn't been happy for months, and that I should cease to be happy the moment that Bryan appeared."

That was all her little confession came to, and in my young wisdom I thought what a fool the man was, that all that was necessary was for him to appear, for him to be as lit up as she was, for him to cry : " What a day for a walk ! " and take her hand in his. But all he had done at Harpenden station was to tap his bulging despatch-case and say : " My word ! We're going to have a busy week-end of it ! " And so they had, and she had hated going to the station to meet him ever since.

8

I disliked Mr. Bryan Graves the more I saw of him. He always came down to the Rowans on Saturdays full of new thoughts about the taxation of land values or the Sunday closing of beer houses or some other public matter, but I have never known a man so entirely without private and personal matters to discuss. I insisted on calling him " Sir " though he always called me Alice or even at times Miss Openshaw, and I had, whether I wished it or not, to join them at meals. Usually, these ended with a quarrel between me and him. He would address his pronouncements to me rather than to Judith, and more often than not I disagreed with him, and said so. He pretended to be amused, saying : " Well, if that's what the Great British Public thinks ", or " If that's how women will talk when they get the vote ", and so on ; but more often than not I said what I did merely to annoy him, not meaning a word of it or, more often not knowing what he was talking about. But there I was, Alice, one of the family, as one should be in all decent collections of human beings, or so he said, and I was resolved to take the burden off Judith, who had plenty to do with her everlasting typing. So I defended the Sunday opening of public houses, though I had not been in one in my life, and told him that I thought he was talking nonsense about the taxation of land values. I knew that he was hopping mad with me, but his smile never wavered, though it took on a pitying tinge, and I never succeeded by a hair's breadth in making him alter an opinion once he had formed it. And why should I ? I did it only to annoy him.

9

So we got through that summer, and the autumn came, and one Saturday I suggested to Judith that we should go blackberrying. I had done it once or twice with my mother, wandering in

Cheshire, and I knew how to make jam. For once, Bryan would not be coming home on the Saturday morning train. He would lunch in town and catch one that brought him to the Rowans late on Saturday afternoon. Judith would be in plenty of time to meet that, for blackberries were abundant and we had not far to go.

I was the keener for this expedition because I knew it would displease Bryan. The week-end before this, he had spread himself abroad on the importance of state factories. The wicked people who were called capitalists were to be bought out, or otherwise dispossessed, and the State was to have a high old time supplying the citizens with all they needed at cost price. As usual, Judith had nothing to say, and, as usual, I talked to annoy him. Weren't there already, I asked, lots of things that people could have at cost price, but they were too lazy to make them. " What about blackberry jam ? " I asked. " My mother and I used to lay in what we wanted for nothing. All it meant to us was the cost of the sugar. There must be scores of things like that, but people are too lazy to make them. All your grand schemes would make them lazier still."

He smiled at me in his patronising way. " My dear Alice," he said, " believe me, the state ownership of the means of production would be for the benefit of us all."

" You always talk, sir," I said, for I loved to call him " Sir ", knowing how often he said he disliked it, " about some wonderful scheme. You are talking now about the means of production. I am talking about blackberry jam."

" I am talking," he said, still smiling, " about dispossessing capitalists. That would be for the good of all of us. *You* dragged in the blackberry jam."

It was one of those fool arguments that he liked, and now, in a moment of madness, I said : " Capitalists ! What do you call yourself ? How would you like to be dispossessed ? "

This was in the days before Members of Parliament received wages like everyone else, and I had asked Judith about it. " Oh, Bryan is comfortably off," she said. " His little house in London takes some running, and then there's this." And she told me that though Bryan's father, dead now, had been a Methodist parson, his uncle, the parson's brother, had gone into stockbroking and died both a bachelor and a rich man. He left everything to Bryan, who was now living on a comfortable £4,000 a year. And so, when I used the word capitalists, his face darkened for a moment, but he called up his smile pretty soon and said : "I despair of knocking any sense into your head. I am a great believer in votes for women, and I condone even their militant tactics, but heaven help us poor men when women get the vote. It will be one irrelevancy after another until we've educated them."

Then, casting his beam on us both, he added : "Now, go and have a walk in the moonlight, the pair of you. I'll see to the washing up."

So he ended the little debate with the pretence that we were all one family, and that he did his bit.

We took him at his word, and went for a stroll on the moon-washed road, leaving him rolling up his sleeves and murmuring with his forgiving smile : "Blackberry jam!"

10

The next Saturday was fine, and, when we had done the bit of work that so small a house demanded, we set out with a basket and crooked stick each. We took our lunch, too—sandwiches and so forth wrapped up in napkins. We dawdled all the morning, and it was not till lunch time that we came to a really good spot with dewy bunches on the hedges all about us. The day was not only fine but hot, and we decided to eat our sandwiches, have a rest, and then gather the berries. They were so plentiful that we could fill our baskets in half-an-hour.

Well, we ate, and then we settled beneath some trees, and in no time Judith was asleep. But for some reason or other I could not sleep, and I took my Tennyson, which I had slipped into the basket, and was soon deep in "The Passing of Arthur", which I had been through many times, and still thought one of the most wonderful things I had ever read.

I put down the book when I had done and looked at Judith who was sleeping beside me, and decided not to awaken her. She was thin and drawn, and I thought a good sleep was what she needed. So I lay at her side, gazed for a while at the green branches laced above us, and, without knowing it, drifted into sleep myself.

I was awakened by Judith shaking me. "Get up! Get up!" she was saying. "D'you know the time?"

I yawned, rubbed my eyes, and gazed at her leaning over me. She was smiling, and it was a rare thing in those days—a smile on Judith's face. "We've forgotten Bryan!" she said. "He'll have arrived at Harpenden by now and there's no-one to meet him!"

I didn't know then that this was the first time in all their married life that she had not been at the station to welcome him home for the week-ends, to discuss with him as they strode to the Rowans the contents of the precious despatch-case and all the things she would have to type.

I was glad to see her smiling, and said: "Well, what do we do? We're all members of one family, aren't we, and a member of a family is surely entitled to sleep under a tree."

"We'd better get back quick," she said, stuffing the debris of our picnic into her basket. "Never mind the blackberries."

So we went back the way we had come, but there was no question of getting back quick, because we had walked a long way that morning, and, for all her sleep, Judith was tired. It was a dusty and rather bedraggled pair that presented itself at the Rowans. We found Bryan laying the tea-table. He did not mention Judith's absence from the railway station, did not mention the absence of both of us from the cottage. He merely said: "You'll need a cup of tea after your long walk." And he poured out the tea for us.

But in bed that night I could not rid my mind of Judith's smile; I couldn't help wondering whether her absence was a salutary shock to the little man. He had been fairly quiet, for him, at dinner that night, but immediately after the meal the rattle of Judith's typewriter had sounded from the room that was called the study.

II

I have said that, when we went on our blackberry picnic, I had stuffed my volume of Tennyson into my basket, and I have mentioned the study. The fact was that by this time I was a reading being. With the permission of both Bryan and Judith, I went into the study whenever I liked and took from the shelves such books as I thought would interest me. They were few enough. Judith was not a reader. Apart from a few old Sunday school prizes and things of that sort, she had nothing. Bryan's contribution didn't amount to much. There were masses of pamphlets and blue-books, masses of stuff that made heavy political going. All these I rejected, for neither *Jessica's First Prayer* nor Ricardo's *Principles of Political Economy and Taxation* had any appeal. But that uncle who had been so good as to leave all his money to Bryan had also given him the complete novels of Dickens. These I found in a corner, covered with dust. I hadn't the least idea what they were or what they were about, but they were alongside Forster's *Life of Dickens*, and I read this first. And then conscientiously I read through the novels in the order in which Forster mentioned them, beginning with the *Sketches by Boz* and ending up with the unfinished *Edwin Drood*. I was an animal that had found its meat. I learned more about financiers from Mr. Merdle, more about politicians from a score of characters, than Bryan was able to teach me in all his lectures. Indeed, I became like the person in one of the novels who "wants to know, you know ", and with Dickens and Tennyson I hadn't made a bad beginning at knowing. I was in some danger of becoming like Bryan himself : I thought I knew everything. However, I was soon cured of that.

In all this time I had heard nothing from Mr. Mell. He was in his last year at Balliol, and why he should have bothered with me I don't know. But there were times when I was hurt and unhappy that he did not write. He wrote occasionally to his Aunt Judith, and he never failed to add a line in which he asked to be remembered to me or inquired " how Alice is getting on." But I always had the feeling that he had " added a line ", that it was only politeness on his part, and that he didn't care whether I was alive or dead. I didn't want a message from Mr. Mell, passed on by somebody else. I wanted a letter to me from Mr. Mell.

However I didn't get one, and I had to make do with a young man at Harpenden free library. We spent a long time, with me leaning over the counter, talking of this and that, and as I was always ready to pick anyone's brain, if he would place it at my disposal, I took his advice about the books I should read. In this way I came upon Taine's *History of English Literature*, and by the time our blackberrying picnic took place I had read Taine from end to end and, with the help of the young man from Harpenden, had got hold of many of the authors whom Taine wrote about.

12

Bryan was not a travelled man, and he was much excited about the scheme of dashing to Germany on what he called " a fact-finding expedition ". He was incapable of saying simply that he and a few other people had decided to have a look round in the hope of seeing how the German people lived. It had to be a fact-finding expedition and he was full of this expedition when he came home a week after the blackberry outing.

It was his own idea. There had been much talk about Germany and her warlike ideas. Concerning that fact, at any rate, Bryan had made up his mind without leaving England. It was just poppycock. The Kaiser was a boastful, pretentious fellow, apt to give himself military airs, but one word from the German trade unions would be enough. The members of the unions to a man would refuse to support any nonsense, and that would be that. This was as clear as daylight to Bryan, but it was not clear to everybody. However, one or two of these people only needed to see it to be convinced, and then Britain and Germany could settle down without the pinpricks and innuendoes which of late had been far too abundant.

So Bryan, who came home most week-ends full of ideas that meant work for Judith, came home that week-end with letters to be written, invitations to go out, and all sorts of things to be done concerned with the fact-finding expedition.

He knew one or two German trade union leaders, to whom he often wrote, though he had never seen either ; and all was soon going as he wanted it to go, save for one fact. Judith had no intention of going with him. She had become reconciled to his demands upon her so long as they were made at home.

Perhaps, a year ago, she would even have gone abroad with him and done all that was expected of a secretary. But during the last year she had begun to see Bryan in a new light, as a task-master to be obeyed rather than as a lover to be joyfully worked with, and I think she consciously chose the fact-finding expedition as the occasion for making this clear. She typed a lot of letters during the first week-end about the G.F.F.E. This was Bryan's name for the German fact-finding expedition, for he shared the opinion of many that a thing became more important if its name were expressed in initial letters instead of fully spelled-out words. Perhaps it was his one grain of political wisdom that he realised how important things could be made to sound when they were not set out fully as their rather unimportant selves.

So the G.F.F.E. was launched that week-end, and during the week Bryan worked on it in London. Soon all was in order for twenty or so men and women to go to Berlin, Hamburg, Essen, Cologne, and a few other places, where they would meet employers and workmen, professors and soldiers, and be cosseted, coddled and comforted to their heart's content.

Bryan had a good deal of luggage, and a cab came from Harpenden to take him to the station. I went with Judith to the garden-gate to see him off. He did not kiss her good-bye. I think he regarded kissing with disfavour—a habit indulged in by rather undeveloped people. I should have loved a man to say to me at such a moment : " I shall miss you no end," but Bryan, with a cocky motion towards his Panama hat, said " I shall miss your typing. There'll be any amount to do when I get back."

But he never got back. The G.F.F.E. was to have crossed from Harwich to the Hook of Holland and to have gone thence to Hanover as its first stopping-place. But it didn't even reach Harwich. By a stroke of luck, though several were injured, only one was killed when the engine jumped the rails. But that one was Bryan.

Chapter III

There would not be many more days like this. Autumn prolonged itself, and I was glad to have a breathing-space. All the family had come to Bryan's funeral, but now they were gone. Judith was to spend a week or so with her brother, Mr. Conybeare, in Cardiff. Meanwhile, the cottage was mine and I made the most of my liberty. For the first time in my life I had no one to think of but myself. Sometimes I walked all day long, past cottage gardens full of beehives and dahlias and chrysanthemums, under the blue sky, along the fringes of woods, where the beech-leaves were turning to gold. I would sit among them, looking out over wide territories and sometimes I would read and sometimes I wouldn't, for the great joy of that moment was that I could do as I liked.

One day I decided not to go out at all, but to spend it with a book in the garden of the Rowans. I have explained that the garden was at the back, looking over a valley, and the cottage stood in so isolated a lane that no one was likely to come that way. So I settled down soon after breakfast, and this time it was a new endeavour altogether.

That morning I had been looking through the room called the study. Usually it was an unrewarding room, with bound numbers of political pamphlets and things of that sort in it ; but now and then its dark corners, unswept and unlighted, would yield treasures that one had not expected. In it I had found Defoe's *Moll Flanders* and *The Plague Year*, and, rummaging in it now, I came upon a book called Chardenal's *First French Course*. It was quite natural for me to assume that Taine and the young man from Harpenden had taught me all that was to be known of English, and that I could go ahead now with French. But it was altogether too sweet a day for Chardenal. I sat there in a

46

deck-chair, with a deplorable " rustic " table at my right hand,
and it wasn't long before the book was on the table and my
attention given to the departing swallows, the stream down in the
valley, to the droning of bees and the falling of leaves too tired
to keep a hold on the branches, falling now with tired surprise that
the earth, not the upper air, was their destination.

So, without having opened Chardenal, I was soon asleep,
and I suppose I wasn't bad to look at. I had put on a dress of
light-green linen ; my feet were bare, and my red hair, that
I had not bothered in any way to " do up ", was a curtain behind
my head. It was thus that Julian Brogden found me. The
sense of a presence roused me, and there was no need for a
tentative cough or two that he gave.

I opened my eyes to see a young man who was tall rather
than short, thin rather than stout, fair rather than dark. Indeed,
the first impression of Julian was that he was rather something
than something else. He was that sort of young man—an
average type. He was leaning on a silver-headed malacca cane
and wore a straw hat.

" I am looking," he said, " for Mrs. Bryan Graves."

" I am the servant here," I said, forgetting all that Bryan
had ever taught me. Mr. Brogden did me the favour of looking
as though he doubted it.

" Mrs. Graves," I told him, " has gone to Cardiff to take a
holiday with her brother. I don't know when she'll be back."

I made to give him my chair, but he said : " Don't bother
about that, please," and brought one from a pile that was leaning
against the scullery wall. " I don't suppose," he said, " that you
could provide such a thing as a cup of coffee ? And do please
join me."

Leaving my book on the table, I went to the kitchen to make
the coffee. When I returned, his hat and stick were on the grass,
he was smoking a cigarette and Chardenal was in his hand. He
murmured as I approached : " J'aime, tu aimes, il aime, nous
aimons, vous aimez, ils aiment." " Why," he asked " do they
always choose that verb as an illustration ? " As I didn't know
one word of French from another I didn't answer.

" Well, be that as it may," he said, stirring his coffee, " I
suppose I ought to have written to Mrs. Graves, asking for an

appointment. Then I shouldn't have found myself stranded like this. However," he said, smiling for the first time, " I wanted a day in the country, and I've got one. Tell me, Miss——"

" Openshaw. Alice Openshaw."

" Tell me, Miss Openshaw, *are* you a servant here ? "

" I suppose I'm more of a companion to Mrs. Graves."

" Well, let me introduce myself. I'm Julian Brogden, just become a junior partner in a law firm—Breckenridge and Breckenridge. We had the handling of Mr. Graves's will. It wasn't read, as you know, at the family gathering after the funeral."

" I don't know. I didn't attend the funeral and I wasn't at the family gathering."

" Well, it wasn't," said Mr. Brogden. " That's what I wanted to see Mrs. Graves about. However, it'll have to wait till she comes back. Now, concerning Chardenal . . ."

I didn't know a thing about Chardenal. It was just a book that I had found in the study and that I hadn't opened. I said so. " It's just a book I picked up in the study. I've read all about France in the *Encyclopædia Britannica*. So I thought I'd see what French was like."

He sipped his coffee and smiled. " It's like that, is it ? " he said. " l was like that myself once. But I soon learned that I got along better if there was someone to guide my infant footsteps."

" Oh," I said, " there's a young man in the Free Library at Harpenden. . . ."

" I dare say," he conceded, " that the young man in the Free Library at Harpenden is all very well in his way. But believe you me, learning French is another matter. There is, for example, the question of accent. You ought to find a master."

I liked Mr. Brogden. He talked very easily, and it was a long time since anyone had done that to me. Bryan Graves had always talked as though he were annoyed because I didn't agree with every word he spoke. Judith didn't talk much, and she wasn't interested in the things that interested me. Of course, there was Mr. Mell, but Mr. Mell seemed now a long time ago, and I didn't expect that I would ever see him again. So I took advantage of my audience now that I had one, and told Mr. Brogden that I had learned " everything " about English literature from Taine in four volumes and that now I was going on to French.

" If you want to pick up a bit of French," he said, " I think I ought to send my sister Laura to see you. She's going back to France any day now, and you may be just the sort of person she's looking for. Frankly, I don't see any future for you here."

He got up, taking his hat and stick from the ground. " Well," he said, " I'll be writing to Mrs. Graves. Good-bye, and thank you for the coffee."

2

I ought to tell here something of Mr. Julian Brogden and his sister Laura. She was a year older than he was, and they were the children of a doctor in Whitechapel. Doctors in Whitechapel did not, in those days, make much money, especially if they were like Dr. Brogden, who gave half his services for sixpence or nothing. When he died, he left little beyond a widow and these two children. There was just enough to send Julian to school and to put him after that as an articled clerk in a lawyer's office. Laura was sent to France. She wanted to be a teacher of French in a girls' school, and, unlike most teachers of French, thought it would be an advantage to learn the language in the country to which it belonged. So she went to a Madame Coignet in Paris, whose educational methods were years in advance of her time. They consisted of little but talking intelligently to a cosmopolitan bunch of girls who were at liberty to wander where they liked, provided that they wandered in places where they were liable to hear good French. So Laura wandered with the rest, and went to law courts and public meetings and art galleries and theatres and did a lot of reading and learned her French as if she were a French girl. She had now one more year of this sort of life to go.

Julian meanwhile had passed his law examinations and had recently become a partner in the firm of Breckenridge and Breckenridge. The last of the Breckenridges was dead, but the ancient name was kept for what it might be worth, which was a good deal. It was in the time of the now dead Breckenridge that Bryan Graves had made his will. Needless to say, Judith had not discussed this will with me, but she had not either—alas !—discussed it with her husband. She had assumed that all, or as much as makes no difference, that had belonged to Bryan would belong to her ; but, true to the end to what he considered his principles, he had left her enough to " get by ", and the rest he had scattered over crack-brained political societies of one sort and another, all guaranteed to do little more than print pamphlets for the edification of the already deluded.

Whether the last great Breckenridge, who was concerned with this will, had tried to persuade Bryan to be sensible we shall never know ; but there it was, and it was left to Julian Brogden to enlighten Mrs. Graves on where she stood. It was small wonder that he had said to me : " I don't see much future for you here."

3

I could have stayed with Judith. She had after all £1,000 a year, which was, in those days, more than enough to " get on " with. She had, too, the Rowans, and announced her intention of staying there and selling the house in Westminster. She could have contested the will, but she did not do so, because, I have since decided, she sub-consciously wanted nothing further that Bryan had been involved in or that he wished to do. He was an episode in her life, a shining one at first, but one that got duller and duller, because he was concerned with humanity and not with human beings. I didn't for a time see the Rowans after that, but I was glad to notice on one of my visits that Judith had had the tiles stripped from the roof, and thatch put there instead. She could sit in her garden, and watch the swallows that nested in it, and think of all the years she had wasted in the belief that she could reform them and reform the world.

But I met Laura Brogden long before that. She came, unannounced, soon after Julian had called. I was taking a stroll in the dust that then passed with us as a side-road when I saw this dark well-dressed girl coming towards me. She was about my own age, perhaps a little older, and my own height, but as dark as I was fair, with blue eyes that were almost black. She said : " You are Alice Openshaw, aren't you ? " and when I said that I was she smiled. "Julian was quite right," she said. "He told me to look out for a mass of red hair."

I was wearing no hat, so the identification was not difficult. "You ought to take it in hand," she said. I was to learn in time that Laura could see few things that didn't need taking in hand. But they were almost always small personal things, not the world-problems that had bedevilled Bryan Graves's life.

We were not far from the Rowans. "Come and sit down," I invited her. "I'll make a cup of coffee."

We were soon sitting before the rickety little table in the garden, with that great roll of country before us, and she asked : "How is Chardenal getting on?"

I hadn't opened Chardenal since the day of her brother's visit, because, rummaging in the study, I had come upon a small eye-straining edition of Keats that was tucked away, never read, in a dark corner. I had left it, when I went for my walk, lying on the table in the garden, and now I picked it up and it fell open at the Ode to Autumn. I remembered how, when first I found it, I had brought it out here and ruffled the pages, not expecting to find much, and, beginning to read in a lazy fashion, I came on the words of the Ode. I recalled how I had rushed in to get my Taine, how I had found Keats unwritten about, merely dismissed in half a line for his " sickly or over-flowing imagination ", and how, in a moment, Taine had fallen, never to rise again. Pages and pages about Tennyson, nothing about Keats.

Well, I have learned since then that there is something about most people, poets and peasants alike, and Tennyson has come back where he belongs, and so has Keats. But in that moment I was in a Keats fury, which is the way I have come on most things, and I held the neglected dark-covered little volume out to Laura. She ruffled the pages, her blue eyes smiling, and she sipped her coffee. "So that's how it is," she said. "Chardenal is superseded, eh? We'll have to take you in hand."

"But isn't he wonderful?" I asked.

"I suppose he is," she said coolly. "Not that I've read much of him."

So my hopes of a good excited talk about Keats slumped, and

we sat there not saying much, but, as I realised later, calming down.

" Julian tells me," she said at last, " that you were looking at Chardenal when he met you. So he jumped to the conclusion that you wanted to learn French. However, conclusions are bad things to jump to, unless you've got something to go on."

" Oh, but, Miss Brogden . . ."

" Laura, please. And I'll call you Alice."

" Well, I *do* want to learn French. I want to learn *everything*."

Laura smiled again. " Don't be such a bore," she said.

She was cutting the ground, great shovelfuls of it, from under my feet. But I liked her and poured out another cup of coffee for her. Then she said nothing for a time, but sat there drinking and looking about her. Presently I said : " Well, I'd better take these things into the kitchen and wash up."

" Now that's something I wanted to ask you about. Can you be trusted to wash up ? "

" Well, if I could be trusted with Lord Llanelly's dinner-service," I said, " I can be trusted with a few old crocks ! "

And I told her of Lord Llanelly's present to his daughter and how I had washed it up on the evening when I ran away from Mrs. Lilywhite's, and of how I met Mr. Mell, and all that had followed from it. And now I was talking like a human being, and I felt that Laura preferred me that way.

" And where were you before you went to Mrs. Lilywhite's ? " she asked.

Soon I was giving her my whole life story, which, when you think of it, didn't come to much after all. I was surprised, indeed, that it came to so little, because I had been in the habit of thinking myself an important and remarkable being. I finished my brief story feeling rather small, a bit nervous of this well-dressed good-looking girl, and rather for the want of something to say than for any other reason I asked : " Well, what about taking a few hard-boiled eggs and some sandwiches and walking somewhere ? "

And that is what we did, and it was when we were sitting on a fallen tree, far from the cottage, that Laura began to tell me what she was after. Simple enough ; but unlike me, she refused to be swept off her feet and wanted to know what she was doing.

" Taste and see " was my way, and if I liked what I tasted I
was in it up to the neck. Otherwise, I was not a horse but a
regular mule led to the water, and nothing would induce me to
drink.

Fortunately, I liked what Laura had to offer. It was simply
that I should go as a servant-girl to France. She reduced it all
to logic. She talked of francs and translated them into pounds,
and I saw at once that I should be getting much less than Judith
was giving me; indeed, I should be slightly below the level of
the Lilywhite pittance. But Laura thought that the advantage of
hearing French, and nothing but French, spoken around me
would more than compensate for this. And, taking one swift
look at the proposal, I was inclined to agree with her. " And
you'll always have me," she said, laying a hand affectionately on
my knee.

" When do we go ? " I asked. I was, as usual, excited and
ready for anything. If Laura had said : " Now. Pack your
bag," I would have been with her. But she said instead : " You'd
better write to Mrs. Graves and give her a week's notice in the
usual way. No banging the door this time."

And I had no sooner waved her off at Harpenden than I ran
back to the Rowans and wrote the letter. Judith was with her
brother in Cardiff, and a day or two later I had a rather cold
answer from her, in which she didn't wish me luck in my great
enterprise, but said I must do as I liked. " If you must go and
throw in your lot with foreigners there's nothing I can do to
stop you."

I don't think this would have abated my enthusiasm in the
least, but what pleased and excited and encouraged me was that
by the same post there came the first letter I had received from
Mr. Mell.

" My dear Miss Openshaw," he said. " You perhaps know
that I have now finished with Oxford and I am at home with my
parents for a little while, before going on to see my other aunt,
Mrs. Graves's sister, who lives in Cornwall with her husband,
Mr. Frank Melvill, the novelist. Your letter has come for my
Aunt Graves and she is none too pleased with you, which is a
tribute of a sort, because she wouldn't want you to stay unless she
was looking forward to seeing you again. However, you must

53

on no account consider what she would have you do. (So, you see, this letter is *very* private !) I must say that for my own part, I was not surprised but pleased that you have decided to go to France as a domestic servant. A lot of nonsense is talked about domestic service, which is as good as any other sort of service, and I don't suppose you will be a domestic servant for long, but that what you have in mind is simply to be in some place where French is talked all about you. In that way you will learn the language ; and it's the best way I know. When you have learned it to your own satisfaction, we shall see. But don't forget to read plenty of good English, too, which is quite a useful language ! Don't bother to answer this letter. Yours sincerely, Melvill Conybeare."

"Don't bother to answer this letter" so clearly meant "Don't answer this letter" that I forebore dashing to Bryan's writing table to say to Mr. Mell that I was indeed not forgetting "to read plenty of good English". I wanted to tell him all about Keats, but decided that perhaps he had heard of him at Oxford or somewhere, and that, on the whole, "don't bother to answer this letter" had an undertone I had better respect.

4

Laura came again in a day or two, and it was as though she had been an old friend. She was my opposite, calm whenever I wanted to boil over, circumspect where I would have dashed at things. "I haven't yet written to Madame Coignet," she said. "I thought you had better know all about her before you make up your mind."

I was, of course, longing to tell her that I had heard from Mr. Mell, but decided against this. Instead, I said that I had heard from Judith, that my "notice" was accepted, and that Judith was going to stay for a while in Cornwall, with her sister who was married to Mr. Melvill, the novelist. She said that she had heard of him, indeed had read some of his books. "He really is very good," she said in her calm way. "He writes very well, and his books are worth reading. Not that my opinion is worth much. But I get hold of his things whenever I can."

But it was of Madame Coignet she wished to tell me, and she did so while we strolled about the country that afternoon. " Don't think you'll have a soft time with her," she said. " She's a tough old nut and she'll get the last penn'orth out of you. But nothing is spoken in her house except French ; and, if you want to learn it, that's the way to do it. All the Chardenals in the world won't do for you what you'll learn without thinking much about it. And don't expect me to have much to do with you, either. There'll perhaps be ways and means, but on the whole you'll be just a servant girl, not one of what she calls ' my young ladies '."

Laura did all she could to make me say " no " to the Coignet household, but my mind was made up. Let her point out a thousand snags if she felt it her duty to do so. I rode over them all, and we parted on the understanding that she would write at once and say that she had got just the girl that Madame was looking for.

5

I'm not going to pretend that I was happy in the Rue d'Eglise. Indeed, there were times when 1 felt like banging the front door as I had done in the Lilywhites'. Madame Coignet turned out to be like most people I have met. She knew which side her bread was buttered on. She was as nice as pie to the " young ladies " from England and America and Italy and Germany whose payments were helping to keep her, but it was another matter with me. I was costing her a pittance, and I had to work for it. " And why shouldn't you ? " said Laura. " You are learning the language, and that's what you came for, isn't it ? The rest of us have to pay for the privilege. You do at least get a small wage, and what's more you get plenty of argot from the other servants. I have to dredge it up in the Halles."

I also got red hands and broken finger-nails and not enough to pay for decent clothes to wear on my rare nights off. It was on these occasions that I met Laura as friend meeting friend. There was a hole-and-corner feeling about it, for she wasn't supposed to meet me at all. But we had ways and means. We would meet in remote places, and I was, as she said, learning the language. It was a point of honour at Madame Coignet's that nothing but French was spoken. After all, that is what the " young ladies " were there for. To the old girl's credit I must put on record that her own French was perfect and melodious. And, as Laura said, I learned the argot. I learned to distinguish between the one and the other. Without boasting, merely as a matter of fact, I found that I had an aptitude for the language, and my two years in France were well spent. I didn't go to England once during those years, and I saved my money for my holidays. They were only a week each, and there were two of them. I spent them in roaming about in the cheapest way, and I could exchange back-chat with railway porters and tramps.

Why Madame Coignet wanted an English servant at all remained a mystery. I solved it, rightly or wrongly, in my own way. Laura was one of her favourite pupils, and it is my guess that Laura and her brother Julian cooked it all up between them, that Madame no more wanted me than she wanted the moon. But those two found me both friendless and with a battered Chardenal and they arranged the scheme between them. It was with Laura that the scheme of the English servant girl originated, and Madame Coignet, severe in most things, was talked (or written) over. When I frankly charged Laura with this, just before she returned to England, leaving me to fend for myself, she merely smiled and said : " Well, if that's the way you want to explain it, there's nothing to stop you," and not another word could I ever get out of her on the matter.

6

It was at the end of the summer term in 1913 that Laura Brogden returned to England for the last time, and now (though necessarily I had seen little of her) I was as lonely as when she and her brother had found me at the Rowans when Judith had gone away. While the house was full of young ladies who were learning how to come into a room and how to leave it, how to curtsey, how to play the piano, how to sit in a chair and how to get out of it, I was scrubbing the stairs and polishing the brass and generally behaving as I had done at Mrs. Lilywhite's. But I was not unhappy as I had been there. I was learning something, if in the most menial conditions, and I was always happy when learning, though it did not occur to me at the time that the two things had much to do with one another.

Anyhow, there I was, red fingers, swollen wrists and all, taking my ease on a seat in the Bois de Boulogne. It was one of my rare afternoons off duty, and it was now the end of June with the sun shining. It had been a fine summer. The brilliant weather seemed as though it would never end, and it was good just to be sitting there, watching the smart frocks that swished by me and thinking that this was an improvement on the Llandaff Fields in Cardiff where I had occasionally dallied with Mr. Ronald Lilywhite. I felt immensely older than I was then, immensely more experienced, when all of a sudden my age and experience tumbled about me, and I was in a moment the stupid red-headed servant-girl of my Cardiff days. Grave, walking slowly as though he were pondering immense matters, Mr. Mell Conybeare was coming towards me.

I think he would have passed by without seeing me, but leaning against the bench, furled, was a parasol that I had bought in a second-hand clothes shop. With a gentle movement of my foot I caused this to fall to the ground, and, in bending down to pick it up, I let fall, too, La Bruyère's *Caractères* that I had bought in a tattered condition on the Quais and had been rather listlessly turning. Startled from his reverie, Mr. Mell saw the parasol, the book, and a red head bent over them. " Pardon, Madame," he said. " Permettez-moi." And in an instant his eyes were down on a level with mine, looking into them.

" Mr. Mell ! " I cried, with what I hoped was a good imitation of complete surprise.

" Why, Miss Openshaw ! " he said.

He sat on the bench at my side, and took in, I thought, every detail of me : my rather frayed cuffs, my red wrists, my dilapidated parasol. For a moment he did not speak, then he said : " I knew you were in Paris. My Aunt Graves told me you were coming here. I seem to remember writing to you about it. But I thought you'd be gone long before this." He added with a smile : " I didn't know that you were still here and reading La Bruyère."

" It's a long way from Tennyson," I said, hoping to call his

57

mind back to those old Cardiff days, "but it all started from there."

"I refuse to be held guilty," he said. "But tell me. What are you doing here?"

I looked at him sideways. He was well-dressed and carried a cane with which he scraped at the path. I told him, and in my pride and self-assurance, I told him in French. It was a shot in the dark, but I found that he spoke French nearly, but not quite, as well as I did myself. I told him of how, accidentally, I had come upon the Brogdens and of all that had happened since.

"And after this—what then?" he asked.

I didn't know, and said so. I had come to Paris to learn French, and after that I had no more idea of what I was to do with my life than the man in the moon.

He was silent for some time after I had finished my story; then he said gravely: "It may not be your own decision. It may be decided for you. Don't you think so?"

I was puzzled by this, and I suppose my face showed it, for he asked: "Don't you read the French newspapers?"

I said that I glanced through them—that was all. In the little time I got to myself there were other more important things to read.

"Haven't you been reading, for example, what they say about this assassination in Sarajevo—the heir to the throne of Austria?"

"Oh, that!" I cried blithely. "But these people are always killing one another."

He tapped the book on my knee. "I think," he said, "you had better put La Bruyère aside for the moment. There may be more important matters calling for attention."

Then he told me something about himself—how he had worked for a time, after leaving Oxford, in the Foreign Office in London, and how, recently, he had been given a job in the British Embassy in Paris. "Still, I am here, as I was there, little more than a clerk. But one lives and learns, as you have found out for yourself. Even a clerk need not be unaware of what is blowing on the wind. So, my dear Miss Openshaw, I advise for the moment a little more attention to maps and the daily papers and a little less to La Bruyère. Well, we may meet again."

He got up. I thought, as I, too, rose and stood before him,

that he seemed very tall. He threw up his left arm and looked at a wrist-watch—one of those things that were then becoming fashionable—murmured something about an appointment, shook my red hand, and was on his way.

I sat again on the bench and watched him pass out of sight, and I suppose here I ought to write that my limbs were trembling, that my legs were like water, or something of that sort. But, rather to my own surprise, they were not. If I felt anything, it was a mild anger, but soon that passed, too, and I felt more like laughing than anything else. It had all been so gentlemanly, so perfect, that it amused me : the stoop for the parasol, the recognition of me, red wrists and all, the refusal then to be surprised or in any way discomfited, the brief conversation. " We may meet again." But I didn't think he was very keen on it. He hadn't even asked my address.

So I sat on the bench and turned him over and examined him as though he had been a pebble in my hand. His sense of duty had been perfect. Everything he had done had arisen from that. He had found me flat on the Lilywhites' path, and had picked me up and borne me off to his father's house as he would have borne a fallen sparrow. He had read bits of Tennyson to me because he thought they were in my mental range, and he had walked gravely with me in the Llandaff Fields, even offering me his arm. When I was fit to go, he had taken me to the Graveses' house, and when Bryan had died and I had resolved on going to Paris he had written to me. " I seem to remember writing to you about it." I smiled as I recalled how much his letter had meant to me, and to find how he " seemed to remember " writing it. Still, it had been his duty to write, and he had written. I took up my battered La Bruyère and set off for Madame Coignet's.

7

I should have starved during the first world war if it hadn't been for Laura Brogden. I was one of a rush of English people to make a last-minute homing. Laura had, in the meantime, become a teacher of French in a day school for girls not far from her mother's house in Golder's Green. We had written often to one another during my last year in Paris, but I think she was unprepared for the shabby down-at-heels creature whom she met at Folkestone. But she said nothing about all that : merely took me as a friend to her mother's house. She rigged me out with her own old clothes which more or less fitted me, and when she was at home, which was only in the evenings, she talked to me. The Coignet régime had been so strict that I had literally got out of the way of talking English, for, after Laura's departure, there had been no English people to talk to. But that was overcome, and we talked usually in English.

Her school was at Mill Hill, no great distance away. She talked at times of trying to get me a job there as assistant French mistress, and this put me in a dilemma. I hated the thought of it. Why I had ever learned French I don't know, but I had learned it, and she could not understand that I had no wish to put it to what she called a practical use. But I disliked the idea of being among a lot of girls. Yet the Brogden household was not blessed with money and I was paying nothing for my keep. Julian Brogden had married, and was, moreover, enlisted in the Artists Rifles. He was away in a training camp and I saw nothing of him. For most of the day I was thrown into the company of Mrs. Brogden, who was an ageing woman, inclined to be neurotic, who didn't like me, and who could not understand Laura's goings-on. She more than once said so—to me, but never to Laura, who held the house together. She protested mildly to me about everything I did, but let me do it, so that soon I was a slavey once more in all but pay, scrubbing floors and blacking boots. It was a small house, one of a row, brand-new. The evidence in it was of people who just " got by ". Only my affection for Laura enabled me to put up with it—this and my sense that being a servant did in some way make up for my never receiving a penny. My heart woke when Laura came home late in the afternoon, but alas ! all too often with girls' exercises to go through. But this was something I could help her with, often halving her work ; and then we would go, however late the hour, for a walk together.

Even with that consolation, I wondered how long I could endure my life. The small respectabilities to which Mrs. Brogden became more and more addicted as the war stretched her nerves tighter and tighter were wearing me out. The hang of a curtain an inch or more to right or left became as important to her as protocol to a Minister, and the blinds had to be run up to a precise point. I, who was satisfied with giving a curtain a casual tug and a blind a run for its money, found that little things were beginning to hang on me like a weight, and I forgot the real things behind Mrs. Brogden's ways. An only son in the forces, a daughter whom she rarely saw, her own widowed state, would have explained it all ; but I was impetuous and wrong-headed and did all I was told with a frown.

I don't think I could have lasted long in the Brogden household ; but I had not to endure. A chance came, and I managed on my own feet to get through the sad long days of the war.

8

On Laura's birthday, towards the middle of 1915, she took a day off from her school on the pretext of illness. It was all eye-wash and we went furtively to town to celebrate. It was characteristic that she paid for everything, even for her birthday lunch ; and that didn't put me in a good temper because, as is the way with human beings, I was feeling more and more resentful against a benefactor, yet there was nothing I could do about it. Laura understood me as her mother never did, and put up with me, even twitted me on my bad temper. We walked about the town for a while, had the celebratory luncheon at one of those restaurants that belong to a chain store company, and, as we came out into Regent Street, almost collided with a young man who was hurrying by. " Well—you ! " he cried, and raised his bowler hat.

That was my first meeting with Evan Bond, in whose office I was to spend the weary years of the war. He was a friend of Julian Brogden and, it is my guess, for what it is worth, that he would have liked to see more than he did of Laura. But Laura was a " career woman " if ever there was one, and, though she liked Bond well enough, it was never as a husband.

It was some time since they had met, and there was much to talk about, especially Julian whom Bond had not seen for some time. So we were taken back into the tea-shop, drank more coffee, and at last got on to the subject of Bond's war-time job. He had been turned down for the Army, and continued to be, though he presented himself with great regularity during the years which followed, when government " funk holes " were periodically cleaned out. He had now been appointed to a staff that concerned itself with French newspapers and periodicals of all kinds. And it was on this staff that I spent the war in an orgy of translation. It didn't take Laura long to persuade him of my qualifications, and once I was there I stuck there. It was at all events a living, and it taught me a lot about putting one language into another, which is a harder job than you might think and did my English as well as my French no harm. I continued to live at the Brogdens', but it pleased me now that my lodgings were not free. His Majesty's government paid me a pittance, and some of this went every week to Mrs. Brogden.

9

It is not my intention to write about that war. It was, as we all know, the war to end war ; but, mysteriously, there has been another since, and I suppose that is the one people talk about if they want to talk about war at all. Clearly a war to end war, which was supposed to have done its job properly and now turns out to have done nothing of the sort, doesn't deserve to be talked about.

Anyhow, the beginning of 1919 found me out of work again, and now there was no question of going back as a free lodger to Mrs. Brogden's. Julian had been killed in the war, and how Laura managed I don't know. Julian's widow, a feckless young thing who had neither money (save her pension) nor talent for making any, had imposed herself upon the small house at Golder's Green ; Mrs. Brogden had become a more and more querulous hulk on the brink of dissolution ; and Laura, padding each day to her school at Mill Hill, was in many ways an inspiring, yet to me, somehow, a depressing figure. I had saved a few pounds, and, with this in my pocket, I set out to take a holiday in Cornwall and think of my position.

There was just a hope of making a little money. I had become acquainted in our Whitehall office with William Dunbar. He was a dry old thing, well over service age, with a loving and intimate knowledge of the French language, and he had in peace time done a good deal of translating for a publisher. He was hoping now to take this up again, and was particularly interested in the novels of Philippe Frémont, none of which had ever been done into English. An English publisher had given him two to translate, and one of these he entrusted to me to take with me to Cornwall.

Chapter IV

It was in May of 1919 that I set off for Cornwall. I was twenty-three years old. Though most of my life had been spent as a domestic servant, I was better educated than most women of my age. I had taken, quite naturally, a great liking for literature, both French and English, and knew those languages inside out. I knew a good deal else, the things that come naturally to a human being as life goes on.

After the wartime in London I was not looking my best. Most of the time I had spent cramped into a small office, and my face was thin, pale and drawn. My hair was as red as ever, my eyes as green ; but no, I was not looking my best.

I took the Riviera Express as far as Plymouth, and there got on to the platform with a rucksack thrown across my shoulder. I wanted the sort of holiday I had had twice while I was with Madame Coignet—a holiday of vagabonding without any objective. There were two things in my favour. One was that, in those days, people walked. It was not at all unusual to meet someone attired like myself, footslogging along the roads, especially in a county like Cornwall. And that was the second thing about it. Cornwall then was rarely visited except by those who took it on its own terms and did not expect it to provide all the accessories of their daily lives. If they wanted those, they knew where to find them and went there ; but now all these things must follow them and be with them for ever. And so Cornwall, as once I knew it, is destroyed, and you might as well

63

put the " quaint old Cornish town " idea out of your head and be done with it. The Cornwall I write about doesn't exist. It marches with the times, God help it.

I spent that night in a Plymouth lodging-house, and crossed the Tamar into Cornwall next day. I had no idea in my head except a much-needed holiday on the open road, and then, when my little money was expended, a return to some large town where I might earn my daily bread.

The war had added to my accomplishments the ability to use a typewriter, but typewriters were as scarce as everything else at that time. To buy even one that had been made from bits of others cost the earth.

However, this did not worry me. I have never been of a worrying disposition, and as I trudged through Cornwall there was plenty to occupy me. It was May time ; there were no cars to speak of on the roads, and the year was at its best. Glimpses of dark-blue sea, birds singing in the air, flowers in quantities and of sorts I had not known before, ample food in cottages, and the novel by Philippe Frémont, read during a rest by the roadside now and then, filled my mind. At nights I would knock at a cottage door, and I hadn't to knock often before I found a night's lodgings. I didn't brown in the sun, but my complexion, such as it was, brightened in the spring weather, and soon I was feeling as fit as I had felt in my life.

So I came to Falmouth and from there went westward, driven on like a lemming that must find the sea at last. I had made up my mind that I would go right through to Land's End.

On the day after I left Falmouth I found myself on the Helford River—an arm of the sea, subject to the tides. There I stayed in a cottage, crossed the river the next day, and made an arc through the country on the other side. I had brought, as usual, a few sandwiches for my midday meal, sat down on a roadside bank to eat them, and then finished Philippe Frémont's novel. I had been on the road, hither and thither, for ten days, and for the first time I felt a wish to stay where I was, for a day or two at any rate, for, strangely for me, my head was aching. I was in wooded country, wonderfully quiet. It was some time since I had seen a soul. A stream gurgled past my feet and lost itself in the elms and sycamores that were all about me. I lay on the bank, hatless, my hair streaming on the grass, and fell asleep.

When I awoke, the feeling I had had earlier, of not wanting to go on, came over me afresh; but I got to my feet with the idea of gathering my scattered belongings. A dizziness in the head caused me to sit down suddenly, and then I was aware of a man watching me from the other side of the road. He crossed over to where I was sitting with my head in my hands and asked: " You feelin' a bit bad, midear ? "

I was by now feeling very bad indeed and could do no more than nod my head.

" You was lyin' there sound asleep when I passed an hour ago," the man said. " An' when I come back 'ere you are still."

He looked at me speculatively, and then asked : " Where's your 'ome ? Can I get you there ? "

I mumbled that I had no home—that I was walking. I could say no more.

" You better come with me," he said firmly. " Never mind all that ole stuff," as I made another effort to assemble my things. " That can stay where it is. No thieves about 'ere. I'll gather it up later. Now you put your arms round my shoulders, midear."

I got somehow to my feet, shivering all over, and did as he bade me. My legs seemed to drag like iron. There was not far to go. Although I didn't know it then, the man's cottage was at the roadside, just round a corner. I was aware of his talking to a woman whom I took to be his wife, of a perilous ascent of stairs, and of being stretched out in a bed. Then curtains were drawn, and I knew nothing more save a sense of peace and quietness, and a drifting upon sleep.

I slept all that afternoon and night, and the next day I was aware of the woman coming in now and then to shake up my pillow, and wipe my sweating forehead, and settle me more comfortably between the sheets. She tried me with a little warm milk, a little broth, but food was repellant to me and I took nothing. She came again late in the afternoon with a man whom I vaguely took to be a doctor, and who was a doctor. He felt my pulse, put his hand on my forehead, and was gone like an apparition. The next day I took a little food, felt my fever ebbing, and slept till the sun was going down. I was able when I woke to notice my things piled neatly on a chair, and the shadow of leaves playing upon the ceiling. The woman came then, and I smiled and gave her a word. " I'm being a nuisance," I said.

If I had announced that I was the Queen of England she could not have been more gratified. She gave me back my smile, and just at that moment the doctor came again. He went through his routine, and then stood back, smiling, too. " She's through the worst of it, Mrs. Davies," he said. " Let her sleep plenty, now, and give her a bit of nourishing food now and again."

I drifted into sleep, and felt so much better when I woke the next day that I announced my intention of getting up and being on my way. Mrs. Davies had brought a bowl of warm milk, and she boosted me up into a sitting position with the pillows behind my head. " Don't be so daft," she said. " You'll drink this and stay where you are for a day or two."

I drank the milk, and what is more I tasted it and thought it good. " Now you lie back again," Mrs. Davies said, " and thank your lucky stars that you was found when you was."

I sank back to please her, and as soon as she was out of the room I got from my bed, anxious to try my legs. They were like rubber and I collapsed on to my knees, clutched the sheets, and managed to haul myself into the bed.

The next day I ate a little solid food, and Mrs. Davies at last volunteered some information. " It's this ole 'flu," she said. " People are dying off like flies." She looked immensely pleased that people were dying off like flies. She was a small rosy woman and she had a small rosy smile. " I never catch nothing," she said with satisfaction. " Davies, he guessed what it was at once, and he said : ' Hospital's the place for her. We'd better get her there in an ambulance.' ' She'll stay where she is,' I told him. ' Hospitals ! People dies off there like flies ! ' "

She watched me eat a little roast beef and a potato, and said : " That's better ! Now I'll tell you what you're going to do. You're going to sit outside in the sun. That's what you're going to do, and then I'll turn this old room out."

She helped me to dress and put a vast shawl round me. " Now you put your arms on my shoulders and we'll get down them ole stairs in two ticks," she said.

And so we did, though it seemed more than two ticks to me. She went before me, shorter than I was, and, clutching her as though she were a small pack-horse, I got down the stairs and through the open door. There, in the minute front garden, I found a deck-chair and more shawls. Mrs. Davies packed me up to her satisfaction and then surveyed me with her small rosy smile. I was glad to be sitting, glad that the adventure downstairs was over. " Now I'll give that ole room a turn-out," she said, already rolling up her sleeves.

In the days that followed I did a lot of sitting in the garden, a bit of walking on legs that gradually got stronger, and I listened to the birds singing and the stream flowing. It all passed into me, and I began to be unhappy. It was so beautiful after the long lists of young men dead, after the stuffy London office, after the little house in Golder's Green. I would soon have to go back. That was the thought that haunted me. My small reserve of money was running out. I would have to pay the doctor and the Davieses. Good-bye rewards and fairies. I must, somehow, get hold of a second-hand typewriter and set to work. For a time I played with the idea of finding a room in a cottage in that delectable part of the country and there, with my typewriter, getting on with my work. But that notion faded. I would have to keep in touch. And this thought of keeping in touch, knowing all the right people, being on the spot, nauseated me. I didn't want to go back.

" You take my arm, my ole dear, and let's have a little walk," said Ben Davies, watching me as I sat one day in the garden on my deck-chair. " Time you was stirring a bit."

It was. The doctor had made his last visit. All I needed now, he said, was Feeding Up and a little gentle exercise. I shuddered as I thought of his bill, and took Ben Davies's arm.

There was a path through the woods, and the stream left the roadway and flowed along this path, and it was soon obvious to me that the trees were carefully tended and were part of someone's private domain. Here and there, amid the now fully-leafed elders and elms, were trees of a rarer sort, camellias that filled the woods with blossoms of white and pink and red, and feathery mimosas whose bloom was already fading, and lilacs and shrubs whose names I did not know. Alongside the stream were primulas and the gold knobs of water-buttercups, and the air was full of singing birds.

There was a bench by the stream, and when we reached this Ben Davies said : " You'd better sit down and rest a bit, my dear. I'm just going on now to 'ave a look at the 'ouse. I'll be back when you've rested your carcase."

I was on good terms with the Davieses by now. I had told them of my walking holiday, and how I would soon have to be getting back to London. They had both spotted Philippe Frémont's novel and were full of wonder at anybody being able to read " them ole foreign tongues." If I had been a visiting princess from some alien court I could not have been more respectfully treated and they could not have resisted calling her " midear ".

I asked Ben now whose were these woods that he trespassed upon so freely, and whose was the house that he was going to see. " Oh, this all belongs to the Boss," was all he told me. " I keeps an eye on the woods. An' it's 'is 'ouse I'm going to look at now. He's been away all through the war. Never come back once. But he's due any ole time now and I better see everything's in order."

" Then it'll be best for him not to find me here," I said, my mind playing with the idea of some old captain or colonel with a gun over his shoulder and a dog at his heels. " You go and see the house now, and I'll get back when I'm rested."

2

I wanted to make this job of translating Philippe Frémont's novel a good one, as an insurance for getting more work of that sort, and so I had brought the book with me. I was a pretty fastidious writer of English because—hardly by choice, but it had so happened—I had read little but classic authors, and in them I had been ranging for years, both in poets and novelists. There were phrases in Frémont's book of which I wanted the flavour as well as the mere sense, and I worked on these for awhile when Ben

Davies was gone, trying over a sentence or two on a writing block I had with me. But my mind was not yet fully recovered any more than my body. I quickly tired, put book and writing block down on the bench at my side, and, lulled by the singing of the stream and the songs of the birds, was soon asleep.

I was awakened by a sense of someone sitting beside me and opened my eyes in alarm. He was a tall man, slightly taller than I am, and I am rather tall, wearing an old tweed hat, a tweed suit, and with an ash stick propped by him against the bench. He was dark, thin and moustached. Philippe Frémont's book was in his hands and he had my writing block on his knee. I had underlined certain sentences in the book in pencil, and he was looking from these underlinings to what I had written. Seeing that I was awake, he said with a smile : " You know, all that Frémont is saying here is : ' The sun was still shining, but darkness came upon them as though a cloud had suddenly blotted out all that light.' Don't you think that is better, simpler ? "

I was too flabbergasted to answer his words. Instead, I said foolishly : " I have been ill. I was resting for a moment. I hope I'm not trespassing."

He said : " Yes. I know that you have been ill. I came a bit sooner than I was expected and met Ben Davies up at the house. He told me you'd been staying in his cottage and that I'd find you here."

He got up, stuffed all my papers under one arm, and offered me the other. " I'll see you back to Davies's cottage," he said. " We'll talk about Frémont later. You still look a bit washed out, you know."

We walked slowly back along the path. I was a little afraid of him. He was not the captain or colonel I had been expecting, but he was the owner of these woods and burgeoning trees and all that my eye could see. And for all the smile that lighted up his face when he wanted it to, he was, in repose, sad and tired-looking.

We came out at last by Ben Davies's cottage, and there was Mrs. Davies hanging garments on the bit of line that stretched across her front garden. She looked at him in amazement for a moment, then cried : " Oh, Mr. Melvill, you're back ! "

" Yes. I'm back. I've got a hundred things to do at the house.

I've just delivered this lady. Look after her. Now give us a hug, and I must be off."

And, to my amazement, the old thing hugged him, laughing and crying at the same time. He hurried off, and I looked at her, and could only say : " You called him Mr. Melvill ? "

" Yes," she snivelled.

" Mr. Frank Melvill ? "

" Yes."

I collapsed into my accustomed deck-chair, and sat there trying to pull myself together, while Mrs. Davies's drawers and pinafores flapped on the line above my head.

3

I had heard Mr. Mell speak of Frank Melvill, the novelist, who had married Judith's sister, Jane. But there was no reason why Mr. Mell should speak much of him, and Judith had hardly mentioned him. She was not a reading woman. Frank Melvill was her sister's husband : that was all. But I had been crazily excited when I heard that there was this relation in the family, because, for some reason or other which I had never analysed, people who wrote books were to me as gods. And so I had read those of Frank Melvill's books which I could get hold of, and my excitement did not diminish.

There was much that I did not know then and that I have learned since. I might as well set it down briefly here. Frank Melvill was an artist's son. His mother had died so soon after his birth that he scarcely remembered her. What he could remember, and always with joy, was growing up with his father in St. John's Wood. I can picture them as a pair very like me and my mother. Nothing much mattered to them except this life together. The boy went to St. Paul's school and the old man worked at his pictures, which were mostly in black and white, to illustrate stories in the magazines so plentiful at that time. It was a quiet, hard-working life for both of them, and they were in perfect accord till the time came when Frank was of university age. Then he said that he didn't want to go to a university : he wanted to be a journalist. " A journalist," he argued, " sees everything. I want to know how people live. And I don't want to be a journalist for ever. I want to write books. But I've got to *know* first."

"Well, there's no harm," the old man argued, " in knowing, to begin with, how young men live at Oxford."

But Frank was obstinate, and it happened that that winter's night old Melvill entertained at dinner a friend of his who was the editor of a magazine for which he did most of his drawing, a man that he was very anxious to keep in with, as they say. And into the pocket of this man's overcoat, as he solicitously helped him on with it, the boy slipped a story that he had written, with a note asking for advice—was it any good ? ; did the great man recommend him to keep on with that sort of thing ?

The story was no good. But it was a turning-point. There was a long pow-pow between the editor and Frank's father, who was persuaded that the boy at any rate could write, and that, when a few corners were knocked off him, he might do the job well.

There is no need to go into Frank's journalistic career. He had " worked himself up " from a weekly in a Yorkshire village to a London daily, and in ten years had indeed, as he had wanted to do, " seen everything ". His father had died, leaving him a few hundred pounds, and, with this for his only financial backing, he had taken a room in London's East End and there produced his first novel *Outcasts*.

It was successful enough to persuade him to go on, and soon after writing his second book he met and married Judith's sister Jane. This was not long after Judith's own marriage to Bryan Graves, and the sisters saw little of one another, for Frank had taken Jane off to Cornwall and there settled down to his own job. Unlike Judith's it was a happy marriage, but it did not last long. While I was in Paris, just before the war broke out, Jane died.

4

These were all facts which I heard of slowly. What I remember of that day when I first met Frank is the joy of the Davieses on his return. It was like him to appear suddenly, without warning. He had spent the night in Falmouth, come on to Helford in one of the taxis then available, and was rowed across the Helford river. The river breaks up into a number of creeks all but dry at low tide. But it was high tide then, and so he came to Dros-y-Mor at the head of the creek. Dros-y-Mor is the house that he had built there. Where the water ends, he and Jane had found, years before this, a ruined cottage which they had transformed into the house in which they settled down. He bought, too, Davies's cottage, separated from the house by the woods, and the Davieses now lived there, rent free, as his handyman and woman. All through the war they had little enough to do save keep the house dusted and aired and the stream sweetly running, and the woods cleared ; but now, as Ben Davies lost no time in announcing, things were going to be different. " You better get along, midear," he said to his wife, " and cook a bit of dinner for to-night. And you, Miss Openshaw, you're invited to go up an' share his dinner, if you feel like it."

I didn't a bit feel like it. For one thing, I was not yet up to eating a dinner of any sort. A bowl of Mrs. Davies's porridge would have suited me far better. I was still feeble on my feet, and the exercise I had taken that day was enough. And, for another thing, I was afraid of Frank Melvill. I wonder if you understand that ? He had been kind and considerate that afternoon, but now that I knew who he was I was afraid of him, as I am to this day of any men or women who have distinction.

But I went.

I should have liked to dress up in radiant clothes, but I had none. There was nothing but what I had stuffed into my rucksack, knockabout rags, and in these, at seven-thirty that night, I went, on Ben Davies's arm, and made my first acquaintance with Dros-y-Mor.

In the few days since I had been allowed to take a little exercise I had not been much farther than the Davieses' garden plot and the fringes of the wood. It wasn't much of a wood. You could walk through it in a quarter of an hour. But it was a lovely one, full of flowering shrubs that had been planted among the trees that originally stood there. And I had not known that a short walk would bring me out to a house. As I went slowly that evening, leaning heavily on Ben Davies, along the path that followed the stream, the flowers were lovelier than any I had imagined, and among them the birds were fluttering at their business of settling down for the night. I said not a word, torn between my emotions of fright at the meeting ahead of me and joy in this present moment.

And then the woods thinned out and the house was before us, lonely, but lonely amid so much loveliness that I could only stand and gaze. The tide was high and the creek was full of quiet water. The sun was all but set, and it turned the cloudless air into a vast mauve curtain, and pinned to that was a sliver of new moon, going down behind the sun. And standing on a platform of turf, with the water before it and the sleeping woods behind, the white house glimmered, silent like everything about it, its curtains drawn. Ben was anxious to take me in at once, but I said : " You go in now. I'll come in a moment."

I stood there alone. Dros-y-Mor has now become an accustomed house to me, but I wish to write of what I saw then. I stood with my back to it and looked upon the creek. This twisted a hundred yards or so from the house, so that I saw little of it. But I saw and I felt the quietness : the fields that sloped down to the water, the heron wading along the shore, a tree here and there, mirrored in the glass of the water, a swan making for the bank with a flotilla of brown cygnets behind it. The water ended at my feet, arrested by a wall that had been built up of the local stone, and to my right stone steps climbed to this grassy platform on which I stood. It had that day been shorn, and the smell of cut grass was all about me, filling the air which trembled now on the verge of night, with the new moon going down. I turned and looked at the house that had been behind me, long and low and white. The tall trees, bursting into full leaf, rose behind it, sheltering it with great arms, birch and elm and sycamore. The stream that ran through them here met the sea. A ghostly tinkle of water, as it tumbled over one edge of the platform, was in my ears, and there, glimmering now, their gold turning dark, the king-cups grew.

Curtains were pulled aside ; a French window was opened ; and Frank Melvill came quietly across the lawn. He was dressed, as he had been earlier in the day, in tweeds, but now he had no hat and I saw that his hair was turning grey.

" Come in, Miss Openshaw," he said. " Mrs. Davies will be dishing up in a moment or two."

I followed him through the French window, which he shut and drew the curtains across. It had turned rather cold, and I was glad to see that a fire of logs was leaping in the open fireplace. It cast shadows on what I saw to be a rather large room. Then Frank touched a switch and a chandelier in the middle of the ceiling filled the room with light.

" Oh, what books ! " I involuntarily cried.

It was an oblong room and, save at this end where the fireplace was, it was shelved from floor to ceiling, and on the shelves were books and books and books. I had not seen so many books since I had known the young man at Harpenden, and, having uttered my exclamation, I was speechless with joy. When I found my tongue again it was to say : " I suppose this is where you write."

" No," he said. " There's an old shed in the woods that I knocked up myself. That is where I write."

There was a deep red-leather chair on either side of the fireplace, and he seated me in one of these. " Excuse me for a moment," he said. " I'll see what Mrs. Davies is up to. I'll let her know that she can serve up now when she likes."

I watched him go out of the room, a tall, sad, greying man. But I was too much excited by the room itself to take much notice of him. A gallery, reached by stairs, was at the back, and evidently from that ran a passage in either direction. To bedrooms, I guessed. Then there was this end where I sat before the fire, with a few pieces of porcelain on the mantelpiece, and for the rest, save for the French window, were books and books. I longed to get up and examine them, but nervousness held me in my chair. I could but look about me, marvelling. Then, in a frame among the porcelain, I saw the photograph of a woman. I had got up to look more closely at this when Frank Melvill came back quietly into the room and said : " She was my wife. She is dead."

I had heard of her. I had heard that Mr. Mell occasionally came into Cornwall to stay with his Aunt Jane, Judith's sister. She must have been alive when I met him in Paris, just before the war broke out. There was nothing I could say. Nothing about her, at any rate. I said: "I knew her sister, Mrs. Bryan Graves."

I don't think he heard me, for he had taken down the photograph and was looking at the dead woman. I can only say that he was looking at it in a *consuming* way. I wished that a man would look at my picture like that.

Mrs. Davies butted open the door with her knee and began to put the dishes, for the meal was set here in this splendid room which had a small table near the fire. "Now put that down," she said, as wheedlingly as a mother, "and get this food into you. And Miss Openshaw had better not overeat, almost as soon as she's out of bed. I've just brought a bit of something special for her."

Frank put down the photograph and drew my chair up to the table. He sat facing me. I don't know what he ate, but for me there was a little fish and bread and a glass of wine—nothing more. It was a rather melancholy meal, because, whatever he ate he ate little of it, and, infected by his mood, I merely toyed with the fish and left my glass half empty. I remember the fire, and the photograph on the mantelpiece, and Frank slipping into deeper and deeper gloom. He addressed hardly a word to me, and this did not help, because I thought it was my fault and that I ought to sparkle. I never felt less like sparkling in my life. There was a shaded lamp on the table, and he switched this on and turned off all other light in the room, so that I was aware of the books about us as row upon dusky row. When he had finished playing with his food and I with mine, Frank suddenly said: "Will you excuse me, Miss Openshaw? I think I'll have to go to bed now. Ben Davies is in the kitchen and he'll see you through the wood."

He got up and pulled out my chair and I said: "May I come some other time to see the books?"

"Come when you like," he said. "No one uses this room except for meals. Bring your translation with you. You can work at this table. Have you brought a shawl or a warm coat? I expect you'll find it a bit cold in the wood."

"She can have an old coat of mine," said Mrs. Davies, who was in the room. "I've got one in the kitchen, and I'll let Ben know that Miss Openshaw is going at once."

A moment later Frank saw me off with a formal handshake, and I was very quiet as I leaned on Ben Davies's arm and walked through the dark wood to his cottage. He had brought a torch whose light bobbed around our feet. I went gladly to bed, feeling more exhausted than I had been for days. I dreamed of walking down corridors of dark books, on and on.

I did not at once accept the invitation to go and see the books, nor did I take my translation along. Instead, I felt that I had had a set-back, and I spent the next day sitting in a deck-chair in the Davieses' garden, with the happily warm sunshine falling about me. Now that Frank was back, Ben and his wife had little time for me. She was up at the house most of the day, and he was doing whatever it was that he had to do. I was glad to be left alone, with a glass of milk and a dry biscuit or two on a wicker table beside me. During the afternoon Mrs. Davies found time to sit beside me for half-an-hour, and in that brief time she was capable of communicating a lot, for she was a great chatterer. I learned, for one thing, of the death of Jane.

It had happened during my last days in Paris, just before the war broke out. Judith had come to spend a few days with her sister ; and Frank, with a book finished, had gone to London, as he always did at such a moment, to hand it over personally to his publisher and to meet a friend or two.

" It was a lovely day," said Mrs. Davies, " and them two took a dinghy down the creek and to the river. There's some good beaches there where no one comes, and they used to go down there and bathe and then row back. Not that that Mrs. Graves could swim. She used to splash an' paddle about near the shore, but Mrs. Melvill she was a swimmer an' would go right out."

Well, that was all that was needed for the tragedy. " No one comes " was right enough that day. There was no one to answer Jane's cry of alarm when, far out in the river, which was so blissfully at rest with the tide high, cramp overtook her. While that poor Judith went beating about in the shallow water, and shouting for help, and no one came, the body at last grew still, and sank, and was never seen again.

5

So there was no funeral, no grave, no ceremonial. Frank did not for a time come back from London, and then he had little to say to Davies and his wife. The war came, and he disappeared. All he told the Davieses was that he was going back to London. Thence he wrote a day or two later to Ben saying that he had joined the army. He was a fit hale man, whose hair had not yet greyed, and he gave his age as less than it was. It was nearly a year later that he went overseas. He was always very reticent about his war-service, but I gathered from him bit by bit that he had done enough, and it was a man whose hair was greying who found himself, a lieutenant, in a base hospital when 1916 closed. That was the end of active warfare for him. For the rest, he was promoted to a captaincy with the business, which he disliked, of showing the great something of the fighting. Politicians, authors, publicists of one sort and another—" even actors ", he would say with a bitter smile—were thrust under his wing for " a visit to the front ". Despising himself, despising them, he would take them as near to danger as he dared—nearer, sometimes, than his orders gave him any warrant for. So he saw the war drag to its end, and here he was, back at Dros-y-Mor, as undemonstratively as he had gone, suffering from influenza like any common mortal.

6

It was only when I heard that he was suffering from the influenza that then was fatally sweeping the world that I realised that, for me, Frank Melvill was not, and could never be, a common mortal. As I sat in the sunshine on the day after taking dinner with him, Mrs. Davies told me that he had kept to his bed. " He's got a temperature and we've sent for the doctor," she said. " I shouldn't be surprised if it's this ole influenza that everyone's gettin'."

It was late that afternoon that Dr. Nancarrow appeared at the garden gate. " I hear you've been spreading infection," he said severely, and this voiced so much that had been in my own

77

mind that I began to tremble at his words. He pulled up a chair alongside mine, and his old country face broke into a smile. " No, no," he said, " don't take on about it. I was having my little joke. Foolish of me."

He felt my pulse, asked his routine questions, and patted my hand. " You're all right," he said. " I sha'n't bother with you any more. But don't you start worrying about him. He's caught this bug somewhere in London, I shouldn't be surprised, before coming on here. Or in the train, perhaps."

He looked at me thoughtfully for a time, as though wondering whether I was the sort of person he could confide in. " I've known Frank a long time now," he said at last. " Ever since he came here, in fact. Knew his wife, too. You've heard how *she* died, haven't you ? "

I said that I had heard that very day from Mrs. Davies.

" All right, then," he said. " You can guess why Frank joined an infantry regiment, can't you ? "

I nodded. I could guess, well enough.

" Very well, then," said Dr. Nancarrow. " He didn't succeed. But that's the difference between you and him. He doesn't care if he dies, and you very much wanted to live. See ? "

I nodded again, glad to have the doctor's assurance that I had not carried the germ, distressed beyond measure by all else that he had told me.

He shut the garden gate and hopped on to his shabby bicycle. " Keep away from him till I give you the word. He's not going to die of this damn' lot if I can do anything about it."

After that, I saw little of the Davieses for a day or two. They slept at the house, and I had the cottage to myself, getting stronger, making myself a bit of gruel now and then, taking a little exercise, and finding at last that my legs were not elastic. I even tried to get on with my work of translation, but that was no good. I could think of nothing but Frank. On the third day Dr. Nancarrow stopped at the garden gate, a more than usually broad grin on his face. " It's all right now," he said. " He knew me this morning. ' Well, you old fool,' he says, ' you've pulled me round again'."

Dr. Nancarrow seemed very pleased with this dubious testimonial, and rode off at once, leaving me to digest the news.

I got up and walked for a time in the wood. It seemed a different place than it had been for the last few days. The young larches were greening, the stream had a more cheerful voice, the birds were singing everywhere. " So they would be if he were dead," I told myself. But he was not. He had turned the corner, and I knew it if the birds and the trees and the stream didn't, and all of a sudden, where I had first met him, on the rustic seat, I sat down and cried. And my tears were more revealing than joy would have been. Did he remember me ? Had he asked for me ? I was strong enough to hope that he had not, that he was aware of little but a blessed coolness after his burning days and nights, that he wanted nothing now but sleep. All the rest could wait. But I loved him so, and his sad grave face, that I prayed the waiting would not be long.

7

Now that Frank was back the Davieses, as they had done in Jane's time, spent all their days at the house and came back to the cottage only in the evenings. I began to feel a nuisance and a hindrance, and suggested to Mrs. Davies that the time had come for me to be paying her and moving on.

" Move on if you like," she said. " But who's been saying anything about paying ? Ben picked you up when you was lying by the roadside and brought you in here. You didn't ask, did you ? We've done nothing but give you a bed. A scrap of gruel's about all you've et—no more than a sparrow."

" Well, there's the doctor's bill to pay," I insisted.

" Never you mind the doctor's bill," she said. " That's being looked after."

I had done such dusting as the spick and span place required, and was giving her a hand with the beds. My strength was back. I felt like walking again.

" That's being looked after," she repeated, smoothing down the counterpane. " But there's such a thing as manners. You ought to wait."

" What have I to wait for ? I can pack my rucksack and go. It's time I was getting back to London."

" All the same, if I was you, I'd wait," she said darkly.

"Tell me frankly," I said. "Has Mr. Melvill been asking
for me. Does he expect to see me before I go ? "

But she was not to be rattled into a straight answer.

"You wait," she said. "And as for doctors' bills, that's a
few shillings—neither here nor there."

She got up and surveyed the bed, her hands on her hips.
"That'll do," she said. "Now I've got to get up to the 'ouse.
If you're gone when I get back, that's your business. Go if you
want to. No one's stopping you. I don't suppose Dr. Nancarrow'll have you arrested on the road for his bill."

She went, and I dallied for a moment in the garden. She
knew as well as I did that I was eating more than " a scrap of
gruel " now. I had just put behind me a breakfast of two eggs,
and bacon, and plenty of toast and marmalade. I went indoors,
and wrote a letter to her and Ben, thanking them for all the
kindness they had shown me. "And I hope," I added piously,
"that Mr. Melvill will soon be out and about again. Please
give him all my thanks for his hospitality to me when we met."
I sat looking at my foolish latter, wondering whether there was
anything else I ought to say, and added : " Please thank Dr.
Nancarrow, too."

Then I sealed the letter, put it where she was sure to find it,
and shoved my things into my rucksack. My holiday was over.
I looked at my map, resolved on a sweep round the head of the
Helford river, and thence to Falmouth. There I could take the
Riviera Express back to London. I would send the Davieses a
little present when I got there. I was full of virtue.

I suppose it was my virtue that led me into the wood that lay
between me and the house. After all, I owed a good-bye to the
place where I had found comfort in those days when my legs
were jelly and I could crawl just as far as the seat that was half-way
along the path. I sat down now on the seat, with my rucksack
on the path beside me. I was still there when Frank came from
the direction of the house, very slowly, stick in one hand, the
other resting on Ben Davies's arm. I got up then, and he sat on
the seat. " This is as far as I can go, Ben," he said. " Thanks
for seeing me so far. Come back for me in half-an-hour. Unless
Miss Openshaw will see me as far as the house ? "

I nodded, for I was too full for speech. He was thinner than ever, white and exhausted, wearing his old tweeds and his tweed hat.

" They haven't been looking after you," I cried, when Ben Davies was out of earshot.

" Is that why you were running away ? " he asked. He poked my rucksack with his stick. " Sit down," he said.

I sat beside him, and we didn't speak. He looked at everything, listened to everything, as though he hadn't looked or listened for a long time. The wrens and the tits and the blackbirds and thrushes ; the gentle ripple of the water ; the camellias and the lilacs. I hardly knew at that time one thing from another. I have learned them all since.

He didn't want to talk, so I was silent, but gradually I became aware that he was happy and rested in my companionship. It was only after a long time that he said : " Coming back was harder than I thought it would be. And then this."

I understood him to mean the illness that had come so suddenly on him, and I said : " You are through the worst of it now. Take things easily. In a week or so you will be as well as ever."

" I wonder," he said ; and at that I cut him short. " Now you'd better get back," I said. " If you want to sit out of doors, you ought to do it on your lawn where the sun shines. This wood is not a good place for you."

He got up obediently and took my arm. " I'll pick up my rucksack on the way back to the cottage," I said.

" So you're not going after all ? "

" Well, I'm in no hurry. Come to that, there's nowhere much for me to go to, and nothing to do when I get there. I might as well see you on your feet again."

So I led him out of the wood, and Ben Davies had anticipated my own anxieties. There was a deck-chair ready on the lawn, with blankets enough to cover a regiment. As I had thought, the sun fell here. When we had made him comfortable in the chair we left him gazing out at the tide which was beginning to fill the creek. I went into the house where Mrs. Davies was preparing the mid-day meal.

" Oh, so you're not gone ? " she said. " I thought you'd be half-way to Timbuktu by this time."

" I think I'll wait till Mr. Melvill is quite well, if you'll put up with me a bit longer."

" As you like," she said.

I went back then, and tore up my farewell note to her, and got on the road. I walked for the rest of the day, eating in cottages, and got back as the sun was setting, feeling as well as I have done in my life.

8

That scourge was world-wide. In all countries people had been dying in thousands. My own attack had been light compared with Frank's, and to him it had come on top of the long anxieties of the war. However, he recovered. The sunshine endured. Each day he took a longer walk, and now, on his insistence, I accompanied him, and then sat with him on what he called the quarter-deck where Ben Davies kept the lawn fine and close. My recollection is of the smell of grass and long times of peace.

Then one morning he said : " Miss Openshaw, are you a girl who could put up with a little scandal ? "

I was rather alarmed, but glad that he was able now to talk of this and that without exhaustion. " I could stand it as well as most people," I said.

" You ought to go now. There's no reason why you should stay. But I've been turning over a few ideas in my head and I want to start work again. My wife, you know, was my typist. When I was done with my stuff she used to type it, and she answered most of my letters, too."

He found it hard to talk of his wife, and there was a long silence between us. I broke it by saying : " I know all about your wife and how she died. You needn't talk about her unless you wish to."

He said simply : " I knew it would be lonely coming back here, but I didn't think it would be so lonely as it is." He added inconsequently : " Of course, I could post my stuff away to a typist, but I don't want to."

" Well, what do you want ? Do you want me to stay and be your typist ? It would be very awkward. I can't impose on the Davieses much longer. There's hardly room for themselves in that small cottage, much less me. I'd have to find lodgings somewhere else, and where I'd do that in such an uninhabited place I don't know."

" We'll talk about it again, then."

" No," I said. " While we're on the matter, let's talk about it *now* and have done with it."

He permitted himself a pale smile, but it was not so pale as it had been. He was getting better. " You're a determined young woman, aren't you ? " he said. " That's one of the things I like about you."

" I'm determined enough to be able to put up with the ' small scandal ' that you speak about. I suppose that would arise if I lived in the house ? "

" It certainly would," he conceded.

" Well, then. I'll live there."

" Thank you," he said. And that was all we said about that.

9

I returned to London the next day in order to settle my few affairs there. I was rather surprised at the smallness of my property. So far, I had gathered little in my journey through life. There was not much that wouldn't go into a few parcels that could be sent by post. Then I finished and delivered my translation and was ready to depart. I sat down on the truckle-bed I occupied in Golder's Green and laughed. It had not occurred to me before what a mobile creature I was. I seemed to have no more property than a snail that carries everything on his back. A few books, a few dresses—that was about all. As for money, I had hardly a penny. At the Lilywhites' and at Madame Coignet's I had got little beyond my food, at the Rowans, not much more. His Majesty's Government, during the war, had not fallen over itself to be generous. I suppose I was the nearest thing to a pauper that ever was. But I felt young and happy, though I was not so young as all that. I sat on my truckle-bed and counted the few parcels round me, and came to the conclusion that all I had was inside me. I had a great knowledge and a great love of both English and French language and literature. I had mooched about the picture galleries in both London and Paris. I knew a lot about men and women. I had learned to use a typewriter. Well, it would have to do. In the morning I would be off. I had said good-bye to Laura Brogden, and there was nothing to do now but use my last few pounds on a third-class ticket to Falmouth and a first-class dinner in London. I had promised myself that, and I did it. There was some satisfaction in the thought that I would be a beggar-maid to Frank's Cophetua.

10

I was away for a week, and I gave no notice of my return. It was a great pleasure to address my parcels to Miss Openshaw, C/o Frank Melvill, Esq., at Dros-y-Mor. Then, with nothing but what would go into my rucksack, I made the journey and spent the night in the cheapest lodging-house I could find in Falmouth. I was away early in the morning in order to catch the tide at Helford, and, once across the river, found myself for the first time being rowed up the creek. It was now June, and the peace of the quiet fell upon me. The busy traffic of yachts in the river was left behind, and there was only this creek whose end I could not see, for a twist hid the house. There were the fields sloping down to the water, and a few trees in them, and cattle lying in the shade, and on the water a heron was wading along the banks and there was a swan of lovely arrogance. We seemed at every pull of the oars to be plunging deeper into peace, and the only sound was the water dropping from the blades and the grunting of the rowlocks. It was at the noon of the day that a final twist of the creek brought the house into view—long and white and drenched in sunshine. Somewhere at the heart of it was Frank Melvill, and I knew again, what I had known all along, that it was Frank I had come to seek, and that if I had found him penniless in a desert it would have made no difference to me. " Is that the house ? " I foolishly asked.

" Ay, that's the house."

The creek ended in a wall, and running to the edge of the wall was the lawn that Ben Davies kept so beautifully cut. Skilfully the boatman brought us sideways-on to some steps. I paid him his fee, took up my rucksack and mounted the steps

84

slowly. It was very quiet. I could almost hear my heart beating, and I was only then aware that it was beating faster than it usually did.

No-one knew that I had arrived. Why should they, seeing that I had given no time for my arrival ? Ben and his wife were presumably in the house. Frank, I hoped, was well and working. I wanted to see him at once, for no particular reason, but for all the reasons in the world. So I watched the boatman out of sight round the bend of the creek, shouldered my rucksack, and went into the wood. Deep in it was a shed. Perhaps Frank would be working in it. I had been told that it was his work-place, and once I had peeped inquisitively through the window. There was a table made by nailing a few planks to trestles. In front of this was a wooden kitchen chair, and beneath it was a bit of cocoa-nut matting.

The shed was some distance from the path beside the stream and it was easy to overlook it, impossible to guess its purpose. Normally, I supposed, he would have trodden a path by his comings and goings, but he had been away for four years and more, and as I stood by the water and looked towards the shed there was nothing but a growth of moss and a few woodland flowers. Carefully stepping on the moss and avoiding the flowers, I advanced and peeped through the window.

There he was. His back was to me. His feet were on the table, and he was smoking a pipe. A neat pile of quarto sheets was by his right hand, and a pen stood upright in an inkstand. The picture of the man perfectly still in the bleak little room was as different as anything I had ever imagined when I had thought of an author at work. I raised the latch and stepped into the shed. " I'm back," I said, smiling with all my joy at seeing him again.

He did not get up, but turned his head to look at me. " So I see," he said.

His face was so unsmiling, so unwelcoming, that I was in a dither. " I thought I'd come and see you at once," I stammered.

" Not here, please," he said. " No one ever sees me here. Shall we meet at lunch ? At one o'clock."

The last words were so precise an instruction that I hitched the old rucksack a little closer to my shoulders and went the way I had come, shutting the door quietly. Quietly, yes ; but inside I was raging. I was back in Cathedral Road, Cardiff ; I was back at Madame Coignet's. I had been spoken to as if I were a servant-girl. I would never forgive him. Why hadn't I banged the door behind me ?

Because I knew I had been a fool. I sat on the seat by the stream, and gradually my rage calmed and I felt my eyes stinging with unshed tears. Soon I let them go. They drenched a handkerchief, and it was while I was rummaging in my rucksack for a new one, angry with him, angrier with myself, that Frank found me.

" It's there, right under your nose," he said, indicating a bit of muslin that I had turned out on to the seat.

I picked it up and dried my eyes. " In a few moments," he said, " I should have got a start into a book that's been worrying me for a long time. Then you come along and put the whole thing out of my mind. Hasn't anyone ever told you to keep away from the shed ? "

" I ought to have had more sense," I mumbled. " But you were very rude."

" I was also very angry," he said, " as angry as you apparently are with me. But take it as a rule—will you ?—that no-one, no-one whatever, sees me when I am at work."

" How on earth was I to know that you were at work ? " I demanded. " You looked very comfortable, with your feet on the table and all."

" They would soon have been under it," he assured me. " But that's enough now. When I'm in the shed I am at work, unpromising as I may look. No-one comes there. Is that understood ? "

I nodded.

" Very well, then. Now come and see what we've done for you at the house."

II

I ought to say something about the house. When Frank bought it, it was a ruin standing above a ruined wall. He rowed up the creek with Jane on their honeymoon, passed into its silence and

86

peace at the noon of a midsummer day, and, rounding the bend, saw the ruin amid the nettles and charlock that ramped there. They climbed the tumbledown steps and ate their lunch looking on the water; and while Jane slept Frank explored. A door hanging askew on its hinges led him into the place, and it didn't take him long to determine to buy it if he might. His father had recently died, and he had inherited a little money. His first book was being a success, and he was determined to live far from London and its meaningless brouhaha. He stayed in London till Dros-y-Mor was finished and, save for the war years, he had been there ever since. The wall was built up, the steps were made good, and all that remained of the old cottage was the splendid room where his books were kept. This had great height, for the upper floor was removed and a gallery put up above at the back. A fireplace, a table or two, a few chairs and the bookcases running right up the walls : that was all that remained of the old building. On either side a wing had been thrown out. In one were the kitchen quarters. In the other, reached by a short passage, was a visitor's bedroom. When you climbed the staircase from the library you found that the gallery led right and left. At the end of one of these short passages was Frank's bedroom ; at the other was a spare room that the Davieses occupied on the rare occasions when they spent a night in the house.

Jane did not see the place till it was finished and ready to be lived in. Frank came down from London each week-end while the work was in progress, and stayed at the Davieses' cottage. He had happened upon it one day when strolling through the bit of woodland which he had bought and added to his small property. The stream entered his wood from a side-road, little more than a track, and not far beyond this point he found the cottage. The neatness of the garden first attracted him, the straw bee-skeps, the laden fruit-trees, the well-disposed vegetables, and perhaps the cooking of Mrs. Davies. Anyway, it did not take him long, being the persuasive man he was, to induce Ben and his wife to become his handyman and housekeeper. He bought their cottage, and there they lived, rent free ; and, once Jane was installed, they came daily to the house.

This, then, was Dros-y-Mor as I came to know it. This was the place I entered with my rucksack on my back, on the morning when I had crashed into the shed and Frank was annoyed with me, and I with him and with myself.

12

Mrs. Davies came in from the kitchen to say that lunch was ready, and Frank said: "You'll have to make it stretch a bit. Miss Openshaw has come." And to me he said: "Chuck that thing into a corner," meaning my rucksack.

I chucked accordingly, and Mrs. Davies, before returning to the kitchen, showed me where my room was. We went out of the library, along the short passage-way, to the new room that had been built there. "This little place opening off it is a closet," Mrs. Davies explained. I was glad that she hadn't adopted the modest modern way of calling it a toilet.

"All right," I said. "I'll look at the room after lunch. Now I'll just wash my hands and come right in."

There was a wash-basin at which I performed my ablutions, as the toilet school would say, and then I went back to the big room which was library, dining-room and everything else. We ate shoulder of mutton with red-currant jelly, new potatoes and cabbage. Then there was a rice pudding and nothing else. I was glad to see that Frank was eating heartily again, and so was I. I eat like a horse when I am well.

When we had finished this simple meal, Frank lit his pipe and, over a cup of coffee, came to the point. "I'm sorry," he said, "if you thought me rude this morning."

"I have known politer men," I said.

He grinned. "You won't have to go far to find politer men than me. But now you know. That is my work-place, and whether I work in it or not is nobody's business. I go there every morning when I am writing a book, and when I am there I'm not to be got at."

"Yes. I understand that. You made it very clear."

"Good. I tried my best to do so. There is a path through the woods and you are welcome to go on that whenever you like. But keep away from the hut. Now there's one thing we haven't discussed, and that's money. There's nothing much to do here. I loathe typing, and that's about all it comes to. Let's get it quite clear. When I'm going full kick I write about a thousand words a day. Well, I suppose you can do that on a typewriter in an hour. Four copies. I could send it out, and in that way I'd save money. But I dislike the idea of the stuff going from under my nose till it goes for good. So there'll be that to do. Then there are a few business letters. Any personal ones I write with my own hand."

I could see that he disliked it all very much. It was something he had to talk about and get over. I disliked it as much as he did. The thought of taking money from Frank was odious to me.

" I'll work for my keep," I said. " Come to that, and now I think it over, I've never done anything else since I left the Lilywhites."

It had not occurred to me before, but it was true enough. At Bryan Graves's I had been " one of the family ", in name anyhow, and that had justified Bryan in paying me what he would have paid any grown daughter, and that was little enough. At Madame Coignet's I had worked with a purpose, and that purpose had been achieved, but, goodness knows, there had been no money in it.

But all Frank asked was : " Who were the Lilywhites ? I've heard Melvill, my nephew, speak of you once or twice, and my sister-in-law, too, Mrs. Graves. And that's about all. Let's go outside while Mrs. Davies clears this lot. We can talk on the quarter-deck."

So we did that. We went through the French window and sat side by side in wicker chairs and I went right back to the beginning. Manchester, Cardiff and Mr. Mell and the Lilywhites. Judith and Bryan and the Rowans. Laura and Madame Coignet and Paris. The war and my long weary labours during that time. He didn't say much, except : " You have done very well. I wish a lot of women had an education like yours. Much better than Roedean and a frisk round Oxford. So you're quite out of touch with the Lilywhites now ? "

" I haven't seen or heard of one of them from that day to this."

" But they're the most interesting family of the lot," he said. " The old man is dead, you know. What became of his wife and the girls I don't know. But Ronald's in clover."

I looked at him very much surprised. " How on earth do you know about them ? "

" Well, I read the papers now and then. There was an article about Ronald in one of them the other day. Mark my words, we'll see a few people like him before we go much farther. It was one of a series of articles about great financiers who have come out of the war. I wonder whether you distrust great financiers as much as I do ? "

" I haven't had the pleasure of knowing any."

" Well, neither have I, come to that, but they always bob up out of a war, you know. You should have stuck to Mr. Ronald. You'd have been a millionaire's wife by now. Just give 'em a generation or two to get honest and be appointed to the peerage, and there they are—the backbone of old England."

He knocked out his pipe on his heel and I saw that he was smiling.

" But tell me about Mr. Ronald," I urged him.

" Well, anyone with a ship or two and a bit of what it takes could make a fortune out of the war. Even you, with your harum-scarum sort of education, ought to know that. Old Lilywhite took Ronald into his business, which was mainly shipping, and I suppose to his own surprise the boy settled down. Some time before the war started Ronald was made a director of the company. He had more sense than to join an infantry regiment or anything of that sort. Or, as the article I was telling you about put it, he was found indispensable to the war effort. Especially when old Lilywhite died half-way through the war. Ronald became managing director then, with his hands on the whole thing."

" I can't believe it ! " I said, with a mind full of Ronald's exploits in Llandaff Fields, and of a night when he borrowed from me the price of admission to the Cardiff Empire, and never paid it back.

" No. I'm sure you don't believe it," said Frank. " But there it is. You ought to have stuck to Mr. Ronald. He's got an estate somewhere in South Wales and—the last sign of affluence —he owns race-horses. Can't you see him on a course, wearing a top hat and striped trousers with a gardenia in his buttonhole ! You didn't know when you were well off."

He pondered Master Ronald for a while and then went on : " D'you know the chief thing about rich men ? They never know when they have had enough. There are two or three of them in England now, whom I could name, who are after all they can lay their hands on. Your Mr. Ronald is one of them. He's buying up all sorts of things right and left. And d'you know the dangerous thing about them ? They are doing it with other people's money. What does Mr. Ronald know about cotton ? "

" Nothing so far as I know."

" Well, he's bought a few mills, and he's having a go at theatres and music-halls. Those are just some of the things that earn him a place in any list of the great financiers of our day. Well, you'd better go in now and have a look at your room and the house in general. I'm off for a walk."

I watched him go along the woodland path with his ash stick, and then I went to inspect my bedroom, sitting-room and office combined. As I have said, it opened off a short corridor that led from the one splendid room of the house. The window overlooked the quarter-deck and the creek. Under this window was a table, a typewriter upon it, and a ream of typing paper with a box of carbons. There was an easy-chair in front of the fireplace, which was an electric one, with a hanging-lamp so that one could sit there and read in comfort. Pushed against the back wall was a single bed with a cretonne-covered counterpane, and alongside this, too, was an electric lamp, so that, if I felt like it, I could read in bed. The cretonne was repeated in the window-curtains. A small chest-of-drawers and a small book-case, unfilled as yet, made up all the other furniture in the room, which was carpeted up to the skirting-board in sage-green. A door opened upon my small lavatory, and that was all. But it was splendour compared with the room I had had at the Lilywhites' or with Madame Coignet. Indeed, it was the best room I had had anywhere in my life. The only disorder was that the parcels I had sent by post were tumbled on the bed and my rucksack was thrown into a corner. I undid the parcels and put my few bits of finery into the chest-of-drawers, which was still all but empty when I had done. Most of the parcels contained books, and these I arranged in the bookcase—my Tennyson, my beloved Keats, the Oxford Book of English Verse, a few novels in English and French. Then,

91

stuffing all the wrappings into a waste-paper basket that was near the typing table, I stood back and looked about me.

There was a knock at the door and Mrs. Davies came in. " Well, what d'you think of it all ? A fine ole time we 'ad arranging everything to suit Mr. Melvill."

" I thought you'd done it all to suit me," I laughed.

" Well, you, too, I suppose," she said with her hands on her hips, looking about her. " But him chiefly."

I rather puzzled Mrs. Davies. Before Frank had come home, while I was still recovering in her cottage, she had learned a lot about me. She had learned that I had been a servant-girl, a fact which I never concealed from anybody. It seemed to me as honourable a job as any other, though a scandalously underpaid one, and we are reaping the harvest of that now. But Mrs. Davies, who had been a servant herself in her time and knew the indignity with which servants are treated, never could make up her mind whether to call me midear, or Miss Openshaw, or Madam. So " You, too, I suppose," about summed up her attitude to me, and if " him, chiefly " gave an order about me —well, that had to be obeyed. Not that Frank was lavish with his orders. I never knew a man who, more than he, found a suggestion enough.

13

The next morning Frank went to the shed. This time, no-one disturbed him. I don't remember ever being in the ramshackle place again while he lived, except to drop his morning coffee on the table and steal out. But I had learned, and did not forget, that it was a holy of holies. " You'd better take your breakfast alone," he said ; so I put it on a tray and carried it to my own room. I put the typewriter on the floor and ate at my work-table. I was learning. I took care not to return with my tray till he had had a chance to go. I guessed, and rightly, that he loathed so much as a word while he was taking his breakfast. His morning's work had already swallowed him up, was demanding some shape and substance. When he came back that morning he put a few quarto sheets in my hand and said : " Well, that's a beginning. Four copies."

He was blithe enough at lunch time. It was a happy thing about Frank that he did not, as it were, carry his books about with him. So long as work was in progress he was completely unapproachable in the mornings. Thereafter, he seemed to forget that the writing of a book had ever entered his head.

That afternoon we walked. " I've never employed a secretary in my life," he said. " Better make some use of her as a walking-companion." But he had been thinking about me, all the same. In the course of our walk he said : " I use a bank in Helston. You'd better come with me next time I go there, and open an account. Then I can tell them to pay your wages into it weekly. It'll save a lot of bother."

It certainly saved him what would have been the anguish of paying me every week. He didn't ask how much I wanted, but, later, when I saw that he was paying me four pounds a week and " all found ", as they say, I was more than satisfied.

So we settled down at Dros-y-Mor. I typed every morning what he had written the day before, and then, in the afternoon he walked. If he didn't want me to go with him he said so, and the same freedom was allowed to me. As often as not I stayed at the house, or wandered on my own. And then, one evening the dinghy arrived from Helford river.

14

We had finished dinner and had taken our coffee on to the quarter-deck. The tide was coming in, and what had been a thin trickle of water under our wall was gradually deepening. We sat there without speaking, for in such moments there is nothing to be said that isn't trivial. The sky was a-flush with small pink clouds. The birds had done their singing. There was not much singing even in the sunlight at that full time of year. The tide wasn't rising with the vigour I had sometimes noticed, but was gradually deepening—a tide " that, moving, seems asleep ". However, it was talking in its sleep, all sorts of little sucks and gurgles ; and the swans that lived on the creek were floating like white phantoms.

Then, round the bend, came the dinghy. A sailor was rowing it, necessarily with his back to us ; and, facing our way, was a man in evening clothes, with a light cape thrown over his shoulders. Frank, who was smoking his pipe, asked through one side of his jaw : " Shall we go in ? Looks like someone from one of the big yachts in the river."

It did, for, as the dinghy drew nearer, I saw that it was all spick and span, with the painter cheesed down, with the paint-work sparkling, with the rowlocks, that were of brass, polished up to the nines. I knew Frank's dislike of being casually accosted, and so understood his wish to vanish, but I said : " Let's see who they are. It'll be rather pointed if you go in now." With a grunt of acquiescence he sat where he was.

The dinghy, the outside beautifully varnished, was now almost at the steps, and the man in the stern, taking a cigar out of his mouth and knocking the ash into the water, said : " That'll do, Wilson."

Wilson backed water, and rested on his oars.

Suddenly I knew who the posh gentleman was. He had filled out and was inclined to the florid and wore a moustache. He had an air of owning not only Wilson and the dinghy but the water thereabouts and all that thereon was, including the landing-steps, Dros-y-Mor, Frank himself. " I'll get in," I said with affright.

" You'll do nothing of the sort," Frank said. " You told me to stay here, and you'll stay with me."

The man in the dinghy now shouted : " D'you mind if I come ashore and stretch my legs for a moment ? " and without waiting for a yes or no, he said : " Put her into the steps, Wilson."

Wilson did so, and in a moment Ronald Lilywhite was standing on our little quay. The tide was now about full, for it was a spring tide with the quiet water almost lapping the grass where we sat on our deck-chairs.

" Nice place you've got here," said Ronald. He looked about him with a proprietorial air, as though at any moment he might buy us up. " Just having a look round after dinner on the yacht," he explained. " Tide just right."

For the first time, he looked us full in the face, annoyed, I think, by Frank's silence. But now he saw me, and gave a start. I suppose his instinct would have been to repudiate me, to forget all that once had been ; but (allow me to say this) I had grown into a beautiful woman. My red hair had lately been bobbed, which was coming into fashion then, and I was wearing a green dress. He stared at me.

He was standing on the edge of our quay, and Frank got up lazily and stood at his side. " You seem to know this lady ? " he asked.

All of a sudden, this was the old Ronald. He let out a laugh and said : " Know her ? I should think I do. She's Alice Openshaw, isn't she ? She used to be a skivvy of my mother's in Cardiff."

" Skivvy ? " said Frank.

Ronald saw that he had used the wrong word and attempted to recover himself. But there was no time. Frank pushed him in the chest, and he went backwards. He had not far to fall, for the tide was well up now. But he made a great commotion. However, he was a good swimmer. I remembered how he had used the Cardiff baths a lot. A stroke or two landed him at the steps, where the bewildered Wilson took him aboard. Frank put his arm under mine and led me back to my chair, whence I had started in alarm at seeing the turn things were taking. We watched Wilson row round the bend, and just before they disappeared Ronald turned in his seat and shouted : " You'll hear more of this, sir ! "

Frank re-charged his pipe. " I doubt it," he said. " But even if I didn't, I'm glad I did that. It's not a word one human being uses of another, especially when I had brought this lady out here for no other purpose than to ask her to be my wife."

15

I don't know what I should have said then. I realised that, all through the summer, I had been engaged in a war against my own feelings. Frank, as a man,—a man, too, with whom I was in such close contact, walking sometimes in the afternoons, sitting here on the quay or in the library at night—had besieged my imagination. Sometimes he talked of the books on his over-flowing shelves, though he talked little of books. " I leave that to Mell," he said once with a grin. " I just write 'em." And as I typed each day what he was writing now I realised that he did indeed " write 'em". I am not much of a critic. In any case,

I was prejudiced by being so close to the author. But I could not help all that. I could not help a worshipful feeling creeping over me, till I realised that life without Frank would be hollow. And this was where my warfare began, for I knew that all this must be bottled down, suppressed, by no means allowed to appear. So I handed him his typed sheets each day as calmly as though they had been the accounts of a company, and each day there was, on the mantelpiece in the library, the photograph of Jane. When all was said and done, she had been for more than four years dead ; but what did I know ? How strong were the bonds between them, even now ?

But I found myself using all a woman's tricks and snares, and despised myself for it, but couldn't help it. For one thing, I had always been careless about my clothes. Not that I had ever, in all my life, had money to buy much. But even such as I had, I, as often as not, did not put on. Even my hair, which was something, I neglected. Now I found myself dressing for dinner, brushing my hair to show it off at its best, and in a dozen ways making myself as personally attractive as I knew how.

Frank took no notice of it. At any rate, I thought he didn't. Even my proposal to index and arrange his books was turned down. " A fine mess that would be," he said. " Leave the old jumble as it is. Then I'll know where things are."

So it was. I walked when he wanted me with him. I stayed, or walked by myself, when he didn't. Above all things, I avoided the appearance of thrusting myself under his notice, except in that one small matter of my clothes. I bought a pair of golden evening shoes to go with the green dress I was so fond of ; and one night, when I didn't put them on, he asked where they were. " They go well with that dress," he said. It wasn't much, but it was something.

And so, I say, I don't know what I ought to have done when Frank, almost casually, said that he had taken me out that evening for the purpose of asking me to be his wife. But at that moment Ben Davies came out of the house. " The ole electricity 'as failed," he said.

Frank got up. He was very proud of the electricity, which wasn't usual in a rather remote country house at that time. It was a private installation, and the generating plant was in a stone hut in the middle of the wood. Normally, this was a situation that he would have looked into personally, but now he merely said : " Well, see that there are plenty of candles where they will be wanted. Then you and Mrs. Davies can get off home. Call on that chap in Helston about it in the morning."

It was characteristic of Frank that he couldn't ring up the " chap in Helston ". Electricity, yes. But a telephone, no. " I don't want every jackass in the neighbourhood getting at me."

So Ben Davies went, and the tide lapped quietly at the wall, and a full moon climbed slowly out of the eastern sky. The cattle in the fields alongside the creek were beginning to lie down under the trees, and the only sound was the heart-breaking cry of curlews now and then falling into the dusk. Frank said : " I suppose I am a good ten years older than you. Perhaps I had no right to say what I did to that eminent financier."

I said nothing, and he put an arm round my waist. " But I couldn't stand it," he said, " when the toad used that abominable word. Was it wrong of me ? "

I was shivering all over, watching the moon getting bigger and bigger, listening to the sad crying of the birds. " Was it ? " he insisted.

" Nothing you do," I said, " can ever be wrong. To me."

He led me towards the house which was now dark save for the pricking here and there of a candle-flame. He shut the French window of the library behind us and shot the bolt. I turned to the passage leading to my room, where a candle was burning on a table, and this I took up in a hand that trembled. Frank blew out the little flame and put the candle-stick back on the table. Then he drew me into the large room and took up a light that stood there. Supporting me with one arm, he led me up the stairway to the corridor at the end of which, I knew, was his bedroom. Half-way along it he blew out his candle, too, and we entered a room that was now flooded with moonlight.

16

Mrs. Davies came at eight every morning. At seven, I was in my room and in my bed. When she appeared with the customary cup of tea she said : " Mr. Melvill's going off to Truro early to-day. So you can stay in bed if you like. He's having his breakfast already. Nearly finished. And Ben's gone over to Helston to see that man about the electricity."

I had been wide awake. I hadn't slept at all, though I pretended a great drowsiness. Goodness knows what I had imagined. It seemed to me that last night's bliss must be written all over my face, all over every inch of Dros-y-Mor. It was a comfort to hear her speaking of normal things. Frank was going to Truro. Ben was going to see a man about the electricity.

So I yawned and rubbed my eyes. "Don't bother then about breakfast for me," I said. "I'll make do with this cup of tea and a biscuit or two." I snuggled back beneath the bed clothes, glad when she was gone. And then, indeed, I slept and did not wake until she shook me by the shoulder. "Lunch is nearly ready," she said. "I'll be laying it in a quarter of an hour."

I must have looked as though my very sleep had betrayed me, as indeed my dreams would have done, but she said no more, and, dressing quickly, I went in to my solitary meal.

17

In the afternoon I took a deck-chair and sat on the quarter-deck, watching the water over which Frank must return. There seemed nothing else to do except watch for Frank. He filled my imagination. The sun streamed down and the water, at our end of the creek, was only a trickle. I knew that there would not be enough to bear him home till dinner-time, but I sat and watched it, as urgently wishing it to flow as Canute's courtiers wished for it to ebb. I wondered whether I would have wished to upset the habits of nature if it had not been for last night. But there *had* been last night, and that had taught me that I should always feel this emptiness, this hollowness, when Frank was away. I thought of his face on the pillow in the moonlight, so much at rest, so peaceful, and I felt proud that I had put on it a touch of fulfilment that I had not seen on it before. I thought of Jane, who had been more than four years dead, and of the four years, of danger, of restlessness, of emptiness, through which he had passed. And there I sat, longing for him to be back, for the tide to flow. There was an old dinghy, not a bit like the polished thing in which Ronald Lilywhite had appeared, kept always tied up to the steps that led to the quarter-deck. Frank used this on the rare occasions when he wanted to go across the river to Helford. Thence he could always pick up a conveyance to Falmouth and so get by train to Truro. And it was this old boat which I now sat awaiting as anxiously as though it were King Arthur's barge with a crew of queens.

It came, when I was out there in the evening, as most things come if we wait long enough for them, and very commonplace it was—a boat that needed painting, that was inclined to be wet, with a man rowing slowly as he smoked a pipe. But it was Frank who was rowing. As he came round the bend he turned, and saw me there, and waved. Oh, all these little actions—so small, so usual, a man waving from a boat—but I was filled with emotion as though Drake had come back after circumnavigating the world.

I knew from the state of the tides that he would return after the usual time of our dinner, so I had told Mrs. Davies to make it a little later. " As if I didn't know as much as you do about them ole tides," she grinned ; and now I ran in and told her that Frank was in sight. She had laid the dinner-things and got busy in the kitchen, so I returned to help him quite unnecessarily to land. And there he stood on the quarter-deck, the man I had not seen for all those hours—oh, months, years—and he said nothing, but put an arm through mine and led me into the large room. I had put on my green dress and my golden shoes and my hair was neatly brushed, but he took no notice of any of it. He merely said to Mrs. Davies : " Fetch Ben, and come back here with him, will you ? " And when they were both there, he took my arm a little closer and said : " I've been over to Truro to-day, as you both know. What you didn't know was that I went to see the registrar. I've fixed everything with him and I'm going to be married next Thursday. Miss Openshaw here will be my wife. Now I'll go and have a bit of a wash, and then we'll have dinner at once. I see you've got the lights on again, Ben."

Ben nodded mutely.

" Good man," Frank said, and went upstairs to his room.

The news was too astonishing to the Davieses to allow them

to say much. Rather vaguely they wished me luck, then shot off, as I imagined, to have a good talk in the kitchen. I was as astonished as they were. He hadn't even asked me to marry him ! Well, perhaps he had in his own way. He had told Ronald plainly enough !

Chapter V

We did not ever again see Ronald, who had, in a way, precipitated this crisis. Frank told me that, when he arrived in the river on his way to Truro, the handsome yacht had vanished.

On the Wednesday night we slept in Truro, were at the registrar's in the morning, and were married. I don't remember anything about that. I only remember that Frank had told me to bring such things as would go into a rucksack and a solid pair of shoes, and he did the same. After the ceremony, we took a train to Plymouth and stayed there for the night. The next day we began our wandering honeymoon. We struck on to Dartmoor and strolled across it and fetched up at Exeter. Then we walked all over Devonshire and Somerset and ended at Porlock, overlooking the grey water of the Bristol Channel. Frank, like me, was an untiring walker. It was not till we were in Bristol that he said : " I think we'll take train from here to London. We can get out into Hertfordshire and see Jane's sister, Judith. Mrs. Bryan Graves, that you lived with at one time. I haven't seen her since her husband died."

2

I'm afraid I tend to see everything through Frank's eyes, and I must record that he loathed big hotels and all the ceremony that was connected with them. That was why we found ourselves in a very small one in London, one that was compatible with our rucksacks and, by now, wayworn shoes. Not that we spent long

in it. We had no sooner eaten our evening meal than Frank said :
" Let's go out and have a walk."

Anywhere was a walk to him ; it didn't matter whether it
was over the granite headlands of Cornwall or through the back
streets of London. " I hate books that stink of a study. You
can always *see* something if you go out for a walk."

We rambled through the streets on the north side of the
Strand and presently came out on to the Embankment. There we
walked for a time and presently sat down on a seat giving a view
of the river. It was getting towards dusk ; the lamps had just
sprung alight above their dolphins, and on the water and beyond
it, on the south bank, there were lights. In the sky, too, the lights
began to come out, so that I remember it as a night when there
were lights everywhere, above us and around us and on the barges
that slid quietly over the dark water. Frank took my hand, and
we sat there like any other sentimental couple, with nothing to
say to one another but much to think.

It was while we sat thus that we watched a couple leaning on
the wall not far from us. The man's arm was round the girl's
waist, and now and then they kissed. They had clearly forgotten
those who came and went on the pavement behind them. No-
one existed except the man for the woman, the woman for the
man. Their faces were so close together that it was impossible
to recognise them, and it was not till they had stepped away
from the wall and begun to move, coming towards us, that Frank
exclaimed : " Mell ! You, of all people ! "

I was as surprised as he was. " You, of all people." The
words summed up all I had ever thought of Mr. Mell, though
I had thought less and less of him as the years went by. I was
seventeen or so when he sat at my bedside and read the *Idylls
of the King*, gave me an arm through Llandaff Fields, and landed
me on the Graveses. He, I suppose, was then twentyish. Save
for my back-street adventures with Ronald Lilywhite, I had
never met a man who took any interest in me, and I regarded
Mr. Mell with a reverence that could easily have become something else. There was a gravity about him that was a new quality
in my experience. He was, to me, like one of the Arthurian
knights that he read about. I am afraid that he became dangerously
like Galahad ! But, after the short adventure with the Graveses,

he had passed out of my life save for that one meeting in Paris on the eve of the war, and at last almost out of my imagination, but, if I recalled him, which I did less and less, it was as a rather solemn young man, the last man in the world I should have expected to find with a girl on the Embankment, his face at times dangerously close to hers. I realised with a shock that I was now nearly twice as old as the girl he had read to in a bed in Cardiff.

But, if this was something of a shock to me, it was an even greater shock to realise, as they came closer and halted on the pavement at Frank's words, that the girl with him was Laura Brogden. She was re-arranging a hat which his kisses had knocked endways. And here was Mr. Mell saying : " Let me introduce you to Miss Brogden," and Frank, making room for them on the seat, replying : " Let me introduce you to my wife."

Though Mr. Mell—Mr. Melvill Conybeare, to give him his right name—had been called after Frank, who had married his Aunt Jane, they had seen little enough of each other, and there can hardly have been two men more different. Mell was all scholar. He had known public school and University, and after that the Foreign Office ; while Frank had wanted, and obtained, the liberty that the rejection of these things brought him. The two had not met after Jane's death. Mell was surprised now to learn that I knew the girl who was to be his wife, and that, indeed, I had lived in her house for some time. He was always surprised at the odd chances that happen in life ; quite at home with all the things that follow one another, like university following school and a Methodist minister being shifted to a new town every three years. It was a natural sequence of things that had landed him in the Foreign Office, for that was where he wanted to be, and all his sequences led to what he wanted and worked for. The one thing that appeared greatly to surprise him was that he was engaged to be married. " You know," he said more than once, " I hadn't *intended* to get married. At any rate not for a few more years. I had intended to be an Ambassador first." All this with great seriousness, as though he were genuinely puzzled. " And now I've asked Laura to marry me. Only a few moments ago, in fact. And she said Yes." He couldn't get over her saying Yes.

" Well, what did you expect me to say ? " Laura asked him, examining her still ringless finger ; and that reminded me that Frank had never given me an engagement ring. Not that I expected one, Frank being Frank. He was far more likely to think of my rucksack and the state of my shoes.

" I didn't know what you'd say," Mell answered. " Of course, I hoped it would be Yes. But it's all so unexpected."

It *was* unexpected, as I learned in a moment or two. It happened in this way. The war had come and gone, and all through that time Mell had remained at the Foreign Office. It had become his habit, whenever he could spare the time, to go out to Harpenden once a week to see how his Aunt Judith was progressing. She was a widow, she was living alone at the Rowans, she was his aunt. All these things added up, for Mell, to a duty, though he had no great feeling for his aunt, but a duty was something that a man discharged. Thus it was only in times of crisis that he didn't go to the Rowans once a week. When the war ended, he continued to make his weekly visits. A few weeks ago, he had met Laura Brogden there.

I had been neglectful of Laura. The sense of duty was not so strong in me as in Mell. Besides, I had other things to think of. Since I had said good-bye to her on going down to Dros-y-Mor I had not once written.

And so it happened that one week-end she had gone over to the Rowans to ask Judith, whom she had never met, whether she had news of me. She was more faithful to me than I had been to her. Judith, who had not forgiven me for, as she thought it, deserting her and going to Madame Coignet's, knew nothing of my movements and was able to give her no information. But a friendship of sorts sprang up between the two women, and Laura more than once called at the Rowans. It was during one of these calls that she met Mell, whose sense of duty was disrupted, and who now met Laura instead of his Aunt Judith at week-ends. Poor Judith was altogether distracted by the turn events had taken. To her despairing cry : " But why can't you meet Laura *here* ? " there was, I fear, only one answer.

All this I gradually learned ; but there was only one thing blindingly clear : that the girls' school at Mill Hill would soon be advertising for a new French teacher.

There were, of course, that night the usual formalities : me congratulating Laura and Mell, and they congratulating me, and everybody, it seemed, congratulating everybody else. There were plenty of couples leaning and kissing on the wall, and it is surprising that, in the general atmosphere of good will, we didn't go and congratulate them all. However, that would have been a bit too much to ask of Mell, who hadn't yet quite got to calling Laura by her Christian name, and now informed us that he must get Miss Brogden to her underground station and see her off to Golder's Green. He said that he would be calling on his Aunt Judith at the Rowans at tea-time in a day or two, and we arranged to meet him there. When they were gone, Frank said : " D'you know I've omitted part of the protocol ? I saw Mell eyeing your left hand, and it was only then that I realised that I had never bought you an engagement ring. I don't know that our marriage is quite sound in the eyes of the Foreign Office."

I said : " One of these days you shall go to Cartier's and buy me a massive emerald surrounded by small but excellent diamonds. Meantime, I'll do with a wedding ring."

So we leaned on the wall again, and Frank kissed me, and we forgot, as near as maybe, Mell and Laura ; and I knew the tone of his voice when he said : " Let's get back to the hotel."

3

Frank had written to Judith at the Rowans, telling her the date and time of our call, and she was waiting at Harpenden station to greet us. I didn't know what to expect, for it was a long time since I had seen Judith, but I certainly had not expected the gay creature who met us as we stepped off the train. Gay but old. That was the horrid thing about her. She was much older than Frank, and had aged during the war years, and there were wrinkles round her eyes and lines at the corners of her mouth. But, in common with thousands of women at that time, she had taken to cosmetics and was dabbed all over the cheeks and lips, and she extended to us a claw-like hand that was finished off with talons that flashed scarlet. It was a lovely day and I was wearing no hat, which is perhaps why I was surprised by the juvenile-looking structure tottering and tumbling on her hair which was dyed, and was bluish. Her very voice had acquired a new note, and as she came forward a shrill falsetto greeted us. It kept up a chatter all the way to the Rowans, to which she took us in a taxi. She didn't walk any more. She talked of neighbours and bridge-parties, and of holidays with her friend, a certain Connie Lee-Smith, till I was dazed and confused. The one thing she didn't do was congratulate me and Frank on our marriage. I don't think she really considered us married. She never understood how Frank could be married to anyone but her sister, and, as for me, she didn't concede that I was quite the sort of person to marry at all.

The Rowans was not the house I had known. It had been bad enough in my time, bleak and forbidding; but now it had a ghastly welcoming air. The garden, back and front, was all set out in little formal squares in which flowers stood on parade with not a weed between them, and as we passed up the gravelled path to the front door she chattered of her love for calceolarias and lobelias, this and that. Everything she spoke of was referred to in superlative tones. She " loved " or " adored " or " positively worshipped " everything about her.

Inside, the house was like this new Judith : all gimcracks and knicknackery. She hadn't gone " all modern " as they say, but had fallen back on Victoriana, which, she assured us, was "coming in" again. So there were silken bows on the chairs, and plush photograph frames on the mantelpieces, one containing a picture of Mell ; and here and there card-tables were folded and thrust against the walls. " Cards are such a Solace," she assured us, with almost a reverence in the capital S, " and really we play for very small stakes. Connie Lee-Smith and I are usually partners, but we lose very little." At the thought of her small losses, she giggled—yes, positively giggled like a Victorian miss.

I was desolated, and I think Frank was too, though he kept up a conversation of sorts ; and I longed for Mell to come and put us all out of our misery, for I found nothing to say, nothing at all. He came at last, having walked up from the station, and Judith embraced him and told him he was a naughty boy not to have brought Laura. He looked at her gravely and told her of his engagement ; and then she was even more girlish and said she was not sure she could forgive him, " because Laura, you know, I am almost certain, stole dear Alice from me and sent her away to be a servant girl in that horrid Madame Coignet's house."

I had not known till then that I was dear Alice; but I was quite certain that we were all invited to note those words "servant girl". But Mell answered manfully, though with a slight blush : " I think I could forgive Laura anything, especially placing Alice at Madame Coignet's, which did her no end of good. She speaks French better than I do."

" Oh, French," cried Judith, brushing the matter off her slightest notice. " Well, now, I've got a jolly surprise for all of you. We're going to tea with Connie Lee-Smith. I must just dash upstairs to put on a face, and then I'll be with you. I think we can manage to stagger to her house without a taxi. Do you mind ? It's only ten minutes' walk."

So we staggered, Mell chivalrously taking his aunt's arm, and Frank and I dawdling a little behind. Connie Lee-Smith's house was on the ridge, like Judith's, and it was, as she had promised us, only ten minutes' walk away. It was new since my time, a house twice as big as Judith's, with twice as much garden, and having an appearance of trying hard to have twice as much of everything. There were twice as many lobelias in the flower-beds, and twice as many bees were making a buzz twice as loud as you would hear anywhere else. There were twice as many windows, and there was twice as much ivy on the brick walls. A general air of twiceness hung about the whole place. Connie Lee-Smith was sitting on a deck-chair overlooking the valley, looking twice as large as life. She was a childless widow, older than Judith, with an appearance of having taken much trouble to conceal the fact. Her face was large and fat, and looked like a newly-painted house front. A Pekingese was asleep at her feet, and I am sure that he would have yapped at us twice as loud as any dog between here and Timbuktu, but he was so over-fed, like his mistress, that he was incapable of yapping at all. " Oh, you must forgive little Ching-Ching for not getting up to greet you," said Connie Lee-Smith, " but he's having his afternoon siesta."

Her hair, like Judith's, had been dyed blue and there was about her a look of sluggish good nature. She waddled before us into the house and we took tea in the drawing-room. She was all butter to Frank, whose books she praised to the sky, but he drew her out enough to make clear that she had not read one of them. Judith's chatter ceased ; she looked worshipfully at Connie Lee-Smith. It was obvious who was the guiding spirit of that strange partnership. It would need only a shocked exclamation from Connie : " But, Judith, your hair ! " for her to rush forth and have it transformed till it glowed like the summer sky ; and one glance round the drawing-room was enough to establish whence had begun the passion for Victorian knicknacks. Even the maid-servant, who handed us little cakes as we sat here and there in rickety chairs, wore a detestable servant's cap. I writhed, remembering the Lilywhites, and when the girl was addressed as " Smithers " and told brusquely to replenish Mrs. Melvill's cup, I writhed again, remembering You and Openshaw.

Frank discovered an engagement in town almost as soon as tea was finished. There was a train from Harpenden which we could catch. " Oh, why didn't you tell me ? " cried Connie Lee-Smith. " I could have had the car at the door. My man could have run you there in no time."

But Frank professed a love of walking, and we walked, leaving Mell dutifully holding the fort. " So there's a man, too," said Frank, breaking the silence when we were half-way to the station. " Well, well." And this " well, well " was the only comment I heard from him on Judith and Connie Lee-Smith.

4

This was the only time that Frank had interrupted the writing of a book in order to go away. It was his custom to drive at the task daily until it was done. But his marriage to me and our honeymoon were an exception—an exception, however, that came to a sudden end. A restless desire to be at work seized him, and it was that very night, when we had returned from Judith's, that he announced : " We won't walk back. We'll take the Riviera Express in the morning."

So it was that we hurried back, and in March of 1920 two things happened : the book was finished and Raymond came into the world. When I was able to sit up in bed and Dr. Nancarrow allowed Frank to see me, he said : " I don't know what I am prouder of—you or Raymond or the book."

I was proud of the book. It was the first that Frank had written after a long silence, and it had a good reception ; but I was prouder of Raymond. He had a fuzz of hair that promised to be as red as my own, and it was useless for Frank to point out that all children were born with finger-nails. " Even Connie Lee-Smith," he said, " was born with finger-nails, though a pretty mess she's made of them." But nothing would convince me that anyone was born with finger-nails like Raymond's—so beautiful and rosy and so formed—well, like finger-nails. " Why, he's born almost grown-up," I objected ; to which Frank replied with a grin : " You've got a lot to learn about babies yet."

" Well, I've learned to have this one without much fuss. And now get out. I'm going to feed him."

But that was a ceremony at which Frank liked to be present ; and he watched me as though a woman had never suckled a child before.

5

In the autumn of that year 1920 Miss Pritt joined us. Mell and Laura were married in London, and Frank and I went up to town to be present at the wedding. After all these years I met Mell's father again—the Methodist parson whose presence took me back to Cardiff and the night of the Lilywhites' conversazione, the night of the banged door. He was an old man now, a superannuated minister, which means one who has retired, will not know again the whirl of shifting every few years, but gives a hand where it is wanted in the place where he has settled. As, in this case, that was at a seaside town in Norfolk, we were not likely to see much in the future of Mr. Conybeare or of his sister Judith, who, his wife being dead, had now become the companion and housekeeper of her much older brother. Judith was there at the wedding ; and she confided to Frank that she would find it easier to leave the Rowans because she had " fallen out " with Connie Lee-Smith. Connie accused her of having done something or not done something which she should have done or not done in a game of bridge, and one thing led to another, and there it was : a beautiful friendship ended. So she was going now to console her brother's lingering years. His income, as a super-annuated minister, didn't amount to much, and what Bryan Graves had left her would make all the difference, especially as she was investing the money carefully.

All this Frank confided to me, with his own dry comments, but I didn't myself see much of Judith because I spent such time as I could with Laura. It was from her that I heard of Miss Pritt. Miss Pritt was eighteen years old, the oldest girl of the school from which Laura had now resigned. " I've had her in my French classes and she's quite hopeless," Laura said. " Indeed, she's hopeless at anything to do with what's usually taught in a school. But she's mad on being a nurse. I don't mean a hospital nurse. She wants—heaven knows why—to be a children's nurse in what she calls a good family. Do you think you're good enough ? "

" Well, we'd do our best to live up to her," I assured Laura. " Who is she ?—a princess's daughter ? "

" No. She's a boiler-maker's daughter, and she's been brought up in a ghastly family. That's why she wants to be in a good one. And she has something that's becoming quite tradi-tional—a kind heart, which, I may remind you, is more than a coronet."

I interviewed Miss Pritt, who had regrettably been given the Christian name of Zaza. This might be a testimony to her mother's addiction to the cinema, but I felt it would be a bit out of place at Dros-y-Mor, and was glad to find that she was prepared to hide this dreadful secret under the name of Emily. It would be at once a tribute to my love of Miss Brontë and something more in keeping with our way of life. Frank and I took at last to calling her Em, and as Em Pritt she shall henceforth be known.

I was not sorry to be back at Dros-y-Mor, where Mrs. Davies had quite efficiently been looking after Raymond during our brief absence. The only change made was that the room at the other end of the gallery running over the library became Em Pritt's ; and Raymond, whom we had taken to calling Ray, was shifted with his cot thither.

6

It would be agreeable if this book were full of psychoanalysis and dreadful things as Ray grew up, but he grew up a normal boy and, I think, we were normal parents. We were able to persuade the education people that he could safely be entrusted to us, and I taught him to write and read quite easily, and talked to him a lot in French so that he was almost bi-lingual. Frank taught him to add, subtract and divide, and in his room there was a large globe of the world, so that he came to know a good deal of what lies outside Cornwall. A favourite opening was to take someone like Columbus or Drake, and say : " Now let's have a look where old Columbus went to," or " Let's see how Drake got round the world," and there, with a twist of the globe, was a geography and history lesson combined, with all the lands and seas coloured for him to look at. So far as tides and ships were concerned, he had only to look about him, and that goes, too, for birds and beasts, flowers and trees, and all growing things.

Most of these lessons, if you can call them such, happened in Ray's room. And Ray's room was simply a version of Frank's own writing-room in the woods. Ray had learned to respect that room, and never went near it ; but he counted on our showing the same regard for " Ray's Room". It was knocked together by Ben Davies in the wood, and had its easy-chair, and a work-chair, and a table and a book-case. To this room, at his invitation, I would go each morning and give him his lesson, and he spent hours in it alone or with Em Pritt, who had taken a great liking to him, and he to her.

So far as outdoor things went, they were all about him, to choose where he liked. He rowed the dinghy ; he swam like a fish, always with no clothes on, for we taught him to know his body and to be unashamed. And so he grew up, rather lonely, but his very loneliness threw him into adult company ; rather grave ; and startingly, with his red hair and fair complexion, like me.

7

It was in 1925, when Raymond was five years old, that we learned from the newspapers (which, you will recall, had hailed him as "one of our great financiers") that Mr. Ronald Lilywhite was arrested. We had not seen him since, a few years before, Frank had quietly pushed him over our quay wall, but we had read of him in the news. He was buying up everything: mills and theatres and businesses of every sort: with money that poured upon him from those who were impressed by "one of our greatest financiers". They all wanted something for nothing, and, as this is not granted in this world, they joined him in general ruin. Then it was good-bye to yachts, race-horses, houses in town and country. What Ronald did when his five years in gaol were up I never knew. That was the end of him so far as I was concerned. I never heard of him again.

But we heard of Frank's sister-in-law Judith. Her brother, the Reverend Mr. Conybeare, did not long survive his super-annuation. It had been a comfortable one enough, with Judith to look after him and with Judith's money to ease his way ; but he was found dead in bed one morning, and that was the end of him. I felt the natural sorrow that one feels for the death of an old man, a sorrow for the brevity of human life rather than for an individual, though some sadness, too, for him. He had been kind to me in his way and had not prevented Mr. Mell from doing his duty in snatching me from the maw of the Lilywhites. But it was into this very maw that Judith fell.

She remained in the house on the East Coast for some time after her brother's death, finding a new Connie Lee-Smith to make life endurable, playing bridge, and defying her age, and at last thanking her stars that her new friend had heard of Mr. Ronald Lilywhite and the way in which he was dishing out God's plenty to all who had money to lend him. Judith went down when so many went down on the bursting of the great bubble.

8

It was in a letter from Laura that we heard of Judith's plight. I suppose I was related in a sense to Laura, being married to her husband's uncle, but I never thought of her save as a dear friend. I rejoiced in her good fortune. When she married and became Mrs. Melvill Conybeare, she and her husband found Melbourne Square " going down " badly, and were among the first to buy a house cheaply in that now prosperous locality. They tidied it up and made their home there. What Mell did in the Foreign Office I did not learn, for he was never one to talk of his affairs and Laura was as closed on that side of their lives as he was. All I knew, and all Frank knew, was that he was now the head of a department and he was talked of with respect into which a little awe was creeping. His hair was turning white and the gravity of his carriage deepened with the years, though, on the few occasions when I saw him, I thought he was still a bit Arthurian, the sort of man who would rescue a maiden and read bits of Tennyson to her in bed. Or was he, as Frank had once said, a shade—just a shade—of a prig ? Whatever he was, I would never forget that he was the man who had rescued me from the Lilywhites, though I was on the way to achieving that rescue myself. I had, at any rate, banged the door.

9

Frank and I accepted Laura's invitation to stay in Melbourne Square during our time in London. It was in Kensington, and very much, save for its shabbiness at that time, like other London squares—rows of Georgian houses with a garden in the middle. There were planes growing in the grass, and, this being autumn, the paths were patterned with falling leaves. But it was a quiet place, with a pale blue autumnal sky overhead, and few motor-cars as yet to disturb us with horns and banging doors and general clangour. Mell had gone to his office, with a rolled umbrella, though the day was fine, and a black felt hat, and Frank had taken the opportunity to have lunch with his agent. So Laura and I sat on a seat in the garden with the leaves falling on us and about us, and we discussed poor Judith.

She had become Poor Judith now, in every sense. She had hardly a penny, she was getting on in years, and she was in general the sort of woman whom one calls poor this, that or the other.

"Mell thinks," said Laura, "that she ought to come to live with us. After all, he says, it was at her house that we met."

Certainly something must be done about Poor Judith, but the reason why she should come to Melbourne Square seemed to me so typically Mell, so much something that he "ought" to do, that I burst out laughing. It was not well received, and I understood that what Mell suggested in Melbourne Square was the gospel in that part of the world.

"I've seen her," Laura said. "Mell and I went over last week-end. She's a pitiful old thing, and Mell thought that we ought to have her. After all, she's got no one else now—no husband, no sister or brother. Just Mell, and though he's only a nephew he feels very strongly that there's room enough here to give her a place of her own. She was always glad to have him at the Rowans, and there's such a thing as paying one's debts."

It might have been Mell himself speaking, and, indeed, I felt, Mell *had* spoken, and that was that.

"Well," I conceded, "she'll find plenty of Connie Lee-Smiths, I should think, in Kensington. She shouldn't be too much of a strain on you."

"Of course," said Laura, almost shyly, "there'll be a nursery soon. She'll have a grand-nephew to occupy her attention."

At that, I kissed her. "It doesn't show," I said. "When is it to be?"

She blushed all over. "Really, Alice, you do say such things."

For the first time, I felt superior to Laura. Was I not the mother of a five-year-old son? Could he not already swim and tell an oak from an ash? Could he not trace with a chubby finger a complete circumnavigation of the globe? So I talked to her like a mother, though she was older than I, and I learned that Mell, who settled all things in advance, had already decided that his son should enter the Foreign Office and be called Matthew Conybeare. But we weren't talking about Mell's son after all. We were talking about Belinda—Belinda Conybeare.

10

With Em Pritt at Dros-y-Mor, Ray was in good hands; and so we stayed to see Poor Judith installed in Melbourne Square. We all took to calling her that, as though she had been baptised " Poor ". Her quarters were snug enough. They were on the first floor, looking out over the falling leaves of the Square ; and though they were only one room, it was a large room that made an excellent bed-sitter. I went into the shops now and then with Laura to buy this and that which would help to make her comfortable, and this was always at Mell's suggestion who knew as well as any old woman what belonged to comfort. " But don't exhaust yourself," he always said to Laura in the hall, taking up his hat and rolled umbrella. " She is in your hands, Alice. Mind you look after her." And off he would go with a despatch-case as inseparably attached to him as a brandy-barrel to a St. Bernard dog in the Alps.

Meantime, Frank prowled about London. He was a great prowler, both in London and at home, and if you asked him what he went prowling for, he knew no more than you did. " Oh, I don't know," he would say. " Things come back to me when I want them. Things I've thought about and people I have seen."

We were all there except Mell when Judith arrived. I hadn't seen her since the day when we took tea at Connie Lee-Smith's, and she looked much the same—an ageing woman who was working hard to keep age at bay. The same sort of hat tottered on her dyed hair, and falling down in a green cascade on her breast was a torrent of jade beads that clicked as she moved. Laura, on Mell's instructions, paid the taxi-fare ; and, when there had been kisses all round, took her up to show her her room, to which Frank had carried the bags.

I went with the pair of them and watched Poor Judith enter her new home. She would miss the sight of the sea, she assured us, and found the falling of the leaves " rather melancholy ", but she approved the springs in the new easy-chair, and there was only one thing that she asked for. That was a card-table. " I don't play bridge any more," she explained, " only Patience. I do find that such a consolation."

"There isn't such a thing in the house, dear Aunt," explained Laura. Judith wasn't her aunt, but she was Mell's aunt, and, as that was what Mell would call her, Laura had decided that she must do the same. "Mell and I never play, but we can easily get one. Just there is the place for it. It will get all the light from the windows."

I left them, unpacking bags, putting a photograph of the late Reverend Russell Conybeare, in a silver frame, on the mantelpiece, and making the room habitable. Frank was prowling in the hall. "I think we'll go home in the morning," he said ; and that was my desire, too.

When Mell came in that evening, we told him of the arrival, and Laura said : "She's gone to bed now, tired out after her journey."

"I'll just go and say good-night, then," said Mell, and vanished up the stairs. He was a long time gone, and I solaced the waiting with a vision of him reading Aunt Judith to sleep with *The Passing of Arthur*.

Chapter VI

It all went very much as I had expected. Judith found a Connie Lee-Smith called Mamie James-Villiers, and under Mamie's guidance joined a bridge-club, Mell paying her debts. Occasionally there were winnings, but she was a reasonably expensive aunt, for the losings were greater than the winnings, and then there were her food and clothes and the installing of the radio, which at least kept her in her own room. Laura was very patient with her, but drew the line at letting her have anything to do with Belinda.

Frank and I saw nothing of them, but a weekly letter from Laura to her relatives at Dros-y-Mor kept us informed. Or were we relatives ? I have never quite sorted it out. Frank at least was Mell's uncle, and Mell was married to Laura, so I suppose he was her uncle, too, and I was her aunt and Belinda's great-aunt. But, as I say, I have never understood relationships, and felt rather resentful at being a great-aunt.

A typical letter from Laura ran like this. " Dear Alice.— I've just come in from giving Belinda her daily airing. We left Poor Judith in her room trying to get some foreign station. She is over-joyed when she gets one, though, for all she makes of it, it might be the man in the moon speaking. I think it was Bucharest she got to-day. Anyhow, I interrupted an excited out-flow of gibberish, and she waved me impatiently from the room, with her finger to her lips, lest I should interfere with something utterly incomprehensible to her. Her hands, you know, are covered with rings, which, coupled with their dashes of red here and there on the finger-nails, give a great air of authority to her semaphoring. She waved this signal in the air, towards the bright day outside, thus giving me to understand that it was a good day to take Belinda for a walk. So I left her fiddling with her little knobs, which now and then produced outbursts of darkie music— you know, tom-toms and all that sort of thing— which, I suppose had authority because it came from Manila or somewhere—Dear me ! Where is this sentence getting to ? Anyway, I went out with Belinda, and it was joyous in our little Melbourne garden where all the trees are fully out. Then we went on as far as Kensington Gardens.

Mell was home quite early to-day, so he was able to give Belinda her bath, which he loves doing, though he's not often in time to do it. We had a lovely evening to ourselves, for a scribbled note from Poor Judith said that, after all, she had decided to go to a ' bridge-tea ' at her club. She didn't get back till after dinner, the wicked old thing, and then she had lost, so Mell had to dip his hand in his pocket again. He and I look forward to visiting you in the autumn, though Mell will have to stay at the office for some time and will arrive later than I shall. Ever, Laura."

2

This arrived when Belinda was three years old, and Ray was eight. There was a hard time ahead of me, because, when this holiday was over, Frank would take him away to a prep school in Devonshire, and, though Devonshire was the next county to ours, it seemed a long way off. We had said nothing to him yet, and I had no doubt that when the time came he would go with the stoicism that had become his habit ; but Em Pritt and I were down in the dumps.

Em, during the last five years, had grown into our lives. The small room, which had housed both my bed and my typewriter, was abandoned when Em joined us, and for some time now it had been hers. Ray slept in the room which they had for a while occupied together. I did my typing and everything else in the big library-room. Frank didn't care where anybody slept. So long as he had his writing-room in the woods and could stretch his legs in the big room when he felt like it, all was well with him.

Ray, as I have said, had a room in the woods, too. It had been early impressed on him that he must on no account go to Frank's room. This had so thoroughly sunk into his red skull that nothing would please him, when he was of an age for such matters, but a room in the woods for himself.

" So long as it's a good way from mine," Frank agreed. And so the boy helped Ben Davies to knock together a shed that was not unlike Frank's, roofed with the same sort of shingles, and furnished in much the same way. Here, in a small bookcase, he kept *Kim*, and *Coral Island* and things of that sort. Here on the plank table, he kept his globe and anything else he was interested in at the moment ; and he rudely chalked on the door: " Keep out unless asked in." I was asked in most days to help with the lessons ; but on the days when I was not asked, and my men had retired to their work-places, I felt there was little left for me save to get Ben Davies to knock me up a shed, too, and go there with my knitting. But, as I didn't knit, there was not much sense in that. So I would type Frank's bit of stuff in the library, and then, if the tide was right, have a swim or pull an oar in our creek, and sit there, when the tide was out, looking at the mud and thinking of my two men keeping me in idleness as they bent over their tables. There was only one cloud in my sky : soon one of the sheds would be empty.

I would sit through those idyllic summer days, planning

what to do with the incursion that was to break upon us. Mell
and Laura, with a cot for Belinda, would have to share the room at
one end of the lofty corridor—the room that was now Raymond's.
He had volunteered this solution, offering to sleep in his shed.
Happily, he was a boy who didn't fear night noises. The cries
of owls and curlews wouldn't worry him, and a folding canvas
bed had been ordered for him to sleep on. There remained only
the question of Poor Judith. Where she was to sleep worried
us for a time, but Em solved the question by saying that, if the
Davieses didn't mind, she could have their spare bedroom—the
room in which I had come through my influenza in days that
seemed now remote, before Frank had returned from the war.
The Davieses didn't mind that, or, it seemed to me, anything
else. They were a good-natured couple. And so it was arranged
that Judith should have Em Pritt's bedroom. We were all ready
for the only bit of entertaining that we had ever done.

3

Mell, as I have said, came later, so there were only three to be
met when the Riviera Express arrived at Falmouth—Poor Judith
and Laura and Belinda, who could toddle. Frank took Ray with
him, leaving me behind to make a few last-moment preparations.
I watched the two of them go off in the dinghy. Ray was a good-
looking boy, fair as the morning, lanky for his age, with grey-green
eyes sparkling under his red crop. He turned in the stern when
they reached the bend of the creek, waved, and they were gone.

I sat in a canvas chair on the quarter-deck in the blaze of the
late summer weather, and for the first time I wondered whether
I had thanked God enough for the luck that had been mine.
Soon they would all be about me : Mell who had picked me up
from the path in Cardiff and had been like a dutiful brother to
me and taught me to read, letting in a slit of light through what
had proved to be an enchanted door that could lead to anything ;
Poor Judith who had taken me in then and been kind to me in
her way, though sorrow enough was soon to fall on her own head;
Laura who had had the sense to kick me out of my niche and had
given me the opportunity to learn something of a wider if dingier
world. And then I had met Frank, and I think I was modest

enough to realise that this had been the most fortunate stroke of them all. He had come back to what must have looked to him like an empty life. He had come back from an experience that had sickened him, which had not done what it had promised to do, as war never does, but as love does always, which had knocked the bottom out of the world as he thought he knew it. All this had meant an emptiness that he must face without the support of a loved wife. And I had been there. I did not diminish all that had been in my favour : we were both ill, both interested in the same sort of things, though with a mighty division lying between the qualities of our interest. But I was conceited enough to believe that I had been good for him, an understanding wife, who had known when to leave him to his own angels and devils. And all this was sealed by Ray, who now held us in a bond that I believed would never be broken.

And there was Em Pritt. What were we to do with Em now ? She had pushed Ray about in an old go-cart over our indifferent roads. She had been a good friend to him in all the joys and small sorrows of his growth, and she had been, as likely as myself, the one invited to his shed when he felt like inviting anyone. She had grown up with the child. She had learned as he had learned—even to swim ! It was a great sight, Em proceeding like a porpoise through the water while Ray flashed about her like a minnow. She had learned the names of trees and flowers so that she should not seem to Ray to be behind him in knowledge, and I had been touched, when walking alone one day, to come upon Em and Ray at the place, a mile from us, where our stream made its first bubbling emergence from the earth amid ferns and moss. There they were, and Em was explaining to the boy that thus the mightiest rivers had their beginning. She would miss him, when he went to school, as keenly as any of us ; but there was the sad fact that we had no further use for Em. There would be no more children. I felt certain of that. So what were we to do with Em ? I knew that one of the first calls of Ray, when he came home from his first term, would be " Em ! Em ! Where's Em ? " Could we say that we had ruthlessly cut away part of his life ?

I felt, rather than saw, that Em was at my back as I turned these matters over in my mind that morning when I sat gazing at the water on which the boat had disappeared. "Come and sit by me, Em," I said without turning, and she pulled an old chair up at my side. I looked at her, and there wasn't much to look at. She was half-way through her twenties, a roly-poly girl who hadn't been blessed with looks, though her healthy well-fed life with us had at least improved on what we had taken over. And yet there was everything to look at—everything that mattered: honesty, and devotion, and innocence, and, at this moment, a great sadness. Her eyes were grey, her nose was snub, her mouth too big. But my heart went out to Em.

"I wanted to ask," she said, pulling out the words with difficulty, "for a reference."

"Why on earth do you want a reference?" I asked, knowing well enough.

"There'll be nothing for me to do," she said, "when Ray's gone."

She had always called him that, and I for one would have hated to hear her call him Master Ray or, as he grew, Mr. Ray. It would have diminished them both.

"You'll get no reference out of me," I said, "or out of Mr. Melvill, come to that."

Em was abashed and crestfallen. "Why?" she asked simply.

"Because we both know you too well."

She turned that over in her simple mind, and found no flaw in it. "I've done my best," she said. And then: "All right. I'll stay till these people are gone, and then I must look out for myself."

She was sitting on an old seat that would hold two at a pinch, so I got up from my deck-chair and put myself alongside her, and my arm round her waist, and said: "The trouble with you, Em, is that you're too good."

"Then why won't you give me a reference?" she asked doggedly.

She could never see what was under her nose, and so I had to make myself plain. "Because we want to keep you, Ray or no Ray, as long as you care to stay with us."

Even at that, she was full of doubts. "But what will Mrs. Davies say, with me about the place all day long?"

"I don't think you'll have any trouble with Mrs. Davies. You never have had, have you ? "

" No."

" Very well, then. Stay and chance it as long as you like. Any time you want to go, you can go. But don't bang the front door."

And to smooth a moment that was becoming embarrassing, I told her of my adventure at the Lilywhites', to which all she said was : " But I could never be such a one as you. Fancy letting a young man read to you in bed ! No, I could never do a thing like that ! "

4

Judith arrived in all her glory. Frank was there, too, with Ray and Laura and the young Belinda ; but Judith could not forget that this had once been her sister's house, that Frank had once been her sister's husband, and that every chair and book and ornament had once had its accustomed place. From the little I had heard of Jane, there wasn't much in common between the sisters, but an instinct for tidiness is something they shared. Frank was slap-dash. Everything to do with his work, everything to do with his precious shed, had to be just so ; but, outside his work, he was another man.

Judith fussed. While the others were out walking or swimming or rowing she stayed at home to see that all was in order. A dozen times a day she put Jane's photograph an inch to the right or left, picked up Frank's matches from inside the fender and put them into an ash-tray, went up to pat the beds, saw that there were new flowers in the vases and that these had fresh water every day, and even slid the pictures on the wall hither and yon. She straightened mats and fiddled with blinds and curtains, and all that Frank had to say was : " So long as she keeps out of my shed between nine and one I don't care a damn what she does. She'll be gone soon."

Mell came down, and our party was complete. I had seen little of Mell at any time, though, scarcely knowing it, he had been a great force in my life. But he had always seemed sober-sided and set in his ways. This was the first time I had watched

him day after day for a fortnight, the first time I had watched him
with the cares of office (if one may put it that way) cast aside. He
was pale, with an official and metropolitan pallor, when he arrived,
but this soon passed under our Cornish sun, and I was glad to
observe a Mell that I had not known before. For one thing, he
was a swimmer, and this endeared him at once to Ray, and so did
his knowledge of every bird and tree and flower. He was even
invited into Ray's shed where he gravely approved of a map of
Cornwall, with all its ridges raised, in plasticine. It was my
duty to be a mere boatman, when the tide was high, rowing him
and Laura, Ray and Belinda, to some spot where they could dive
off the boat. " Now," he commanded me from the water one
day, " take off all Belinda's clothes and throw her in."

I was startled by the order, for Belinda, like me, had hitherto
been a mere spectator of these pranks in the water ; and she was
of an age now to raise her voice in protest. She did so, setting
up a frightened squall, and I felt more like comforting her than
taking off the few rags she was wearing. Laura joined me in
begging Mell to have a bit of sense, and Ray, paddling like a dog,
watched the outcome. " Well, lower her in as she is," Mell
commanded, " clothes and all," and to Belinda he said : " Now
drop on Daddy's back and have a ride."

This was a new Mell to me—one determined to have his own
way, and one who was prepared to call himself Daddy in the
process. I had never thought of Mell as Daddy. Father was the
least I should have called him, if not something altogether
almighty. As the tide was running out and we were in fairly
shallow water, I leaned out of the dinghy with an armful of
squealing Belinda, and firmly placed her on his shoulders. " Hold
on to my hair," he ordered ; and at once struck off with her to
our steps. It was not far to go, but an anxious convoy, Laura
and Ray, kept to port and starboard of him, and when he was
able to stand up, he swung Belinda to arms' length and laughed
into her face. All the terror had gone from it. She merely cried :
" Do it again, Daddy ! " and there was I condemned to row her
out time after time, place her on his shoulders, and follow slowly
after. And so in a few days Belinda was swimming like a dog in
shallow water, and all Mell had to say was : " That's the way
I was taught." He always wanted a precedent.

So, mostly, we messed about in the boat on the creek, and swam, or walked inland, in the morning, leaving Frank in his shed, for even in this holiday-time the hours between nine and one were sacred to him. But in the afternoon he and Mell would walk together, and I imagine that at times their conversation was pretty grim ; but, whatever it might be that they discussed, they kept it to themselves, and even, now and then, walked off again after dinner, if they came in to dinner which, once or twice, they did not.

Em Pritt pottered about and helped the Davieses, and Poor Judith, when she had finished her tasks indoors, keeping everything straight, would sit in a chair on the quarter-deck, with patience cards spread out on a table, and rarely got beyond that. She hated the water, and who could blame her ? She had watched her sister drown. So there she would sit, regretting that we had no radio, no bridge-club in sight, longing, I imagine, for Mamie James-Villiers, thinking us all a pretty poor lot, and clicking her jade beads like a rosary. Even under our sun, she was for ever at her cosmetics and thought we were all indecent because we allowed Belinda to mess about in the water with nothing on, save a skin which was soon the colour of ripe mahogany. Her hair, which was kept cropped, was as fair as flax and fitted her like a cap.

So Judith was not with us when we made our visit to the river on the last night of the holiday. We were to have a beach-picnic on the spot where she had seen Jane drown. It was only later that it occurred to me that it was a spot evocative in Frank's heart, too. Far-ranging as his walks were, they had never taken him in that direction. I do not think he was exorcising a ghost. That ghost would always be, for him, beloved and lived with. He could live with it there, as well as anywhere else. So he came with us, saying nothing.

It is a small beach on the Helford River. Looking to your left, you see the water running among the hills. To the right you look at the sea, boundless, and, that night, serene and benevolent. Frank and Mell said they would walk overland and meet us. The rest of us piled into the dinghy just as the tide was flowing, making the journey possible : myself at the oars, Laura, Belinda and Ray. It was a spring tide that would bear us easily back. We took an old kettle full of water, a screw of tea, a hamper filled with food and crockery.

I rowed down the creek. It was the sort of evening when you do everything quietly. Summer and autumn were hand in hand. Not a leaf had yet been shed by any tree, but you knew that, exhausted by summer, all would be falling soon. All would be gone—our visitors, the leaves, Ray. The light slanted from the west and the birds had long since ceased their singing. Even the children were quiet, and Laura was trailing her fingers through the water, as though it were a fabric melancholy to the touch.

So we came out at last on the wide river where a few small sailing-boats, drowsed by the evening and the absence of wind, were coming in so slowly that here and there you saw their crews helping them along with oars. Their sails were like broken wings, and we had not yet come to the time when every boat has its engine to help it over that last lap.

We turned to the right, and there was the bit of beach, with Frank and Mell sitting by a fire they had made, smoking their pipes, meditative like everything else that night. They got up and pulled us in, and then at last the children's tongues were loosed as they ranged here and there picking up bits of dry wood beyond the high-tide mark and making a pile to keep the fire going. Soon it was blazing well and I put on the kettle, while Ray and Belinda gathered large flat stones to serve as tables, setting out a plastic cup and saucer and plate on each. Laura made the tea in a large metal tea-pot, and we all sat round to see what Mrs. Davies had put into the basket. I forget what it was. All I remember is the odd solemnity of the occasion. Whatever Frank and Mell had been discussing, it held them in a serious mood that communicated itself to me and Laura. Ray and Belinda were the only bright members of the party, and, when they had eaten, ran like turnstones upon the beach, gathering up shells and pretty bits of coral, stowing their finds in handkerchiefs knotted at the corners. But I recall that, as the sun went down and a small chill came into the air, we four adults sat round the dying fire with little to say, until Frank outed the flames with a few handfuls of sand and said : " Well, here endeth the picnic. Mell and I will walk back. We'd make rather a load in that dinghy." They lit their pipes, took up their sticks, and went.

Belinda was more tired than she would admit, and went to sleep in Laura's lap as we turned again into the creek. It was darkening quickly. The shadows of the trees fell across the water as I rowed rather fast to beat the tide, which was falling now. The faithful Em was waiting at the steps as I made it, and bore the sleeping child straight upstairs. Ray retired to his bed in the woods. Poor Judith had long since gone to hers.

5

Baker's Place in North Devon was very much like scores of English prep schools at that time. It was a country house that had been built on to here and there as need arose, and looked a snug enough place amid its trees and fields. Frank had been over once or twice to see the headmaster, Mr. Twyford, whom he knew slightly, for they had been together at St. Paul's as boys. On the last occasion he had spent a week-end there, and Ray with him. Mrs. Twyford was French by birth and took the boy for a long walk, in the course of which she satisfied herself that his French was all right. Mr. Twyford, too, had rambled with Ray towards the sea, and what they talked about I don't know, but I came to know Mr. Twyford, and from my knowledge of him I should say there were traps in the conversation, hidden snags and difficulties that Ray got over well enough. The boy was used to nothing but adult company and would not have been scared by grown-up questions. We had not come to the happy day when every child must have reached, by identical steps, an identical status. There was still room for a bit of variety, and so Ray was enlisted as a suitable boy for Baker's Place.

Frank was silent enough as we set out on the journey. I had impressed on Em that there were to be no tears on parting, which is why Em, I suppose, was absent from the quarter-deck, getting over her grief in some quiet part of the house. The Davieses waved us off as Frank took the oars, and they waved us down the creek. At the bend, Ray turned ostensibly to wave to them, but in reality to take a last look at the only home he had ever known. He had swept and garnished his hut in the woods the day before, and had entrusted me with the key. " Use it while I am away," he conceded, " but see that nothing's out of place." I did, as faithfully as any custodian of a shrine. I dusted his plasticine map of Cornwall, his globe, his few books, his writing-table, and his " Notes on Birds observed In and About Dros-y-Mor, with particular remarks on the Habits of Cygnets."

We took the branch line from Falmouth to Truro, but there we did not, as I expected, get into another train. " Let's go down into the town for a bit," Frank mysteriously said. So we left the boy's bags in the luggage-room, and went down that street paved with granite, through the granitic town, to the head-waters of the Falmouth River ; and, near there, was a garage into which Frank peeped and shouted : " Anyone at home ? "

There was a most oily man at home. He climbed out of an inspection pit, wiping his forearms with cotton waste. " Well, there she is, Mr. Melvill," he said, and indicated the car standing above the pit. " All ready for the road and Joe will be here in a moment. How d'you think she's looking ? "

Frank grinned rather wryly. " Like the herald of a new age," he said. " You ought to put a banner on her bonnet : ' Here goes the age we knew.' But we'll have to put up with these damned things, I'm afraid, from now on."

Ray was tremendously excited. " Is she yours, Dad ? " he asked, and without waiting for an answer began passing a hand lovingly over the shining mudguards and the other bits and pieces of the monster. The man called Joe appeared and " Hop in," he said. " See how comfortable the seats are. Ready any time you like, Mr. Melvill."

Mr. Melvill thought at last that some explanation was due to me. " I've been making all my journeys to Baker's Place," he said, " by train. Three changes, believe it or not. And at one of them you wait for more than an hour. We'd not see Ray from one term's end to the next if we didn't have some way of getting at him. How long does this thing take, Joe ? "

" I've been looking it up on the map, Mr. Melvill. I reckon one hour and a half to two hours. Two at the most, barring accidents."

" You see ? " said Frank. " We can go over now and then to see how Ray's getting on. Twyford has no objection. I'll have to learn to drive the thing. However, Joe's going to do the driving to-day. Let's get in. Joe, we're going to call at the station first for the luggage."

I got in, speechless. I wasn't used to motor-cars. Now and then I had hopped into a taxi, but since settling down at Dros-y-Mor I had hardly seen a car once in a week. I didn't look ahead. I didn't foresee the day when these things would put paid to the Cornwall I had known. I was, on the whole, proud but nervous. Frank was sitting next to Joe who was at the wheel. Ray, along side me, was on his toes with his head stuck between them, imbibing knowledge.

" Now, here's a bit of straight road, Mr. Melvill, and nothing on it. What about taking the wheel ? Get the feel of the thing. I'll stop her. You start her."

So we went on, through Lostwithiel, to the ferry over the Tamar at Plymouth, now Joe driving, now Frank, with Ray all the time exciting and restless. " Why can't you beat her up to sixty, like Mr. Joe, Dad ? "

" Sixty's nothing," Joe replied. " You can safely touch eighty in this bus."

" Not for me," replied Frank. " This is the first time I've been at a wheel, and thirty'll do for me. I can start her and stop her and make her go. I reckon that's enough to be going on with."

We were at Baker's Place precisely in two hours, left Ray with Mr. Twyford and a few of the boys, ate lunch at an inn, and were back in Truro by the middle of the afternoon.

" I'll run you to your house now," Joe said. " You'll see how quick the whole process is."

" You'll have to bring her back again if you do. I've got no garage built yet."

But Joe, whose name was Duncombe—Joe Duncombe—was all for showing off the car, and so, for the first time, we missed the row over the creek. He made a circular détour and brought the car to a stand at Ben Davies's cottage. " I don't think we can go any further, Mr. Melvill. What roads ! Why, there's hardly room to turn her round ! "

" Don't worry about that," said Frank. " I expect the roads will be seen to. It's only a matter of time."

" Yes," I said, feeling a bit dizzy with the day's doings. " It's only a matter of time, I suppose, before we have a telephone and a radio."

6

Ray was not a demonstrative boy. There had been no tears, not even a kiss. Just a hand-shake as he strolled over to Mr. Twyford, and his schooldays swallowed him up. I was glad to see that Baker's Place was a fine old house, standing in good countryside with plenty of trees and a river running through the grounds. It was cheering to know, as Frank assured me, that Twyford was mad, of all things, about otters, and that Ray would be welcome to share such enthusiasms. At any rate, I pretended to think it cheering. But I missed the boy, and life as autumn closed in on us seemed empty and Frank's bit of typing a welcome diversion. I was glad when the time came for the first log-fire, and we drew the curtains at night, and Frank and I sat together in the evenings, talking or reading.

Em Pritt was in low spirits, too. The fact was, there was little for her to do. She had been a good companion for Ray and Ray for her. With him gone, she mooched about the place, getting in the Davieses' way, doing this and that, and nothing in particular. She spent her afternoons down on the site of the new garage. This was being built just opposite the Davieses' cottage. Frank's bit of woodland started there and, ominously to me, a few trees were pulled down and the garage was to be built just inside the woodland. Joe Duncombe now and then drove the car over, gave Frank a lesson, and cocked an eye at the progress of the garage. He was a dark-skinned, dark-eyed young man, in his middle twenties, good-looking, and mad about motor-cars. Em Pritt was there whenever he called. I was there, too, one afternoon when autumn was touching winter, waiting for Frank and Joe Duncombe to come in from a lesson. I was nervous about Frank. The fact was that he knew no more about cars than I did, was rather afraid of them, and had bought this one in a whim. It was something to get to Ray with, but we had not yet visited Ray.

There was a garden round the Davieses' cottage where vegetables were grown for the table at Dros-y-Mor, and that day Ben, who was digging in the garden, came across the road and joined me and Em as we looked at the place where the new garage was to be. He was in a glum mood, and this came out in his first words. " I bin here," he said, " longer than Mr. Melvill, and I've gazed out of them ole windows at them ole trees as long as I can remember. When there *was* trees." He looked at the stumps and the beginning of the foundations, and repeated " When there *was* trees."

It was clear that Ben Davies was not in favour of a car, a garage, or, beyond all things, of a youngster like Joe Duncombe usurping the attention of Frank Melvill. I had sensed, too, that the Davieses, now that Ray was gone and there was not much for her to do, resented Em Pritt. They had always done all that Frank wanted, served him with devotion, and now there was this girl, there was this man Duncombe, there were these trees that had been there time out of mind and that now were stumps, rotting teeth stuck in the earth.

" And now, I 'ear," he said, " they're goin' to change all that lot an' 'ave room for *two* cars."

I soothed him as best I could. " But that's only a precaution, Ben. There'll be only one car. The room for another is just in case."

" But it'll mean a bigger building," Ben broke out, " an' a fine sight that'll be from my flamin' windows which 'ave always looked on trees."

It was the first time I had heard even a mild swear-word in Ben's mouth. He himself seemed to feel that he had gone too far. He kicked at the dust of the by-road uncomfortably with his boot, then went back to his garden and to his digging.

All might have been well if the gentle Em Pritt had not thought this the moment to be alert and sprightly. " There's one thing I know," she shouted over the hedge. " Ray'll be glad of the car. He's up to date. He's modern. We'll be able to get out of this place now and then when he's back."

This brought Ben Davies to the hedge. " No one's asking *your* opinion," he said, all his heat returning. " We know why you're always mooching about the garage whenever that chap from Truro's knocking around."

It was a home thrust. Though nothing would induce Ben to call " that chap from Truro " Joe, or see in him anything but a vague embodiment of all the disasters that might be expected from a chap in a large city, as mighty as London to Ben, yet I knew as well as he did why Em was always to be found where Joe Duncombe was. Still, the matter was now becoming personal and undignified. I told Em to get back to the house and see that tea was ready, ignored Ben's muttered comment that Mrs. Davies was well able to look after that, and wandered alone to meet the travellers, disconsolate and miserable.

I had gone about a half-mile when I met the car, with Joe at the wheel. He pulled up to let me get in, and I noticed that one of the gleaming new mudguards was badly dented. Frank, who was sitting alongside Joe, said nothing about it. Nor did Joe. Nor did I. The Sunbeam was pulled up smartly where the garage was to be, and Joe reversed her. " Well, see you to-morrow, Mr. Melvill," he shouted, and was gone. Ben Davies had vanished from his garden. Frank and I walked together through the woods. He was limping slightly.

Mrs. Davies brought the tea into the library. Em Pritt was nowhere to be seen. Another bit of resentment, I thought. She was annoyed that I had sent her back to the house just when she might have had a glimpse of Joe—perhaps even a word with him. I stretched the moment out as long as I could, asking Frank to clear up a point in the manuscript I had been typing that day. There was no need to do it. His writing was as clear as the morning ; but I thanked him, and then asked : " What's the matter with your leg ? You seem to be having some trouble with it."

" Oh, that's nothing," he answered in an off-hand way.

" Is it anything to do with the car ? "

" Well, yes. I was driving. Getting on very well, too. I turned the corner where the Tregannock Arms is, and there was a brewer's lorry delivering beer. Too far out in the road. The thing ought to have been much closer in to the pub at a spot like that. Come to that, the road could do with a bit of widening."

" Well, come to that," I repeated his phrase, " we could get at Dros-y-Mor quicker if we cut the woods down. Have a garage on the quarter-deck."

For the first time since our marriage—and that was a long time now—Frank was annoyed with me. His face darkened. "Anyway," he said, "I hit the thing. Just grazed it. I'd have cleared it if it had been in its proper place. No harm was done. None whatever. I just bruised my leg against the dashboard. These things are bound to happen when you're learning."

"I suppose that was Joe Duncombe's consolation?"

"It was. He says the mudguard will be as good as new when he brings the car over here again."

"D'you know what I'm worrying about, darling?"

"There's no need to worry about anything."

"All the same, I *am* worrying. Just about this—will *you* be as good as new every time you come home?"

Mrs. Davies came in and cleared away the tea-things. Frank got up and lit his pipe. "You don't need to worry about *me*," he said as the match went in and out. "Or are we quarrelling about the car?"

I resorted to the North Country reply: "I'm not arguing: I'm just telling you."

Frank smiled at that. "Well, you'd better come and have a look at this leg now. A bit of ointment or something."

It was a nasty bruise. I fixed it up, and nothing more was said at that time. But I was not surprised when Ben Davies appeared on the quarter-deck the next morning. Frank was walking up-and-down, a habit with him for a few moments before disappearing into his shed. Ben knew, as well as the next man, that his appearance was forbidden—that Frank was on no account to be spoken to till his morning's work was done. I had so got into the habit myself that I was as mute as a fish during breakfast time and was glad to see Frank out of the way. Watching him now out of the window, and seeing Mrs. Davies coming along like a whole platoon of troops supporting an attack, I myself hurried through the opened French window to find out what this portended. Not that I didn't know. I knew all too well.

"And 'er being as near to ninety as makes no difference, we thought it our duty to go an' look after 'er few remaining years," Mrs. Davies was saying in a well-rehearsed manner.

The lady in question was Mrs. Davies's mother "over to

Gweek ". We had heard of her before. She had lately been widowed and lived alone in her cottage at Gweek—" and seein' as she's lately taken to tumbling about," said Mrs. Davies who seemed to have learned her part better than Ben, " we thought as now was as good a time as any other to give notice. It's our duty to 'er, and Ben can always find a bit of work to do in gardens."

That was the last chance to keep the Davieses. The old lady at Gweek, from all I had heard, was a spry body, ninety or not, as well able to look after herself as I am. The " tumbling about " was an artistic touch which I admired though I didn't believe in it. The old lady had a son of sixty who lived next door and who, or his wife, was in and out all day long. It was only a week ago that Mrs. Davies had been boasting to me about the old lady over to Gweek. She had been asked to go in and live with her son, but she had refused with spirit to do so. One way and another, there was no very good reason why the Davieses should so suddenly decide to go and comfort her last years. Moreover, Frank's work was already ruined for the morning, so that if ever there was a case for compromise this was it. He had only to say : " Well, Ben, you know you're doing what you ought not to do at this time of day, but seeing that you *are* here let's talk the matter over." Something like that. But, instead, Frank went into a raging temper, which with him showed itself in a whitening of the face and a working of all its muscles. Then he simply turned on his heel and walked through the wood. He spent the morning mooning about the garage, deciding this and that.

He had been a good employer. The Davieses had had a soft billet with excellent pay and a free cottage. So long as the household work was done, they could come and go as they liked. Indeed, the more they were out of the way the more Frank was pleased with them. He would have liked to employ a couple of invisible djinns, but these were human beings, which, as I saw it, was the root of the matter. Davies had known those trees for a long time. Indeed, he had always known them. He liked trees and he didn't like motor-cars. He liked to look out of his cottage windows and see them standing there, emblems of a world that didn't change much. To see, when he pulled his curtains of a morning, the trees gone, a building, and a mechanic washing down a car, wasn't something that he welcomed.

I could have put all this to Frank and a compromise might have been reached. But Ben's precipitate appearance on the quarter-deck, his fighting manner, and Frank's reaction to it, made this impossible. Moreover, I knew that in Ben's mind, as in Mrs. Davies's, too, all this evil was summed up, as evil tends to be, in a person. The person was Joe Duncombe. Although he was often outside their cottage, they rarely spoke to him. And, by transference, seeing Em Pritt's obvious interest in Joe, the resentment went over to her—the last person in the world able to speak for herself.

Sitting on the quarter-deck alone that morning, I saw clearly enough what a tangle of human emotions and motives lay behind the quarrel. The garage had merely touched it all off. But here, as in everything else, the heart of the matter lay in men and women, what they wanted, and what they didn't want. The Davieses wanted to stay put, rooted in the fields and woods. Joe wanted what he thought of as a glorious future of wider roads, trees felled wherever they stood in his way, bigger and better motor-cars, and a more modern world all round. Em Pritt wanted Joe, at any price. As it happened, Joe wanted Em, and that was the solution we at last found.

Chapter VII

The old lady over to Gweek, as old ladies of ninety will, died very suddenly and for no reason that could be discovered except that she was ninety years old. Reason enough. This happened soon after the Davieses had moved, but moved they had and that was that. Em Pritt and Joe Duncombe were married. We gave them a month off, with use of the car, for a honeymoon, and for a wedding present furnished their cottage, or rather let them furnish it according to their taste but at our expense. I wasn't sorry to have Frank to myself for a month. We shut the house and went off for a honeymoon of our own, with rucksacks on our backs. Frank had finished his book. It was springtime. We took a train through from the Hook of Holland to Berlin, and there got on our feet to have a look at the country which was causing headaches throughout Europe.

We didn't stay for long. Dubious night-clubs, a febrile population, a sense of something boiling up to nobody's good, made us glad to be out of the place and walking in a saner air in other lands.

It was on a morning in May that we found ourselves once more in London. I rang up Laura from our hotel, cadged an invitation to dinner that night, and reported to Frank that she seemed to have something up her sleeve. We discovered, when we had been in the house in Melbourne Square for five minutes that this was the future of Poor Judith.

Mell was there when we arrived, but Judith was not. She had gone to spend the evening in some women's club that she had joined, and when Frank expressed surprise at this, Mell said : " I expect she sensed that we should be talking about her. I'm being sent abroad, you know."

He said it as calmly as he said everything, but his gratification was not to be concealed. He was to go to a ministry in a foreign capital. " I'll only be a dog's-body there as I have been here," he said, his pride shining through his self-depreciation. " Of course, I'll take Laura with me, and the brat, I suppose."

(The brat, Belinda, had been put to bed.) " I can't take Aunt Judith."

Laura was as excited as Mell was calm. They were to go to a South American capital. " Of course, it might lead to anything." Mell spoke both Spanish and Portuguese.

I think she was already seeing herself as His Excellency's lady. But the next step was always the thing to Mell, and the next step, for the moment, was the disposal of Poor Judith. He was refilling the wine glasses as he began to make her position clear. " Of course, she hasn't a penny of her own, thanks to her pathetic faith in my old friend Ronald Lilywhite of Cardiff. She was only one of many that that shark lured down his ample gullet. Still, there was little I could do for her except give her a home and a

shilling or two to spend. Well, I've done that. What's to become
of her now ? "

Frank and I looked at one another across the table. We
were thinking the same thing. We didn't want Aunt Judith.
Mell considered us with an ironic smile twisting his mouth. " I
spoke," he said, " of my old friend Lilywhite of Cardiff. You
remember the family, Alice ? "

I thought of them all, even including that odious old woman,
Mrs. Gregson, to whom I was You. I thought of the fall on the
path and of how, when I had nothing, Judith took me in. Now
she had nothing, not even Bryan. But I was honest enough with
myself to admit (in my mind) that I didn't want Judith, and
I knew that Frank didn't want her. She had grown into a dis-
agreeable old painted woman. We had nothing to offer her save
our quiet, our trees, our water. There wasn't a bridge club
within miles. " Of course we'll have her," Frank said. " We'll
do our best to make her comfortable."

Mell looked at us with the same ironic smile. He might have
been presiding at the signing of an alliance between two nations
who didn't like one another very much, but whom necessity had
thrown across each other's path. " Well, I don't suppose you'll
see her to-night," he said. " She won't be back till late. I don't
sail for a month or so. There'll be plenty of time to make arrangements." And then he went on to tell us as much as he thought
we ought to know about his new job.

2

Joe Duncombe was back with Em and the car when we returned
to Dros-y-Mor. The car shone. You would not think that it
had been to the North of Scotland and back, with many a détour.
Em Pritt, as I could not help calling her to myself, was shining
like the car. You would imagine that Joe had given her an
occasional rub down with whatever it was that he used to induce
brightness. She greeted us, wearing a cap. What had been
to me a symbol of slavery was to Em a crown. A cap, or anything
else, is what you make it. I pointed out to Em that it was
unnecessary. But nothing would make her come in to serve
a meal unless that glory was upon her head.

135

It was her sign that the Davieses had departed and that she was in command.

By the middle of June Mell was gone, taking Laura and Belinda with him. Judith was left in the house in Melbourne Square to see the furniture into store and, if possible, to arrange a " let ". This had now been done, and, after a good deal of correspondence, we were to pick Judith up in London and bring her to Cornwall. The journey was to be broken at Ray's school where we should take part in such jollifications as half-term permitted. These consisted chiefly in seeing the boys run to the point of exhaustion over a sacred mile, a cricket match in which the boys could be counted on to defeat the Old Boys, and an out-of-doors tea-party at just such a time as you would like to take your son for a walk upon the countryside.

However, there we were, with Joe Duncombe wearing the chauffeur's uniform which he insisted on when he was taking the car for more than a mile, Em Pritt seated beside him in front, and me and Frank at the back. It had not ceased to be a wonder to Em that Joe knew the way to London. She herself had carefully marked out the route on an inch-to-the-mile map in case anything went wrong. She was secretly hoping that it would, so providing her with a way of saving the situation. The map was spread out on her knees, and her hat, despite the windscreen, was unnecessarily protected by several yards of muslin. And all these were endearing idiosyncrasies to Joe. He even consulted the map now and then, but this was not without a secret wink to Frank, as one old soldier to another.

3

While Joe Duncombe and Em went to stay with her parents, and he was getting over his surprise that such forebears could produce a paragon, we addressed ourselves to Poor Judith. She was staying in a small hotel where we found a room, too, and when she had kissed us both redly she asked : " But where is the car ? "

We explained that we had left it with Joe Duncombe, who doubtless would like to take his wife's parents for a run or two.

" Oh, but I was so looking forward to calling with both of you on Mamie James-Villiers," she cried.

" We can go in a taxi," Frank explained. But that was not the same thing. " There's *something*," she said, " in calling in a chauffeur-driven car—something you don't get at all by arriving in a taxi."

We soon learned that this was the main thing about Judith in her present state of development. Now that she was, almost literally, nobody, she had a great desire to be somebody. Even Frank, who was somebody, though he seemed the last person ever to realise it, was, whenever she introduced him, " *my* brother-in-law, Frank Melvill—the famous novelist, you know." She had already made several " friends " among the old ladies who frequented the rather shabby drawing-room of the hotel, and Frank had to endure a number of these introductions, always followed by the explanation : " And do you know what he's done ? He's actually lent his motor-car to his chauffeur ! Silly boy ! " She would have tapped him on the arm with her fan if she possessed such a thing. As it was, she rattled her jade beads and did all she could to look like a duchess in reduced circumstances. She had taken to a lorgnette through which she looked at him fondly, though more disparagingly, I thought, at me. For two pins she would have added : " And this is his wife— would you believe it, once a general servant, both to me and in some queer place in Paris." She never quite got to that, but I imagine it was only fear of Frank's wrath that headed her off. She could never forget that Frank had married Jane, never forgive me for having intruded upon *her* brother-in-law.

However, we got over it all, even including the visit—in a taxi —to Mamie James-Villiers, a poor old thing who lived in a flat at Kensington. She was another nobody, surrounded by the gestures and the possessions of a somebody. She shed a rheumy tear or two as she bade us " take great care of Judith in your wilds of Cornwall, because she's rather precious, you know." It was Mamie James-Villiers who induced me to take a more lenient, a kinder, view of Poor Judith. She was a representative of so much, of so many nobodies, tottering as bravely as they could through a few last shabby meaningless years.

4

Ray was growing up. We found him wearing long trousers, giving orders concerning the rolling of the cricket pitch to various small fry wearing short ones. Judith succeeded in blotting her copy-book at once by calling him darling and kissing him. Both the words and the action made him blush furiously and evoked grins behind small paws. Frank tried to set the matter right by calling him " old man " and bearing him off, this being a parents' day, to tea in a neighbouring farm garden. Joe took Judith for a drive in the motor-car round the surrounding countryside, and Em Pritt came with us. As we sat at a rustic tea-table and Ray and Em consumed great quantities of Devonshire cream and strawberries, I looked at my son. He was becoming absurdly like me, with his ginger hair, green eyes, and height beyond the ordinary. Frank tried to draw him out, with small success. " Well, how do you like it here, Ray ? Does the place come up to your expectations ? "

" Oh, it's so-so. You know."

" And what are you learning now ? "

" Oh, the usual stuff, you know."

" Been on any otter-hunts yet with the Head ? "

" You'd drive him mad if you used any such word. We don't hunt. We observe. It's one way of getting round him. We're doing a dig at the moment."

" Ah ! What are you finding ? An ancient camp ? "

" We don't know what it is yet. Except that it's not a camp or a burial mound. Maybe a Roman villa. We're finding some interesting mosaic pavements."

And then he was off with Em again concerning his hut in the woods at Dros-y-Mor and all that was therein, which she was supposed to keep swept and garnished. " We'll do this site in plasticine when I get back," he promised her ; and Em, who didn't know what a site was, and hardly who the Romans were, or a villa from a burial-mound, was greatly pleased by the promise. She and Ray wandered back to the school together, leaving us to follow when we thought fit.

We sat for a while amid the wreckage of the tea-table, and

watched the swallows, and listened to the hum of the summer's day, and I said : " Thank you for giving me a son, Frank."

" Don't mention it, madame. Anything to oblige. D'you know what I most like about him to-day ? "

" His hair, like mine."

" That Em's company makes him happier than having a ride in the car with Aunt Judith. Did you notice how she tried to get him ? "

" Yes. Poor Judith ! "

5

We did our best. We gave Judith the room at the end of the corridor opposite our own. We put an easy-chair in there and a card-table and a few packs of patience cards. There were heavy demands on Joe Duncombe's time, for almost every day Judith dolled herself up and went for a ride. She insisted on dressing as if she were in London. She spent much time at her mirror " making up ", and her jade beads, her lorgnette, and a bluish hat that flopped on her head became known to us like the backs of our hands. The country bored her. She never asked Joe to take her to Land's End or on to the downs, but to such towns as Cornwall offered—Truro, or Helston, or Bodmin—and there she would take tea and pine for Kensington. Frank and I, who walked most afternoons, asked her often to come with us, but the sight of our ash sticks and heavy shoes daunted her, and she never once accepted our invitation. She preferred to be riding, or tottering on her high heels, and it was useless for me to remind her of the times at the Rowans where we had walked the day through. She said that she had " grown up " since then.

It was a mild winter. Frank had begun work on a new book, and thus he was at liberty to disappear each morning into his hut in the woods. We took our afternoon walk while Judith rambled about the house or rode in the car, and then there was the evening. This, which had been our best, was our worst time. With an early evening meal behind us, with a log-fire burning, Frank and I had been in the habit of sitting in the library, talking to one another, reading to one another, or reading to ourselves, finding in the silence all the companionship we needed. Occasionally he would put his hand on my knee and ask : " No regrets ? " and I would smile at him and he knew that of all the actions of my life there was none I less regretted, none I looked on with more fulfilment and pride, than in having married this rather grim, rather silent, husband of mine.

Now all this was ended. Judith would carry the card-table down from her room, plank it in front of the roaring logs, complain of the cold, tell us what she had seen in some café at Truro or St. Austell, and generally wreck our serenity. She always " changed " for the evening. Frank and I never did. With a new face, a new dress, she was the same old Judith, and I was almost glad when the crisis came.

It came, as crises will, suddenly. She was deep in a game of Demon Patience, letting us know whenever a Red Queen was turned up that went on to a Black King, and so preventing our minds from being on anything of our own. She got up to reach a match-box from the mantelpiece, having become a heavy smoker of cigarettes. She was confronted by Jane's photograph in its heavy silver frame and picked it up and stared for some time at it. Frank said quietly : " Put that down, Judith, please. I never allow anyone to touch that. Not anyone."

She put the photograph back, and said, almost to herself, " I was the last person to see her alive."

It brought back into our quiet lives what Frank, for all these years, had tried to forget : the scene of anguish on the beach, the last despairing cry, the white arms beating the silent water. He had tried to forget, but he had not forgotten, and I had learned to know the moments when he remembered. They were moments when I could do nothing but be with him in a very special sense. I could long ago have put the photograph in a drawer. I could, for that matter, have burned it quietly ; but I knew that I could never conceal Jane from him, never burn her out of his memory. She would always be there : the woman who had preceded me, and I sometimes wondered whether she would not always precede me.

The silence was so painful, so obvious, that Judith became aware of it. She swept her four rows of little cards into one pack and slapped them down in a pile in the middle of the table. I could see that in a moment a lot of grievances had rushed to her mind, and prayed that she would not now say anything that would make a bad situation worse. But, like most prayers, that one was unanswered. " I'd like to know exactly what my situation here is," she said, " so that I may keep it, and not make any more mistakes."

No one answered, and she went on : " I drive by myself every day, and no one ever offers to come with me. It's almost as though you were ashamed of me, or disliked me."

" We have offered, day after day," I said, " to take you walking."

" I'm speaking to Frank," she said, rattling her beads at me in her agitation. She looked at me with so much dislike that the sound of the beads was a rattle-snake's warning that it was about to strike.

" I am the sister of Frank's wife . . ." she began, but Frank intervened.

" You are not, you know, Judith," he said quietly. " You are Jane's sister. Alice is my wife."

· " At any rate, you are my brother-in-law, and you forbid me to pick up my own sister's photograph."

" I'm sorry, Judith. Perhaps I spoke harshly to you. But it's just one of those things. I hate anyone touching that photograph but myself."

" You were quick enough in finding a substitute for Jane, anyhow."

" A little more than four years," Frank said. " A longish time for a lonely man. But I didn't take Alice as a substitute. I took her for herself."

The words were quietly spoken, but I knew that they were the last words on this subject, that Poor Judith was finished. We had seen the last of her.

6

Among other things, I was Frank's secretary, as you know, and I kept carbon copies of all his letters. Not that he wrote many. Having done his writing for the day, he was content to call that enough, so that he wrote hardly one letter in a week. But here is one which he wrote at this time to Mell.

"Dear Mell.—I am sorry to say that we have failed with Judith. You had one great advantage over us. You went out to work every day; and she had friends, a club, and all the advantages of civilisation. In these backward parts, we lack these, and we have had her all the time, with few of the things to which she had become accustomed. An occasional wrestle with a muffin at the end of a motor-car ride to Truro or St. Austell is about all we could arrange for her. She would have liked us to share these heady joys, but Alice and I preferred to go our own way, which, as you know, is not a very exciting one to people accustomed to metropolitan delights.

"It is not to be wondered at that, in these circumstances, Judith became restless and unhappy and allowed to develop a dislike of Alice that I have always been aware of. Even this might have been put up with if it had been kept under control, but it broke out in circumstances that I need not bother you with.

"I have now made other arrangements for her that I hope will not be too displeasing to you and Laura. I invented some business that took me to London, and there I called on Mamie James-Villiers, with whom, I imagine, you are not unfamiliar. With the name, at any rate. Alice and I had been there with Judith before the move was made into Cornwall, and I formed two impressions : one, that in their way these old ladies were attached to one another, and the other, that Mamie James-Villiers was, as we say, living on a shoe-string. Her little Kensington flat was a pretty shabby place; and, surrounded by relics of a grandeur that was evidently a thing of the past, she was just ' getting by'. She and Judith have been faithful correspondents since Judith has been here, and I imagine that a trickle of discontent has flowed from Cornwall to Kensington. Anyway, amid the faded Georgian mirrors, the worn-out Aubusson carpet, and the tarnished silver, it was not difficult to persuade her that there would be advantages if she and Judith shared the flat and the expenses of it. Indeed, over a cup of tea in a Kensington tea-shop, she welcomed the scheme and undertook that she would be the first to open the matter to Judith.

"You will think that Uncle Frank is a plotter of the deepest dye, but I am trying to act like a reasonable being. Judith is unhappy, my work is interfered with, and Alice has to put up with us both. There is not a point in common anywhere. And please don't think that this is to lay any extra burden on you and Laura. It will cost me more to have Judith in Kensington than to have her here, and this cost will be gladly met. It will be better all round. Judith will be happier in London ; we will be happier in Cornwall ; and (if this means anything to you) Mamie James-Villiers will be happier to have a friend and to keep her ancestors' portraits.

"I am glad to know that you find the new work to your liking. Alice and I send love to you and Laura and the Brat."

7

It was soon after Frank had written this letter that Judith, having read one of her own, announced : "Mamie James-Villiers wants me." The post tended to be late in those parts, and this was at luncheon. The morning was a bad time for Judith. Frank was at work in his hut ; I was typing in my room ; and there was nothing left for her to do except dawdle on the road, awaiting the post-girl. No word came to her from the great world except an occasional letter from Laura, or one in the large florid hand that we knew was Mamie's. Mamie's were read again and again, as a starving man, if he could, would bite again and again on his crust. I shall never forget the joy there was in those few simple words : "Mamie wants me." I think for the first time I realised one of the agonies of growing old : the sense that nobody wants you, that to be put up with, unwanted, tolerated, is the most that you can expect.

"Read Mamie's letter," Judith said. She handed it to Frank, who read it and handed it to me. He had told me what he had done during his visit to London, and so the letter was no surprise to me. But it was a pleasure. There could be no doubt that, though she was playing her part in a scheme that had been proposed to her, Mamie was writing sincerely and from the heart.

"Well, what do you think you ought to do ?" Frank asked. Even in such a moment he was too honest to add : "We should miss you, you know."

Judith was brighter than she had been since the affair of Jane's photograph. She was almost merry. "Well, I'll have to answer the letter, to begin with," she said. "It would be heaven to get back to Kensington."

"So you want to leave us. At any rate, you wouldn't *mind* leaving us ? "

Judith answered frankly : " No. You have been very kind to me, Frank. But there's nothing to *do* here, nothing at all. You haven't even a radio. But there *are* points I'll have to think out. I don't see, to begin with, how on earth I am to pay my share of the rent. Oh, that Lilywhite man ! I wish I had never heard of him."

Frank did not answer that hearing of a person was one thing. Putting your money into his sieve was another. He merely said : " I think that could be arranged."

"I could write to Mell. He is always most generous."

"No. You must on no account write to Mell. At least, you mustn't write about money. He has Laura and their infant to think about."

"Well, you've got Alice and a great growing son."

"Let me and Mell settle it between us, then."

She agreed, but I knew that all the money would come out of Frank's pocket. This was his scheme, and he would see it through. However, living down here, and living as we did, cost little, and Frank was well-to-do. His last novel had been filmed, and Christopher Lyndhurst wanted to make a play of it. "We'll go up to London together," he said to me that afternoon when Judith had gone to her room to write to Mamie. "We'll see Judith settled in, and there'll be a chance for me and Lyndhurst to talk about this play."

Christopher Lyndhurst was a man in his middle thirties. He was one of the last of those who believed that a play was a play, not a medical excursion into sodomy or incest or children being knowing with their parents and telling them where they had gone wrong with their lives. He had written a play or two of his own, but his main occupation was in transforming other people's novels into his own medium. He had been successful in this, and Frank, who admitted that writing a play was something he could never do, was anxious to meet him.

It was an October day when we set off. We left Em Pritt behind. Joe ran us to Truro where we got on to the Riviera

Express and then he returned to Dros-y-Mor. It was all to
Judith's disliking. She would have preferred to make the journey
by chauffeur-driven car, but Frank's motoring days were all but
ended. Mine had not begun, save as a victim.

8

Mamie was an " honourable ", but (unlike Mrs. Lilywhite, who
was also an " honourable ") she could trace her family back
for a long way. She was one of the last of them. Two deaths,
one taking place in the 1914–1918 war, had come inconveniently
close to one another, and two sets of death duties had done the
rest. Mamie had little left except her family portraits, which
were worth a bit, the family having seen its rise when Romney
and Gainsborough were painting. These pictures, a survival of
bits and pieces of family furniture, and an income that was just
about enough to keep a pet rabbit in lettuce, was all that remained.
Frank and I, with Poor Judith, took tea with her. The tea was
served in porcelain made by Spode and was poured from a Leeds
tea-pot. A little silver urn containing hot water buzzed and
spluttered on the table. The walls, whose paper was in none too
good a condition, were bright with the family portraits and with
small water-colours that attracted my attention because strange,
almost transparent, figures hovered among substantial trees and
made their way along roads that one could have walked on. I
asked Mamie who had painted these, and with pride the old girl
admitted that they were all hers. " I have a lot more in a portfolio," she said, as her almost transparent ivory hands flickered
over the tea-pot. " They are visions I see. I see them often,
but not every day. It is such a comfort to know that we are
watched over and accompanied by spiritual essences."

The figures were all of pretty girls, wearing a little diaphanous
clothing, and, if one had to be haunted by spirits, they were
pleasant enough.

" An odd thing about them," said Mamie, " is that they are
all like me in youth. But some of them are male figures. There
is one that is remarkably like my nephew, who was killed on the
Somme when a seventeen-year-old lieutenant. He comes again
and again. I keep him in the portfolio. He was a brave boy, a

credit to the family. He died trying to take a German machine-gun. Of course, he is not really dead, or I wouldn't see him so often. But they say he is dead. At any rate, his name appeared in the casualty list. You know, those ghastly columns that used to be in *The Times*."

The autumn evening was closing in and Mamie switched on the electric light. " Well, there's one thing," she said briskly, " now that dear Judith is here I sha'n't have to think so much about the electric light bills. We'll be able to switch on much earlier. Oh, I am glad that you've brought her ! We shall have such *fun*. We'll have a jolly time this very first night putting all her things away."

It was clearly an invitation to me and Frank to go, leaving them alone to their jollifications. We walked for a time round Kensington, haunted by memories of Thackeray, and Frank was depressed and dispirited. The autumn night was full of falling leaves. A chill little breeze blew up, and his depression communicated itself to me. " Will they be happy together ? " I asked.

" God knows," he said. " God alone knows."

9

Christopher Lyndhurst had asked us to dinner, and we joined him in the Ivy. Neither of us had met him before, and we both liked him. He was in his middle thirties, one of those dark good-looking ugly men, if you know what I mean by that. He had a square face with prominent cheekbones, dark eyebrows and hair. He was carefully dressed, unlike Frank, who thought no more of his clothes in London than he did out of it. People used to go to the Ivy to stare at celebrities, and I was glad to see a satisfactory amount of staring going on as we made our way to our table.

We didn't discuss the book at all, and I enjoyed myself noting the difference between the two men. There were Frank's cuff-links, for example, that looked as though they had come from Woolworth's, as they had, and, Christopher's of silver crossed with blue enamel. There was Frank's old rag of a tie, and Christopher's which declared that he had once been in the

Guards Brigade. But they wore their clothes with equal indifference. Christopher was a gourmet, too, and ordered a gourmet's dinner, to which Frank did justice, unaware of what it was, with an air that suggested he would be just as much at home with blood puddings.

" I've just been settling a sister-in-law," he said, " with a dear old dame in Kensington," and he gave an account that drew from Christopher the remark : " It might be my aunt, Mamie James-Villiers."

So we were not without conversational resources. It turned out that Christopher was one of the same family, an " Hon " like all that bunch, but keeping it dark. " I've taken the name I go under by deed poll," he said. " All that old game is up, and the sooner we realise it the better. But Aunt Mamie holds on. A pity she hasn't got a few nephews who've become stockbrokers. That's what that dead and doomed lot go in for mostly. And a good thing they're making of it. But Aunt Mamie and 1 go in for the arts. Has she shown you her pictures ? "

We said that we had indeed seen her pictures, and Christopher admitted that he had a few in his flat, which he hung whenever a visit from Auntie was threatened. " I wish she'd give me the Gainsboroughs and Reynoldses instead," he said. " I'd sell 'em like a shot."

" I don't so much mind her transactions with the spirit world," he went on, " as her literary inspirations. Now *there's* something that does set my hair on end. I expect you've met 'em, Mr. Melvill—the people with the finest story in the world ? All you have to do is write it and go fifty-fifty with the royalties."

Frank said he had indeed met them and that he had a short way with them.

" Yes," said Christopher. " Very nice when you don't know the people and all is done through the post. But it's another matter when the person concerned is Auntie and she turns up *in propria persona* and wild with inspiration. I've lost several fortunes through not seeing eye to eye with her about what will or will not go on a stage. Her plays are always a mixture of Oliver Lodge and Maeterlinck. Now I ask you . . .! And she doesn't write a line. It's the idea that matters. She says so."

We went on to a theatre after dinner, and it was not till we were parting for the night that Frank said : " When you're ready to work on my book, you may care to do it at my place in Cornwall. It might save time, having me on the spot."

10

It was not till the Christmas holidays were over and Ray had gone back to school that Christopher came. Ray had suddenly shot up broad and tall, with a voice that had passed the cracking stage and was now full and clear. It was January. In the autumn he would be going to Oxford. He would be an undergraduate, as Mell had been when he picked me up from the Lilywhites' path. True, Mell had then been in his last year. Ray would be a freshman. But he would be an undergraduate as Mell had been then. I got no comfort from the reflection. I was as old as Poor Judith had been when I joined her at the Rowans.

Judith had settled down. We heard from her but rarely. Her life and Mamie's seemed to be divided between bridge and the spirits. They belonged to a women's club whose members divided their time between listening to " tea-talks " by rising poets and novelists and playing bridge. The rising poets and novelists cost us nothing, except a prayer that they would eventually rise ; but the bridge required Frank to dip often into his pocket, and, whenever he did so, a letter came from Judith calling him " the best brother-in-law in the world." He was very patient with all this, but not so patient with the curiously smudged photographs which showed Mamie's nephew with a radiant cross above his head, or, of all people, Bryan Graves, attended improbably by mystic females who seemed to be luring him on to indiscretions he would never have committed while living. But, as I say, they were rather smudgy creatures, and a hint here and there of a wing or two among them perhaps involved an intention to lead him up rather than on.

However, we hoped the best for Bryan and prepared ourselves for the more earthy coming of Christopher Lyndhurst. He came as January was opening with the camellias in the woods in bloom, and with a primrose here and there, and with the magnolia stellata that sheltered behind the house beginning to show its white buds. We had told Ray of his coming and of his purpose there, and

Ray had magnanimously given him the freedom of his hut for working in. " Tell him to be careful of the plasticine record of the dig," was his only reservation.

However, Christopher did not use the hut. He arrived late on a January day, having, to the delight of Joe, driven himself in a two-seater car from London. It was the first time Joe had had two cars in the garage, and he was as proud as a trainer with a string of thoroughbreds in a stable. There was an inspection-pit in the garage, and Joe's head sticking out of it is associated in my mind with that visit. But I was of the opinion, and am still, that the way to arrive at Dros-y-Mor was by water. To cross the river from Helford in a dinghy, to enter the creek, to feel the quiet more and more enfolding you, to make the last turn and see the white house dreaming on its platform with the trees behind it ; that was the way to come to Dros-y-Mor. But more and more people have forgotten so now. I often took that way myself, and I learned to scull, standing up in the boat and facing towards the house, for the sheer joy of seeing it draped in wistaria in spring, surrounded by hydrangeas of many colours as the year drew on, always apparently immovable and beautiful.

But as it happened on that January day Frank and I had wandered through the woods and had just come out by the garage when Christopher's car drew up. It was a red-enamelled sportive-looking thing with a hood that could be lowered, and it was lowered now, with Christopher at the wheel, wearing furry gloves and looking weather-beaten. " Hallo, Mr. Melvill," he exclaimed. " Rotten roads for the last mile or two."

Joe was hanging about to take charge of the car. It was a remark after his own heart. He would have fully agreed with G. K. Chesterton that " the rolling English drunkard made the rolling English roads ", but he had no use either for rolling drunkards or the roads they made. He would have liked a road that ran straight and flat from Charing Cross to " his " garage at Dros-y-Mor. From the beginning, it was obvious that Christopher was the man for him.

However, Frank said : " We do our best. We like to be a bit hidden. I apologise, but I'm afraid you'll have to walk for a few hundred yards. Bring the bags along, Joe, when you've put the car away."

Christopher got out of the car, pulled off his big glove, and shook Frank by the hand. He kissed me on both cheeks. I hadn't been accustomed to the casual London kiss, and was both surprised and alarmed. But it was consoling to see the way Christopher walked through the woods. They meant something to him. The evening was closing in, and the flowers burned in the darkness. The running of our stream could be heard. Here and there, already, primroses were at our feet, and a fragrance was on the air. When we came to the quarter-deck he walked right across it and stood with his back to the water, looking. The white house glimmered and an owl began its tremulous crying. It was at this moment that Em Pritt switched on all the lights in the big room whose windows were uncurtained. The light streamed across the grassy quarter-deck, falling on the stone tubs in which the hydrangeas would bloom, and on an old iron well-head that Frank had brought from Italy, and on a bronze faun, half-concealed behind the white flowers of a camellia. At last with a sigh, Christopher walked towards the house. " Better than my rooms on the Cromwell Road," he said.

II

Christopher was with us for a month or so. We all three break-fasted together, and then Frank made for his hut in the woods, I went to the room that was my " office ", and Christopher worked in his bedroom. In the afternoons we walked, and in the evenings, when the lights were on and the log fire crackled on the hearth, Frank and Christopher discussed the play : what had been written that morning and what was proposed for the next day. Not that Frank took much hand in that. " I'm not a dramatist," he said. " I've tried to write plays and they're not my thing. They all go flat. This is your job, Chris. You asked for it and you've got it. Still, I like to hear you talk about it, and I'm here to answer any questions."

And so, with his pipe going, his chief contribution was to listen and approve, though I knew that he would have preferred to have his mind vacant of everything except the job he was on at the moment.

I was busy enough, what with Frank's daily stint of novel

and Christopher's daily stint of play. Frank's contribution did not bother me, for he wrote fluently in a clear hand with scarcely a correction in half a dozen pages. But Christopher's was another matter. His hand was crabbed, his corrections were many, and there came, as there was bound to do, a morning when I was beaten. I looked at the blotched and muddled manuscript, could make nothing sensible of it, and my typewriter clicked to a standstill. I had been well brought up as an author's secretary. I should not have taken my difficulty to Frank while he was at work. I should simply have called it a day and left it till his mind was disengaged.

I decided to take my difficulty to Christopher.

He never dressed properly till the midday meal, coming down to breakfast in pyjamas, red leather slippers and a black silk dressing-gown with a scarlet pocket and scarlet cuffs. There was a silken scarf as a rule wound round his neck. So I found him. Em Pritt had been up during breakfast time and set his room to rights. The bed was made, an electric fire was burning, and the room was full of cigarette smoke. When I knocked and went in he was sitting at a table in front of the window, too small to hold much more than the quarto sheet he was working on. The floor about him was littered with other sheets bearing his scribble. I told him of my difficulty which he soon cleared up, and then said, in an unsteady voice : " This is the first time I've seen you without Frank being about." As he said this, he took my wrist and tried to lift it to his lips, while his ugly pleasant dark face was curiously twisted. I allowed him to kiss my hand, determined at all costs to keep the moment light. " Well," I said, " now you've had the pleasure of seeing me without Frank being about."

" I love you very much."

" You must get on with your work," I said, trying to keep my tone as level as if I had been telling Ray to get on with one of his plasticine models. " I'm interrupting you and getting in your way. If it's any consolation to you, I like you very much."

" Couldn't we contrive something ? "

" No. We must contrive nothing."

" You couldn't come to London to see your Aunt Judith ? "

" She's not my aunt. She's Frank's sister-in-law. And I should dislike seeing her."

" This is a silly little scene," he said, " not a bit like some of the scenes I've been working on."

" I'm sorry I can't make it more like one of them," I said. " Now I must get on with what you've written."

I took his manuscript with me and sat at my typewriter, but not a word could I knock out for the rest of that morning.

No more was said about it, and it stands to reason that I said nothing to Frank. It would have disturbed him at a time when he must not be disturbed. Not that I would have said anything to him at any time. The chief emotion in my heart was gladness that there were men who still found me desirable. I had been living for perhaps too long almost literally in the woods. I put on my golden slippers and green dress that night. I had had them for years, but I was gratified that Frank still liked to see me in green with a touch of gold. " Don't you think," he said, " that Alice is looking uncommonly well this evening ? "

Christopher looked at me as though noticing me for the first time. " Oh, yes," he said. " She looks built for a motor-car made for two." They both laughed at such an odd conceit, and then went on to discuss the play.

12

A day or two later Christopher returned to London, taking the finished play with him. He had had his car out the day before, and had mysteriously said that he had some business to do in Plymouth and would be back by dinner-time. It was at dinner that he produced a case of pipes for Frank—" my perfect host " —and for me, with much preliminary unwrapping of tissue-paper, he had bought a spray of leaves and flowers, wrought in gold, each flower having a zircon at its heart. It was an absurdly expensive present and he made quite a ceremony of fastening it to my dress. " For the perfect hostess and secretary," he said. " And now we'll all drink to the success of the play, and," he added, looking hard at me across the table, " to the success of its adapter."

Frank re-filled our glasses. " To the success of the play

and its adapter," he said. " To the success of the play," I said.
The play *was* a success and little more need here be said about
it. Attempts were made to dramatise other novels by Frank,
but none appeared on a stage. Not that Frank minded that.
He would have liked, as novelists before him would have liked,
to see his books on the stage ; but primarily he was a novelist
and didn't much care what happened after he had done with
them. The main thing about this particular adaptation was that
it introduced me to Christopher Lyndhurst.

Chapter VIII

Mell was for a few years in South America and was then recalled
to London, where he wanted to be and where for some time he
remained. It would not have surprised me or Frank if he had
become an ambassador. He had all the airs and graces and,
while not giving a drop himself, could extract blood from a stone.
He was, when it suited him, most forthcoming ; usually he was
the most reserved of men, keeping such secrets as he had under
double lock and key.

He had not sold but only let the house in Melbourne Square,
Kensington, and now took possession of it once more. Frank
and I gave him and Laura time to get their furniture out of store
and then proposed ourselves for a visit. Ray was to join us. He
was at Worcester College, Oxford, and it had been a hard job
to persuade him to spend part of his long vacation in London.
Whenever we called on him at Oxford we found his rooms cluttered up with objects that had come out of his " digs " : skulls
that horrified me, and tiles and jars and arrow-heads, beads and
bits of barbaric jewellery. It had become the passion of his life,
and if we ever tried to get him on to his intentions when he came
down from the University he would tell us gravely that, so far as
he could see, archæology was the only subject in which he was
really interested, of which he *knew* something.

He and some other men were engaged at the moment in a
" dig " not far from St. Albans, but he might, he told us, spare
a day or two to be with us in London. He could leave the
direction of the work to " Sandy ".

" Sandy ", whose name was James Sanderson, was becoming
at least as important a person as Ray's parents. I remembered
how, when we had first abandoned Ray to school life in Devonshire, he had disappeared with a skinny boy who was similarly
abandoned. This was Sandy. Beginning their school life
together, they had clung to one another, discovered an equal
passion for the " digs " that the school organised, and distin-
guished themselves by making a large-scale model of what the
school region had probably looked like in Roman times. Sandy,
who had a step-mother and no father, was not, I imagined,
particularly happy at home. He spent a large part of every
summer holiday with Ray at Dros-y-Mor, and they went on to
Worcester College together, firmly welded by the years. Sandy's
step-mother was now dead, leaving him a wealthy young man,
for the father's will had given this second wife only a life-interest
in what was a considerable sum of money. This money was now
Sandy's, and if there was one thing which interested him as
much as archæology it was the Stock Exchange. The *Financial
Times* came to him by post every morning when he was with us
at Dros-y-Mor, and it was a sight to watch him poring over its
columns. " Digging can be an expensive habit," he explained
to us gravely. " It's as well to do it out of profits and leave the
capital alone."

He had filled out since we first watched him and Raymond
at school. He was in his early twenties, a well-built fair youth,
blue-eyed and well-dressed. Now that his step-mother was dead,
without any perceptible regret on his part, he hadn't a relative in
the world. " And that," he would declare, " is a desirable
position to be in, don't you think ? I've got excellent brokers,
and that's enough for me."

Brokers played a large part in his life, and he was an expert
with motor-cars. Frank's car, which tended to live a solitary
life in the garage, was constantly in demand while Sandy was
with us at Dros-y-Mor. " Do you mind if Ray and I borrow
the car this morning ? " he would ask Frank. " I want to hop

154

over to Helston to ring up my brokers." He didn't understand how we could do without so desirable an instrument as a telephone to keep us, as he called it, " constantly in touch ".

He had, we gathered, a flat of his own in London—" Just a place where I hang out and keep a telephone," he explained. " I should hate to settle. I'm up and down all over the place on digs."

2

However, we *did* use the car when we went up to town to pay our promised call on Mell and Laura. As usual, we took Em and her husband with us. They were quartered in a small hotel in Kensington and Joe presented himself at Melbourne Square each morning for orders. These were usually quite brief. " Oh, take Em for a ride somewhere."

Mell was not at home when we arrived, nor was the Brat, as Frank and I called Belinda. Laura was alone, and, I thought, not improved by her few years in South America. She was thinner and more taut, and her skin had a burnt-up texture. However, she was Laura, and she welcomed us literally with open arms. I imagined that, whatever Mell had been engaged on over there, it had involved a good deal of entertaining, and it was as our hostess that Laura received us. " Now do sit down and rest yourselves," she said. " You must have had a tiring journey. You can see to your things later. Belinda sends her apologies for not being here to meet you, but she'll be in to tea. And I've asked two old friends to be here, too. Poor Judith is coming with that old soul whose flat she shares—Mamie James-Villiers."

" So you've already got round to seeing Judith again ? " Frank asked. " She was unhappy with us."

" Well, Mell thought we'd better see her as soon as we could. She's hardly a stone's-throw from us. And quite happy. The two old ladies seem very attached. And how is Ray ? He must be quite a man now."

We explained about the " dig " near St. Albans and assured her that Ray would be looking in soon. " Probably with his friend James Sanderson."

155

We were explaining who James Sanderson was, and a parlour-maid was clattering cups and saucers on to a table, when Belinda came in. She stopped our conversation. I don't know how she " took " Frank, but I was for a moment tongue-tied. I could only stare.

Belinda was a beauty. Whatever the South American sun had done to Laura, it had ripened Belinda. She was a peach, ready for plucking. She would then have been about eighteen or nineteen years old, with a nose that tended to be tip-tilted, dark eyes and skin, slight in build but over-brimming with vitality. She was fashionably dressed. She came straight up to Frank and me and kissed us. Such warm lips ! " I remember you both," she said. " I remember holidays at Dros-y-Mor, and being thrown overboard and made to swim. How is Ray ? "

There was not a trace of embarrassment about her. If Laura had seen much service as a hostess, Belinda must have been always at her side. " Now please sit down," she said, not giving us a chance to answer anything. " You must have some tea. I positively rushed home to join you. Mother, I'm dying for a cup."

Everything about her was right : all the little things : her shoes, her handbag, her hat, which she flung on to a sofa, her gloves which she drew off with an air, her stockings. Her finger-nails were lightly coloured, and she knew how to apply cosmetics. I was all against coloured finger-nails. I was all against cosmetics, having before my eyes the dreadful example of Poor Judith. But with Belinda they seemed right. She had a low sweet voice. She stole the picture. Laura faded into the background, and this, it seemed to me, she consciously and willingly did, anxious and happy to display her lovely daughter.

" Don't you think," she asked unnecessarily, " that Belinda's looking well ? "

We both agreed that Belinda was looking well, and I felt some of Laura's own reticence : the reticence of the middle-aged in the presence of youth and beauty. But it was one of the girl's endearing characteristics that she quickly brushed off any reference to herself. " Now do tell me," she said, " all about Dros-y-Mor. I shouldn't blame you if you thought I'd forgotten all about it.

But I haven't, you know. I remember everything. I remember Ray's shed in the woods, and his models that he wouldn't let me touch, and the little stream and the flowers. How is all that ? And the creek, so lovely. Are there any houses built there yet, or are you still isolated ? I'll have to come down with Mother to see it all for myself—before Daddy carries out his dreadful idea of sending me away to the Sorbonne."

I noted that Mell was Daddy, and that he already had schemes for his daughter.

" We'll be glad to have you both down there," Frank said. " We're still Crusoes. You shall see for yourselves. As for Ray, you'll meet him soon, I hope."

3

They met sooner than anyone expected. The drawing-room in which we were taking tea was at the front of the house and my chair gave me a clear view of what was happening outside. I was the first to see the red two-seater draw up and Ray and James Sanderson get out. They were dressed, as they always seemed to be in these days, in old flannel bags and pullovers with scarves of silk carelessly knotted round their necks. Frank heard the car door bang at the same time as I did, and exclaimed : " Good lord ! They're here ! "

Belinda glanced through the window. " Good lord, indeed," she said. " What a pair of vagabonds ! I recognise Ray. Who's the other man ? "

But there was no time to explain about James Sanderson. Already a bell was pealing through the house, and a moment later, with clay on their shoes, James and Ray came into the drawing-room. They saw Belinda and they were tongue-tied. But only for a moment. I remember the rather hurried introductions and then Sandy saying : " Oh, but this is too bad ! We are a pair of sweeps. We're doing a dig, you know, Mrs. Conybeare, near St. Albans, and this morning new tools were needed, so we hopped into the car to get them in London. There's a good shop for all that sort of stuff. The car's cluttered up with it. Then Ray suggested we should come on here to see whether his father and mother had arrived. Just that sort of call—you know. We had no intention of staying. If you'll allow us, we'll make a formal call later, all dressed up to the nines. We're not fit to be in civilised society."

He was going on, impelled into speech by his own nervousness, fiddling with his scarf. " Sit down," Belinda said. " You must have some tea." She was as calm as he was flurried.

Ray was seated opposite Belinda. " I remember you," he said. " You've changed a lot. But I remember you. I used to pull your hair as you swam in the creek at Dros-y-Mor."

He seemed to appreciate his own daring in saying any such thing.

" Well, you'd better not pull it now," Belinda said. " It cost a pretty penny to have it done."

We were out of it—Frank, Laura and I. " This is a new chapter," I was thinking. " This is a new generation."

We could only look on. They had no eyes for us, the three young people. We were only an audience.

" But, look here," Ray was saying. " We'll have to get back. The chaps will be expecting us. But, Father and Mother, I do hope we'll see you over at St. Albans before you go back ? "

It was the first time he had ever invited us to see the glories of one of his digs.

They pushed back their chairs. " And you'll come, too, I hope, Miss Conybeare ? " said Sandy. " And Mrs. Conybeare, of course ? "

Of course.

We all promised to see what could be done. A moment later the red car was buzzing off like a high-powered wasp.

4

Mell was late that day at the office. He did not come in till nearly dinner-time, and we waited for him. Laura insisted that we should stay and have dinner with them, but Belinda did not join us. She was, Laura said, taking dinner in the West End with another girl and two young men, and then going on to dance. She came down, clad in glory ; and, soon after, one of the young men, to whom I was introduced (but I forget his name) came for her, dressed, as she was, for an evening's festivity.

They got into a taxi-cab together. There was no clay on *his* boots.

But the memory of Belinda, all lit up, faded when Mell came in. He was tired, overworked and solemn. He greeted us with his usual grave courtesy and even treated me to a kiss. There was more white than black now in his hair, and I remember the meal that followed chiefly because of its funereal quality. He hardly spoke a word, and there was a moment when the telephone rang and he was out of his chair before it had stopped ringing, saying : " That's for me."

When he came back he was more serious than ever, and I began to feel as though I were at Dros-y-Mor, and Frank great with book, and myself not venturing to open my mouth.

It was a grim dinner, and the dismal thing was that Mell's mood communicated itself to Frank who was all but mute. Laura and I did our best. I put leading questions about his work in South America, hoping to lure Mell in that direction, but South America seemed now, to him, a long way off, and at last both Laura and I were bogged down into the general gloom and silence. Then he got up, wiping his lips with his napkin, and said : " I'll have to get back to the office for an hour or so to-night. Like to stretch your legs, Uncle Frank, for part of the way ? "

When they were gone, Laura and I went into the drawing-room and looked at one another. " What's on Mell's nerves ? " I asked.

I think Laura felt the tension more than I did. " Mell never talks to me about his things," she said. " You know he's rather highly thought-of in the Foreign Office these days ? Of course, he wouldn't say anything to you about it, or to Frank, for that matter, but he knows what's going on, and I have to content myself with reading his face and his actions like a barometer. I don't like what I'm reading in these days. You know he was sent out to the Embassy at Berlin lately ? No, of course you don't, and I shouldn't mention it. He was there for nearly a week. All that came through to me was a cryptic remark about Belinda."

" Belinda ? Why about Belinda ? "

" Well, you know he was set upon sending her to the Sorbonne ? He just dropped me the hint : ' Go easy on that

Sorbonne business with Belinda. She may not go, after all.'
It was so hush-hush that I haven't mentioned it to the child."

I asked if they had called yet on Judith and her old friend,
and Laura said that they had. " We found Mamie in one of her
ghost-hunting moods. She has been seeing them and painting
them like mad lately, and, of course, we had to look at the new
pictures. I have never known Mell so impatient. He was as
nice as pie to the old ladies, but as soon as we were in the street
he burst out in a way that is quite unusual with him. ' Ghosts
enough in the world,' he said, ' without inventing them.' And
then one of his grim silences."

Frank returned in about an hour. He had walked part of the
way to the Foreign Office with Mell, " and then," he explained,
" I had a bit of a dander about the streets on my own."

It hadn't, I gathered, been a very comfortable dander. Mell,
in his own non-committal way, had given him at least something
to think about ; and our walk back to our hotel had all the
brooding quality that had overhung our dinner. I wished he
would talk to me, but Frank never talked to me about his most
secret things. We were happily at one on a certain level of our
lives together, but he never mentioned his books to me, never
mentioned what he was most deeply thinking and experiencing.
I often wondered whether these things had all been open between
himself and Jane, but that, too, was a ground on which I never
intruded. I only knew that the photograph in the silver frame
still stood on the mantelpiece at Dros-y-Mor, and no one, not
even I, moved it an inch.

When Joe Duncombe called for his orders in the morning
they were brief and emphatic. " We'll all be moving back to
Dros-y-Mor to-day."

Chapter IX

Books enough have been written, and will be written, about the Second World War. This is not one of them. I want merely to record our narrow provincial bit of the world-experience. We were, in a sense, out of the world, stranded, literally and figuratively, at the head of a creek. But our world, such as it was, went to pieces.

I was fifty-two years old when the war started. Frank was a good deal older. His reticence extended even to his birthday. It was never celebrated or mentioned, though I knew from *Who's Who* that he was in his middle sixties. We had losses and gains because of the war, and the greatest loss to us was that Frank never wrote another word. It was a wonderful time for writers. Their books sold during that war as never before, but Frank took no advantage of it. His old books were re-issued and sold well, but a new one—No. He said nothing to me about it, but I knew that he was a heart-broken man. The first war, with its consequences of poverty and unemployment and misery throughout the world, its failure to do what it had said it would do—the war to end war—the rise of rascally financiers, had been the theme of his writing for some time. Now apparently he was reconciled to the world going to the devil in its own way. The fall of France, the invasion of the Low Countries, had no effect upon him. He did not become either excited or depressed. He had his own things to think about. His son and James Sanderson were among the many who had ferried small boats to and from the beaches of Dunkirk. Both joined the Navy soon afterwards.

There was that to think about, and there were Judith and Mamie.

We had received a letter from Mell, who remained throughout the war with Laura at the house in Melbourne Square. He pointed out with good sense that the fewer people there were in

London the better, barring those who had no option in the matter. Judith and Mamie had seen nothing of bombing, to speak of, but that was sure to come, and he thought it his duty to get Aunt Judith out of London. He had at last prevailed on her to make the move, but she would not go unless Mamie went with her. " So, my dear Uncle Frank, hard as I find it to shift a burden off my own back on to yours that has borne so much in its time, this is to ask whether you and Alice would receive the two old ladies until further notice. They could, of course, go into a hotel in the North or West if they had any money, but they haven't much between them, and I fear there is no option to asking some friend to take them in."

This, like all other matters in those days, I took off Frank's shoulders. We could take them in well enough. Joe Duncombe was gone. He had found some job with the Air Force, having to do with aeroplane engines. He remained safely on the ground throughout the whole war, which did not prevent Em Pritt from imagining that every day he was in the thick of battle. So, with everything left on my hands, I had brought Em into the house. She slept in my old secretarial room which was unenlivened now by the sound of my typewriter. Every morning, so ingrained had the habit become, Frank would go and mooch about in his hut, among the trees. What he thought about in those lonely and desolate moments I never knew, but gone for ever was the old lively moment when he would return with a few quarto sheets in his hand and dump them down on the machine with the cheerful air of a morning's work well done.

So I shut up the cottage opposite the garage, and it was my intention now to dump Judith and Mamie there, so that they might have one another's company and be no embarrassment to Frank.

But it was not to be like that. I had gone down to the cottage one day to give it a look-over. It was a two-bedroomed place, though more than one had never been used in my time. I intended to have a bed shifted down from the house and put, with a bit of other furniture, into one of the rooms, so that Judith and Mamie could have a bedroom each. I had settled these matters to my satisfaction and come out again into the small garden when, from near the garage, I saw a soldier looking the house up and down. He wore a captain's badge of rank and crossed the lane to speak to me. He saluted me and asked : " That cottage unoccupied ? "

I said that it was unoccupied at the moment, but would soon house two old ladies who were coming down from London.

" You Mrs. Frank Melvill ? " he asked.

I said that I was, and to my surprise he then embarked on an essay on Frank's books. He had read pretty well all of them and knew what he was talking about. However, I was guarded, and wondered how much he was trying to ingratiate himself with me, and said to soothe him : " You must come some day, if you remain in these parts, and have tea with me and my husband."

" It's very kind of you," he said, " but I shall be gone. I'm here for only a day or two, and I shall be very busy."

Joe had knocked up a bench in the front garden, so that Em could sit there, and now Captain Thomson, as he introduced himself, asked permission to sit and, as he put it, to " have a few words."

" There's nothing secret about this," he said. " Everybody'll know of it in a day or two. I've been sent over to find a site for an A.A. battery, and just here, at the edge of that bit of wood, there's the place I've been looking for, especially as the cottage is unoccupied."

He looked apologetic, and I suppose my face was the cause of it. Here, where at least we might have expected peace and quiet, the two things left that Dros-y-Mor could offer to Frank, two things above all others that he most needed now, we were to have the rattle of guns, the sound of exploding shells, the war on our doorstep.

Captain Thomson nodded across the road. " What's in the garage ? " he asked.

There was nothing in the garage. As soon as Joe was gone Frank had sold the Sunbeam and given the money to the Red Cross. This, too, I explained. " The men who were not on duty could kip down there," Captain Thomson said. " A couple of officers could use the cottage. The battery'll be just over there on the fringes of the wood."

There was nothing I could say about it.

" You never know," Captain Thomson explained, " just how

163

important the Helford River may become. We may need to guard it pretty closely. I'll come along to the house and explain all this to Mr. Melvill. But I'm afraid it'll have to go through."

The last thing I wanted was to have Frank worried by any such matter. "Leave it to me," I said. "I'll do all the explaining that's necessary."

"Well, if we may do that——"

He seemed relieved, but I did not miss the force of the "we". It suggested endless resources behind him.

2

Frank was not disturbed when I told him the news. He seemed hardly to take it in. He was, I remember, engaged on an extensive course of re-reading. He was going through all the novels of Dickens at the moment. "A pretty good man, this," he said. "A pity he was so damnably sentimental. Or was it just the time he was living in ? After all, he was a pretty tough nut himself. The Victorians were like that—tough nuts who were ready at the drop of a hat to shed oceans of tears about some little Joe or Nell. You deal with this Captain Thomson, will you ? "

He was in that mood now. He hardly walked at all, and the sticky problems were left for me to deal with. At the moment there was the problem of Judith and Mamie James-Villiers. They were due in a day or two, and I had hoped to head them off into the cottage. Now that dream was ended. They would have to share the bedroom at the end of the corridor up aloft, where it had been my intention to put Em Pritt. We should have to move a bed into my secretarial room for Em ; and we might as well. For it was clear that my secretarial life was ended, bar a letter or two that came for Frank and that he would read listlessly before throwing it over to me. "Answer this feller for me, there's a dear. Tell him I'm dying. Tell him I'm dead. Tell him anything."

3

Em was my stand-by. She grieved about Joe. She was fearful that he was daily in danger, but she never forgot me. She never forgot Ray, who was an able-bodied seaman on a battle-ship, and she never forgot my anxiety about Frank. He was there, under her eyes, and she could weigh a situation up. She did not mention him, but she knew what I was enduring. She took off my hands whatever she could. "Don't you worry, now about them old ladies. I'll see to them. I'll go and meet them this afternoon."

And so she did. It was Em who met Judith and Mamie when they arrived at Falmouth station. It was she who conducted them to Helford and brought them in a boat over the river and up the creek. It was Judith who exclaimed on the quarter-deck : "Well, we're in safety at last ! I did think some member of the family would have met us at Falmouth—you or Frank."

I kissed her, trembling with annoyance, and it was old Mamie who said : "It's very good of you, Mrs. Melvill, to have us. Especially now. I expect you've got a great deal on your hands."

She toned Judith down. But there they were, the boatman going quickly away to use the tide. They were surrounded by all sorts of boxes and bags, on which Em Pritt descended. She whisked them away to the room at the end of the gallery. Judith followed her, empty-handed, and I was alone with Mamie, watching the water flowing out, the evening coming down. The dear old thing took my arm. "It is very, very kind of you and Mr. Melvill to have us," she said. "Now don't bother too much about Judith. I'll look after her. You know, between you and Mr. Mell Conybeare, you spoil her. But I think she'll be all right."

Mamie may have had glimpses now and then of strange spirit creatures that were invisible to me, but she could see what was under her nose. Comforted by the assurance that she had got Judith weighed up, I led her through the library, up the stairs, and to her room at the end of the passage. Judith and Em were already busy, putting things into drawers and wardrobes. "Look, Mamie," Judith cried, "only this one room between the two of us. Well, we'll have to do the best we can."

"We will, Judith darling, we will. We shall do very nicely."

And, turning to me, she gave what passed with her for a wink. I left them to it, and went down to find Frank.

4

He was nowhere about, so I went into the wood. He was not in his hut, as he often was in those days, doing nothing, dreaming, I imagine, of past glories ; so I sat for a moment on the seat not far from it where he had come upon me for the first time. I dreamed of that odd encounter, of the discussion we had had about Frémont's novel, in those days when Frank's hair was grey, not white, and there was no Ray or Belinda, and not much else except us two and our great love for one another. My great love for him, anyway. I wondered anew, as I had often wondered of late, whether Jane had meant more to him than I did, whether she would have handled better the situation almost of estrangement, that now existed between us. Here was Jane's sister, but, somehow, I did not think that that would help things between us.

It was now so dark in the wood that I could not see the stream that was almost at my feet, but I could hear its ghostly murmur as it made its way over the pebbles on its way, like the rest of us, to the sea. Then I was aware of someone coming through the wood from the direction of the garage. It was quite dark now. Lights were forbidden, and I made my way in the direction of the sound, knowing, as I did, every inch of the path. Then voices were heard, and one of them was Frank's. To my surprise he was saying : " We don't want you here. I know that my wife has made all the necessary arrangements, and we shall have to put up with the consequences. But we don't *want* you. Not one little bit."

A voice, which to my surprise I recognised, answered : " For that matter, we didn't want to come. The war wasn't our making, you know, and we would gladly have been out of it. But here we are, and we'll make it as light as possible for you. We sha'n't be a nuisance."

I stood petrified where I was, for the voice was undoubtedly Christopher Lyndhurst's.

They came into sight, dark forms just recognisable. Christopher's arm was through Frank's, and he seemed to be almost supporting him. I went forward to meet them, as though I had heard no voices, and said : " Hallo, Frank. I thought I'd find you here."

It was dark enough for me to pretend that I did not recognise Christopher, and he did not introduce himself. He merely said : " Mr. Melvill came along to see how we were getting on at the garage. I was just giving him an arm through the woods. Perhaps you'll see him home now."

Christopher strode off in the direction whence he had come. I took Frank's arm, and felt that he was leaning heavily on me, and silently we made our way to the house. He gave no explanation of what they had been talking about, but I knew that this was the affair of Ben Davies over again. Ben had hated to see " his " trees cut down and what was, to him, all the noise and messiness of a garage arising in their place. Frank, in my absence, had been down and seen the guns and all that they promised of a deeper disturbance. It had hit him, as the garage had hit Ben, off his balance. How far off his balance I did not know, but I knew I had a sick man on my hands. Especially when Frank, having sat for a moment or two in his chair in the library, said listlessly : " I think I'll go to bed. I don't feel very well."

Em Pritt, who had been hovering in the kitchen, listening for my return, came into the library at this moment, and only the sight of her brought back the memory of the two old ladies. My preoccupation with Frank had put them out of my mind. Em was sanity incarnate, and, as though she had known my need, her first words were : " You needn't worry about them two to-night. I've got 'em straight into bed. It was a tiring journey for 'em. I've just taken 'em up a warm drink and a few sandwiches."

" Em," I said, " Mr. Melvill isn't feeling very well and wants to go up to bed at once. Give me a hand with him."

We supported him, one on either side, up the stairs, and Em left me to get him into bed. He did not once speak to her or to me, but flopped like a log between the sheets and was asleep in no time.

5

What with the arrival of Mamie and Judith and Frank's breakdown, I did not feel much like eating. Em Pritt and I sat together in the big room, lit a fire of logs, and had a pot of tea and some sandwiches on a table between us. Now and then she crept upstairs and was able to report that both the old ladies were sleeping, and now and then I looked in on Frank who, too, was sleeping soundly. Em, happily, hadn't a penn'orth of imagination, and talked of this and that, mostly of Joe, and what seemed to me an interminable evening at last drew on to midnight and I sent her to bed and crawled upstairs myself. I got in beside Frank, occupying as little room as I could so as not to disturb him, and slept badly. But I must have slept a little, because it was Frank himself who awakened me as the light was seeping into our room soon after seven o'clock.

" How are Judith and her friend ? " he asked.

I had been wondering, as I fell asleep, what should be my first words in the morning, how to explain that he had not been at home to greet them on their arrival. I sat up in bed and looked at him, and he seemed as well as he ever was in these days. " Don't worry about them," I said. " They've had a good night's sleep. They were both rather tired and went early to bed."

" But I was not here to greet them," he said. " I went off for a bit of a walk in the afternoon, and then—well, here I am ! What happened ? "

Not a word about Christopher Lyndhurst, not a word about the guns. It was all too clear what had happened. At some time during that " bit of a walk ", possibly on meeting Christopher, probably on realising the insanity of men who had loosed all this on the world again, his memory had gone. There was a blank time in which he had said everything he thought, to Christopher and the rest of them : said it in an oblivion from which he was now awakening.

" You must have been excessively tired," I said. " You got home soon after Judith and Mamie had gone for a rest, and you said you wanted to go straight to bed."

I told nothing of how Em and I had put him there, nothing

of the dead-weight he had been in my arms, nothing of that encounter with Christopher in the wood.

I pulled a dressing-gown about me. " Now you get on with your shave," I said, " while I have a quick bath."

It was a quick one indeed. I was down in the big room in no time, and there found Em Pritt putting breakfast for four. " Not a word to Mr. Melvill when he comes down," I whispered urgently. " He's quite well this morning, but not a word. Do you understand, Em ? Not a word to him or to the old ladies."

You could count on Em. " All right," she said. " We'll manage between us."

6

There was a great surprise at breakfast. Mamie addressed Em Pritt as Mrs. Duncombe, and continued so to address her as long as she stayed with us. Em took it with pride. It was the way one addressed a house-keeper. But to me Em was Em Pritt always—a friend on whom I counted. " Mrs. Duncombe," said Mamie, " you mustn't bother over-much about me and Mrs. Graves. To begin with, we'll make our own beds and keep our own room tidy. We're used to doing it, and we'll go on doing it here. We've made a good start this morning, and there's no reason whatever why you should go into our room. A very nice room, too, with a view of trees."

I think she had been coaching Judith, who now broke in : " And there's the washing-up after meals. Mrs. James-Villiers and I have decided to give a hand with that on alternate days. You'll have to show us your kitchen."

" Well, you're model visitors," said Frank. " I wish I was a model host. I was not here to greet you when you came yesterday, and I apologise for being so remiss."

I was relieved to hear that the old ladies had determined to be useful, as little of a nuisance as possible ; but it was Frank I was watching with the most care. It was clear that he had no idea that he had been down at the guns the day before, no idea that he had met Christopher Lyndhurst. I remembered that Christopher had once told us that he was " a sort of a nephew " to old Mamie, and I tried now a shot in the dark that might rouse his memory. "You will have company down here," I said to Mamie. "Did you know that a relative of yours, Christopher Lyndhurst, is with the men who look after the guns ? "

" Christopher ? " Frank cried. " How do you know that ? I had no idea——"

But Mamie cut in : " Christopher Harris ? I see him rarely. I know he calls himself Lyndhurst, but that's only a name he uses when he writes anything. A young sister of mine married a man named, of all things, Harris. No wonder the poor boy doesn't like it. Well, she's dead now, and so is her husband, and I didn't know that Chris had anything to do with guns. Indeed, I know very little about him. He doesn't quite believe, I think, in my things."

I took her to mean the fairies and other spiritual presences that appeared in her water-colours ; but I let that go, with my eye on Frank who seemed as surprised as Mamie to hear that Christopher was among us. At least, I hoped he was. I had nothing to go on but a voice, speaking in the darkness of the wood.

" Well, Christopher or no Christopher, you must make yourselves at home," he said. " As for me, take no notice of me. Just let me go my own way. For one thing, there's a shed in the woods where I work every morning. If you'll excuse me, I must be away there now."

He scraped back his chair and took himself off, though little work—none that I ever saw—was he doing now. " I must look Christopher up later in the day," he said, as he passed out of the room. " How on earth Alice got on to him before me I don't know."

That is something he must *not* know, I thought ; and once Judith was in the kitchen with Em Pritt and Mamie was upstairs in their room, I set off in the direction of the garage.

It was a dull day, with not enough wind to stir the dead and dying leaves that lay all about my path. Fortunately, Frank's shed was not on that track. It lay to my right, pretty well hidden, and once I had passed the spot where he might have had a glimpse of me, I hurried and was soon through the wood, with the garage on one hand and the cottage on the other. I paused for a moment, thinking of all that had arisen out of that spot, for here was the bank on which I had lain down and whence Ben Davies had picked me up. And a few days later I had met Frank. And now there was Ray, goodness knows where, and there was Frank, moodily pretending to be doing I knew not what.

As I stood on the by-road thinking of these things, an incongruous smell drifted out of the cottage—fried bacon of all smells—and a young man in a private's uniform came out of the garage. " Pardon me, Miss," he said, " but you're not supposed to be loitering about here."

I had nothing but a voice to go on, nothing but a dark form seen in the woods last night, but I took a chance and said : " I have a message for one of your officers, Mr. Lyndhurst."

He looked at me blankly. " Never 'eard of 'im," he said.

The foolishness of my imagination, built up on a voice and form half-seen, rushed upon me. I was on the point of retreat when a voice behind me cried : " Good morning, Alice ! "

I turned, and Christopher was leaning out of the cottage window whence the smell of half-burned bacon was still drifting to my nostrils. " This lady is all right, Potter," he said. And to me : " Come on in and share my breakfast."

I crossed the road and entered the cottage. Christopher, wearing a lieutenant's uniform, came to meet me and led me into the front room, where a table was laid on trestles and where his bacon was getting cold. " This is our dining-room," he explained. " Another officer and I share this and sleep upstairs. He's gone now to give the guns a once-over. The men kip in the garage. By the way, the name Lyndhurst drew me to the window. That's a pen-name, you know. Any time you want me ask for Mr. Harris."

He grinned, and I thought of Mamie. " My younger sister married a man named Harris."

" I wanted to talk about Frank," I said.

His laughing face grew graver. " Yes. I guessed it was you who took Frank off my hands in the wood last night. I've been expecting you."

He looked at the ruins of his breakfast. " Well, never mind this lot now. Let's take a walk. I'm off duty for the next hour or two."

So we went out, and the man Potter gave us a smart salute, and we said nothing till we had walked along that by-road on which the cottage stood and come out on the main road. Then he said : " Frank was a bit of a surprise last night. He was as nice as pie to me and Cotterel—that's our other officer—as we showed him the guns and what we have done with the cottage and garage. And then, when I was seeing him home, he starts this harangue as we were half-way there. I thought he'd gone suddenly quiet, and then this broadside, which I expect you heard."

" Yes, I heard every word of it. You know what had happened to Frank ? "

" I could make a good guess," he said, and then we walked quietly along, as though we were both pondering what this guess came to.

" I think," I said, " that he was all right when he was talking to you and Mr. Cotterel—at any rate, as right as he's likely to be in the present circumstances. He loathes this war, because it shows him what he has suspected since the last one—that men are incurable."

" Have you ever read Macaulay's Essay on Bacon ? " he asked.

I told him that I hadn't, wondering what Macaulay had to do with what we were discussing.

" Well," he went on, " Macaulay says that Bacon's career was ' a chequered spectacle, of so much glory and so much shame.' And that's how the spectacle of men must look to whatever gods may be. The sooner Frank realises it, the better."

Christopher looked at me very gravely. " We're a pretty poor lot," he said, " but we have our moments."

" It's too late now," I said impatiently, " for Frank to think nice thoughts. He woke up this morning without the least idea that he met you last night. Such thoughts as he had, he expressed to you. Then his mind closed on the lot of it. What happened between you and him is gone from him as completely as though it never was."

There were berries growing in the hedges, and Christopher swiped at them with a small stick he carried. He looked deeply troubled. " There's a lot in what Frank feels about this," he said. " I'm not so young as all that. I can remember the last lot. I was at school at the time. Pretty well half-starved we were, and the older boys were no sooner out of school than they

were in the army. Killed off like flies. Well, what do I do?
Say nothing to Frank when I meet him?"
"That's what I've come to ask you to do. Leave Frank to
me. If you meet, just put up with him."
"I said nothing to Cotterel last night when I got back.
I was too dumbfounded."
"Well, go on doing that."
We turned then on our tracks, and I told him that Mamie
and Judith were with us. "You'd better come and meet them.
What about lunch to-morrow?"

7

You'd think Ray was the First Sea Lord of the Admiralty. He
was wearing a sub-lieutenant's uniform, all bright and glittering
in the morning air, fresh from the hands of Messrs. Gieves. It
was a good luncheon party. Ray, who had been sent from what
he called his battle-wagon to that place where they train officers
on the South Coast, had passed out in this glory and had said
nothing to us about it. He was given a week's leave and had
travelled overnight to Falmouth. In the morning he had made
the short journey to Helford, and was rowed across the river.
And here he was, coming up the creek.
For a day that was verging on winter, it was unusually warm.
Old Mamie, wrapped in shawls, was sitting on the quarter-deck
with her easel before her, and with her water-colours had been
drawing the water and the fading trees and the pale sky, and was
now putting in a few figures that I failed to see but that were,
she told me, apparent to her spiritual sight. She was unlike most
artists, not minding if she was watched as she worked and keeping
up a chatter about what she was doing. So there I sat and kept
her company and listened to her, while Judith was in the kitchen
helping Em Pritt to prepare the lunch to which Christopher was
coming. Frank was in his shed in the woods, and then, coming
round the bend in the creek was this ancient dinghy, with a
Helford fisherman pulling, and this smart young officer sitting
in the stern, which means that he was looking our way. He
waved as soon as he saw us, and for a moment I could not believe
who was waving. My eyes misted, and he was as insubstantial

173

to me as one of the figures that Mamie had been drawing. But I *knew*, though I could not see him ; and I drew out my handkerchief and brushed my eyes, and he was lightly leaping ashore, and saying to the boatman : " This old skiff could do with a lick of paint, couldn't she ? "

" Paint is easier said than done these days," answered the ancient. He pocketed his fare, put about, and went the way he had come.

And there was my son, with his arms round my neck, and me not caring now about the handkerchief, but unrestrainedly crying. He was so tall, so bronzed, the uniform was so becoming, and his lips were on my cheek.

Old Mamie shed a few shawls as she got up. " Introduce me to Lord Jellicoe," she said, missing a war or two.

He saluted her, and there was a babble of explanations as Christopher came round the house on to the quarter-deck. Then it was Em Pritt's turn. She must have seen him through the kitchen window, and now she was running out, wiping her hands in her apron as she came, and " Oh, Ray ! " was all she could say. He bent and kissed her ; and Christopher, who had joined the knot of us, said : " A privilege of the Senior Service."

Judith was the next to come, so that Ray was saluting and kissing right and left, and then, it being now near lunch time, Frank came gravely from the woods, looking on the ground. There was a catch at my heart as I wondered what he would say, whether he would spoil this moment, but he lifted his eyes, saw Ray, and ran. I was reminded of the patriarch in the New Testament who saw his son from a great way off " and ran and fell on his neck, and kissed him." But Ray was no prodigal. He was enjoying his moment, shining in morning glory, nor did Frank kiss him. He took him by the hand, gripped it tight, and, speechless, they looked into one another's eyes. I think they both knew that all this was show, that behind it was reality, and that the reality was not so pretty as the show.

The moment broke when Ray said : " Em, you've got a full house, I understand. So just heave my bag into my hut when you've got time. I'll sleep there. How is Joe ? "

Em, for once, had little to say about Joe. She wiped her eyes on her cuff and ran into the house. Mamie and Judith followed her, and Frank turned to Christopher. " Well, you're a surprise," he said. " Alice told me that you were down with the guns and that you were looking in to lunch."

He introduced Ray, which I had forgotten to do, and asked : " And how is that young feller Sandy that you were so thick with ? "

" I haven't seen him since Dunkirk," Ray said. " But we write to one another. He's a hand in a submarine. However, never mind Sandy. He can look after himself. Now what about a good cut off the fatted calf ? I'm starving."

I had been counting on this lunch to see how Frank reacted to Christopher. It would have pleased me if, that blank in the mind forgotten, they had met as friends, both interested in books, and had found matter for argument in their common preoccupations. I had forgotten that Frank disliked booky arguments, and, anyway, it was my son who stole all the attention. During that leave, I don't think Frank saw Christopher once, save at that luncheon. " You must excuse me, Chris," he said, " but I'll be out and about with Ray. Plenty of time for us old stagers to get together later."

I looked across the table to the old stager who was sitting between his aunt and Judith. He was a little less than my age, and he had taken great trouble over his appearance. The life he was leading had taken off his pallor. He had put on a uniform that, evidently, he kept for special occasions, and he seemed younger than he was, younger than I, who was oppressed by anxieties and cares. I had not expected Ray or, I think, I should have polished myself up a bit. It was rather a bedraggled person who met Christopher's eye across the table. It was not till Christopher was going back to his guns that he managed a whisper in my ear : " Don't go out with Ray and Frank this afternoon. I've arranged with old Dr. Nancarrow to make a call. And don't forget, will you, that if you want me I'm only a stone's-throw away."

8

Dr. Nancarrow lived in a small house not far from the cottage which Joe and Em shared, and which, for the moment, was handed over to the officers of the guns. He had retired long since, and lived with a housekeeper looking after his few wants. A younger doctor had bought his practice, but had been swallowed up by the army. So it was that Dr. Nancarrow, eighty now if a day, was back at work. He was to be seen pedalling an old bike, which looked the same one I had known when he treated me, hither and yon about the countryside. He was still hale though white-haired, much given to the cultivation of delphiniums in his patch of garden. " If it hadn't been for this damned war eating up my time," he said, " I'd have grown a green one by now," though why anyone wanted a green delphinium I did not understand.

Frank and Ray had invited me after lunch to accompany them on a long walk, but, with Christopher's words in my mind, I invented some household excuse. " Well, we'll just bash on regardless," Ray said, and off they went, Frank looking happier than I had seen him for some time. " Expect us when you see us," he said. " But I don't think we'll be back soon."

The old ladies had got into a routine which included an afternoon nap ; so I didn't think I should see them for some time. Giving Frank and Ray a good start, I went into the woods and sat on the seat where I first met Frank. It was becoming historic now, and like most historic things, it had undergone a good deal of restoration. Indeed, Joe had made it as good as new and had put a back to it, on which I gratefully leaned, for the excitement of the day had worn me out. Dr. Nancarrow would have to come that way, as, barring the access by the creek, that was the only way to get at us.

And there he was, strangely comforting, with his red face, his white hair, and his blue eyes. He sat at my side, took my hand, stroked it, and said : " You're not looking well, Alice."

He had taken to calling me Alice, just as he always called Frank by his Christian name. " Now take your time and tell me all about it. That chap at the guns has given me a hint. It's about Frank, isn't it ? "

It was comforting to me to let myself go. I had said nothing to Judith or Mamie, and my troubles were all bottled up. Now they came tumbling out, as Dr. Nancarrow's hand stroked mine and the stream murmured over the pebbles. I told him everything, and the great thing was Frank's loss of memory, the horrid gap in his comprehension of what was happening under his eyes. When I had finished I took out my handkerchief and cried. It all seemed so inevitable, Frank being what he was and his history being what it was. He had believed in a bettering world. The world was not bettering. I said so to Dr. Nancarrow.

" Of course it's not," he said. " All we can do is occupy ourselves, like that chap in Voltaire, with our gardens." He was silent for a while, then he said: " A doctor's garden includes his patients, and as far as I am concerned that includes you and Frank. I want to be honest with you. There's not much I can do for Frank. What the man at the guns told me was not my first knowledge that he's taking the war badly. I was cycling not long ago a good way from here when I came upon him sitting on a gate. I got off to pass the time of day with him, and he didn't know me. He said this was a fine bit of countryside and he wouldn't be surprised if he settled down in it. I needn't go into the whole conversation, but it's quite clear that Frank was years back, when he first set his eyes on Dros-y-Mor. An escape, if you like, from the present into the past."

I listened to him, trembling.

" How long can this go on ? " I asked.

" I know no more than you do," he said honestly. " It's the first time that a thing like this has come my way. You know what a country doctor's life is like. Delivering babies, and then watching them through small-pox and measles and chicken-pox. That's about the line."

" Then you can do nothing ? "

" Neither of us can do anything," he said. " Except keep an eye on Frank."

I told him of Ray's sudden appearance that morning, and he said : " Well, now that this son of his is at home I don't expect anything will happen. But when Ray is gone, guard Frank, and so will I, and we'll let one another know how things are going. Honestly, my dear, I'm out of my depths. You could have another opinion."

The thought terrified me. " And have him put in an asylum? " I burst out.

" Nothing of the kind. Nothing of the kind." He continued

to stroke my hand. " Now calm yourself, Alice. I've told you
all I know, and you've told me all you know. Let's go on doing
that. We'll manage. We'll manage."

9

I'm not going to talk about Ray's leave, except to say that it
was very precious to me. The old ladies were nothing for
walking, and kept to their routine, but Frank and I, with Ray,
made it a walking holiday. Sometimes, we took Em with us.
We would start off after breakfast, take our lunch, and stay out
till the evening was coming on. Occasionally it would rain, but
that didn't trouble us. There were plenty of barns and out-
buildings to shelter in, and, even if there hadn't been, it would
have made no difference to us. We were walkers, and always
had been, and we were never happier than when we were on our
feet with nothing to do except look at all the things there were :
clouds and the sea and the rocks and the lichens and the gulls
flying and calling.

Frank seemed to me to be happier, though quiet, but he had
always been quiet, soaking things up like a sponge and saying
nothing about it. Occasionally, we would even go down to the
guns and have a talk with Christopher, who had the sense to
prattle of indifferent things.

Christopher came up to the house to take dinner with us on
the last day of the leave. Em dined with us that night. Old
Mamie, of all people, said she would serve the dinner and eat
when she could. She was a percipient old thing, and for all her
love of spectral presences could see better than most of us what
was under her nose. " Now you sit down and have a good meal
with Mr. Ray," she commanded Em. " I believe you're fonder
of him than any of us, and you haven't had a meal with him
since he's been at home."

So a reluctant Em sat next to Ray at the table, mute as could
be, but proud and satisfied. She even took a sip of wine as we
drank his health, and I think I was the gloomiest person there,
though I took care to conceal my gloom. It was all, to me, too
much like the last supper. The kiss of Judas could not be far off.
Ray had said nothing about his destination except that he was

178

to report for duty on a destroyer. Beyond that he did not go, and the very name was to me loathsome. A destroyer : a thing that destroyed. " I've got to catch the Riviera Express in the morning," was all he could tell us.

" You could catch the train at Hayle," Christopher now said. " There's an old bus that I've got an option on. I could run you over there in no time. What about it ? Pick you up with your baggage in the morning outside Em's cottage ? "

This was agreed, and, though it was a ramshackle car with a canvas hood that you put up and down by hand, it was a capacious one, belonging to the old breed. It had to be, because we were all there to see Ray off : Frank and Chris, Mamie and Judith, Em and myself. With Ray, that made seven of us, but we packed in somehow, under a sky that was all lowering and wintery, swishing through fallen leaves till we reached the high road. We seemed to be treading all our summers underfoot.

Well, we saw Ray off. There is no need to go into that except to say that Em wept and the rest of us were determinedly cheerful till the train was out of sight. Then we looked at one another with our real faces, and they were all sad.

" Now, hop in, and I'll have you back in no time," Christopher said ; but Frank answered : " Alice and I will walk. Take the others back."

And walk we did. We didn't get to Dros-y-Mor till the evening meal was about to go on the table. It should have been like old times, with the open road before us and the sky over our heads. How often we had walked and walked like that, saying little, but happy beyond words. Now we still said little and were not happy, like redwings in a cold winter who will be lucky if they find shelter for the night. I don't remember even where and when we ate. I suppose we did so at some half-way house, but it is all gone from me, and nothing remains but the memory of that long trudge through the wintry day, the last walk that Frank and I were to take together.

10

In the morning, to my surprise, Frank was quietly cheerful. He went off, as he always did after breakfast, to his hut in the woods.

But for a long time now, nothing had come of those morning sessions. I had maintained my old habit of entering the shed at eleven o'clock, putting a cup of coffee at his hand, and slipping unobtrusively out. This day, to my great joy, he was writing. I said nothing, but left him to it. I was so elated at finding him working again that I did not at once go into the house. I walked in the wood, the trees all a-drip with the moisture of the night, and I could have cried for happiness. I was back in time to greet him on his return to the house just before one o'clock, and without a word, just in his old manner, he handed me four sheets of quarto paper. He made no remark about being at work again, and acted as though this delivery of precious manuscript were normal, had been going on for day after day. But luncheon was ready. I dumped the pages down near my typewriter, and promised myself the happiness of reading and typing them after lunch.

Mamie and Judith had gone for their afternoon sleep. Em was in the kitchen. I stole into my old office, which was now her bedroom and where my typewriter was still kept on a small table beneath the window. I sat down to read the manuscript quickly before typing it, and I had not read far before all my joy and pride were shattered about me. There was an alteration here of a word, there of a phrase, but this was a novel that Frank had written long before. He was merely remembering, not creating. And he did not know this. All through the morning he had existed half a dozen years ago, doing, in a suspension of consciousness, what he had done then. With my eyes swimming in tears I put a sheet of paper into the machine and began to type. *Shadows We Are.* A Novel. By Frank Melvill. Chapter One.

It was soon done, and having done it I told Em that I would be out till tea-time. Mamie and Judith were still in their bedroom. Frank had gone for his afternoon walk. I went through the woods alone. There was no sign of life at Em's cottage and I walked on to Dr. Nancarrow's place which was not far away. I found the old man in his greenhouse. With the care of a dissector, and with a very sharp knife, he was cutting up delphinium roots and putting each into a small pot. He rubbed his hands on a cloth and said : " Well, Alice, you don't look too good. We'll have to send you along a tonic."

It was the last thing I wanted to hear. I thought I was being so brave, that my face gave nothing away. The old man's words undermined me, and I sat on a wicker chair that he kept in the greenhouse and wept. He fussed over me like an old hen. "It's Ray, eh ? These leaves are a damned thing. Do more harm than good. Pull the nerves all to shreds. They're harder on those who are left behind than on those who go away."

I found a voice at last. "It's Ray and—and—everything," I said. "It's Ray and Frank."

"I was thinking of Frank more than of you," he said honestly. "I've been dreading to know how he would take all this."

I told him, and he listened with acute attention. "Then you've typed what he's written ? "

I nodded, too broken to speak. I had come out hatless, and he stood above me, stroking my hair.

"Good girl," he said. "Go on doing that. Type everything he gives you, as though it were the most ordinary thing in the world. Not a word about having seen it before. Can you do this ? "

I nodded again.

"It's all we can do," he said. "I wish there were more. But there isn't. And it'll keep Frank happy. As happy as he's likely to be. Tell him, if you like, that you're feeling rather under the weather and that you've been up to see me. I'll look in with a tonic for you when he's likely to be at home. So we'll keep an eye on him together. Above all things, go on with the typing."

I left him, feeling comforted that someone shared the secret with me.

II

I was glad now that we had asked Mamie and Judith to be with us. Unexpectedly, Mamie was a strength to me. They looked like a pair of old macaws, what with their bedizenments and fal-de-lals and Mamie's hooded eyes. But she saw more than she seemed to, and a lot of this was mundane. Frank had gone one morning to his shed, and I had retired to Em's room to do my bit of typing, when the door opened and she asked my leave to come in.

To my surprise I was glad to see her. That hour in the morning which I devoted to typing had become a heavy weight. I shouldered it as well as I could, but more and more it was leaving me exhausted. It was not the work. There was nothing in that. It was the daily evidence that Frank was still far from me, living in dreams.

" Come out for half-an-hour," Mamie said, and hooked her arm through mine and drew me into the library and then through the open French window on to the quarter-deck. It wasn't a bad day to be out. We were in mid-winter now, but it was warm and windless. Still holding my arm, Mamie walked me up and down, looking on the grey sky and the muddy waterless creek. " Judith has a bit of a cold," she said. " I've persuaded her to stay in bed." And, having thus disposed of all chance of interruption, she exclaimed suddenly : " Now you can tell me all about yourself. What's the matter with you ? "

I was so sure that I was keeping a good face to the world that I could only say : " Me ? I'm as right as rain."

" Nonsense," she said. " You're getting positively haggard and you're losing weight. You're as thin as a bean-pole. And what's the matter with Frank ? He never has a word to say for himself."

" My dear Mamie, you know as well as I do that Frank was never a chatterer. Naturally, he feels the war and all that it means. Ray, for one thing."

" So you won't tell me."

" What is there to tell ? "

" Everything. Whatever it is that's eating you up. It's something to do with Frank. I can see that very well."

I was sorely tempted to take off the lid, to find a breast to weep upon. But I only stroked her old skeleton claw and said : " Mamie, you're a dear. Do you mind if I say that I'm glad you're about the house ? And you've guessed right."

" Guessed ! " she snorted. " There's no guess about what's under your eyes."

" But," I went on, " this is something that I've got to keep to myself. You'll know in time."

" Another family skeleton," she said. " Ah, well, I'm a bit of a one myself, and I know all about such things."

I kissed her made-up face, and felt comforted.

" Well," she said, " don't add Judith to your worries. I only kept her in bed to have this little talk with you. Though a fat lot has come out of it, I must say. You're as obstinate as a mule. You don't go out much nowadays with Frank. You used to go walking nearly every afternoon."

" He prefers to go alone now."

And that was another thing that worried me. Frank preferred to walk alone.

" Well," she said, " if ever you want to tell me, remember I'm here. God knows I do little enough for my keep, either now or ever. I can at least stand by. So any time . . . That's a promise ? "

" Any time," I said. " I promise to let you know what's going on whenever you can be of use."

" You'll be as old as I am some day," she said unexpectedly. " D'you know the worst of growing old ? You don't feel you're of any more use."

I kissed her again and took her by the bony upper arm. " It's always useful," I assured her, feeling like a schoolma'am uttering a moral platitude, " to have a friend you can rely on."

" Well, I'll go and make Judith a cup of tea."

And off she went on her rather high heels, looking strangely out of place, yet in my very heart.

12

I remember that morning because when Frank came in he had done nothing. It had been heart-breaking enough to type each day a bit of his old re-hash, but now I was to find that there was something worse than that. There was the thought of him sitting in his shed for the best part of four hours every morning, doing nothing. Whatever it was that had set him going on his task had ended as suddenly as it had begun. I would take his morning coffee out each day, and one day he was not in the shed. This had never happened before, and I was at once filled with apprehensions. Where was he ? What had he done ? I put the

183

cup down on his table and went out into the woods. I found him at last in Ray's shed, poring over the raised map of Cornwall, in plasticine, that the boy had made years before.

" This is pretty good," he said. " Where is he, by the way ? Where is Ray ? "

I told him, truthfully enough that I had no idea where Ray was. " Do you want him, darling ? " I asked.

" Well, there's a thing or two I'd like to talk over with him. The way this river rises on Bodmin Moor, for example. I don't think he's got it quite right. Well, it can wait. I suppose he'll be in soon."

" Let's walk till lunch-time," I suggested. " It's a good day for a walk."

He was agreeable to this, and we set off together towards Em's cottage. We had not gone far before we met Dr. Nancarrow, who had been told that Frank was in his shed every morning, and was now coming to the house to have one of his secret talks with me.

" Well, Frank," he asked, " and how are things with you ? "

" Pretty well," Frank answered, " considering the bloody state of the world. No man is an island, you know. At least Donne says he isn't."

Frank was walking a little ahead of us on the narrow path, and we exchanged significant glances behind his back. It was a rational if bitter answer, the answer of a man no longer in dreams.

" They used to talk," Frank said over his shoulder, " of the *trahison des clercs*. We've gone a bit farther. We're living to-day to witness the treason of the scientists. They're poking and prying everywhere. All right if they kept what they're finding under their hats. At least till we were civilised enough to make a proper use of it. But now they're selling right, left and centre. Anybody who is rich enough, unscrupulous enough, or enough ambitious of power, can buy them out. All that they know is on the shop counter."

Those were Frank's last words. He said no more, but walked steadily ahead of us till we came out of the wood. Then, on the lawn, he staggered and fell. We got him on to his feet, one with a hand under each armpit. The French window was open and we took him through. " Don't try to get him upstairs," Dr. Nancarrow said. " Put him down on the floor."

It was an incongruous sight. This was our dining-room, and everything had been placed for lunch. There, at the foot of the long table, we laid him, gathering a few mats to make a bed, a cushion to go under his head. " Keep those old women out," Dr. Nancarrow said.

In the kitchen I found Em, forking at potatoes which bubbled in a saucepan. I put my arms round her and said : " Em, Mr. Melvill is very ill. He's in the dining-room lying on the floor. Now be a good girl. Keep very quiet. Don't go in there."

Em said : " The potatoes was just coming to the boil." She looked at me stupidly for a moment, and I said : " Em, you do understand what I'm saying, don't you ? "

She nodded her head and I left her there, went into the dining-room again, with a glance at Dr. Nancarrow who was kneeling over Frank, a stethoscope to his ear, and ran up the stairs. I thanked God that Judith's " bit of a chill " had prolonged itself and that she would be keeping to her bed. Mamie had just opened the bedroom door and come into the gallery that looked down on the long room. She did not give so much as a cry, and her voice was very low. " I was a nurse all through the first World War," she said. " Let me go and help the doctor."

So Dr. Nancarrow's instructions to " keep those old women out " was useless. As useless as Mamie's presence. Because, just as she gained the room, he stood up and shook his head. " Heart," he said. " Heart and the war."

13

Mell was working himself to death. He hardly took leave while the war lasted ; but he managed to come down for a few days when Frank died. Laura came with him, but not Belinda. She was somewhere overseas with the Wrens. It was a small congregation that gathered round Frank's grave. Judith was, as she put it, all to pieces, and Mamie stayed at home to be with her. So there were three women—myself and Laura and Em—and two men—Mell and Dr. Nancarrow. Christopher was gone—shifted to some other place in the midst of our disorders.

Not far from Dros-y-Mor there is an ancient church with a tree growing through its walls. The tree is still a place of pilgrimage. Thousands of holiday-makers come to gaze on it open-mouthed. Why, I don't know, for a tree growing in a slit of masonry is no uncommon sight. But everything is a wonder to a tourist, though at home it wouldn't be looked at twice ; just as men will gaze with awe at a " personality " on a television screen, though they won't cross the road to see a person. No one pauses to look at a grave.

It was an open slit in the ground that boisterous winter's day when we stood there. A wind was blowing that whipped our clothes about us and whistled through the bare trees. I remember that, and standing arm-in-arm with Em who contributed the only tears that attended his going from us. The rest of us were dry-eyed, stony. I have not been back since. Nothing is there that I want to see.

Chapter X

I was very lonely now. I had little to do. Mamie was a godsend. She insisted on sharing the housework with Em, and she kept Judith out of the way. It had pleased Judith to take this moment to become an invalid. She had come down once or twice after Frank's death, full of innuendoes and hints. If we had called in a " proper " doctor ; if we had done this and that. And the " we " was always myself. The crisis in our relationship arose one evening when she took Jane's photograph from the mantelpiece. " I think," she said, " that I'll keep this on the mantelpiece in my bedroom." I said that I would much prefer that it should stay where Frank had always kept it, and made to take it from her hand. She put it behind her back, and said : " One would think Frank had never had a wife but you."

There was venom in her look and in her voice, and I gave up
186

the struggle of wills. I was too tired to be bothered with Judith any more.

The next day the photograph was back where it had always been. Mamie and I were alone in the library at the time, and she noticed my surprise and gratification. She took me by the arm and led me through the open window on to the quarter-deck—a quarter-deck now that wouldn't have been tolerated in any decent ship, so neglected it was with its weeds and uncut grass, not at all the place from which I had seen Frank push Ronald Lilywhite, years before, into the water. But there was a ray of sunshine and it was a warmish day, and Em had put out a few deck-chairs.

" Sit down," Mamie said, as if she gave the orders in that place, as indeed she did, for since Frank's funeral, a month before, she had more and more taken charge. I had gone to bits with sorrow and uselessness. There was nothing to type now—not even the remembered ghost of an old book walking—and Mamie, with my unuttered consent, was in command. Happily, Em was fond of her and did as she was told ; and Judith had been confirmed in her status of invalid. The night before, when she had come down to dinner, was one of her first appearances among us. Usually, she took breakfast in bed and other meals in the bedroom from which she rarely stirred. On my daily duty visit to her, I would find her, made up to the nines, reading or playing patience in an arm-chair with a footstool under her feet. I was glad when she was taking a nap, for then I could creep quietly out with no need to attempt the contact with her that I was finding more and more difficult. And all this, I knew, though no word had been spoken, was part of Mamie's campaign to keep Judith off my shoulders.

" Sit down," she said now, and let her small weight into a chair at my side. " I've put back your photograph, and I don't think you'll have any more trouble about it."

" It's not mine," I said. " It was Frank's."

" Yes, I know that, and we mustn't forget that it is a photograph of Judith's sister. She was very fond of her sister. Did you know that she had never forgiven herself for Jane's death ? "

I did not know.

" Judith couldn't swim, you know, and there wasn't a soul

187

about. She had to stay and see Jane drown. She has often spoken to me about it in Kensington. She feels there was something that she could have done, or might have done, and didn't do."

She was silent for a time, and then said : " Jane was the stronger of the two. She was physically stronger, and mentally stronger, and, if you'll forgive my saying it, spiritually stronger. I know. I've talked with Judith often enough. And you know, too. You have known her for a good many years. She still clings to Jane. That is why she wanted the photograph. However, I've made her see that you have some rights, too. It was a difficult job. She could not understand how Frank could find any sort of compensation in you."

The old thing gave me a sidelong look that was half a laugh, and I said : " I expect you feel that, too. I feel it myself."

" Well, you needn't," Mamie said. " I've seen you and Frank together in London. He never had much to say, to you or anybody else, but I *know*. Forgive my saying that, but I *know* when people are in accord. And so, as far as Frank is concerned, you've nothing to worry about. That may help you to understand poor Judith better. You can afford to be very kind to her. Well, I'll go and help Em with getting the dinner ready."

She laid a hand on my knee, and I knew the truth of the saying about virtue going out from one person to another. Then she gave me her half-sweet half-mocking smile and went into the house.

I sat alone for some time, feeling the better for this queer conversation. I suppose the world would have called Mamie a useless old hanger-on, a woman who did nothing, one of those whose removal would have been all to the good of this bustling up-and-coming century. Still, it was a comfort to have her about, and embedded in the word comfort is strength, and I was the stronger because Mamie was there when strength was what I needed.

2

We saw strange sights in the Helford River, strange structures afloat and ashore, that, though we didn't know it, were aimed at the invasion of Normandy. They went; they did their job; and in time the war ended.

I had from time to time heard from Christopher, who had been moved hither and thither and who now was in the North of England, and I knew that Ray was safe and that Belinda was expecting soon to be discharged from the Wrens. Considering that war is war, never so beastly as to-day, we had come out of it as well as we could hope for. Only that poor boy James Sanderson had been lost, and would trouble stock-brokers and " digs " no more.

Joe Duncombe wrote to Em from some place in the North African desert where he had been cannibalising wrecked engines, and Em was trotting now and then along the path through the woods, putting in order the cottage from which the gunners had departed. Everybody who was left was looking forward to the peace.

Even Mamie James-Villiers was considering a return to London. " It will be the best place for Judith," she explained. " She's never been happy here. I know, my dear Alice, that it's not your fault and that you've done your best for us. But poor Judith needs crowds, and the sooner we're settled again in a little flat in Kensington the better for her."

I knew that " for her " were the operative words and that the best in Mamie came out when she was the servant of someone else. Ever since Frank died she had been splendid. She had done more than her share of the house-work and she had been a nurse to Judith. From being an imaginary invalid, Judith had become one in fact. She rejoiced in Dr. Nancarrow's visits, kept to her room, and became a horrid old skeleton. Oppressed by my own real cares, I had little sympathy for her imaginary ones, and if it had not been for Mamie, trotting up the stairs from one room to another, the household would have gone to pieces. But, from the scant news that came to me out of London, I imagined that " the little flat in Kensington " was a daydream and must long be so.

My news came mainly from Laura, and at last she wrote that Mell was " taking a few days off " and that they were both coming to visit me at Dros-y-Mor. It was the best news I had had since Frank's death. It galvanised me. I realised with a sense of

shame that I had, as they say, let myself go. And my home, too.
I had a vision of Mell's disapproval. He would look at the place
like an owl, saying nothing, but oozing contempt. I remembered
an occasion just before the war when Frank and I had been in
London and Belinda, just going out for the night, had asked her
father why he did not dance. His reply, uttered gravely, was Mell
incarnate and had become a classic with me and Frank. " My
dear, I do not propose to cavort with sweating hoydens." Even
at this distance of time, the words set me laughing. Well, Mell
should not find a hoyden, sweating or otherwise.

They were coming in a week, and during that week I toiled
like a slave. I visited the garden shed and found a hook with
which I laid waste the long grass and the weeds of the quarter-
deck. Then I ran the mower over it, and laughed to think how
unlike I was to those Tennysonian maids to whom, so long ago,
Mell had introduced me, as I kept the sheet well up to my chin at
his father's house in Cardiff. But, when all was said and done, it
was Mell who had sent me off to the Rowans, had set me on the
path, who was the first lever to move me along such way as I had
come. The least I could do was to show that I had not become
a slut. A mown quarter-deck was not much, but it was something.
Anyhow, it was the point at which I woke up and realised that
there was a Ray as well as a Frank, a future as well as a past.
And in Mell, who belonged to my beginnings, was the one continuing, if infrequent, streak in the whole odd pattern.

I was walking the path through the woods, thinking these
things, as that week was half-way through, when a man in a
great hurry came bursting into my sight just as I was approaching
the place where the garage had been built. He was brown and
bearded and full of health and energy. Over his shoulder was
a canvas bag, stuffed to breaking.

" This is a private path," I told him. " It leads only to a
house."

For answer, he slung the bag off his back and produced the
most horrible jumper I have ever seen. " Made by genuine
African natives of genuine camel hair," he said. " That's for
you. The rest is for Em."

" Oh, Joe ! " I cried, and like a Mellsian hoyden I flung my
arms round his neck and kissed him. " Oh, Joe ! You're back ! "

"I am that," he said, grinning through his beard. "You can keep Africa," he conceded generously. "This is all right for me. Where's Em?"

"She's at the house, I hope, getting lunch. You'd better run."

And run he did. I watched him go round the bend of the path, and never did Noah more thankfully welcome back to the ark a dove with an olive leaf. Back! They were coming back! And then it struck me how odd a dove Joe was, with his brown skin, his great beard, and all. I leaned against a tree and laughed. I pulled myself up as the laughter was turning to tears and walked towards the house as sedately as I could on feet that wanted to run. I was just coming out on the lawn when Em appeared, clinging to Joe's arm. Her face was warm and excited. "Please can I have the day off?" she asked, like a child who wanted to go nutting. "Miss Mamie says I can show Joe what I've been doing at the cottage."

"Hadn't you better have lunch first?" I asked.

"Not if you can spare me," she said sedately.

I could only bow my head in acquiescence, and Joe, Em, the beard and the bag disappeared along the path.

3

I was a girl of seventeen when I first met Mell, and he then, I suppose, was a young man of twenty or so. But such was the gravity of his manner, and so immeasurably was he my superior in knowledge and all other things, that I had always looked upon him as much older than I. But his appearance surprised me when he came down to Dros-y-Mor after the war. I was now a middle-aged woman, and looked it, but Mell was an old man.

When he and Laura arrived, a day or two after Joe's return, it was a white-haired responsible person that I received. Belinda was with them. She had learned to drive a motor-car and had brought them down by road. Fortunately, what had been a garage and then a billet for the men at the guns, was now a garage once more. It had been Joe's earliest concern to clean the place up and make it fit to receive the monsters whom he still worshipped. With his beard shaved off, and looking more like

the old Joe, he had lectured me on the importance of the garage.
" You'll see," he said. " In a few years' time people will go
nowhere except by road. There'll be no crossing the old Helford
River in a boat. People will arrive here by the back way. Bad
enough to walk through the woods to get at the house. Tire
'em out, that will, at the end of a long journey." Even so short
and pleasant a stroll seemed formidable to Joe, who soon made
clear that he expected me to buy a car of my own, if only for his
convenience.

Joe had risen to the rank of sergeant, and it was with a
sergeant's authority that he was lecturing me on these matters
when Mell and his party arrived. To please Joe, but with small
pleasure to myself, I was wearing the jumper that he had brought
home for me—" the very spit and image ", he said, " of one I've
brought for Em." Certainly, he could not have paid me a higher
compliment, but, what with the jumper and my excited expectations of visitors, I must have looked what is called "a sight ". I
had not thought they would come so soon. I had looked forward to
getting up to the house and changing and receiving them in some
style. But there it was, and there was Belinda, looking as cool
as a cucumber and very beautiful. She was wearing an old duffle
coat fastened with wooden toggles, a grey skirt and no hat. Her
hair had been blown by the wind all day, for the car was one of
those in which you could put the hood right down, and it had been
right down. But she looked a beautiful girl, golden from the
sun of the Mediterranean, in which she had spent most of the
war.

" Belinda came home unexpectedly," Laura said, " so we
brought her along. I hope you don't mind."

I kissed them all and said I didn't mind, and indeed, after a
wartime spent with Em and the old ladies, it was good for me to
look at youth again. Laura was unchanged, but Mell, as I have
said, looked more than his age. He had always done that, because
of his quietness and gravity, but now there was something added,
something more than his white hair and his slight stoop. I asked
him formally how he was, and as formally he replied : " I am
very well, thank you."

" You can leave all them old bags," Joe said. " Me and Em
will carry them up to the house later. I'll put the car away."

He gave the car a critical look, as though it were the most important member of the party. "You can get a good many m.p.h.
out of her, I should think," he said.

Belinda gave a light laugh. "Well, I frightened Daddy and
Mummy here and there," she conceded.

We started up the path. Mell and Laura went first, and
I followed with an arm through Belinda's. "I ought to remember
all this," she said. "But I don't. I suppose I was only a baby
when I came here. What are those little hut places, for example?
I don't recall them."

"One of them," I explained, "belongs to my son Ray. He's
in some south-coast town now, cleaning up his destroyer so as
to hand her over all ship-shape to the Admiralty. Then, I suppose,
they'll have finished with him and he'll come home and be
looking for a job. I expect you remember him?"

"Vaguely," she agreed. "He and another man were interested in digging up ancient civilisations, weren't they? There
was some scheme for going out to St. Albans to see one, I remember. Then all this lot came along."

"Yes, and the other man was lost when his submarine was
bombed."

"I wonder," she said, "when people will start digging up
our civilisation, such as it is?"

"You don't seem to think a lot of it?"

"Not over-much. What's that other hut for—the one we're
coming to now?"

"That's where my husband used to do his writing."

"Used to do . . ." It was all over now, and I hadn't looked
into the hut since Frank died. It was not that I regarded it in
any sense as a shrine, a holy and unapproachable place. I simply
had never had the heart to look at it.

"Is it locked?" Belinda asked.

"No. It was never locked. It's simply got a latch."

"May I look in?"

We stepped over the stream—it was as narrow as all that—and
trod down the mosses. "I have a particular reason for wanting
to see it," Belinda said. "You're sure you don't mind? We
had all sorts of books sent by the Red Cross to the other end of
the Mediterranean. Someone had packed in the works of your

husband. I read them again and again. I thought they were marvellous."

My heart warmed to her. We stood before the shed and I lifted the latch and put my shoulder to the door. The old hinge creaked noisily, came away, and the door fell inwards. We stepped over it and gazed. There was little to see. Years had passed since that door had been opened. It was a dim bleak room of boards with a trestle table drawn up near the window. The woods had been neglected and the trees had encroached, so that the place was very dark. The roof, covered with tarred felt over the shingles, had sprung a leak through which rain had dripped on to the table. There were a few quarto sheets on it, and they were twisted and mouldy with the wet. A pen, an ink-stand that contained a dry powder. A chair—an old Windsor chair that was now rickety in one leg and stood askew. I thought of all the times I had crept like a mouse into the shed with Frank's eleven o'clock coffee. I had put it at his elbow, kissed the back of his neck, and stolen out.

We stood for a moment in silence, watching a spider that had dropped a thread from the ceiling on to the rotten paper on the desk, and was now swinging in a small draught. Then I turned to go. Belinda said : " Thank you for showing me. May I have this ? "

She took up the pen that was stuck by the moisture to the rotting blanket that covered the table. I nodded, too overcome to speak, and she dropped the pen into a bag she carried. " Not," she said, " that I'll need this to remind me of Frank Melvill. He was my salvation, you know, out there. Well, let us go." And then, putting an arm through mine, she added, as we stepped over the fallen door : " Why seek ye the living among the dead? "

She kept her hold of my arm, and I noticed that where Frank had trodden a path to the shed all sorts of mosses and small growing plants were now springing up. I was comforted by the girl's presence as we went to join Mell and Laura at the house.

4

They had been travelling since early morning and it was now afternoon. We refreshed ourselves with a cup of tea, and then Mell said : " Alice, my dear, if you don't mind I'll lie down till dinner-time. I'm rather tired."

He and Laura were sharing the bedroom at one end of the corridor, and Belinda at once jumped up and put a hand under his elbow. " I'll see you comfortable, Daddy," she said, " before I unpack."

He went rather heavily up the stairs, paused at the top to look down on the three of us who were left in the great room, and then disappeared from sight. Judith was still in bed. She came down only for dinner. Mamie said : " I expect you two will want a good talk. I'll see to these few cups and saucers."

Laura and I moved out on the quarter-deck, and I said : " It'll be a good thing when Em has got over having Joe at home again. Mamie does more than her share."

The tide was coming into the creek, and we listened for a while to the water slapping against the stones. " What's the matter with Mell ? " I asked.

She replied rather wearily : " He's worn out. He needs a rest."

I took her hand in mine and said : " I know that. But there's something else. What is it ? "

" Well, we don't get any younger, do we ? "

" I know that, too. But, bless my soul, Mell is only a few years older than I am myself. There was a time when that seemed immense. I was seventeen when I met him, and I suppose he was about twenty. It seemed an age, but it doesn't any more. If anyone asked now how old Mell was I'd say ' Oh, a man of about my age.' And I feel as if I'd go on to a hundred."

" You haven't been in the thick of it," Laura said.

I had lost a husband, and I had just come in from stirring up his dust. I had had a son on the seas, but I had not been in the thick of it ! True, I had not been, as Mell and Laura had, in bombed London, but there was more in her dejection than all this. However, I could pry no longer, and I left it at that. Perhaps silence would bring it out of her. And so we sat there till suddenly she said : " You do well to remind me of the first time you met him. Because you formed your opinion of him then, and it hasn't altered much. He was a sort of man you'd never met before, and you've always imagined him to be a man who climbed over all obstacles and reached all his goals."

It was true enough. That was how I had seen Mell. Our meetings had been few and far between, and there was nothing to suggest that I had been wrong. And now here was Laura saying : " Well, I had the flesh and blood of him to deal with, and Mell's a very disappointed man."

Put briefly, " so far and no farther " had been Mell's career. At the beginning, his prospect had been boundless. He had said nothing much about it, but he had seen himself moving forward, almost inevitably, step by calculated step, to the top of his profession. His was to be the final voice to which Foreign Secretaries would listen. Almost anonymous, he was yet to be the power behind important decisions.

Well, it hadn't worked out like that. He had reached the end of his tether. One by one, other men had passed him, and he now faced the knowledge that he had gone as far as ever he would go, and that it was not so far after all. Laura did not say so, but I guessed that what Mell had lacked—and I was able to look at him now more impartially than when I was a servant girl in Cardiff—was any touch of brilliance. He could overcome a difficulty that meant a plodding determined application, but insight was another matter.

Belinda had come out and joined us on the quarter-deck. She pulled up a chair and asked : " Who is the old lady who takes her ease comfortably in her room while the rest of us are busily washing up ? "

" It sounds remarkably like your father's Aunt Judith," I said with a laugh. " She says, whenever there's a job to be done, that she's only in the way. A useful belief if you want a quiet life."

" So that's Great Aunt Judith, is it ? She was coming down as I came out. And who's this, just rounding the bend of the creek ? "

She had seen him before me or Laura, so wrapped up had we been in our discussion of Mell. But the moment she spoke I saw him and I ran down to the wall against which the tide was now full, and I cried : " Ray, oh Ray ! "

He was alone in the dinghy, pulling vigorously. He turned and, as soon as he saw us there, he waved. I had forgotten that I was a hostess, forgotten everything except that my heart was pounding and that my face was disfigured by tears as I ran down the landing steps. He said : " I'll tie her up here and take her back at high tide to-morrow. I borrowed her from an old chap in Helford."

He was still in uniform—one narrow ring and two broad ones round his cuff—Lieutenant Commander Ray Melvill. He tied an expert knot, threw some bags up on to the quarter-deck, and then stepped ashore and kissed me. I hugged him for so long that at last he gently put me from him. " And who are these ladies ? " he asked.

It was Belinda who answered. " I am Belinda. We met, I think, before the war. And this is my mother."

He saluted them gravely. " Yes," he said, " I remember. I was with old Sandy at the time. You were coming out to St. Albans to see a dig we had there. So you're Belinda, eh ? "

They went before me and Laura into the house.

Chapter XI

That was my war. With the coming back of Ray, it seemed all over. We settled down somehow, with Mamie and Judith in my bedroom, with Mell and Laura at the other end of the corridor, with me accommodated somehow in my old typing-room, and with Belinda in the second bedroom at Joe's cottage. Ray slept in a sleeping-bag in his hut. It was a squeeze, and I realised that Dros-y-Mor was no place for entertaining. But it wouldn't be for long, I assured myself ; a new life was beginning for all of us. Not that it ever is. We were all embarked on the only life we should ever know, flowing like the stream of Dros-y-Mor through this and that, to meet the creek at last.

But we could at least put the more painful past behind us, and I was glad that this was Ray's thought as well as mine. He had come home in June, and a lovely June it was. I was walking through the wood one day when I saw Frank's shed with the door lying on the ground where it had fallen on the day when I took Belinda to peep within. It was with some idea of propping up the door that I approached the place and found Ray looking about him. He had shed his uniform for good and was wearing flannel bags and a pull-over of navy blue wool. His hands were in his trousers pockets, and he was looking at the spider's web, and the dust, and the damp. " So this is it," he said. " D'you know that this is the first time in my life that I've ever been in here ? It was always a holy of holies, and I knew I had to keep out. Old Em always used to say ' Oo, not there, Ray,' as though going in would desecrate a shrine. Not much of a shrine, is it ? "

He was tall and fair and I wanted to kiss him, but I knew he disliked this. " You can come in as much as you like now," I said.

" I don't want to," he answered. " I was in a sense saying good-bye. I hope you won't mind, but I never want to talk of him again."

" Neither do I. So that's understood between us."

He looked puzzled, as though not knowing how to put what he wanted to say. " I'm not callous," he said at last. " We'll always remember him. But not talk of him. Anything but that."

" Anything," I agreed.

He looked at his wrist-watch. " Now I must hurry off and meet Belinda. She's at Joe's cottage. We're going for a long walk."

He went, fairly sprinting up the path, so anxious not to talk of the past, so eager to meet the future.

It was a day of encounters. I sat on the seat where, years before, I had first met Frank, home from another war, and this time it was Mell. He came upon me just as I watched Ray disappear, my son going to meet his daughter, and he joined me there. He was looking altogether better. His stay at Dros-y-Mor had put some colour into his cheeks, and daily walking had given him something of a spring to his step, so that he now seemed more like Belinda's father and less like her grandfather. His gravity remained, but it was now the gravity of a middle-aged man, not of an ancient.

"Was that Ray I saw vanishing along the path ? " he asked.

I said that it was, and that he was going to meet Belinda at Joe's.

"I'm rather worrying about Belinda," he said.

"Well, there was a time when you were worrying about me. Do you remember ? In Cardiff."

He allowed himself one of his bleak smiles. "I didn't worry long about you," he said. "I just palmed you off on to the Graveses. I'm afraid I washed my hands of you. But Belinda's another matter. What are Laura and I to do with her when I retire ? "

"Oh, well, there are a few years before you begin to think of things like that."

"No. That isn't so," he said. "I've talked it over with Laura, and we've decided that this is as good a time as any to retire. I haven't made the headway that I expected in the Foreign Office, you know."

He said it as a statement of fact, not with any regret or animosity that I could discover in his voice, and he didn't dwell on it. "The war was pretty hard on me," he went on. "You caught a whiff or two of it, I expect, down here, but London was another matter."

He didn't dwell on the matters that had caused it to be hard on him, but I could guess : the bombing, the ruins, the fires.

"I haven't seen London since the war started," I told him.

" But I can well imagine it all. I don't suppose I should know the place if I saw it again."

" Well, we needn't go into all that," he replied. " But a man's entitled to a few years of quiet at the end of things, a few years to think about this and that, perhaps to write about them, and the long and the short of it is that I've handed in my resignation."

I didn't like the sound of that. " A few years of quiet at the end of things." How old was Mell ? I had always thought of him as immeasurably older than I was, but was he so old after all ? I was now at a horrible age, but I didn't feel it. I felt, still, years stretching before me—not " a few years of quiet at the end of things," either.

" Laura and I," he said, " have decided to take a smaller house. We shall sell that house in Melbourne Square. It was always absurdly big for us, and luckily it's escaped the bombing. We'll find some small place, and that's why we're worrying about Belinda. Of course, she won't stay with us. D'you remember Bryan Graves ? "

I cast my mind back, and was surprised how far I had to cast it. I recalled the fussy little man and his depressed wife who was now Poor Judith, and my own impertinence to him. But I couldn't recall him clearly, and said so.

" One of the things he was mad on," said Mell, " was equal rights for women. Well, they've got them now with a vengeance, including the right to be conscripted for the Army, Navy and Air Force. But I was talking about Belinda. She'd have been with Graves pretty well all the way on this matter. She'll want to go out in the world, and I don't see that we can stop her. Not that we'd want to."

" I expect that's something she'll settle for herself. I think you and Laura worry too much. Look at me," I boasted.

And Mell did literally look at me. My red head was bare. I was wearing, for one thing, Joe's abominable jumper, but I was happy. Frank was gone, which was something I thought I'd never get over. But I had got over it. Ray was back. I knew the best and the worst, and, so far from looking forward to Mell's few quiet last years, I was still capable now and then of surprising in myself sensations not unlike those that had made me bang the

Lilywhites' front door and cast myself on the winds of the day. I had come, somehow, through two wars, and I was not such a fool as to think that this last one promised us anything much beyond a troubled world for many a long year to come. You can't stir a pot to such an almighty seethe, and then watch it at once settle down to a good meal for all. But each life was a thing in itself, to be lived as one could live it ; and anyone who believed that equal rights for women, or any other sort of rights, would make a ha'porth of difference to essential things, was welcome, so far as I was concerned, to cherish these dear delusions.

"Mell," I said, "we've known one another for the best part of half a century, but, d'you know, we've not before now exchanged more than half-a-dozen or so of words. I've never been to you more than a red-headed street urchin who should be indoctrinated into the gospel according to Tennyson."

He smiled, and it was rarely that one saw a smile on Mell's face. "Well, now," I went on, "I'm your hostess and I prescribe a good walk. As for Belinda, let her do her worrying for herself. So far as I've seen her, she's quite capable of it, as capable as I've been myself. And I'm a good sample of a girl you've set on the right track by letting her do what she liked. We all do, anyway, in the long run. So why interfere ? Interference is as likely to wreck a life as to make it."

We took a walk through the summer woods, where the birds were silent now and the stream's was the only voice. We came out by Joe's cottage and walked into the open country, and a mile or two farther on met Ray and Belinda. But they were not, after all, walking. They had taken Mell's car out of the garage, and heaven knows where they had been speeding to. Now they were returning, and they were good enough to stop and offer us a lift back. We let them go alone, and we continued our walk, and were all the better and saner for it.

3

It was greatly to our surprise, when we were returning for lunch, that we saw two cars outside the garage. Mell's had been parked within, but a second car was on the road outside with a man bending over the open bonnet. He looked up on hearing our approach, and I saw that it was Christopher Harris, or, as he called himself when he wrote, Christopher Lyndhurst. I had not seen him since the garage had been the quarters of his men and he with a fellow-officer had lived in Joe's cottage. He was now in civilian clothes, and he had not changed in appearance.

I introduced him to Mell, who had not met him, and I was rather hard on him for his stingy letters all through the war. " You let us know," I said, " whether you were alive or dead. That's about all."

He answered airily : " Plenty on my plate without writing letters ", but all this was now to be put right. He was out of the army, he explained, and was taking a motoring tour of the west country before settling down—" so far as a second-hand bus and motoring restrictions will let me. Being so near, I decided to look in and see you and Aunt Mamie," he said.

" That's very good of you," I conceded ; but in my heart I was glad to see him. He was a link with Frank, and the dramatising of Frank's novel, and with many things that I wanted to remember.

" Well, I daresay we can squeeze an extra one in at lunch," I told him. " I'm afraid you'll have to leave the car where it is, and walk through the woods. It'll take you at least a quarter of an hour. Can you walk that far ? "

He grinned at Mell. " Do you know this woman well, sir ? "

" Pretty well," Mell said gravely. " She married an uncle of mine."

" She was always the boss hereabouts, but I'm rather fond of her."

" You might do worse," Mell conceded, generously for him.

In the big room we found Belinda and Ray drinking sherry. I introduced Christopher, and we joined them in a drink, and then old Mamie came in and greeted Christopher as though she had seen him yesterday. She kissed him and said : " Oh, so you're here. I knew we'd be seeing you soon, because I had a vision of you yesterday. Judith is on the way down."

The two facts seemed equally important to her, and she began at once to busy herself with laying an extra place at the table.

Then Laura came down the stairs, with Judith leaning on her

arm. Laura was deferential to Judith, for she never forgot that this was Mell's aunt and that it was at the Rowans that she had first met him. Ever since she had been with us, she had showed the old lady every attention, which Judith accepted as no more than her due. " It's so nice to feel," she once said, " that one is treated in Frank's place as is one's right."

Dros-y-Mor would ever be, to her, " Frank's place," and I rather an interloper in it, although Frank, long before her coming, had made the place over to me. I was in some doubt as to how far Judith was a *malade imaginaire*, making the best of her situation, and how far she was merely an ageing and rather pathetic and tiresome old lady. Dr. Nancarrow, who spared her a moment now and then from his delphiniums, said : " She's a bit of an old fox, she's a bit of a sick woman, but which would be the more accurate diagnosis I don't know. But I do know this : you've got her for good."

However, there she was, and there were more introductions and we settled down to lunch.

Mell asked : " How is the car running to-day, Belinda ? Don't forget you'll have to drive us to London to-morrow."

Their brief holiday was over, and soon Mell's resignation would take effect.

"I should have thought, sir," said Ray, "that Belinda might have stayed a bit longer while you are settling things in London."

" Now, Ray, we've had all that out this morning," Belinda said. " For one thing, Father drives, when he drives at all, with half his mind on the state of Europe, and Mother's no driver. There must be somebody competent about."

So they had been having it all out, had they ? I saw Christopher grinning at me across the table. He, too, had caught the implication of the words. " I should think," he said, " a father and mother are a small sacrifice in so admirable a cause."

Mell permitted himself a smile. " In this matter," he said, " I am an Abraham and claim the right to sacrifice my child."

" You needn't worry," Belinda assured him. " We've settled that point. I shall drive you home."

"That provides a good opportunity for me," Christopher said. " I take it there will be a bed going. May I stay for a day or two now that, at long last, I've come back to Aunt Mamie ? "

He gave me such a look that there could be no doubting who was the Aunt Mamie referred to. It was agreed that he should stay, and that night I came down to dinner wearing a green dress, golden shoes, and the rather startling piece of jewellery he had given me long ago.

4

Mell, Laura and Belinda were away early in the morning. We all, save Judith, walked down to the garage to see them off, and found that Joe, glad to have a car to mess about with, had filled her petrol tanks and brought her out on to the road. " Sweet as a nut," he said, and looked disparagingly at Christopher's second-hand job that remained in the garage. He gave the mudguards an extra wipe, stowed the luggage in the boot, and joined us on the road to see them off. Joe could not get over having been reduced to the status of a handyman : keeping the path clear through the woods, cutting the grass on the quarter-deck, cleaning the windows. He gave now a glance at Christopher's car in the garage, and conceded : " Better than nothing."

There was the customary kissing and waving, and, almost before we knew it, the road was empty. They were gone. Joe disappeared towards the house, and Ray said : " What am I to do all day long ? "

Mamie had gone, holding on to Joe's arm, and Christopher said : " Well, if you like you can take this contemptible bus of mine for a run. Better than nothing."

" Do you mind if I do, Mother ? " Ray asked.

Christopher, as well as Ray, seemed to hang on the answer. " Well, be back to lunch," I said.

Ray climbed into the car, and with a clashing of gears started her and brought her into the road. Then he was off, round a bend, and out of sight.

" I don't suppose," said Christopher, " that the Navy knows everything about cars. I only hope he's got a driving licence."

He was talking for the sake of talking, and there was an uneasy pause. Then he said : " Years ago, while Frank was still alive, there was a moment when I reminded you that this was the first time you and I had been alone together. D'you remember ? "

The road was empty. Christopher had suddenly passed from being a self-possessed man to one who spoke with diffidence, almost with a trembling in his voice. " Do you remember ? " he repeated.

I nodded. I remembered very well.

" I went into Plymouth," he said, " and bought a present for Frank and one for you—a bit of jewellery. You wore the jewellery last night at dinner. Was that accidental ? "

" Why do you ask ? "

" Because a lot hangs on the answer. If it was an accident, I'll hop into the old bus after lunch and continue my tour. If not—well, I'll ask permission to stay a day or two."

" I wanted to see if you remembered."

" Remembered ! " he cried, almost fiercely. " D'you think I've ever forgotten ? While Frank was alive I took a hold on myself. But Frank has been dead as long as his first wife was dead when he took you for his second."

" Frank had no children by his first wife. I have a son. Isn't my duty to him now ? "

" A son ! " he said, as though brushing all sons out of account. " What do sons do in the long run but clear out and leave you ? What is this son of yours doing now except think hungrily of this daughter of Mell Conybeare's ? I'm thinking of *you*, not your son. We are middle-aged, both of us. But we've a lot to give one another. I'm asking you to marry me. Will you ? Sons can look after themselves. It's what they're intended to do. It's how they become men. Believe me, you won't have Ray round your shoulders for long. Bigger fool you if you wish it and do anything to secure it."

We had walked on towards the house. We paused now on the edge of the stream and listened to its murmur. " You would be bored stiff in a place like this," I said. " Trees and water and birds and the sea. They're not your stuff."

" Do you think you'd stay here ? " he asked. " Not if I had any say in the matter. You'd come back with me to London."

" You're pretty sure of yourself."

He sat on the seat at my side and suddenly put both arms

round me and began kissing me hungrily. Almost to my surprise, though not altogether, I was responding. It was a long time since I had kissed a man. Ray hated being kissed. But only by me, I thought suddenly. He'll want kisses enough before long. And I gave myself more freely into Christopher's arms and heard him sigh with content as, over his shoulder, I looked at the door of Frank's old hut lying on its side where I had pulled it not long before from off its hinges.

5

It was quiet at lunch without Belinda's laughter, without Mell, without Laura. Neither Chris nor I said anything about what had happened in the wood. I merely said that Mr. Harris would be staying with us for a few days. It was quiet because I missed the laughter of the two young people. I thought that I had been too long without laughter. It was time some laughter came back into my life.

Ray, who had been glum, cheered up when I said that Chris would be staying with us. His thoughts, I fear, had been all on Belinda ; but now he said : " I'm glad you're staying for a bit, sir. We'll be able to get about in your car."

It was clear that the notion of being alone with two old ladies and a middle-aged mother had not appealed to him. Chris had other ideas than getting about the country with a growing boy, but I was glad when he fell in at once with Ray's proposal. " Yes," he said heartily. " You know Cornwall as I don't. You'll be able to show me all the good spots."

" I ought to know them," Ray said. " I was born here. Very nice, too, if you've got plenty of money or if you've come down here to retire. But it's no place for a man with a living to earn. I'll have to get up to London soon and begin looking about me."

" What will you be looking for ? " Mamie asked him. " Have you any idea about that ? You won't make a living, you know, out of digging for old bones." She had heard of the " digs " that seemed to be, at one time, the main interest in Ray's life.

" Oh, all that's done with," Ray answered cheerfully. " There must be plenty of openings. It's just a matter of looking about."

It wasn't my experience or my belief that there were plenty of openings after a war, but Chris was right. It was obvious that Ray was ready to fly, and though, even now, my heart wanted to keep him, fly he would, and the sooner I became reconciled to the idea the better. So I let them chatter on, and the longer they talked the clearer it became that Ray hadn't an idea in the world beyond getting to London where Belinda was, and where he would " look about " and there were " plenty of openings ".

6

Ray was gone. He intended, he said, to live cheaply at the R.N.V.R. Club. His gratuity would see him through. I wondered for how long, but nothing would persuade him to live for a while with Mell, who offered him a room. He was going " to stand on his own legs ".

Chris was gone, too. They motored up to town together, and I was comforted to notice that they got on well. " I'll keep an eye on him," Chris said. " I'll let you know from time to time what he's doing."

It was the last evening they were there. Ray had gone after dinner to pack, and Chris and I walked through the wood on to the lane by Joe's cottage, and thence into the country where few if any people ever came. It was a summer night with the sun gone down, leaving a huddle of cloud in the west, a red and pink and violet smother. We leaned over a gate and Chris kissed me. " I can't believe it," he said.

I was half-ashamed of my own emotions—I, a middle-aged woman, with a great son who would soon be looking about him, leaning over a gate and feeling twenty years younger than I was. I was silent, and Chris asked: " No regrets ? "

I shook my head. " Only that you are going."

We were like a pair of country lovers. We listened to the cows wrenching at the grass. We watched a light spring up in a cottage across the field. The glow went out of the sky and we picked our way back through the wood to Dros-y-Mor. Ray had finished his packing and was throwing pebbles from the quarter-deck on to the rising river. " To-morrow," he cried, " we'll be on our way ! To-morrow to fresh woods and pastures new."

I spent a dreary autumn. There were only the two old ladies left, an occasional letter from Mell, Chris or Ray. As I had expected, the plenty of openings that Ray had looked forward to finding were not so abundant as all that. He began to be short of money, and I supplied him. He was meticulous in sending me I.O.U.s. " One of these days," he wrote, " when I am on my feet, all will be paid back," and he noted with joy the occasions when " Chris Harris, whom I met at your place," had taken him out to dinner. " But all goes well," he assured me, " and I am on the look-out. It's only a matter of time, and I have great hopes of a chap named Mapson. Between us, we may surprise you yet."

I remembered the name, and was a bit taken aback to come on it again in a letter from Mell.

" My dear Alice.—In a month's time we leave here—all, that is, except Belinda. So ' all ' boils down to me and Laura. Belinda has gone into the Foreign Office in a clerkly capacity and I have gone out of it. I have felt my Aunt Judith on my conscience, and, as she is getting rather old now for any sort of move or for looking after herself, Laura and I have decided to ask her to stay where she is. Miss James-Villiers is another matter ; and, from the little I saw of her, I should say she will want to be back in London soon.

" I am selling this house in Melbourne Square. Pretty advantageously, too. It has always been rather a white elephant and I don't know why I burdened myself with it in the first place. Perhaps I expected to be of more consequence in the world than I am. Property was at a reasonable price when I bought it, but believe me it is not at a reasonable price now. When you get to London you will be surprised at the dirty knocked-about state of the town. With half the houses gone and with so many people wanting to come back, there's a struggle for accommodation both for homes and businesses. I have sold my place to a young man named Bernard Mapson. How he knew I was about to sell I can't tell you, but he has offered me an irresistible price, and the house is now his. He takes over as soon as I move out, and Belinda will have to find a flat somewhere. That is her wish,

anyhow. Like so many young people now, she wants to be
' free '.

" So that's how things are at the moment."

8

It is from what I found out later that I am able to tell you something of Mr. Bernard Mapson. He was born in the East End of
London, the son of a labourer at the Docks. His mother died
when he was young, and his schooling ended as soon as it con-
veniently could. His father was killed by a beam fallen from
a crane just as the second world war was breaking out ; and, for
an occupation rather than for any other purpose, he joined the
Navy. He was not of what they call " officer quality ", and he
was throughout the war an A.B. He served in the warship in
which Ray, for a time, before going on to be trained in an officer's
duties, was himself an A.B. There they became acquainted, and
once Ray was sent on to King Alfred, the officer-training establishment, they did not meet again while the war lasted.

They did not meet again, indeed, until Ray had left me in
quest of the many openings which he believed to exist in London.
It was about a month after he got there, and he was beginning
to find that the openings were not all that he expected, when he
turned one evening towards an eating-place that was rather
scruffy. He was just about to enter it when he ran into a young
man, dressed rather flamboyantly, who greeted him : " Hallo,
Ray ! "

He was puzzled at first by this young man. He had met
him, but he couldn't recall where. Certainly, he was a man he
was unlikely to have met before the war on any of his digs, though
Mr. Mapson was destined to dig London pretty wide apart.
At last he remembered the man he had known for only a month
or two, and, being anything but a snob, and being, too, anxious
for company, he said : " Hallo, Bernard. So you've come
through all right ? Join me in a sausage roll."

Mapson said : " Not in there. Not on your life. *You* join
me." And, taking Ray's arm, he led him down a street or two
and at last steered him through the door of a very swagger
restaurant indeed.

Ray who, during the short time he had known him, had been made well acquainted with Mr. Mapson's birth and ancestry, sat next to him on a plush-upholstered seat and could not prevent himself from saying : " Look here, old man. D'you think you can afford this ? "

Mapson grinned. " I certainly can't afford," he said, " to be seen eating in the sort of joint you were going into. I've got to be seen where money is and where money is spent. Now what are we having ? "

They were having a very good meal indeed, though Mapson kept off the wine. He was, and remained, a teetotaller, and he did not smoke. " It's an advantage," he explained, " to be able to say to a man : ' Didn't I see you the other night when I was dining at the Blue Lagoon ? ' "

Ray was fascinated by the man, and did not take long to learn something of his story. He had been discharged from the Navy a month earlier than Ray, but a month was a long time to Mr. Mapson. He had no mother to go to so that he might bask for awhile, but he got down at once to looking about him. He looked more effectively than Ray had ever done. He hadn't spent a penny of his money as an A.B., so that he was able to support himself meanly in one room in Whitechapel, and some sort of a job had enabled him to keep his " capital ", as he called it, intact. But his chief looking about had been done when his day's work was over. He had haunted the ruins of London like a jackal. He had, more than most people, a sense that a new London must arise on the old. A hole in the ground, where once a great building had been, fascinated him. He saw a new building arising there, a building with twice as many storeys as before. He saw hotels, office blocks, groups of flats, rising ten, fifteen, twenty storeys out of those holes. He was worried, as Ray had never been worried, by dreams. Not so much by dreams of a new London. That was only an implement. He didn't care twopence for London. But dreams of money, money, money.

It was not till later on in that meal that they got on to Ray's affairs. Ray told him that he had a mother living in Cornwall, but that she would be joining him soon. He told of a " sort of uncle " who would soon be moving out of a Kensington square.

" What's he going to do with his house ? " Mapson asked.

" Sell it, I suppose. He's retiring for good."

" Have you got any money ? " Mapson asked keenly.

" About as much as you have," Ray answered. " All I've got is a living to earn. Doesn't seem too easy at the moment."

" A pity. What are your prospects ? You'll have money some day, surely ? "

Money. Got any money ? You'll have money some day. Money drifted through all that Mapson had to say.

Ray explained that yes : he'd have a bit later on, if he lived long enough. " My father left a life-interest to my mother. Then the capital comes to me."

Mapson's eyes brightened. " Capital ! " he said. " That's the thing. Capital. Look, laddie. I've got a scheme. Suppose you were behind me. Would you mind if I mentioned to a bank manager that you were behind me ? With this bit of capital ? "

Ray didn't at that time take Mapson very seriously. " Well, if my name's any good to you . . ." he conceded, rather grudgingly.

Mapson said no more and paid his bill. " See you here in a week's time ? " he said. " All expenses on me."

Ray laughingly agreed.

That was how Mapson obtained an advance from a bank. The manager was more impressed with him and his dreams than Ray had been. And that is how Mapson bought Mell's house, and in due course pulled it down and caused to spring up on the site of it a block of flats, ten storeys high, and costing the earth to rent. And on those flats was founded the fortune of Mapson Properties, Ltd.

9

" I've sold this place," Mell wrote to me some time later, enlarging what he had already told me once. " I was having a clean-up of old papers, an almighty burn, the other night, when I was asked if I could see a young man named Mapson. I was rather killing time, so I had him sent up. He was a rough diamond, dressed in a ' classy ' suit, with a tendency to mispronounce some words. But, unlike me, he seemed to have no time to waste and he came straight to the point. He understood that I was about to sell my house. How much did I want for it? I asked him how he knew that I wanted to sell, but nothing would draw this out of him. I'm fairly good at keeping secrets myself, and I must say that his caution increased my respect for him, and it wasn't long before I saw that I had an unusual customer to deal with. All he would say was that he had a bank behind him. It seemed to give him great satisfaction to have a bank behind him. ' I can make you out a cheque right now,' he said, ' and we needn't sign any papers till the cheque is honoured.' He thereupon produced a cheque-book and asked, with a frankness which, I must say, delighted me, ' How much ? ' I've never known a young man determined to come to the point without wasting either time or words. So I'll waste no words myself, but say that I've sold this house, given a guarantee to be out in a month, and satisfied myself that the cheque will be honoured. I got into conversation with the young man, who didn't seem the kind of person who would want a house like this, and asked him frankly why he wanted a house in Melbourne Square. He as frankly answered ' That's my business. Your's is to say whether you'll sell.' A determined young man. A war always throws his sort up. Perhaps we'll hear more of him."

" Ever, with my love and Laura's, Mell.

" P.S.—Did I tell you we are not seeing much of Belinda ? She's got a flat of her own, decorated with prints of horrible modern pictures—Klee, and people like that."

10

At about the same time a letter came from Chris who wrote almost daily.

" Dear, dear Alice.—I know that your first anxiety is about Ray, not me. I see him most days, and the other night he came in to see me. (By the way, what a queer association ours is ! You know my address and that is about all, so far as my worldly ' status ' is concerned. Well, this tells you that when Ray called we were able to sit at a window overlooking the Thames. You know I have a Chelsea address. Now you know that I can sit at a window looking on lights twinkling on water.)

" Well, Ray came, and said he mustn't stay long as he was seeing an old Navy friend named Bernard Mapson, and it's about this man Mapson that I am writing now. Ray seems to me to be completely dominated by the man. He talked of nothing else. It was Mapson, Mapson, all the way. I thought at first that the man was at least an admiral, so you may imagine my surprise when I found that he had been an A.B. and that Ray had known him for only a month or so, when he was himself an A.B. serving on a battle-wagon before going into destroyers. Don't ask me anything about Mapson, because I know him only from Ray's words, from which I gather that he is completely on his own, has no parents or known relatives, and has a dominating position in Ray's regard. So that's enough about him, but I thought you'd better know that all Ray's looking about has so far done nothing but bring him into contact with this young man—in his early thirties, I believe—who seems to be the piper to whose tune Ray is now dancing.

" Don't think that I am doing nothing on the boy's behalf. When I learned that he was coming in here to see me, I arranged with a friend to call, so that they might meet, as it were, by accident. I think this man might have helped Ray at any rate to get his feet on the beginnings of something; but I'd no sooner mentioned that someone was coming whom I'd like him to meet than Ray was all for going at once. He'd arranged to meet Mapson, and I was left in no doubt that a talk with Mapson took priority with him above all other matters. So he went.

" I don't know whether he has mentioned Mapson in any of his letters to you, but I thought you'd better understand that there is what seems to be a powerful influence behind him."

The rest of Chris's letter was very personal so I'll say nothing of it ; but, coming on top of Mell's letter about the sale of the Melbourne Square house, it did make me begin to wonder ; for Bernard Mapson's name had not appeared in any of Ray's letters to me.

11

I decided to go to London so that I might see for myself what was happening. I wrote to Ray giving the name of my hotel and asking him to take dinner with me on the night of my arrival. He replied that he would be very glad to do so, and that he would like to bring a man named Mapson whom he had known in the Navy and whom he much wanted me to meet. I had planned in my mind a quiet meal with Ray and a talk which would lead gradually to Mr. Mapson, and this idea of throwing me precipitately into his presence did not please me at all. Mell, Chris and Ray himself had made me very conscious of this young man, whoever he might be, and so I wrote to Ray saying that I was looking forward to a long talk with him alone, and that doubtless we would have an opportunity of meeting his friend later.

Ray had always been a rather solitary boy. Perhaps his bringing up, buried with a few adults in Cornwall, had been responsible for that. He had shown a tendency ever since to cling to one man. At school and in the university this had been James Sanderson, and now that Sandy was gone Mapson had apparently taken his place. My wish to know something about him, to vet him, was understandable enough, though perhaps hopeless, for if I have learned one thing more than another it is that an older generation is wise to keep out of the way of one that is younger and that has its own problems to settle.

When I met Ray at dinner in my hotel his appearance rather surprised me. I had last seen a boy who had come from Mediterranean suns, who had spent the summer gallivanting about Cornwall, and who was in the pink of condition. Now he was paler and thinner, though he had always been thin.

London, if one had not seen it during the war, was in itself enough to take the edge off joy. I had not yet explored it, but had seen enough in my brief journey from Paddington Station. Perhaps, I told myself when I met Ray, it was this which had depressed him—this scene of ruin, makeshift, desolation. Whatever the cause, it was hard going to establish any sort of contact with him, and it was not till after dinner, when we wandered down Norfolk Street and sat on one of the Embankment benches, that I put the direct question to him. " Why are you so depressed, Ray ? You've hardly spoken all the evening."

" Because I'm not getting on," he said.

I tried to jolly him out of it. " What did you expect ? " I asked. " Did you think you were going to conquer London in a month ? "

" There are people who do it anyway," he said. " At least they make a start. They have an *idea* what they want to do, and ideas about how to do it. Oh, I know that there are jobs of a sort knocking about. I've had them offered to me. A few pounds a week for the pleasure of being shovelled into a dead end. I'm looking for something else—something with a future in it, and that's not easy to find."

" There's no hurry——" I began ; and he interrupted me quickly. " That's just what there is. It's the men who get in first that matter. Men who can see the thing that's there under their noses and are on top of it like a ton of bricks."

There was no heading him off from his master-motive. " Like your friend Mapson, I suppose ? "

" Well, he's a sample of what I mean. He came out of the Navy about the time that I did. And he was nothing but an A.B. No education, either, to speak of. But already he's got his foot into things. You should hear him talk ! You'd think that London was nothing but a place for him to buy up and improve."

" I should like to meet him."

" You can meet him to-night if you like. He's dining with a man at the Blue Lagoon. I'm meeting him there afterwards and we're going on to have a talk about things."

" Mr. Mapson will think it a bit precipitate if I turn up with you to-night."

" Well, he's a precipitate chap."

I wondered. I didn't see Mr. Mapson as precipitate. Quick, if you like. I imagined he looked all round a problem quicker than most people. But precipitate—no. That was not the sort of man that Ray had presented to me. I was aware, too, that Ray was under this man's thumb, however it had happened, and that he did want me to meet Mr. Mapson. " What time are you meeting this man ? " I asked.

Ray looked at his wrist watch. " Well, I ought to be getting along pretty soon."

" All right. We'll go together."

12

Taxis were not yet plentiful, but one happened to cruise by us at that moment, and we got in. I wondered what the Blue Lagoon was like. It didn't sound the sort of place that Frank had been accustomed to take me to during my few visits to London with him. Indeed, he had a fondness for coffee-stalls. We were as likely to eat there as anywhere else while Frank " looked about him " as Ray was looking now. However, the Blue Lagoon seemed a harmless place when we got there—perhaps a little bit too " chic ", a little bit too everything, with its dance floor and all, but harmless. We found Mr. Mapson just saying good-night to the man who had dined with him, and Ray introduced me. Mapson was a man of middle height, broad, dark, a few years older, I judged, than Ray. He could, when he liked, have charm. Already he had learned to dress unobtrusively. You wouldn't notice him in a crowd. He said : " So you're Ray's mother ? He promised that I should meet you, but I thought that was to be later. I can understand that you'd want your son for a time to yourself."

I said that that had been my intention, but that Ray had wanted me to meet him at the earliest possible moment.

" Have you dined ? " he asked.

I said that we had.

" Well, let's pick our way through the ruins," Mapson said, " and have a talk in my rooms. Would you mind ? "

I said that would suit me, and found that picking our way meant commandeering one of the taxis that pulled up at the Blue Lagoon's door. " I hope," said Mapson, " to have my own car soon, but this will have to do for the moment." He said it gravely, as a statement of fact.

We made in the Pimlico direction, and I noticed that Ray had little to say for himself. He wanted me to meet Mapson. I had met Mapson. And Mapson could do the rest.

" My rooms ", when we reached them, were nothing to write home about. They were a bed-sitting-room in a rather down-at-heel street, with a hole in the ground, where houses had once stood, at the end of it. Mapson was apologetic. " Do you mind this, Mrs. Melvill ? " he asked. " It's all I can do at the moment. I hope to have a house of my own some day." He had told me outside the Blue Lagoon that he hoped to have a car of his own. He was a young man living on hopes. He lit a meagre electric fire and hoped I was warm enough. It was clear that he had missed a great many things in life and was determined to get them.

He put me in the only easy-chair and sat on a corner of the table. I said, to get the conversation going : " Ray met you when you were both A.B.s on a battleship. He's told me something about you in his letters since meeting you again. For example, that you're going to reform London."

" Well, to begin with, yes," said Mapson without a smile. " But London's not the end of it. If you ask me, the whole country wants shaking up."

And, once started, Mapson's vision of the England of the future began to pour out of him. Hotels, garages, flats, ten, twenty and more storeys high, were to replace all these little buildings that were content to crawl on the ground or raise themselves a stingy two or three floors above it. " Think of a hotel," Mapson said. " Think what it could be—ten, twenty, thirty storeys high, with everything a human being could want under one roof. Garages, a ballroom, dining-rooms, bedrooms, sitting-rooms, all going up in one vertical line ! Think of the ground-rents you'd save. Or take the provinces. I've been around a bit. Some of the towns, for their size, are knocked about worse than London. Take Plymouth. Or look at a town more or less in the country. Take Exeter."

He thought for a while, swinging his legs as he sat on the table. " Or a whole town, come to that," he said. " One that hasn't been knocked about at all by the war. But it's been knocked about by the years, hasn't it ? " he asked. " There are streets in it that ought to go. Just think for a moment. Garages in the basement, a supermarket above that. Think of the traffic for one thing. You could widen the street while you were at it, straighten it out, knock off the angles and corners. I'm not against trees and grass, mind you. A tree here and there, in reason, does no harm, and you could have them growing out of a bit of grass . . . Model towns . . . All the houses centrally heated. Talk about smoke abatement . . ."

"But, Mr. Mapson," I ventured at last to interpose timidly into the rushing stream, "all this means money. Even ruins have owners, and so have the bits of land they are on. You've got to buy all these things before you get to work on them and sell them. Even a hole in the ground in London belongs to someone."

"Don't I know it!" he said. "But these difficulties can be overcome. A start's the thing. Give a man a start and it's like giving him a lever. He can shift anything with it. Now take that chap I was dining with to-night at the Blue Lagoon. He's the owner of one of the holes in the ground that you've been speaking of. Not so far from here, it isn't, either. I think I'm on the right side of him."

We have lived to see it all come true ; but Ray and I guessed nothing of this as we listened to Mapson building what seemed to be dream upon dream that night in a small room in Pimlico.

When we left him we walked back to Ray's club. (People were still walking, though it was soon to be a lost art.) On the way, he asked anxiously : "Well, what do you think of Mapson?"

I didn't know what to think. On the one hand his dreams seemed crazy, but on the other he was a young man whose very energy, whose determination to get what he wanted, rather scared me. "He's a live wire, all right!" I conceded.

"I'll say he is!" Ray exclaimed. "And he likes me, you know. I've been able to help him with one or two things."

He didn't tell me then that it was the prospect of his taking money over when I had done with it that had helped Mapson with a bank manager. That was perhaps a small thing. The bigger thing was the man we had seen Mapson dining with at the Blue Lagoon. He had done well out of the war and wanted to go on doing well out of the peace: How Mapson had got into touch with him is something I never learned, but he had been more impressed than I was with the young man's dreams. He had consented to give his financial backing to a hole or two. With Mell's house, it was a beginning. And a beginning was all that Mapson wanted.

13

I had told nobody—not even Ray, not even Mell—that I was engaged to marry Chris. And I had not told Chris that I was coming up to London. He had bought, of all places, Poor Judith's old house the Rowans. She had long since parted with it, and during the war it had been occupied (as being in a comparatively safe neighbourhood) by the wife of a Brigadier who had been killed in the war's last days. Now she was going to live with relatives in some remote part of Scotland, and Chris had stepped in and bought the house. He had told me about it in a letter which came to me at Dros-y-Mor. " I made a sentimental journey the other day. I took the train to Harpenden and walked the mile or so to the house you have often spoken of called the Rowans. Everything about you interests me, and I was in quest of the place to which a red-headed servant-girl had come soon after being read to in bed by Mell Conybeare in Cardiff. (The chances that man has missed !) Well, in many ways it's not the Rowans you knew. There's been since your time a lot of building in that region, and the Rowans is one of many ' bijou residences ' scattered here and there. But the outlook over the valley is not much changed ; there are some splendid beech-woods still not chopped down, and a rowan tree or two identified the cottage.

" Believe it or not, dear Alice, this great middle-aged gump spent some sentimental moments prowling in the neighbourhood, thinking of that small red-head, with all the world before her, to find me at the end of it. I still can't make out why you did it ! But there it is. You've done it, and this is to say that you're going to live in the Rowans once more ! Let me tell you how it all came about."

And he told me of the Brigadier's widow, and of how he met

her while roaming about the Rowans, and of how he learned that it would soon be on the market.

" And now there it is, all tied up by the lawyers, and this is my wedding present, my dear one, to you, because I've bought it in your name and the place you came to as a no doubt wondering and perplexed girl will be all yours when you've signed a few papers that are being sent on."

The papers had come. I had signed them and the widow was gone. Chris had had his few things moved in from his Chelsea flat, and it was at the Rowans, the next morning after meeting Mapson, that I rang him up to say I was in London.

He was waiting for me at Harpenden station, and, looking out of the train window and seeing him there on the platform, I thought of the many times I had been on that platform with Judith to await Bryan. Two wars had come and gone ; I had been seeing my grown-up son who had been in one of them ; I was in my fifties ; and yet I felt a flutter of the heart as I saw Chris scanning window after window. I jumped on to the platform before the train was fully stopped, and ran to join him.

What is age ? When do we become old ? I felt as young as the girl who landed on that platform so long ago to be introduced by Mell to his Aunt Judith. Christopher embraced me, and he wasn't smiling as I was. I could feel him trembling, and he said : " You've been so long. So long."

It was a good day and we walked to the cottage, his arm through mine. The autumn was coming on. Dahlias and Michaelmas daisies and chrysanthemums and helenium were blooming in the cottage gardens. The swallows had flown and the beech leaves were spinning through the air. There should have been a sense of last things, of melancholy, and London, as a glance had shown me, was in ruins. But I was happy.

Chris pointed out the new houses. Between the wars, when I had not known the place, many had been built, and even the dusty by-road which led to the Rowans was now " made up ". We did not go into the house at first, but Chris led me round the side of it to the garden at the back. The great view sprang to meet me. The land dropping away to the valley, the hills on the other side rising, tree-crowned, to touch the sky. But even here there were changes. A house or two smoked quietly into the air, and some former owner of the Rowans had abolished the rough piece of grass on which Judith and I had been accustomed to sit in our deck-chairs. I thought of Laura's brother, now dead in a war, coming upon me there, asleep with Chardenal's *First French Course* at my side. Now there was a gravel path running among neat beds ; but the rowans, the mountain ashes, were full-berried in the hedges. A " rustic " seat—one of the pretentious things I hate—had been set up amid this suburban splendour, and there Chris and I sat down, and he said : " The Brigadier's lady was a tough nut. She soaked me for this place. However, I managed to sell the rest of the lease on my flat in town."

" From the little I've seen of London," I said, " you'll be able to get a good price there for a rat-hole."

" Yes," he said. " People are scrambling back in their thousands, and there's nowhere to put 'em. I was lucky to get this place. Even in the country—the comparative country —houses are costing the earth. But I don't want London. Not any more. I've spent most of my life in it, but I've got a hunch that the London I knew is finished. Anyone can have it for me. I can work as well here as anywhere. Thank God I'm not tied to an office."

" I'm afraid Ray will be," I said, and told him of Mr. Mapson and the talk we had had in his room. " That man's a comet, unless I am mistaken," I said, " and Ray's tied to his tail. He's full of ideas, and Ray hasn't an idea in his head. He came back to a world that he thought would want him, and his few weeks in London have taught him that he isn't wanted any more than the next man. And now the poor dear's clinging on to this Mapson. Fortunately, for some reason, Mapson seems fond of him and is glad to have him tagging along."

" And fortunately for me," said Chris, " Ray's mother seems fond of me. That's enough of Mapson—even of Ray. Come into the house and see what I've made of it."

I knew it better than he did, though it was a long time since I had been in it. I knew the dark corner whence I had first pulled out a volume of Keats and discovered my Chardenal. All sorts of milestones sprang to my eye ; reminiscences crowded upon me.

"I can be very happy here," I said.

It was all changed. In Bryan Graves's time it had been an office, a workplace, with little in it save the necessaries for reforming the world—blue books and white papers and reports on this, that and the other thing. Now, with Chris's furniture moved in, with his notions of what constituted a curtain or a cushion, it was a home. But it was the old place. It would always be full of memories for me, and I found myself glad to be in a place of memories.

"And this," Chris said, "is the spare bedroom. We can always keep it for Ray."

It was a good bedroom, looking out on to our noble prospect. And I was glad that he had thought of Ray whom I had been inclined to leave to the wolves. But what of it ? The young are the young, and will make their own lives, and the less interference with them the better. I, too, had a life to run—a few more years, I hoped—and I felt no dismay that I was thinking of me and Chris. But I was glad that, in that moment of our supreme happiness, he had spared a thought for Ray.

Chapter XII

Not far from Chorley Wood there was at that time a nice little house. By "that time" I mean a few years after Ray had met Mapson. The house didn't rise in storey upon storey. It was not mere glass and concrete. It didn't in any way catch the eye. It seemed to try, successfully, to fit itself into a couple of acres of garden and to be part of the countryside. It was called White-cotes. Even the garden, though haphazard, fitted the place.

A few noble trees, flower-beds that seemed just to find themselves where they were, all gave the place a homeliness that was not without dignity. There was only one modern touch, and that was not so modern as all that. Behind the house was a garage for three cars.

Mapson had just acquired Whitecotes. There was to be a luncheon-party to commemorate his going in. Chris and I, who had been married for some time, were among the few invited, and the invitation came through Ray. Bernard Mapson left everything of that sort to Ray, whose looking about for one of the many openings which he believed to exist had got no further than Mapson. He was Mapson's equerry. Wherever Mapson was—and he was in an increasing number of places now, and one heard his name more frequently—you would find Ray, and Ray's business was simply to do what he was told. He didn't seem to be faring badly out of it, either. He had a flat of his own ; and, though it was a small place, it was in an exclusive part of London. He went with Mapson here and there about the country, looking, I presume, at holes, or village streets that needed the awkward corners knocked off them, or town streets that could be cheered up by stores and supermarkets and flats rising like towers of Babel into the empyrean. When he wasn't tagging at his master's heels, he went daily to the offices of Mapson Properties, though what he did there I don't know. As I see it, Mapson's fondness for him must have been founded on something that happened long ago when they slung their hammocks side by side in a battleship, stirred anew by Ray's friendly attitude when they met in such different circumstances in London. Ray was certainly the first man who believed in Mapson, though Mapson's belief in himself didn't need much encouragement. Ray was the first who saw what Mapson was up to, and approved of the doing of it, but he was no more capable of himself taking steps to bring that New Jerusalem down to dwell among men than he was of flying.

Belinda came to the luncheon party at Whitecotes, and I had better tell how she and the rest of us were fixed at that time. Judith was dead, of nothing in particular except that she was tired of life. Old Mamie James-Villiers was a tougher person, despite her occasional adventures among the spirits, and had pulled up such roots as she had let down into Cornwall. London, slowly, was recovering from the stunning blow of the war, and London was where she wanted to be, and now was, in a Kensington flat, not much unlike the one she had occupied with Judith. Belinda had a flat in the same house, and, theoretically, Mamie kept an eye on her at Mell's request. Now that he was retired, nothing would have pleased him more than to have Belinda with him, but she, wisely, repelled all the efforts of an older generation to mould her doings.

Mell—heaven knows why—was writing a massive history of the Roman Empire. I think he had given himself this long assignment in order to keep his thoughts off what he insisted on calling his failure to do what he had set out to do.

Judith did not long survive the departure of Mamie, who had never considered her adventure into Cornwall as more than a war-time expedient. Judith just faded away. She never quite forgave Laura for marrying her nephew, just as she had never forgiven me for marrying her sister's husband. So, with a sense of failure as deep as Mell's, this last of his blood relations faded away.

It is a strange thing, considering how she resented my marriage to Frank, but she never forgave my second marriage either. Chris and I were quietly married at a registry office without telling anyone about it till it was over. We did not even have a honeymoon, except that we were happy together at the Rowans. When we did at last break the news to Mell and Laura, they sent us the sort of common-sense good wishes that we expected; but Judith, propped up, I suppose, in bed, wrote to me a hysterical letter in which she said that she couldn't understand how a woman, once married to her sister's husband, and the mother of that husband's son, could have the audacity to besmirch a famous name by changing it for another. But there I was, too late now for Judith's intervention, Mrs. Chris Harris. I never showed him the letter, and, oddly enough, we lived happily ever after.

So we came to that luncheon-party at Whitecotes, a house which Bernard Mapson had insisted on making more realistic by having two or three poles stuck here and there in the garden, with white dovecotes up aloft and white doves in them. Seeing that this was done, and getting the doves for them, had been, I remembered, one of Ray's assignments. There were few guests : Ray, Chris, myself, Belinda and George Ringway. Ringway was the man I had seen dining at the Blue Lagoon with Mapson on that memorable evening when I had gone to his shabby room in Pimlico and heard him in full spate about the New England. How Mapson had got hold of Ringway in the first place, how he had interested him in his dreams, I don't know. But he was like that. It hadn't taken him long to convince me, a pretty tough nut, that he was a man who was going to make a lot of money, though whether he was going to make a success of his life was another matter. Anyway, there Ringway was, a rich childless widower. He had had one son who was killed in the Normandy landings, and now his money stretched before him like a sandy desert. Mapson's proposal was to make this desert blossom as the rose. He made it blossom, anyway. Once he had started with Ringway's money, he needed no one else. Thereafter, he could get money whenever he wanted it.

Chris and I had spent the evening before the luncheon-party at a London hotel. Usually we went up from the Rowans every week, so that we should not become complete country bumpkins. On these occasions it had become our habit to take Belinda out to dinner, thus fulfilling our acceptance of Mell's command to keep an eye on the girl. Mell, I regret to say, believed that all girls should be kept an eye on. He had begun with me in Cardiff, and in my heart I never failed to thank him for that piece of super-vision. But a girl who had not read much more than Silas K. Hocking was no Belinda, believe me. To begin with, Belinda was getting on for being ten years older than I was then, and she was, what I cannot have been at that time, a very striking woman. Chris and I were well used, when we took her out to dinner, to see heads turned in the direction of our table, and we knew it was not ourselves that were being looked at. Belinda's years with her parents abroad, her experience as an officer during the war, her present sense that she was doing a worth while job, her ability to dress well, all combined with her tall fairness to make her a striking and self-contained figure. We were, in a word, proud to be out with her. I cannot claim that, at that time, we *knew* her. She remembered us as the hosts of her parents and herself at Dros-y-Mor and was glad to be with us, but there was an aloofness about Belinda, a refusal to give herself, that we had not overcome. Ray occasionally saw her, and would have liked to see more of her, but she was as self-centred as Mell had been at her age. We were dining with her one Saturday night when Ray and Mapson came into the restaurant. That was the first time that she and Mapson had met. Some years had passed since I visited his room in Pimlico, and this was not the man I had met there. His manner had become quieter; his commerce with people in a different walk of life from the one he had occupied then had not been wasted on a man who was a quick learner. He was a broad, dark man, who had taken since I last saw him to wearing a moustache. His eyes were the most remarkable thing about him. Perhaps the only remarkable thing, for Mapson did all he could to be inconspicuous, to pass for nobody in a crowd. But his eyes, dark like the rest of him, gave one a sense that he saw everything. He could look at a hole in the ground, then lamentably frequent in London and elsewhere, and he could see rising out of it some finished and completed dream, assessed in cash.

Belinda, that night, had put on her most joyous rags. A shade of light chicory-blue was particularly kind to her fair hair, her fair beauty, and that is what she wore. We had taken our places at the table, and she was just drawing off her blue gloves and Chris was immersed in a menu-card when Mapson and Ray came in. They saw us and walked straight across to us, and Mapson said: " I have met your mother and Mr. Harris, Ray. But who is this lady ? Introduce me."

" Well, sir," said Ray, " I don't think she's any relative. But I've known her off and on all my life. She used to visit us with her parents at Dros-y-Mor. She's Miss Belinda Conybeare. Her father is a nephew of the woman who was my father's first wife. Belinda, this is Mr. Mapson."

We were all in laughter at Ray's laboured explanation as she shook hands with Mapson. She knew who he was, for, in the course of our meetings with her, Chris and I had told her about him, and about Ray's association with him. But I think she was as much surprised as I was at the easy way in which that " Sir " had left Ray's mouth in addressing him. This was something

new in their relationship—the Lieutenant-Commander calling
the A.B. " Sir ".

" Will you all do me a great favour ? " Mapson asked. " I
see you haven't begun dinner yet. Will you all join me and Ray? "

Chris and I had seen him and Ray dining in this restaurant
before. This was the first time he had taken much notice of us
—certainly the first time he had invited us to join him. It was
also the first time he had seen us with Belinda. I saw Chris's
eyebrows contracted in a momentary hesitation ; and I thought
of Mell's injunction to keep an eye on Belinda. But she took the
matter out of our hands. " I've never dined in a London restaurant with Ray," she said.

It was a neat get-out ; and Mapson had enough sense not to
say : " But you'd be dining with me." He simply called a waiter,
and we were all fitted somehow round the table that he had
booked for him and Ray. He ordered the dinner, being careful
to consult us all as to our likings. " Will you order the wine,
Mr. Harris ? " he asked. " I know nothing about wine, and
never drink it."

He had placed Belinda so that she faced him across the
narrow table, and his eyes rarely left her face. He was particularly attentive to her, and kept her in the conversation. " Now
tell me what you did in the war." " Now tell me what you are
doing in the Foreign Office." It was always *me*, not *us*.

Belinda was as cautious as Mell, and told him no more than
she wanted him to know, and it was not long before Mapson got
on to his own ambitions. Ray, Chris and I knew that subject
well enough, but to Belinda this was a new topic. She had not
guessed, any more than most people had guessed at that time,
that we were living in a new London, a new England, where
a few men had started a race to be the controllers of the way we
were to live and have our being. She listened to Mapson, en-
thralled, and only interrupted him to say : " I don't like one
little bit of it. I'd much prefer to see the old London come
back as we used to know it."

" You're much too late, Miss Conybeare," Mapson answered,
courteously but firmly. " Think of the thousands of people
who'll be crowding back into London, *are* crowding back into
London. Think of the ground-rents alone. And think of the

motor traffic, increasing every day. Think of the new roads and the buildings that will have to be put on them. You can't stick a lot of one-floor houses on roads like that! All this new accommodation will have to be on new lines. It'll *have* to be, whether we like it or not."

"Well, count me out of it," said Belinda. "Give me my stuffy little flat, which is at the top of a three-storeyed house. And that's high enough for me."

Mapson seemed pleased to meet with opposition, to be able to expound his views to an unbeliever. "Now take airports," he began, but Belinda cut him short. "What do *you* think, Ray?" she asked.

I had noticed Ray. He was not very comfortable. To find someone battling against Mapson, whose ideas he had thrown himself in with, was not a thing that he liked; but neither did he like to be opposed to Belinda. "Well," he began, "there are two sides to the matter, I suppose . . ." but Mapson cut him off short. "There are no two sides to this matter," he said, rather sharply. "You can look where you like—and I'm not talking now of towns that have been flattened by the war; I'm talking about places that the war hasn't touched—and you'll see that they are re-modelling themselves according to modern ideas. And that's upwards, not outwards, with every sort of machine to help in the daily tasks of life. Take it or leave it. It's there."

"Well," Belinda said, "at any rate the modern idea has a hot-gospeller in you, Mr. Mapson," and on this quieter note the discussion ended. Chris rose to go. "We'll be seeing you at Chorley Wood, Mr. Mapson," he said. "It's to be a very quiet affair, I understand?"

"Only a few friends," said Mapson. "If Miss Conybeare would care to be with you . . .?"

"What do you say, Belinda?"

"Well, if Mr. Mapson promises to keep off the new world . . ." Belinda agreed, with a smile at him.

"I'll be good," Mapson promised; and he, too, had a smile as he said it.

The next day Chris drove me and Belinda out to Chorley Wood. She had her own car in a garage not far from her flat, but as we were in town for the week-end we picked her up and went together. We had not gone far and were in the suburban fringe when a smile came over her face and she said : " Uncle Chris," (using the term of address that she always kept for him), " I felt last night that you and Aunt Alice didn't like Mr. Mapson's notions."

" And you were quite right," said Chris, blowing his horn with some vehemence as a small traffic block built up in front of him.

" Neither do I," she said, " but what an inconsistent lot we are ! I've got a car, and here are you driving one. Look at that fool in front now. He ought never to have a car, but there he is."

" I don't see what cars have got to do with it," Chris said.

" But Mr. Mapson does," she said. " At least, he's consistent. He sees that it's all part of the same thing : crowded roads, crowded cities, crowded everything. And crowds have no sense. They're a lot of sheep. They'll cry out, for a time, about everything that Mr. Mapson is doing, and meanwhile they'll want a bit of it for themselves. I expect before long we'll see people going out like this in thousands every day because they don't like the cities Mr. Mapson condemns them to work in. And when they get there—wherever there may be—they'll live in just the sort of places they're running away from, diversified perhaps by a window-box with a few flowers in it and a washing-machine in the kitchen."

" Then you'd better sell your motor-car," said Chris, when the road-block at last broke up. " That'll be your good deed for the day."

" But I sha'n't," she said. " That's just what I'm telling you. We all buy cars to-day because everybody else is buying them, not because we want them. Mr. Mapson knows that everybody—except a few that he doubtless calls cranks—does what everybody else is doing. They may grouse that it's killing all they are after, but they'll go on doing it just the same. He's got us all weighed up."

" He seems to have impressed you," Chris said.

" Up to a point, yes," she admitted. " At least he knows what he's doing. And he's one of the few men I've ever met who know that."

We got into the open country, and she said no more. Whitecotes turned out to be all that the name advertised. The white cotes were sitting on their poles, and the white doves were sitting on the ledges outside, crooling and crooning as realistically as one could wish. There chanced to be blue sky behind them, which made them all the nicer, and I couldn't help thinking that this was just such a house as Mapson would want behind him, to make him all the nicer. There were only a couple of acres of land, but all round it were tall trees, mostly beech, that hid the place from the side-road leading up to it. It was a hide-out in every sense of the word. The house was little more than a cottage, but a neat and trim one, only two storeys high, and the grounds were mostly lawn with a few flaming beds, too hot for my taste, in the front. Mapson himself, in a light summer suit, was waiting for us, and Ray, who seemed to be never far from him, was hovering in the background. Mapson helped us to alight on the gravel sweep, and then turned to Ray. " Run her into a garage, Ray, till she's wanted." Ray obediently got behind the wheel and drove the car off. The garages were cloaked by shrubs.

" We're waiting for Ringway," Mapson explained. " Well, what do you think of the little place ? Might be a long way from London, eh ? "

Whitecotes might, indeed, be a long way from London. Nothing could be seen except the neat house, the shaved lawns, the flower-beds, the white poles and the white doves. A cloud or two, which looked as though their hands were in their pockets, strolled negligently about the blue sky, like policemen on the outskirts of a peaceful demonstration.

" With all this grass," Mapson explained, " it's easy to keep in order. One old Jew looks after the whole place. A professor or something, once, in Dresden. Got out before Hitler got him."

He seemed pleased to have a professor or something working for him in so menial a position.

" Let's not wait for Ringway," he said. " Come and have a look at the house. Ringway's seen it all. In fact, it was he who put me on to this place."

We were just going into the house, which had a good oak door, Mapson and Belinda first, and I tagging behind with Chris, when Ray came back from concealing the car in the garages, as though he had put an unsightly person in gaol. Mapson turned in the doorway and said: " You might see that some little tables are put on the lawn, Ray. I expect people will want a gin or sherry before lunch."

Ray would manifestly have preferred to be with Belinda, or even with his mother, but orders were orders, however expressed, and he watched us go into Whitecotes. We were no sooner in the hall, which was a good wide place, than Belinda exclaimed: " But that's a Vlaminck, surely ? "

And there the Vlaminck was, hanging a little incongruously above an oak chest with two long coaching-horns crossed above it.

" Well," said Mapson, " I want to go in for old stuff in a place like this. Who is this Vlaminck ? "

Belinda said with a laugh : " He's not so old as all that, anyway."

Mapson said : " Isn't he now ? I bought it because it was old, from that Jew of mine—one of the few things he was able to smuggle out of Germany."

" Well," said Belinda, " I congratulate your old Jew on his taste. But you ought to take away those coaching-horns. With a Stubbs picture, or better still, an Alken drawing, they're just possible, but I don't think they look happy in their present company."

Mapson was an honest man. He might have put up a defence of his coaching-horns ; he might have blustered a bit, even pretending to know all about Vlaminck ; but he looked rather abashed and humble. " I don't know much about these things," he said. " I'll have the horns shifted. Will you come and talk to me now and then about pictures ? Ray ought to have known I was making a bloomer."

I looked back through the sun-filled doorway, and there was Ray on the lawn, giving orders about the small tables and the drinks. A man was just getting out of a car, and I presumed it would be Ray's duty to conceal it in the garage. " I think that's Mr. Ringway," I said.

" He can wait. He's seen all this," Mapson said. " Let's do a quick gallop through the house, and then we can join him."

So we did a quick gallop through the drawing-room and the

231

dining-room and the bedrooms and a small room that Mapson
called his office. I noticed on the table some drawings of very
vertical tall buildings, and, more particularly, I noticed that
Chris and I might not have been there. Mapson went ahead
with Belinda in tow, and it was to her that he addressed all that
he had to say. She was pleased on the whole with the house and
was gracious enough to tell him that he was on the right lines.
" Well, it's an escape," he said "—a sort of escape from what
I normally do."

And, of course, it was ; but the sort of escape that would
be increasingly denied to millions as Mapson got into his stride.
Or was the fact this : that the stride had got hold of him, and
that he was being hurried like the rest of us along a road, no
more in control of the situation than a child on the beach, building
sand-castles, is in control of the tides that in their own time
sweep it all away ?

He was greeting Ringway now as though Ringway was the
one person on earth that he had been waiting for, and he drank
water while the rest of us drank gin or sherry. And all the time
his eye was on Belinda, and Ray's eye was on Belinda ; but it was
Mapson who told us where to sit when we went into the cool
dining-room. I was on his right, Belinda on his left, and Chris
was put at the other end of the table with Ray and Ringway on
either side of him. There was a good deal of table between.
A girl, who reminded me of myself on the night of the famous
conversazione at the Lilywhites', served the meal, and I should
like to write that Mapson was a good host. But he wasn't. He
never threw a remark to the far end of the table, and Ringway
was no conversationalist. It was left to Chris to keep things
going there, with such help as he could get from Ray, which
wasn't much, because Ray was watching Belinda a little too
pointedly. At our end, Mapson had more to say to Belinda than
to me. They were much of an age, and I suppose they both
considered me an old stager while themselves were caught up
in the agonies of a lost generation. Mapson, however, seemed
determined that it was a generation on which he should leave a
mark. He talked to the girl of his schemes, his ambitions, the
things he had in hand. He was a one-idea'd man, and at the
moment his idea was to impress her. Belinda *was* impressed,

but it was only with half of herself. The other half was amused by him ; and when she quoted Flecker—" Oh, Hajji, whither wilt thou turn, when thou art there ? "—he didn't know what she was talking about.

I wasn't sorry when it was all brought to an end by Ringway rising, with a solemn pomposity, and saying : " Well, we've come to do two things : to wish our friend Mapson happiness in this new home of his, and to wish prosperity to Mapson Enterprises. So I'll put it all into one toast : To Whitecotes and to Mapson."

We drank the toast. Mapson replied in a few words, and drank the health of all of us in water, and that was the end of the great affair. Ringway disappeared, and Mapson became pure business. " Ray, roll up all those drawings that you'll find on my study table. We'll want them in London to-night. I'm seeing a man there. Can we give Miss Conybeare a lift ? "

But Chris had already got his car out in front of the house and said, quite untruthfully, that we were all three calling on a friend half-way to London. We would have to take Belinda along with us. She seemed in a mood to condone his felony, and said, as we drove off, "Thank you, Uncle Chris. A little of Mr. Mapson goes a long way. But a little, now and then, might be refreshing, don't you think ? "

2

Belinda's flat was in the same building as Mamie James-Villiers's in Kensington. We all looked in to tea on that day when we had lunched at Whitecotes. Belinda was well acquainted with Mamie now, and unofficially watched over her and kept Mell informed of her progress. If you could call it progress. I don't know how old Mamie was, but Chris said he could remember her as a grown-up aunt as long as he could remember anything, and she had certainly reached the age when " progress " was a relative word. She seemed rather to be embalmed in a hard carapace of cosmetics, at a standstill, if not slightly slipping backwards. She had nowadays a small attendant named Rosy Midge. Rosy had suffered from the war as few of us had suffered. She was an only child whose father had been killed, one of those small

233

gnats whom the clashes of civilisation can afford to ignore. The Lord alone knows why wars are fought, but they are certainly not fought on behalf of specks floating in the air like Rosy. Her mother was one of those Mrs. Mopps whom the war glorified when it had need of them. She and the child lived in one room of a house, and the mite, aged two, was in neighbours' keeping while the mother was at work. But this didn't last long, because the house in which they had their one room was squashed flat in the week following Private Midge's death. Rosy was the only thing got alive out of that heap of masonry. How she had survived until her middle teens was something she never talked about and that nobody knew. But now here she was, incredibly cheerful, utterly devoted to Mamie, who, in her turn, was devoted to her. They even shared the same bedroom, for a small cot pushed into a corner was all that Rosy needed. Her growth —and no wonder—seemed to have stopped when she was a child. She was a tiny thing, not rosy, like her name, but rather pale, thin, grey-eyed, a djinn always on hand whether Mamie rubbed the lamp or not. I was very moved that afternoon to see the devotion with which those pale grey eyes followed Mamie wherever she went, as if on the look out for some small service to perform, and by the cheerfulness which seemed to me to peep through a life-time's history of shabby treatment.

Chris and I had known Rosy ever since, mysteriously, she appeared in Mamie's flat, which was now a year or two ago, and Chris never failed to take her some small present, if it was only a bit of artificial jewellery. Indeed, this was his favourite gift, and she wore it jingling about her, though never without a fear that the flat would be " broke into " by jewel-thieves on the look-out for a rich haul. I had grown increasingly fond of Mamie, and was glad that Belinda, too, had a soft spot for her. There was something indomitable about the old thing, though she looked now as frail as a glass goblet, an antique that defied the years, as she poked about the place on her ebony stick.

We took tea with her, and she enquired about Judith, whose death she sometimes remembered and sometimes didn't ; and then Chris and I went one floor up to Belinda's flat, which was a different matter. She couldn't afford original pictures, but she had some excellent prints. Her salary was as small as her means. She couldn't afford carpet, so her room was laid with pale green felt. She had picked up a few good chairs in junkshops and re-upholstered them herself. Much of her stuff had been picked up in junk-shops. Very good she had made it all look. Chris could never resist giving presents, and I remember that that afternoon he gave her a Copenhagen stoneware monkey for her mantelpiece. He casually said that he had " found it " somewhere, though I know that he had found it in the Copenhagen shop in Bond Street, and paid a pretty penny for it.

It was a quiet little flat, with this room just big enough to be a sitting-room, a bedroom just big enough to hold a bed, a bathroom just big enough to hold a bath, and a kitchen just big enough for boiling a kettle and doing a bit of cookery. We lounged in chairs, and Chris asked : " Well, what do you think of Mr. Mapson and his brave new world, Belinda ? "

" Tell me something about him," she said.

So I told her all I knew : how Ray had met him, how I had listened to his dreams in Pimlico, how her father had sold him his house, how Mr. Ringway had lent him money. " He's one of those men," I said, " whom you can't *help* lending money to, once you let him get going on the world as he sees it. He could convince an atheist of the truth of Christianity."

" He'd have to believe it himself first," Belinda said. " That's what I like about him. He believes in something, if it's only money."

" It's all he does believe in," Chris said.

" Well, it's *something*," Belinda told him. " Believe me, Uncle Chris, money is *something*."

She pondered for a while on Mr. Mapson, and then said : " He spends as well as gets, and a place like Whitecotes is, I suppose, a big step up for a man like him. After all, he did buy the Vlaminck. Though I wish," she added with a smile, " that he hadn't put the coaching-horns on top of it."

" He only needs a woman with a bit of taste," Chris teased her.

" Yes, that would help," she said gravely.

There was a telephone in her bedroom, and at that moment it rang. She got up to answer it, and we couldn't help, through the open door, hearing her half of the conversation. " It's very kind of you, Ray, but I can't get out this evening. . . . No, I'm meeting another girl, and we're going to a place in Chelsea for a bit of dinner. . . . Yes, a long-standing engagement that I can't get out of. . . . So sorry. Yes, we'll eat together some other time."

She came back into the sitting-room, looking rather flustered. " I expect you heard," she said, " that that was Ray. The man he was to meet with Mr. Mapson in town to-night has put the meeting off. So he wanted to take me out."

" And you have a previous engagement," said Chris. " We heard it all. Now we must be hopping out to the Rowans."

She kissed us both. " Thanks for the monkey," she said to Chris. " He looks adorable. My first bit of Copenhagen. You're giving me expensive tastes. A bad thing to do to a poor girl."

3

I suppose you think I have said little about Chris, seeing that he was my husband. When I married him I had been for long without a husband ; I thought it was time I had one ; and I married Chris. It was a marriage of convenience if ever there was one, and it was utterly successful. It is not easy for a woman in her fifties to find a man she loves in the old romantic sense. I had a great affection for Chris, and I think he had more than that for me. We suited one another, had tastes in common, and got on very well. I couldn't help thinking at times of the widow in Manchester. She had married her elderly lodger, expecting no more than to be " comfortable enough ". Well, I was comfortable enough, though in a wider sense than that widow would know. Chris and I laughed at the same things, were serious about the same things, more or less liked the same sort of people, more or less disliked the way the world was going. All around us were men and women who had married for love, and every year or two found someone else to love, and found someone else again as soon as they were in tow with the new partner in the merry-go-round. Meantime, without any song and dance about it, we were happy together. Chris knew, as well as

236

I knew myself, that Frank Melvill had a place in my memory that no other man would ever have, just as I sometimes wondered whether Frank's first wife Jane had ever been shaken from the pedestal in his own heart.

I had, what Chris never had, a son to think about, and as we drove that day from Belinda's flat, it was of Ray I was thinking. I had had dreams about Ray, and so had Frank. But they were not being fulfilled. We had seen him, more notable than his father, a shining figure in the world, carving with a relentless will some predestined niche, yet always thinking of the parents who had begotten him and stood aside when his feet were on the right way. But it was not turning out like that. It rarely does. I did not often see Ray, and when I did it was an occasion likely to be marred by some complaint about Mapson. At first, Mapson was the only man in the world, and, being the sort of man he was, he clung to Ray and used him for all he was worth. There was bound to come an end to this stage, for, apart from an introduction or two—which Mapson would now have got anyway—there was not much that Ray could do. He was a handy ear for pouring the dream into when it was only a dream, but now that that stage was passed, there was little Ray was useful for. I will say this for Mapson : he never forgot those early days. He never forgot whatever the kindness had been that Ray had shown him in the bowels of a battleship when they were nobodies together. We hear a lot about the toughness of tycoons, about how they use a man and then throw him out. Mapson was an exception. If there is, indeed, a rule. The simple fact of the matter is that he had now reached a stage when he could have done without Ray, and didn't do without him. The luncheon party we had been to that day showed it : Ray had been there. Mapson had had no scruples about giving him orders, but Ray was a paid man. His flat in London was next to Mapson's and he was supposed to be generally about. It was a strange relationship. He was, in short, a paid companion who did whatever he was wanted to do. He was like a midshipman on a battleship whom the captain has taken a fancy to, whom he likes to have there, and who is useful for doing a score of things provided they have nothing essentially to do with the business that the ship is about.

When Chris and I reached the Rowans that day we sat in

deck-chairs looking out over the valley and I asked : " What do you think of Ray, Chris ? "

This was sensitive ground, for Chris rarely mentioned Ray. He had seen something of the boy during the time when Ray was " looking about " in London, and had indeed suggested this and that, all of which Ray had turned down—not quite the sort of thing his then optimistic mind was looking for. But on the whole Chris regarded Ray as my problem, and indeed I had encouraged this attitude. I didn't want Ray to be any sort of burden to Chris, and for a long time I had been as optimistic as the boy himself, convinced that all the advantages of school and university would at last land him where he wanted to be. But now he had met a stronger personality who had had none of those "advantages" and who was towing him along like a dinghy in the wake of a high-powered vessel.

Chris said : " The question is : What do we think of Mapson? Is he the sort of man Ray ought to be tied up to ? Because there's no doubt that he is tied up to him. In a queer sort of way, they're fond of one another. Ray admires the man's push and go. Mapson admires Ray for all sorts of qualities he hasn't got himself. In a way, he's learning from Ray, and he's a quick learner. Not that he doesn't like the boy for himself. The question is : do you want to encourage Ray to stick where he is, or do you want him to strike out on something on his own account ? "

" You talk all the time," I said, " of Mapson as a man and of Ray as a boy."

" Well, at all events, they're employer and employed. So long as Mapson pays the wages I suppose he's the one who gives the orders. And, so far as I can make out, now that the money's coming in, they're pretty good wages at that. You may not think that this is a star that Ray has hitched his waggon to, but at all events he's done the hooking. He's at liberty to unhook any time he wants to, and find something else."

" You haven't answered your own question—what do we think of Mapson."

It was getting dark down in the valley, and the trains shuttling there to and fro had begun to put on their lamps. Chris spread a rug over my knees and re-lit his pipe. " Well," he said when it was satisfactorily going, "you've asked me—or rather I've asked myself—a lot. I've met the man only once or twice, but I've heard much of him from you and other people. It's like asking me what do I think of the human race. With this war and its consequences not far behind us, and all about us, I think they're an insane lot of blood-thirsty mammals, but the odd fact remains that I like most men and women. I don't like a bit what Mapson is doing and what, if he and his sort aren't stopped, he'll do in the future. He doesn't care a hoot for England or for making it a better country for men and women to live in. Whitecotes tells us that plainly enough. He doesn't want to live in the sort of place that he thinks good enough for the rest of us. What we have seen to-day is only a start. We've seen a cottage. Soon we shall see a house, and before we've finished we shall see one of the stately homes of old England, with Mr. Mapson shut off by acres and trees and streams from the rest of us. To do that he needs money, and, as Belinda reminded us to-day, money is *something*. What he has seen is the great modern way of laying his hands on millions. He hasn't got them yet, but he will have them. I dislike these wolves as a pack. But I like Mapson. He's a learner, and if he's learned to like the wrong things—for other people—he's had plenty of instruction. It's nothing new, you know, for those who *have* to care not two hoots for those who have not. Our grand estates for centuries past have been maintained on urban rents squeezed out of insanitary property, and they have been surrounded by cottages not fit to turn pigs into. If Mapson wants his styes to go upwards, with every sort of gimcrack adornment, that's only a change of method, not of intention. Squeezing money out of ground rents is nothing new. The new thing is sending buildings *up*, so as to get more rent out of the same amount of land. So now you know what I think of Mapson and all his like, and what I think of the sort of star that Ray's hitched his waggon to. And what's more," he added with a smile, " that's the first political oration you've heard on this bit of lawn since the lamented Bryan Graves departed from it. And, what's more still, it's likely to be the last so far as I'm concerned."

4

When Belinda said she couldn't go out with Ray, she was speaking the truth in a sort of fashion. She had told me that afternoon that she was seeing a film—Italian, that all the highbrows were flocking to—with Rosamund Hornbrook. I had been faithful to the charge laid on me by Mell to keep an eye on Belinda, and was glad that she was on good terms with Rosamund Hornbrook. Not that she couldn't have cancelled the arrangements if she had wanted to spend the evening with Ray. Rosamund lived only a street or two away ; Belinda could have got there in two minutes; and Rosamund was a girl who would at once have understood. So I concluded that Ray thought more about Belinda than she thought about him, and that she avoided deepening a friendship which was no more than just that. I knew that they went out together now and then, but the Rowans was far enough from London to leave me in the dark as to what footing they were really on.

Moreover, though such a matter naturally interested me deeply, I had never been one of those mothers who feel it incumbent to approve or disapprove their children's friendships. I had seen enough evil come of that in my time. I did not feel, either, any urgency to let Mell know every last detail about Rosamund. I knew that she was a well-to-do pin-money girl whose father was " in the City ". What exactly Mr. Hornbrook did in the City I couldn't say except that he managed to run a good-looking house and allow his only child a good-looking income. Belinda, much of her age, had met Rosamund at a dance, and from that moment they were rarely apart except when they had to be. Rosamund liked the feeling that she was earning her own living, but all it came to was some sort of job in Fleet Street which consisted of writing paragraphs for a woman's page about fashionable marriages and dances, and who, generally, was who. Still, I suppose she made as much out of that sort of thing as I made in my years during the war out of translating for His Majesty's Government ; and, what with this and what her father allowed her, Rosamund was a well-to-do young woman.

I had met her on the only occasion when, with Belinda,

I had been to her house, one of those Georgian places dotted all over Kensington. She was a small dark girl, very vivacious, and with no illusions about what she was doing. To hear her talking about a certain " flighty young fool " you would not have supposed that the young fool in question was the person of surpassing elegance and charm that she had been writing about the day before. Indeed, it was always good fun to hear Rosamund, when she was not being professional, on some of those whom, professionally, she found so endearing. " About time they *did* marry," I remember her saying once. " As it is, they've only just got time to beat the band to the registrar of births, marriages and deaths." She was no one's fool, and laid her ear in many a secret place.

Chris and I did what we could for Ray. His time was irregular, for Mapson had a habit of going hither and yon to see places, sometimes whole villages, that were " ripe for development ", and on such occasions Ray went with him. But when he was in town we would either dine with him there or ask him to dine with us at the Rowans. " When I leave Mapson and start something on my own " was a constant theme with him on these occasions, and if we pressed him on that matter and hinted that we would be glad to see him on his own, and even that we would do what we could to get him on his own, he was vague and non-committal about what his own was. " Meantime a man must live " was the way he put it. I could only conclude that he had got into a current, a pretty powerful one, and that it was bearing him along, taking him hither and thither whether he wanted to go or not, and that Mapson was more happy in his company than he was in Mapson's. He had thought at first to be an equal partner with that remarkable man, even the dominating partner ; but his eyes were slowly opening and he realised that he was not much more than what is called, I think, a Yes man.

We ventured, soon after the luncheon party had been given at Whitecotes, to ask both him and Mapson to take a meal with us at the Rowans. They accepted, and came in Mapson's car, with Mapson himself driving. I noted that it was a Rolls-Royce, though very modest in colour—a dark blue. Mapson was dressed to match his car, in a dark blue lounge suit that was almost black. But the car was fitted inside with all sorts of gadgets, including a desk that could be pulled out and worked at. He showed it to us with a modest pride. " Ray does most of the driving," he explained, " when we get about. I generally find a bit of work to do as we go."

It seemed to sum up the two men and their relation to one another—Ray driving where he was told to drive, Mapson doing the work that was the object of the journey. We were standing round the car as all these things were explained to us, and Chris said : " You'll want a chauffeur one of these days."

" Oh, we get along very well without one," Mapson explained. " I like having Ray about. When I'm not busy in the back, I get into the seat alongside the driver's and there's all sorts of things we can talk about. You couldn't talk with a chauffeur. No ; it's a good arrangement as it is. Don't you think so, Ray ? We get along all right, don't we ? "

There was not much Ray could say except yes—they got along all right.

I had cooked the luncheon myself. Apart from a woman who spent an hour or so with us in the morning, we refused to be burdened with a " staff ". Chris could push the mower over our bit of grass, and I could do most of what needed doing indoors. Now and then, I even did a bit of typing for Chris, but his work tended to get less and less as what was demanded in the theatre became less and less to his liking, and more and more beyond such capacity as he had. But we got along. He had a small income and so had I. " Money," he used to say, " is the root of all evil, whether having too much of it or having not enough. We are happier betwixt and between."

But I remember that lunch with Ray and Mapson not so much for the roast mutton and charlotte russe which I had managed to knock up, but for some remarks that Mapson made. We sat on the bit of lawn drinking our coffee, and then Chris said he would walk the two along the road to see a house that had started to go up a hundred yards or so from us. Mapson asked permission to stay where he was. " You go, Ray," he said. " You can tell me about it later."

When they were gone we sat in silence for a while, and then suddenly I broke all my rules about letting Ray do what he liked, find his own way in the world, and all the rest of it. " Mr. Mapson," I said, " I'm rather anxious about Ray."

He looked at me, surprised. " I don't know why you should be," he said. " England is full of men to-day who'd give their right hands to be where Ray is."

" Yes, but where *is* he ? "

" Why, he's with me. I can look after him. I'm very fond of him for a number of reasons. I don't think you need worry about Ray."

" You still don't answer my question," I persisted. " I mean what does he *do* with you ? What's his job, and what are his prospects ? "

He seemed genuinely surprised, as though to be in his good graces were enough in itself.

" I like to have him with me," he said simply. " As for his prospects, they depend on my own, and I've got no reason to complain about them. In fact, they're rather more than prospects, you know."

I sighed at the impossibility of getting him any further than that. And then this boy—little more : he was roughly of Ray's own age—leaned over and patted my hand which was old enough to be his mother's, and said soothingly : " Don't worry, Mrs. Harris. Ray's all right."

I gave it up. I could hear Chris and Ray returning from their small expedition. They joined us on the lawn, where Mapson was putting the coffee things on to a tray.

" We must be getting back," Ray said. " Don't forget that engagement this evening. We'll have to change for dinner."

" Ray's been explaining about that," Chris said. " They're going out to dinner to-night. Taking Belinda and that girl she goes around with—Rosamund Hornbrook."

" Hornbrook's in the City," said Mapson, who was always interested in something however remotely connected with the City. " All right, Ray. I hadn't forgotten."

He turned to me with apologies for " dashing off ", and a moment later the Rolls-Royce was out of sight and Chris and I were washing up the coffee-cups in the kitchen sink.

5

It was from Belinda that I heard, some time later, of the dinner-party that took place that night. Chris had gone in to London, and Belinda, without any warning, not knowing that I should be alone, suddenly called on me for afternoon tea. She had been walking, and there she was. I was sitting reading on the lawn when she strolled in from the road and sat beside me. She was full of apologies, hadn't known that I would be by myself, and insisted, after resting awhile, on making the tea and bringing out a few buns and biscuits.

We sat with autumn flowers blooming round us, and I thought that she was turning into something worth looking at : taller than was usual, well-dressed, a person, as so many girls are not. I told her so, and she laughed. "It's nice to have your opinion," she said. "It was not Mr. Mapson's."

"But you got on very well with Mr. Mapson when we went to his luncheon-party at Whitecotes. I should never have dared to tell him that his coaching-horns were out of place above the Vlaminck. He took it very well. I should have thought the least he would do was appoint you his social secretary."

"Oh, but there was no competition. Apart from you, I was the only woman present, and he knew that you had already been snapped up by Uncle Chris. With Rosamund Hornbrook there, it was another matter."

The little dinner in London had been Belinda's idea. "Rosamund had never met Mr. Mapson," she said. "I believe her father had come across him once or twice in a business way, and thought the world of him. You know how these rich people are. They stick to one another. Anyway, when I told Rosamund about the affair at Whitecotes, she was taken with the idea of meeting him. She said she had never met one of these tycoons that are so busy round us to-day, straightening out our roads, building up to the clouds, and digging down into the earth. Of course, she *might* have met him at her father's, "but I don't think he's *quite* rich enough yet to be asked to dinner."

I was glad that she found this a laughing matter. The situation of the financiers who were turning England upside down

might have earned a grim smile even from her father. I let her
go on, and it seemed that she had arranged the matter through
Ray, who would rather have taken her out alone, but thought
that to dine with her and Mapson was better than nothing.

Ray had small difficulty in arranging the occasion. Mapson,
though he kept his own counsel in financial matters, was, otherwise, reasonably gregarious. As I see him, he was, for one thing,
learning, as he would honestly have put it, to conduct himself in
company. He could have plenty of the company of people of
his own sort, people on the up and up, but he didn't much want
them except on business occasions. When he went out purely
to enjoy himself, he liked to be in the society of another sort of
people, and he relied on Ray to find them for him. He was
especially nervous in the presence of women, knowing how full
London was of women who seemed all right on the surface but
were, in effect, looking out for rich men ready to spend their
money on mink and motor-cars. But on this occasion he thought
that Ray's friend Belinda and Hornbrook's daughter Rosamund
would be all right. He was, Ray has since told me, a bit nervous
about Rosamund. He knew of her scribblings in the newspapers
and the last thing he wanted was to figure there, for he was a very
secret man. One did not hear of his presence until he had passed
and gone and left his traces.

As I see Mapson, he was not, in all this, merely a rich man
who didn't want to spend his money on the wrong things and
the wrong people. He was a Puritan who did believe in a decent
society, though, in my view, he went a queer way about securing
one. And he especially believed in decency between men and
women.

That night he and Ray were to meet Belinda and Rosamund
at Belinda's flat, and they called for them in a taxi-cab because
garages are not easy to find near restaurants in the West End,
which was one of the things Mapson was determined to put right
in time.

" Rosamund was keener on meeting him than I was," Belinda
said to me. " I'd met him at Whitecotes, and, frankly, he amused
rather than impressed me. I suppose Rosamund had heard her
father talking about him. Anyhow, she was all dressed up.
You've met Rosamund at my place, you know. She isn't much

to look at, short and dark, but clothes *do* make a difference. I had to do with my tatty old rags, but Rosamund—well ! "

From all of which I could form my own idea of how Rosamund was. I didn't share Belinda's view that Rosamund was " not much to look at ", and I pictured her dark eyes sparkling over a fur collar like those of a small animal looking for prey.

" I must say," said Belinda, " that Mr. Mapson has learned to wear a dinner jacket. He knows the value of tailors, and he was wearing a red carnation in his button-hole. He's got a figure, too. Ray, mind you, looked all right. I remember how, as the dinner progressed, Mapson took from an inner pocket a note-book to look up a date. It was of nice blue paper bound in leather, and the leather was edged with gold. At any rate, some shining metal. And the pencil, which fitted into a little slot at the side, was in a gold case, too."

Belinda was good at these small touches, which helped me to see the four of them there under the soft lights of the restaurant, Rosamund's eyes sparkling the more as she saw that small note-book with its secret entries and the red flower at Mapson's button-hole.

" And did Ray have a nice little note-book ? " I asked.

" Oh, Ray and I were not in the picture," she said. " Rosamund had come out to meet Mapson, and she met him in a big way. You should have seen him laying her cloak over the back of her chair ! Don't you think there's a lot in the way a man handles a woman's cloak ? "

" That's an academic question. Or is it æsthetic ? Or psychological ? How did it all end ? "

" It isn't ended yet," she said. " But if Rosamund doesn't marry Mapson it won't be her fault. I know she's met him since. Dined with him. Without me and without Ray."

" And what does Mr. Hornbrook say to all this ? "

" Oh," said Belinda, getting up to go, " modern girls don't ask Papa."

6

I asked Chris : " What is Mapson ? "

" How do you mean—What is he ? "

"Well, what does he do? One hears him talked about here and there, but he's a hard man to fix."

"As I see it, the harder the better, for him. He's one of those men—there are quite a few of them now—who are *behind* things. And they prefer to be behind. The less they appear, the better they are pleased. They arrange for things to be done, and when it's too late for the likes of me or you to do anything about it, then you can bet there's a Mapson behind it. They find the money. They find the sites where it can be profitably spent, and that's all they care."

"But surely there are architects, builders. . . ."

"They're just the chaps they work *through*. If you can call them architects, that is. It seems to me that a ruler and a set-square are all one needs to be an architect to-day. You draw a tall oblong, divide it into spaces with windows, and there you are. A modern block of flats. Dammit, I'd rather live in the Rowans, poky as it is."

"So would a lot of people," I pointed out. "You're lucky, and so am I. We can live where we like. But there's such a thing as having to be near a job."

It was soon after this that Chris handed over a newspaper which, like most newspapers to-day, contained a "gossip" column. "Read what 'Melisande' has to say to-day. The third paragraph."

"And when I was with Lord Bloomsbury the other night at the Blue Lagoon whom should I see, dining tête-à-tête, but enchanting dark-eyed Rosamund Hornbrook and Bernard Mapson, who is being talked of more and more as a power behind the structure of the new world rising about us. Rosamund is the only daughter of Mr. John Hornbrook, well-known in the City of London. She makes a delightful link between two great powers."

I handed the paper back to him. "And what strikes you as significant about that?" he asked.

"That Mapson and Miss Hornbrook were dining tête-à-tête. That's the first time, I should say, that Mapson has ventured into high society without Ray to support him."

7

I will say this for Bernard Mapson, he always tried to do the right thing. Typewriters, I suppose, were reserved for business correspondence, but personal letters were in his own hand. The first I ever received from him was addressed to me and Chris jointly at the Rowans.

" Dear Mr. and Mrs. Harris.—I expect you will be surprised to hear that I am married, and that Miss Hornbrook is now my wife. We were married at a registry office, and I should have asked you both to be there, only it was a very private affair. Ray came with me, and Rosamund had one friend with her, but that was all, as we wished this to be a personal matter. So now we are taking a brief honeymoon in Scotland, but this won't last long as I have some rather pressing things to see to. But I thought I'd let you know, as you have been kind to me, and Rosamund and myself will be very glad to see you at Whitecotes when we are back. Ever yours faithfully, Bernard Mapson. P.S. We asked Ray and my wife's friend to keep this quiet for a week or so. B. M."

The letter was written on blue paper, with " Whitccotes, Chorley Wood," embossed in white on the top of the sheet. A very thick nib had been used and the handwriting was that of one not accustomed to write much. There was no indication of where they were. Even the post-mark was an indecipherable smudge.

This was a few months after " Melisande " had seen the two dining tête-à-tête, and we had heard nothing from either Ray or Belinda about their having been together since. Evidently, like everything concerned with Mapson, it was " under cover " until too far gone for anyone to do anything about it.

" So we have been very kind to him," said Chris. " What have we done ? "

I could think of nothing except that dingy room in Pimlico —the room in which I had given Mapson his head, let him unfold his dreams. It was now a goodish time ago, and there were not many people then, I imagined, who were willing just to sit down and listen. Perhaps none. He had had, as it were, to beg his way through those opening stages, and I was touched to think that he had remembered, that I had been " very kind " to him. I hadn't known that I was entertaining, or being entertained by, an " angel unawares ", if, indeed, they were angels who were now in full gallop over the face of England. But, at all events, that, I reflected, was how Mapson saw it, and this helped to explain, too, the rather peculiar place that Ray held in his esteem.

" How about Ray ? " I asked. " While Mapson is away, we'd better give him a dinner and see whether the moment is ripe for him to make a revelation to us ? "

" And I suppose," said Chris, " we'll have to look up a wedding-present while we're at it. I can't afford a Vlaminck, but I might go to a pair of coaching-horns. Or will they be anathema to Mrs. Mapson ? "

8

Chris and I had never been asked to Mapson's office. We took a day off, though there wasn't much to take a day off *from*. Chris was no creator, and in those days his talents as an adaptor were not much sought after. Such novels as were being adapted for the stage had a way of becoming " musicals " and that was not in his line. But he did a bit of writing each morning, though he kept to himself what he was writing about, and I did not ask him. For me, I did the housework, read, and lived a rather shameless idle life.

On that day off, we found Mapson's office in St. Peter's Square, Kensington. All we knew about the place was that it was part of the square like any other house ; and when we stood before it, there was little to distinguish it from them. A tiny notice on a brass plate, which you might easily have overlooked, said " Mapson Enterprises ", and that was all. We had arrived " on the hop " and with some trepidation went in, feeling like intruders, for the place had a hidden secret look, as though callers, even on legitimate business, were not welcome.

" I feel as though I were burgling Ali Baba's cave," Chris whispered. He pushed the door open, and we went in. Fortun-

249

ately, we had not to explain ourselves, for just at that moment Ray was coming downstairs.

Fair, rather tall, very well dressed, there he was. It was the first time I had seen him in what I suppose I must call his " office ", and for just a split second before he saw us, we saw him. He looked very young, discontented, and as though seeking something to do. In a moment he had seen us ; the look was brushed off his face, and he came down more quickly to meet us. Just to the right of us was a fine mahogany door. As he opened it, I noticed the inscription upon it. " Mr. Melvill."

It was his name ; but it was also Frank's name, and in a second I found myself thinking of Frank, which I hadn't done for a long time. I was thinking of a hut in the woods at Dros-y-Mor, Ray's hut, and the two of them bent over a table, rough-hewn and home-made, peering at a plasticine model which they had been building in a holiday-time. And I felt that there was something wrong, that something broad and deep separated this moment from that. An innocence was gone from the world. Like a fool, I began to cry.

But it wasn't much. There were only a few tears which I hastily wiped away. Chris noticed them, and set me down in a comfortable chair, but Ray, if he noticed them at all, said nothing. There were two of these comfortable chairs in the room, and Chris sat in the other. Ray sat in an official-looking seat behind a long table that carried a blotting-pad, a pen-tray, and a few bundles of paper done up in a rubber band. There was also one of those date machines that you alter every day. I noticed that this one was a few days behind time.

There was something about the moment that I didn't like, and to break the silence I said : " We've dropped in rather on the hop, I'm afraid, Ray. We happened to be in town and thought we'd have a look at the place where you worked. You've been a long time asking us."

" Well, now you see me in my glory," he said. " This is where I interview people who don't matter. If they matter, I take them in to Mapson or make an appointment for them."

He was talking with bravado, and as he talked he lit a cigarette. I noticed that his hand shook slightly.

" There isn't really much to see," he said, " and you're only just in time, anyhow. I'm afraid Mapson and I will have to part."

Chris could only say : " But, Ray ! I thought you were well settled down with Mapson. I thought you were the apple of his eye."

For me, the moment became more and more depressing. There was something so absurd about Ray sitting behind that official-looking table, in that official-looking chair. He seemed such a child, though I knew he was now nothing of the sort. But I longed to have him this side of the table, on my knee, if necessary, telling me what was the matter. I got up and went behind the table, took the cigarette from between his fingers as if he were a small boy, and put it in the ash-tray. I put my arms about his shoulders, and felt the resistance die out of him. " For God's sake," I said, " get away from this absurd table. Come and sit on the floor at my feet, or let Chris sit there, if necessary, and you have his chair. Come off the high horse, anyway, and tell me and Chris what's the matter."

" Better still," said Chris, " come out of this damned office and have a cup of coffee."

He didn't withstand us for long. " Well, I could do that," he said. " I was just going when you came in."

I felt better when we were under the sane winter trees. It was a bright day, and Ray, without an overcoat or a hat, loped at my side. I couldn't help putting an arm through his, hugging it tight. We kept off whatever was in his mind, talking of this and that, and Chris backed me up with rather meaningless chatter.

So we came at last, in a better frame of mind, to a tea-shop. It was late in the morning, and most of the old Kensington ladies had finished their éclairs and morning coffee. The place was almost deserted. " You see," said Ray, " I can do more or less what I like, come and go as I please, especially when Mapson's away. Which is one of the things I loathe about my life. However, I dare say I could have put up with that. But now there's the matter of this flat."

This matter of the flat was very simple. The ground floor and first floor of that house were occupied by Mapson offices. " Not that there are many clerks," said Ray. " My room on the first floor is rather grand and pretentious. When Mapson's away, and I'm not away with him, I do little but doodle in it.

Then there is another room on that floor where Mapson receives the really important people. I haven't the foggiest idea what happens in it, beyond that. Over that is the second floor, where Mapson and I have a flat each. He's been very kind about that. They're good flats, and mine's as good as his. We don't interfere with each other. We live there our private lives, and you'd go a long way before you'd find a cosier flat than mine is. Well, I'm being chucked out. I must find another flat. Of course, Mapson will pay the rent. He pays everything."

We let him go on. He was in his stride now, getting off his chest his whole life since meeting Mapson. Mapson had been glad to have him at first, glad of the friendship of a man who was of a status different from his own, a man who could introduce him to a little money now and then ; and there was that old friendship in the early days of the war. I had often been puzzled by that and now asked Ray frankly what it was. And it was nothing—nothing much anyhow. " He loathed the Navy," Ray said, " and the chaps knew it, and knew, too, that he was in a blue funk about what would happen if we ever got into action. So was I in a blue funk, if it comes to that, and so were most of the chaps, too, but we put a good face on it, and were determined to do our best. But Mapson wasn't like that. It haunted him, and below decks he couldn't keep off it. He had a whole gang of them shivering with his own fears, and they took what was the natural way out and turned on him. I always stood up for Mapson, and said he'd be as good as the rest of us if it came to the pinch, and one way and another I looked after him. So there was this queer friendship between us. And what's more, I was right. Long after I'd left the ship she was in action, and it only needed a whiff of the real thing to put Mapson on his feet. He was all right after that, though, as it happened, he was never in action again."

All of which tallied with what I had imagined about Bernard Mapson. Combined with his love of money there was a capacity to remember a friend and he hadn't met many in his life. Nor did he meet many again. Ray's association with him in his early days as a financier was much on the lines of that old friendship in the battleship. Mapson, I imagine, was shivering in his shoes, though now he had learned to put a braver face on life. Ray's belief in him, and the small ways in which he was able to help him, had hitched up in his mind with the older association, and explained a lot. But now there was the question of the flat. In short, there was the question of Mrs. Bernard Mapson, who had been Miss Rosamund Hornbrook. I have no doubt that Mapson had fought bravely enough for Ray and the flat, but Mrs. Mapson had won.

Ray fumbled inside his coat and produced the letter that had come that morning. " Dear Ray. We're up here in Scotland, never mind where, and Rosamund and I have been talking about the set-up when we come back. She's been out to Whitecotes with me, and likes the place well enough, though there are some changes she wants to make there. But the chief thing is London. She wants a home there, and is willing enough to have it over my offices. As a matter of fact, St. Peter's Square is a pretty good address, as she calls it. She's seen my flat there, and thinks something can be made of it, but she wants more room. She has sketched out a scheme, and this involves your flat, too. In a word, the two flats will have to be turned into one, with some knocking down of the walls and a lift right through the building, so that there will be private access. Fortunately ours is an end house, so this access needn't be through the offices at all, but could be a lift in a kind of tube built on at one side. I've told Rosamund to go ahead and plan it out as she sees it, and when that is done I'll get in the experts to give the plans a once-over.

" Of course, this means a new flat for you, but St. Peter's Square has a number of houses that have been turned into flats, and as a matter of fact I am the landlord of one or two of them, and I know that there'll soon be a flat available in No. 17. I'll get on to that as soon as I'm back, and anything you want done to it shall be done. In the meantime, I suggest you find any sort of room and start shifting your things, for Rosamund is all set for an immediate start.

" Weather up here pretty good. All the best, and with kind remembrances from Rosamund, Yours, Bernard."

I handed the letter to Chris, and he read it, too. It seemed to me a reasonable letter, even a generous one. Whatever Ray might think, men did get married, and rich men were inclined, in the beginning at all events, to pamper their wives and give them what they asked for. This was especially so if the rich man had been poor not so long ago, and if the woman were such a one as Rosamund Hornbrook, who, from the little I had seen and knew of her, was the sort of woman who liked to strike a bargain. And the letter had thought of Ray. It had made provision for him, though the feeling was growing on me that Mapson had long outgrown both Ray and his usefulness. There was a magnanimity about it, as of a man clinging on to an old friendship, though it meant nothing to him now but the friendship itself. It was clear that he, at all events, thought the letter reasonable and saw nothing in it that would cause offence. But, alas! Ray thought otherwise.

We took a turn through the Kensington streets. " You can spare the time, Ray ? " Chris asked.

" No one will miss me," Ray answered, and he went along with us rather gloomily, evidently making the most of this fact : No one will miss me.

We passed what was left of the morning in Kensington Gardens and then took lunch in a restaurant. No one mentioned Mapson's letter until lunch was over, and then Chris said : " Let's go back to your flat, Ray, and see if we can talk this thing out ? Shall we ? "

It was a good flat, well-furnished, with one long window in the sitting-room looking out on to bare trees. Across intervening gardens were other houses, and Ray pointed to one of them. " Belinda's flat is in that house," he said. " She hangs a hand-kerchief in the window when she's at liberty for a talk or a walk. I suppose that's one of the conveniences I shall have to do without."

I was glad to know that he was in touch with Belinda, but shocked by his depressed tone. " Sit down, Ray," I said, " and let me talk to you for five minutes."

He obediently dropped into a chair, and I said : " When your father was a great deal younger than you are, his father wanted him to go to Oxford. He didn't want to go, and said so, and said why. He had already made up his mind about what he wanted to do with his life, and he went out and did it. There was no Mapson, no Belinda tying handkerchiefs to a window. You've always wanted someone to hold your hand. It has always been Sandy's digs, or Mapson's enterprises, or Belinda's hand-kerchief. I can say all I've got to say about Mapson's letter in two words. He's been too kind to you. He's offering you another comfortable flat, to go on holding your hand. He likes to have you with him, and he's willing to go on paying for the privilege. How long his wife will want him to go on doing that is another matter. Don't you think it's time you pulled yourself together ? And I mean yourself—not Mapson, not Belinda, much as I like her. Find something to do, and do it. Then you can talk to these other people on your terms, not theirs."

Chris was open-mouthed in his chair, the letter in his hand. Ray was both astonished and infuriated. I had never in my life thought I should find myself quarrelling with my son, as though I were a fish-wife. I could see that Ray was longing to give me back such a harangue as I had given him, but he bit on his words and said quictly : " Well, what have *you* ever done ? "

He didn't know even what his father had done. This was the first time I had spoken to him about Frank's early days. As for me, it had been a " thing " between me and Frank that nothing about my beginnings need be known to the boy. I was just his mother, that was all, and I was beginning to wonder whether that, in itself, did not seem honour enough to Ray. I saw him in that cosy flat, enormously self-centred, Mapson's friend, Belinda's companion when it suited him to become so, grieving now because casually, as though he didn't matter, Rosamund Mapson had knocked a rung or two out of his ladder. For the first time in my life some real doubts about Ray began to take possession of me. There had been whisperings in my mind before this. Now they were full-voiced. " Tell him, Chris," I said.

Chris told him. If there was one thing that tickled Chris it was that now, for what it was worth, I was the " chatelaine " of the Rowans to which, so long ago, Mell had led me after my banging of the door in Cardiff. He was tickled, but, I also knew, full of admiration for my achievement. What I had wanted I had got by my own hands, coupled with better luck than comes to most people.

He didn't make too much of it. In his quiet way he told the story, not liking the job much, but leaving out nothing that

255

mattered. His only burst of enthusiasm was when he told how Frank had thrown Ronald Lilywhite into the creek at Dros-y-Mor. " I wish I had been there," he said. " I wish I'd seen that. I should like to have had a boat-hook to hold him under."

" On the whole, Ray," he said, " you've got a pretty good mother, and when you ask ' What have *you* ever done ? '—well, I think you have the answer now. It hasn't been a bad record, all things considered. And, if I may add a word of my own, I think you owe Alice an apology for the question."

" No," I said. " There'll be no apologies between me and Ray. But I am sick of hearing Ray say ' Nobody will miss me '. There are plenty of people who would miss you very much, but I still think you'd better give some thought to making yourself a person who will be missed."

I think we saved Ray, so to speak, as he was going down for the third time. He had been coddled and cosseted so much that this opposition from Rosamund Hornbrook, coming through Mapson, had been too much for him. He had had his own way —and, though he was my son I can't say that it was much of a way—for too long. It was time to pull him up. How we were to do it was the problem at the moment. He made a show of contrition, thanked Chris for the tale he had told, and kissed me in the most dutiful way. I think Chris and I were both wondering how the matter was to be carried on from there when there was a brisk knock at the door and Bernard Mapson entered.

He looked well. His face and hands were browned, and as men do when they return from a successful honeymoon he looked happy and well satisfied with himself. I don't know whether it is any part of the equipment of men of Mapson's sort to be immediately aware of atmosphere, but it was obvious that he knew he had stepped into a moment that was critical.

He took hold of it firmly. He shook hands with me and Chris, and then with Ray, and said : " Well, Ray. I've followed hot on my letter. I didn't intend to, but there are one or two things that called me here, and Rosamund agreed that we'd better get back at once. I left her at Whitecotes and came on by myself. The car's at the door. Would you mind getting in the despatch cases ? I'll be down in a moment, and then I want to have a talk with you."

Ray went, as though glad to be released from our thrall, and, after giving him a moment to get down the stairs, Mapson asked : " What's the matter with Ray ? "

I couldn't help contrasting the two men, and it was on the tip of my tongue to say : " You are," but I held it back. Mapson was on top of the world. I suppose he had by then reached a point at which his career was straight before him, with no more doubts and hesitations. He was a man to be reckoned with, and though I did not like the England that he and his sort were increasingly producing about us, still there he was : a man with an objective, all his powers bent on achieving it. Moreover, he was just back from a honeymoon. He had acquired the woman he wanted, and though I liked Rosamund Mapson no more than I liked a Mapson building or a Mapson " development " scheme, still, there she was, and she was Mapson's. All this success in acquisition was about him like an atmosphere, like a confidence. Like everything that I didn't find in Ray.

" I'm sorry Rosamund isn't here to meet you," he said. " But she's taken it into her head to stay at Whitecotes till I have a flat here fit for her to live in. I'll motor out every night. No distance. Did Ray tell you about the flat ? "

" Yes," Chris said. " He tells us that you're taking this flat as well as the one next door."

" Yes," Mapson said. " I suppose my flat's all right for a bachelor but what Rosamund is after is a town house. It'll amount to that before we're through with it. It'll mean a bit of inconvenience to Ray for just a moment, but I think we can get on top of that."

" Why are you bothering," I asked flatly, " about a bit of inconvenience to Ray ? Surely, he's as capable as the next man of putting up with a bit of inconvenience ? "

Mapson laughed. " It's a way I've got into."

" Let me tell you, Mr. Mapson," I said, " that it's a thoroughly bad way."

Now it was said, and Mapson saw that both Chris and I were in earnest about something. " Well," he said, " Ray's in a special category. You know my story as well as the next man. You've been to my room when I was lodging in Pimlico, and you know what Ray meant to me then."

" Don't let's go into all that. It was a long time ago, and you and Ray have become very different people since then. You have become prosperous and Ray has become a thoroughly discontented idle fellow. Tell me frankly : is he pulling his weight with you ? "

" He's worth his weight in gold to me."

It was the first evasion I had heard Mapson use. " That's one way of putting it," I said, " but it doesn't answer my question. There was a time when perhaps he was worth his weight in gold to you, but you know as well as I do that that time is long past, and that while you have gone ahead Ray has stood still. I'll go so far as to say that he has gone backwards, and that you know it."

Mapson must have had many tough talks in his time, and although, fundamentally and in the long run, they had been about human beings and how they should spend their days here on this earth, it hadn't seemed so to him. It had seemed all about buildings and roads and " schemes " of one sort or another, and I doubt whether he had given a moment's thought to men and women and children, to noise, to screaming traffic, to the death of the England we had known. That was why I kept him to one point : what was to become of Ray ?

" You have," I said, " been kindness itself to Ray, so please, Mr. Mapson, don't think that Chris and I are concerned with what we might call his bodily welfare with you. But if you look at it fairly you will agree with me that he hasn't made a single step forward while you have made a score."

" Besides which," Chris put in, " don't forget Mrs. Mapson."

" I shall know, as I have always known, how to keep my private and my personal affairs separate," Mapson said.

" There is a point where they overlap," Chris assured him. " For example, Mrs. Mapson wants this flat and yours knocked into one. Ray doesn't."

" What on earth has a thing like that to do with Ray ? " For the first time he looked annoyed, even angry.

" We've spent some hours with Ray," Chris said, " and we've heard a lot about his discontents, including this flat. Incidentally, it was an eye-opener to me that a young man, who is supposed to have some sort of job to do, could casually take a few hours off."

Mapson got to his feet. " I must go down now," he said. " There are a few things to be looked to. Would you like me to speak to Ray ? "

He was considerate to the end. He would do nothing without our permission. " Yes," I said.

9

Ray, sent up by Mapson, came to say good-bye. " I'll have it all out with Bernard," he said, in a tone which assured me that he had no idea of what, I felt sure, was the disillusionment before him.

It was getting on in the afternoon when we went out into St. Peter's Square. " Now that we're in Kensington," Chris said, " what about calling on old Mamie ? I haven't many relatives left in the world : this old sort-of-an aunt, one very good wife, and a stepson."

I knew he wanted for a time to jerk my mind away from Ray and his affairs, and I humoured him, for I myself was not averse from forgetting that painful topic for awhile.

Rosy Midge let us into the flat. She said : " I've put her to bed, but the doctor says we've gotter get a nurse in regular or put 'er in a nursing 'ome."

So we had stepped out of one trouble into another. Rosy evidently thought we had heard of Mamie's illness, whatever it might be, and that we had made a call to see how she was.

We went into the sitting-room which, with the bedroom and kitchen, made up the flat. There was a canvas on an easel, and Mamie had evidently been at work up to the last moment. It was an imagined picture of the creek at Dros-y-Mor, with the tide up, and hovering among trees in the background was a spectral representation of Poor Judith. We sat there and looked at it in silence, all faint wavering lines, Judith faintest of all. One or two family Gainsboroughs and Reynoldses looked serenely on at Mamie's last endeavours.

We were both overcome. " Sit down, Rosy," Chris said with difficulty.

Rosy sat down and put a corner of her apron to her eyes. " It wasn't my fault," she said. " I did everything for 'er."

" No, no," Chris said gently. " You're a good girl. Now tell us all about it. What happened ? "

Nothing much had happened. It was simply that Mamie was getting old, that she was fast reaching the end of her tether. She was painting more and more. She had been painting right up to yesterday, and then she had put down her brushes and said that she was very tired. She would go to bed and sleep for awhile. She had eaten nothing, and this morning Rosy had called in a doctor.

" When is he coming again ? " Chris asked.

" He's comin' any time," Rosy said. " 'E should be 'ere any minute. I was worryin' my 'eart out all alone, an' I've been awake all night."

Chris patted her shoulder. " Now you go in and sit with Miss James-Villiers," he said. " I'll see the doctor when he comes."

She went in, and we sat there, thinking how differently this day had turned out from what was in our minds when we left the Rowans. We had thought of having a chat with Ray, and possibly of taking him and Belinda out to dinner somewhere. Well, we had found his life if not in ruins at any rate badly in need of repair. And we had found Mamie we knew not how.

" You'd better go in," Chris said, " and have a look at her. I'll wait for the doctor and bring him when he comes."

I went in on tiptoe. I don't know why, but Rosy, thinking, I suppose, that that was the right thing to do, had half-drawn the curtains so that the room was almost in darkness. Mamie was a hump under the sheets, breathing rather loudly, and, when I put a hand to her forehead, hot to the touch. She knew that someone was there, perhaps even who it was. I don't know, but she smiled faintly. There was nothing I could do, so I brought a chair and sat beside Rosy, holding her hand. The child seemed more in need of comfort than the old woman who had reached some ultimate peace. Rosy suddenly started to cry, the hot drops falling on my hand. She was such a mite of a thing, so proud of her position, and now it had all broken down under her. I didn't want her crying there, so I picked her up, surprised at her little weight, and carried her through the door to Chris. He took her on his knees as though she had been a baby, and I wiped her eyes with his handkerchief. He said nothing, but made comforting noises, and I left them there and resumed my watch.

An hour must have passed before the doctor came, a young man, having, I imagine, almost his first brush with death. He was very quiet, very serious. Chris, leaving Rosy outside, came in with him. He did what I suppose are all the orthodox things with a stethoscope and what not. He spoke in whispers. " I doubt if she'll see the night through," he said. " She's just exhausted, thoroughly tired with being alive. Are you relatives of hers ? "

Chris explained the situation. " I could send a nurse in," the doctor said. " But honestly I don't think a nurse could do anything but watch while she died. I should say it's a matter of hours, if that."

It wasn't even that. She died that evening while Chris and I sat by her bed, and Rosy cried in the room without. In her will, which we found a few days later, she left Chris her father's cuff-links and all the pictures that had been painted by herself. The Gainsboroughs and the Reynoldses were left to the National Gallery.

Chapter XIII

Bernard Mapson found time in his busy life to come out to the Rowans to see Chris and me. He said nothing either to Ray or to Mrs. Mapson, but himself wrote a letter telling us that he would be there on such a day, taking it for granted that all days were much of a muchness to me and Chris, as indeed they were. We were pretty well off, and though we could have done with the Reynoldses and the Gainsboroughs, which were then fetching a pretty penny in the sales-rooms, still, Mamie had made Chris her " residuary legatee ", which wasn't, as we found to our surprise, a bad thing to be. But this came a little later, and it was on the day after the old lady's funeral that Mapson's letter reached us. It merely stated the time of his arrival and took it that that would do for us.

He came the next day, driving himself. He did not stay to a meal, but accepted a cup of coffee as he sat in our small sitting-room, looking down over the winter landscape. I should have given a lot to know what he was thinking as he studied that wilderness of trees and fields : probably how he could have made it blossom as the rose with tall vertical shafts of buildings threaded by motorways, and gay with changing coloured lights.

" I've been thinking," he said suddenly, " that Ray needs a good holiday. With pay, of course. Say for a month or six weeks. You've got a place, he has often told me, in Cornwall."

I told him that I had, and that it was occupied at the moment. Mell had taken Laura there to finish his book.

" Yes," he said. " By that man Conybeare—a nephew of your first husband, isn't he ? "

He knew everything. It was part of the Mapson technique to know everything, even if it didn't seem to matter much, about anything he was concerned in.

" He's the father, isn't he, of that girl Belinda that Ray goes about with now and then ? Mrs. Mapson used to know her."

Seeing that Dros-y-Mor and all that went on there seemed as well known to him as the back of his hand, Chris and I merely murmured our assent.

" What about that ? " Mapson asked. " D'you think you could get Ray fitted in there while he has a good rest ? Frankly, he and Mrs. Mapson don't see eye to eye about her taking over the flat next to mine."

" I'm very glad to hear that," Chris said surprisingly. " It's the first time since Ray has been—what shall we call it ?—one of your *entourage* ?—that he has shown any will of his own. It's your flat. You can do what you like with it. But I'm glad he's reared up about *something*, though I think it's foolish of him to have reared up about that."

It was very much my own thought, but I doubted the wisdom of putting it quite so frankly at that moment. But Mapson was not in the least disturbed. " Of course," he said, " I shall go ahead with the scheme that Mrs. Mapson has set her mind on. But I agree that it's something new to see Ray ' rear up ', as you call it. Frankly, I've been rather disappointed with him. He hasn't shown the initiative that I expected from him. That's why I wanted him to have a good holiday—to pull himself together."

I refilled his coffee-cup, and said: "And when he has pulled himself together, I suppose he goes back to you?"

"This isn't a land of slaves," Mapson replied, sententiously, if inaccurately. "I'd like to have Ray back, of course. I owe much to him. But he can please himself. He's been, all this time, perfectly at liberty to please himself. I just wanted you to know that whenever he likes he can take a good holiday."

We thanked him, and said we'd talk to Ray about it. "I wish you would," he said, and got up. "Now, if you'll excuse me."

We accompanied him to his car and watched him drive off, not in the direction of London. "He's just taken us in on the way," Chris said. "I suppose he's off to see a new bit of England's green and pleasant land ripe for development."

"We'd better ask Ray to come and spend a week-end with us," I said.

"Yes. And then we could all go down into Cornwall together, if Ray agrees. And if Mell agrees, too. We could throw Belinda in as a bit of weight. Perhaps she can get away."

"I've got a hunch," I said, "that the late Miss Rosamund Hornbrook won't be sorry to see the back of Ray."

"I've felt myself that they don't exactly hit it off."

"Well, how would you feel if you were a newly married woman and you saw a young man about your husband doing precious little, all because he was once rather friendly in the Navy?"

"Not having been, at any stage in my chequered career, a newly married woman, I can't say. But I do feel that, for Ray and all of us, there's more involved than knocking down a wall between two flats."

2

I wrote to Laura, and while we were awaiting her answer Ray came and stayed with us at the Rowans. The work of knocking

down the wall had begun and he had nowhere else to go. Chris
and I told him of Mapson's desire that he should take a long
holiday, and he replied : " Well, if he wants to get rid of me . . ."

We had finished dinner and were in our small sitting-room
with the lamps lit, and I had agreed with Chris that he should
make the opening moves. He was rather taken aback by Ray's
tepid reception of our scheme, and said : " You know, Ray, it's
time we talked rather seriously of this. The question isn't so
much whether Mr. Mapson wants to get rid of you, but whether
you shouldn't get rid of him. You've been with him now for
some years. During that time he's gone ahead at a great pace in
whatever direction that he wants to go ahead in. But have you ?
Aren't you rather where you were at the beginning ? Hasn't
the time come for you to ask yourself whether you wouldn't
be better off if you made a clean break with him and began on
a new line ? "

Ray's answer shocked me. Stuffing tobacco into a pipe, he
looked up with a smile and said : " I don't know why you talk
to me in this paternal fashion, sir. After all, you're not my
father."

I should not have been surprised if Chris had given it up then,
if he had flown into anger and told the boy to go to the devil in
his own way. I was never so proud of Chris as when he held up
his hand to stay my own angry retort, and said, returning Ray's
smile : " No. But in the words of the old melodramas, I have
your welfare at heart, my boy. However, we can drop melodrama
on both sides. You needn't call me ' sir ', but just Chris as you
have always done. What about it ? Mapson didn't come
out here for fun, you know. He's always smooth and polite,
but it's as well to look behind his words. He's one of those
men."

Ray's mood of defiance dropped from him as he listened to
these words, so calmly spoken. " Mapson's all right," he said.
" It's Mrs. Mapson."

" Whatever it is," Chris said, " you may depend that taking
over your flat is only a beginning. New wives, you know, don't
like their husbands to have too many friends, especially "—and
he spoke the words remorselessly—" friends who seem to be only
hangers-on. The last thing you would want, I should think,

would be to become any sort of disturbance in Mr. Mapson's married life."

Ray was overcome, though I don't think he saw with what difficulty Chris made his way through his few measured words, how deeply he was stirred beneath the exterior that he fought hard to keep calm.

" I'm sorry for what I said," Ray conceded. " Forgive me. I'm going out for a walk."

He went, dark though the night was, and I sat there thinking that " a walk " had always been Frank's way of meeting difficulties. I took Chris's hand in mine, and said : " Thank you, darling."

" It was hard going," he admitted ; and we sat for an hour until we heard Ray come in and go straight up to bed.

3

Terrible things happened during the war, and they will go on happening as long as there are wars, and after that, too. Rosy Midge was a case in question. Rosy had literally nowhere to go after Mamie died. She was now at the Rowans, a bundle of nerves and apprehensions. It was useless for me and Chris to assure her that " everything would be all right." " Not for me, they won't," she said, and though, thus far, she had fought her way with courage, or at least with persistence, Mamie's death was a blow from which she did not soon recover.

Her devotion to Mamie was absolute, and there she was now, believing herself once more abandoned, a plaything for gods and men.

Chris and I persuaded her to come with us to the Rowans, and she was with us now, a mite of a thing, though, I suppose, she was then in her teens. She was that wonderful thing, so much written about to-day, a teenager, fortunately beyond the age when Authority could take hold of her and tell her to do this and go there. For better or worse, she was ours.

I often thought of the days, when I was little older than Rosy herself, and I was a new-comer to the Rowans, introduced by Mell, and Bryan Graves had wanted me to become one of the family. I don't know what he would have made of Rosy, and I don't know what we should have made of her, if Ray had not said, while we were at breakfast on the morning after Chris had had his talk with him : " I'm going for a long walk this morning. What about Rosy ? She hasn't been for a walk since I've been down here."

Rosy, unobtrusive as a ghost, had been shuttling in and out of the kitchen, and she heard Ray's remark. It was naturally uttered, for Ray had been brought up by and with Em Pritt. It had been as customary a thing for him to go out with Em as with me or Frank. Whatever else he was, he was not a snob. So it was natural now for him to say to Rosy : " It's as good a day as we are likely to get at this time of year, and I don't think we'll have rain. Put a warm coat on, and let's go when you have washed up."

Rosy said nothing, and Ray, with a glance at me and Chris, said : " If my mother can spare you ? "

I was glad he had thought of that, and said : " Rosy could do with a walk. Go now. Go and get your coats. Chris and I will see to the bit of washing-up."

Rosy was still wordless, but she went and soon presented herself wrapped up in a magenta garment that set my teeth on edge. It was clear that she was obeying orders. She had obeyed orders all her young life, and saw nothing remarkable in the present situation. For a moment the thought flashed through my mind of my own secret walks in Cardiff with Ronald Lilywhite. But, whatever Ray might be, he was no Ronald and there was nothing secret about the present situation. But as he took a stick out of the hall stand I said : " Don't overdo it. I don't suppose Rosy is as used to walking as you are. When shall we expect you back ? Are you likely to be in for lunch ? "

" I don't know," Ray answered. " It all depends on the weather, and the sort of walker Rosy is."

Chris and I went as far as the gate and waved them off. We did not return at once to the washing-up, but sat in the drawing-room looking at one another. " Well, what do you make of that? " I asked at length.

Chris was filling his morning pipe and did not answer in a hurry. Then he said : " Frankly, I don't know what to make of it. Is it a smack in the eye for us ? Is Ray saying : ' I can get on very well without your company ? ' Or is it a sign of grace ?

I don't know. But I do know that you were right to let them go. We'd better wash up, and then we can go for a bit of a walk ourselves. In the opposite direction."

And that is what we did. When we got back I prepared lunch, but they did not come in for it. The weather had remained fine. There was even a bit of wintry sunshine and a bud or two on the trees. It was a good day for a walk, but I could sense that Chris was as anxious as I was that this walk should end, that we should know what had happened to the two strange voyagers.

4

By the afternoon post there came a letter from Laura.

"Dear Alice and Chris.—You could not have chosen a better time for coming to Dros-y-Mor. Mell, who sends his love to you both, is on the last lap of his book and is taking a breather before finishing it. I don't suppose anyone will read it except a don here and there, for who, in these days, cares twopence about the Romans and what they did or didn't do ? I could wish for an *immense* sale for Mell's sake, but really he is not interested in sales one little bit, and says there are three people in England, and possibly one in America, whose good word he would like to have. Given that, he doesn't care what happens. I sometimes think he ought to have been a don himself, and that all his years at the Foreign Office were wasted. Certainly, I have never known him happier or engaged on a job more after his own heart. He keeps me busy typing and retyping, for he has a mania for saying just what he means in just the right words. However, you will know about all that when you come—from me, if not from him, for he's as close as a vice about what he is doing. Good Foreign Office training, I suppose.

"Dros-y-Mor is ready for you, and you will find it very beautiful at this time of the year. I often wander through the woods as far as Joe Duncombe's cottage, and I must say that, having little to do with the motor-car, which we don't use once a week, he keeps the woods and the paths through them very lovely. The camellias are in flower, and the mimosa, and things are beginning to sprout all along the stream. Sometimes I have a peep into Ray's shed, but I am only allowed to get as far as the outside of the window. Em Pritt has the door key, which she says Ray ' entrusted ' to her, and she is so serious and solemn about this trust that I dare do no more than peep within. I know that once a week she is there, and gives the place what she calls a ' good go-over ' so that when Ray comes all his possessions, including his truckle-bed, will be waiting as if never left.

" Mell is rather a sybaritic writer, and doesn't use Frank's old shed. He works here in the big library, so now and then I go along to Frank's shed and see that it is kept in the order that you would like.

" We are both looking forward to Belinda's visit and hope she'll be able to travel with you. We'll manage to tuck you all in somewhere, including this strangely named Rosy Midge. So come, please. Ever with love, Laura.

" P.S.—Joe Duncombe keeps the old dinghy afloat, so there'll be that, if it means anything."

Ray and Rosy came back in time for tea, which Rosy insisted on taking in the kitchen. She was very excited, which is something I had never seen in her before. " Oo ! All them trees," she kept saying. " All them trees and fields and woods ! " Ray was tranquil. He had walked something out of himself. He talked calmly, as he had not talked since he had been with us. " I felt like a seasoned explorer," he said, " introducing a tourist to a new land. D'you know that girl has never been out of London ? I suppose, looking from this place, she must have got an idea that she was surrounded by something different, but to be *in* it, that was something else."

It had not occurred to me that there was anywhere in England a person who had known nothing but the London parks and streets, the trees (fast falling, alas !) in London squares, the back alleys and ruined streets. Even in our far off Manchester days, my mother and I had now and then freshened ourselves with a glimpse of Cheshire, its meadows and meres, and nostalgically my mother would tell me of her own girlhood days when this was her world—a world of farms and beasts and harvests. I had heard of youngsters, driven into the country by fears of bombs and fires, who had come back, terrified of the night silences and the night calls of birds, and the absence of all that to them was familiar and accustomed—the corner-shop and the lamp-post and the companionship of the streets. But as Ray talked of their long walk that day it became clear that Rosy was not one of these. She and Ray had seen the beech-woods budding, and newly-dropped lambs in a field tottering on uncertain legs and crying with loud bleats for their dams, and they had listened to birds trying over the opening notes of a new song. At lunchtime they had fed in a cottage, and that was something else Rosy had never done before. The Ritz or the Savoy could not have terrified her more, and she had been silent and withdrawn, merely nibbling and looking timidly about her.

"And d'you know what I'm going to do now, if you and Chris will allow me? I'm going straight to bed. After that long walk a sleep will do me no harm, and I've been sleeping badly of late."

He pushed back his chair, kissed me, and went with a wave of the hand to Chris.

We listened for a time to Rosy clattering with the tea-things in the kitchen, and then Chris said: "Well, thank God Mapson has married a wife who knows her own mind."

I didn't follow his reasoning, and said so. "Mapson was good for Ray," he explained, "while Ray could give him companionship at a time when he had no other, when Ray could help him on to his feet. Once he was there, he went ahead like wildfire and Ray simply tagged after him. Ray is no more interested in what Mapson is doing than I am, but that damned friendship, whatever it may have been, was stuck in Mapson's gullet, and there it was. It was magnanimous on his part. Give him that. It's the only thing I like about Mapson, but I think it was wrong-headed. Give Ray a salary, give him a flat, give him anything that's going. And all the time there was this misbegotten loyalty that kept Ray at his heels. That is why I thank God for Mrs. Mapson. At the moment, she's the only thing that counts with Mapson. As I see the man, he spent too long being able to give nothing. Now that he's rolling in money, it's a sort of self-indulgence to have someone to give to. It was Ray. Now it's Mrs. Mapson. She knows what she wants and she's going to get it. And Ray isn't on her programme."

"But what's all this to do with a walk with Rosy?"

"For Rosy read Mapson at the time when he was no-one,

when Ray was showing him about. That's what Ray has been doing all day—showing someone about, showing new things— and I think he's always best when someone is dependent on him."

" Well, thank goodness Rosy isn't a Mapson. She's not likely to drain him."

" No. I think all he wanted was companionship ; but it turned out better than I expected. Who would have dreamed that he'd strike a girl who'd never seen a cow in a field ? He must have seemed like a magician unfolding marvels."

5

I rang up Belinda in her flat that night and asked her to take lunch with me the next day in Kensington. She was able to do so, and as Chris and Ray had amicably agreed to go walking together that day, I saw them off, helped Rosy with the washing-up and the beds, and then told her that I would like her to go with me. She had every objection off pat. She had never been in a motor-car before, she would be terrified out of her life, who was to be there if anyone called, and so forth.

" I think we'll chance anyone calling," I said. " After all, it will be a perfectly simple matter for them to go away again. I expect, if anyone *should* call, they'll survive not seeing me. As for the motor-car, I always drive slowly, and you'll be quite safe. Now, let's have a look at your clothes."

" Well, here they are, mum," she said practically. " I've got 'em all on."

" No, no. Let's see your wardrobe," I said, for the idea had seized me of fitting Rosy out before we went into Cornwall.

But this was another matter. Rosy resisted, and at last I saw that she was ashamed of the few poor rags that her box contained.

" Sit down, Rosy," I said. " I want to tell you something. No. Put on your hat. I'll tell you as we go along."

We got the motor-car on to the road and Rosy timorously took her place where ordered next to the driver's seat. It was rather a cold morning, and I tucked her under an imitation fur rug. As I started the car she was stroking the rug with an almost frightened appreciation.

"Rosy," I said, "did you know that when I first came to the Rowans I was just about as old as you are ? A lady named Mrs. Graves lived there then. Her husband was an M.P."

Rosy wanted to know what an M.P. was, and when I had explained that it meant a Member of Parliament she was over-awed by the knowledge. She had seen the Houses of Parliament but had no idea of what happened there, convinced only that it had nothing to do with girls like her. "We didn't see much of him," I said. "He came home only at the week-ends, and some-times not even then. But what I wanted to tell you was that I was Mrs. Graves's servant-girl."

"Oo, mum ! You can't have been ! "

I ignored this, and said : "When you were ashamed for me to peep into your box of clothes, I remembered something. When I came here I had no clothes of my own to come in. I was staying at the time in a parson's house in Cardiff. His sister was Mrs. Graves, and his wife had a lot of old clothes that she used to give to poor people. She fitted me out, and I came in a lot of old things that weren't my own. So I very well know how you felt about your old box."

We were humming along nicely, and Rosy's fingers were still stroking the rug. All that I had said was evidently like a fairy-story to her. She didn't know whether to believe it or not. Out of deference, which she had learned too young, having nothing rebellious in her make-up, she preferred to act as though she didn't. "So we are going, Rosy," I said, "to a nice shop in Kensington, and there we are going to buy you a complete set of clothes."

I think I was more excited than she was. All she could say was : "Oo, mum ! They'll see all the old stuff I've got on," but I felt like a girl excited by the prospect of dressing a doll from top to toe. Rosy wasn't much bigger.

It was still early when we arrived at Kensington, and I found a garage to put the car into, and then took Rosy for a cup of coffee. A country cottage with Ray was one thing. This was another. She literally clung to my arm as we passed into those sacred precincts. There, as I had expected, were all the old ladies with bluish hair discussing what would have happened if they had drawn a trump last night and matters of equal importance. The light was rather dim and the electric light bulbs glowed through crimson silk. The carpet was mossy under our feet. If I had been leading Rosy to the altar of Canterbury cathedral she could not have been more subdued. An acolyte in coffee-coloured linen took our order, and Rosy allowed herself at last to speak, or rather to whisper : " Oo, mum ! You'll have to pay for all this ! "

She sipped her coffee as timorously as a mouse who expects at any moment to be chivvied from its crumb of cheese in a corner, and she wasn't sorry when we were on the pavement outside. There she could refresh her soul with accustomed things—the roaring of cars and buses and the come-and-go of people. The sun began a watery shine, and she said : " Now we can go home."

I was glad that at any rate she had said " home " and not simply " back ". Chris and I had tried to make the Rowans seem to her like home, and now she went so far as to tug my arm in the direction of the garage where we had left the car.

" But, Rosy," I said, " we've promised to take lunch with Miss Conybeare. You know her. You've met her at Miss James-Villiers's flat."

The thought of Belinda seemed to calm her a little, and I was emboldened to add : " And then there's the clothes. We must see about them first."

" But that was only one of your jokes, mum," she assured me. " What I've got's good enough for me. Though it would be a joke, too, if I was dressed like you ! "

She gave a little throaty chuckle at the thought of what a rich joke this would be ; and in the midst of that I whisked her through the swinging brass-gleaming doorway of one of the stores. Here again carpet was under our feet. Lighted lifts were shuttling up and down. Endless vistas opened before us, shining with the world's necessaries and luxuries. We wandered through it all. We went up in the lifts. " First floor ladies' undergarments. Second floor carpets. Third floor skirts, coats, blouses and stockings. Fourth floor modern antiques."

Rosy wandered at my side like an intruder into the riches of Ali Baba's cave. She had never seen anything like it : clocks and cutlery, hangings and carpets, books, boots and blouses, kitchens and drawing-rooms all arranged and ready to live in ; clothes, clothes, clothes. At first frightened, then fascinated, then at a standstill, admiring the women's shoes.

An efficient and official woman now boarded us, drifting ships ready to be captured. " Can I be of any help, madam ? "

I took her aside and left Rosy enraptured at the shoes tapering off in a way guaranteed to crush any foot to pulp, and furnished with stilts as though they had been designed for shepherds in the Landes. I told the woman what I wanted, which was briefly to have Rosy dressed from top to toe. " But none of those shoes," I said. " Give her something to walk ten miles in. I leave the rest to your taste."

The appeal to her own taste was enough. " Certainly, madam. I'll persuade her."

" I'll have a stroll round," I said. " You'll find me at this spot in an hour's time. And have all the old clothes made into a parcel and sent to this address."

I gave her my address at the Rowans, and Rosy, with many a longing lingering look behind, was borne away, like a lamb being led to its first shearing.

I strolled, and found myself in the book department. There, well displayed, were " the complete works of Frank Melvill". Frank, to my advantage, was enjoying a renaissance. I lingered for a long time, turning over pages, recalling the very phrases that he had written in the old shed at Dros-y-Mor and that I had typed in my little room. I didn't want these ; I had all his first editions ; but I had the lot parcelled and sent as a present to Belinda, with a note.

Among the pots and pans of a model kitchen I thought of Frank, and what he would want me to do with Ray, and whether he would approve of my mad prank with Rosy. Yes, it was just his line. Any old clothes had always done for him, but he liked to see a well-dressed woman. I remembered how he had admired my green outfit with the golden shoes, and how Chris had liked it, too, and how Chris had come back to Dros-y-Mor from Plymouth and handed me the too expensive jewel. I wondered whether Frank had noticed that, whether he would approve of me now.

But it's no good playing about among ghosts. I was content

273

to leave that to Mamie. I was exhausted by my ponderings and perambulations and sank down on a chair where I had promised to behold the official woman's handiwork. It was good enough, but it was Rosy. She had merely added herself to all the things she was shy of. She came balanced on a sensible pair of shoes, carrying a stylish umbrella, and with a hat that wasn't a crow's nest on her head. I cannot remember what else she wore. But I remember that, when I had paid and we were leaving the store, she whispered : " And everything underneath is as good as what shows, and they gave me a special little room all by myself to change in."

So, with my renovated Rosy, who was Rosy all the time, though made over as Mapson might make over an old building, I went forth. She was longing for rain so that she might open her umbrella. We went to the restaurant where I had arranged to meet Belinda at lunch, and she was there already to greet us. She didn't look half as well-dressed as Rosy, but she was Belinda. She had often met Rosy at Mamie's flat, but she expressed no wonder at the apparition that was at my side, though Miss Midge was evidently expecting that she should do so. She merely shook hands with Rosy, kissed me, and took us to her table. She was rather pale and looked as though a holiday would do her no harm. She enquired about Chris and Ray.

" He's doing nothing at the moment," I said. " He's left Mr. Mapson."

" Yes. I knew that. I've been out to dinner with Rosamund and her new husband. Not at the flat. That's in a state of chaos. Rosamund and Mr. Mapson are living at Whitecotes for the moment. They come in every day, he to his office and she to superintend what is happening at the London place. I don't see much of her now. I think she took me out to dinner just to show off her new husband. You know she used to write little bits in the newspapers about people. She's finding it an agreeable change to be written about instead of writing."

I could well imagine that.

" I think," Belinda said, " she's glad to be rid of Ray. She never liked him. What is he going to do now ? "

" Well, first of all he's coming down into Cornwall with us. Your father has surfaced for a moment from the Romans and is taking a breather. So this is a good moment to go. I expect your mother has written to you about it. There'll be a lot of us: me and Chris, Ray and Rosy, and you, I hope. We'll all fit in somehow."

Belinda looked worried. " Yes," she said. " I shall be there. I've got a bit of holiday due to me, and I can take it now. But you've rather shelved my question. I know that Ray is going to Cornwall with you. But after that, I mean. What is he going to do ? "

" Well, if it comes to that, what has he done since he came out of the Navy ? "

" Nothing," Belinda said. " Nothing but hold Mr. Mapson's hand while Mr. Mapson found his feet."

" And earn a very good salary for doing it," I reminded her. " Mr. Mapson was always most generous to him."

But she wouldn't let me side-step like that. " Yes, yes, I know," she said rather impatiently. " But that's over. Mrs. Mapson doesn't like him and for the moment Mrs. Mapson says the last word. So I mean *now*. What's Ray going to do now ? "

" We'll have to see. We'll have a chance to think. And so will he."

" He tells me nothing."

I was wondering why he should, what occasion there had been for him to tell her anything, when Rosy surprisingly intervened. " 'E tells me a lot," she said. " We 'ad a long, long walk, and 'e told me all about trees and what sort they were, an' flowers an' lambs an' everything."

Rosy, even in her new clothes, was so insignificant a little thing that we had overlooked her, tended to talk as though she were not present. I was aware that her intervention, this reminder that she was there, that she was a human being, put Belinda on her guard, stopped whatever she was going to say, and left her for the rest of the meal talking only of indifferent things.

" Well," she said when the meal was over, " I must be back to the office. Fix it all up with Mother, and take it for granted that I'll be with you. You'll go by road, I expect ? "

I said that we would, and she said : " You'll never get us all with our luggage into that little car of yours. You and Chris go down together, with Rosy. Ray and I can travel together in my car."

This seemed a sensible arrangement, and we left it at that. She had only one other thing to say. Bending suddenly and kissing Rosy, she said : " Rosy, you look sweet in your new clothes."

Rosy, who was not used to any attention whatever, blushed deeply and got up to whisper in Belinda's ear : " An' they're all just as nice underneath."

We were back at the Rowans by tea-time, but Chris and Ray had not returned. We took tea together, and then Rosy said : " I suppose, mum, I'd better change now into some working clothes."

" What you were standing up in won't be back till to-morrow's parcel postman comes."

" I daresay I'll manage," she said. " There are a few old things still in my box."

I left her to it, and went out to meet Ray and Chris. The day was declining, though it was still a lovely evening of early spring, with birdsong and opening leaves—a good time of year, I thought, for being at Dros-y-Mor. It was long since I had seen it, except in the word-pictures of Laura's letters, and I hoped that Ray and Belinda would find it as good as they remembered. Belinda that day had certainly seemed in need of a holiday, and I wondered as I strolled along what she was going to tell me about Ray, what had been on the tip of her tongue when Rosy's presence suddenly stopped her.

I met my men coming along the road, talking and laughing. That was a good thing. They had never before spent so long in one another's company, and all seemed to have gone well.

" You two seem happy," I greeted them.

" We've been swopping war-time reminiscences," Chris said, " and the Senior Service has been keeping me in my place."

He was carrying a bunch of twigs. " We haven't forgotten Rosy and her education. Ray gathered these : hawthorn and beech and elm and a various assortment. We'll put them in a vase in her bedroom."

" I expect you're ready for your dinner. You'll have to do with a salad and cold meat to-night. I've been out all day."

" We've been feeding like fighting-cocks," Ray said. " Any snack will do."

They seemed very happy, and so was I as I went with them towards the Rowans.

6

We set out for Dros-y-Mor a week later. Belinda had arrived in her car at eight o'clock, and she and Ray went away together. It was nearly an hour later before Chris and I and Rosy followed them. The luggage had been stuffed into the car and we were waiting before the house for Rosy Midge. I had said nothing to Chris or Ray about buying her new clothes ; neither had she. Nor had she worn them at the Rowans. Now she suddenly appeared in all her glory, carrying her umbrella.

" Good lord ! " said Chris. " Who is this princess we are taking with us ? Turn round, Rosy, and let's have a look at you."

She obediently turned round, blushing furiously.

" Well, you look a fair treat," Chris said. " I feel honoured to have two well-dressed women in my charge to-day."

I intervened before Rosy had a chance to say anything about being as nice underneath, and told him of our raid upon Kensington. He laughed and said : " That'd better come out of my pocket. After all, I have the pleasure of escorting you both through England. Well, hop in at the back, Rosy. I've put a rug in there for you in case you're cold."

I wedged myself next to Chris, and through a mirror could see Rosy ensconcing herself behind us. It was the almost-fur rug that I had wrapped round her when we went to London. She was stroking the nap with appreciation, and then almost buried herself in it. It didn't take much to bury Rosy. And it didn't take much to make her feel happy. She was going on the first holiday of her young life, and she had new clothes on, and she was in a motor-car. I watched her place her umbrella not inconveniently remote, as though it might rain in the car at any moment, pull her rug about her, and put back her head into the upholstery.

It was a good day. The sun sparkled on the young year,

and I was as glad as Rosy herself that I was going on a holiday. Not that my life wasn't all holiday, in a sense. But it was long since I had seen Dros-y-Mor and Laura and Mell and Em Pritt and her husband. There were many memories to be renewed. There were the old sheds, there were the woods, bursting now with springtime beauty, there was the stream with its primulas, and there were the quarter-deck and the creek. Many memories. I was more excited than a child. A child would not have the memories.

We had to wake Rosy when we stopped at Exeter for lunch. Lulled by the motion of the car, she had fallen asleep with her head in that delicious upholstery. The hotel rather daunted her, as she had been daunted when we lunched with Belinda. She instinctively took my hand, which moved me very much, and strove hard to hold up her head with the best of them as we went into the dining-room. "Order something," Chris said, and he went away for a moment to give some commands about topping up the car with petrol.

"Well, Rosy," I said when we were alone, "are you enjoying yourself?"

"Oo, mum," she answered. "It's like being in 'Eaven. Nothing to do."

It was a new view of Heaven to me—an eternity of idleness—and I was not sure it would suit me if it came my way. But it was Rosy's idea, and I took her hand and gave it a reassuring squeeze; and a tiny hand it was, red and work-soaked, but a child's. I thought of my hands red and work-soaked like Rosy's, when I was in Manchester and at the Hon. Mrs. Lilywhite's in Cardiff, and how I had kept them under the sheet when Mell read to me in bed. And those old memories made me feel very tender to Rosy, sitting there in her new clothes, trying so hard to look as though dining in a hotel were an everyday event in her life. A small event, heaven knows, and one that would soon bore me stiff.

"How old are you, Rosy?"

"Fifteen, mum, so far as I can make out."

I should never have guessed she was so old. But I hadn't been born in an air-raid. I had missed the amenities of modern life.

Chris came back and we ate our lunch, and were soon on the road again. We took the car-ferry over the water at Plymouth, " and now we're in Cornwall," Chris announced.

" I was on this road with a rucksack on my back at the end of the first world war," I said. " It makes me feel a veteran."

" You don't look it," he assured me.

" I walked and walked. It was just such weather as this. And I ended up on the road outside what was then Ben Davies's cottage. I met Frank for the first time."

Chris did not answer. It was not often that we mentioned Frank to one another. It was not till Liskeard was behind us that he said : " I wish I could give you a son."

I knew that he often brooded about that. " You have given me everything else," I assured him.

" Yes," he said. " Everything else."

We were silent after that. A sadness seemed to have fallen on the day. Through the mirror I could see Rosy asleep again, and I myself, like her, was being lulled by the car's smooth running. My head nodded and soon I was asleep.

I wakened when a change in the car's tempo got through to my mind. We were passing over the granite setts of Truro. We ran on for a mile or so beyond the town, and then I said : " Let me drive for a bit, Chris. You have had enough."

" Yes. I am a bit tired. Take her for a while."

He pulled into the roadside and stopped the car. We got out to stretch our legs before going on, and it was just at that moment, when I was about to take my place behind the wheel, that a car coming from the opposite direction went past us at what seemed to me more than normal speed. It was just a flash, but in that time I saw what I took to be Joe Duncombe's face over the wheel and at the back Mell, his arm tight round Laura's waist.

Why ? Why, when they were expecting us, had they gone at such a desperate lick, towards Truro ?

I must have looked, as I was, a mass of apprehension. " What's come over you all of a sudden ? " Chris asked, supporting me in the road.

I could only gasp. " I can't drive. Follow that car. It's Mell and Laura."

"Get in then, quick," he said, and as soon as I was seated he reversed the car and we were in pursuit. Rosy still slept, clutching her umbrella.

Mell's car was out of sight. I watched our speedometer climb—thirty, forty, fifty. At last we saw it ahead, held up by traffic lights just outside Truro. As we approached, the lights changed, and the car shot forward. We, now, were held up in our turn, and it was not till we were bumping over the streets of Truro that we saw it again. We were only fifty yards behind it when it stopped at the entrance to Truro hospital. We drew alongside as Mell helped Laura out. She was white and trembling. I took her arm and shook her, and she looked at me, as though hardly recognising me. It was Mell, grey and haggard but in possession of himself, who said briefly : "We came in answer to a telephone call. An accident, I fear. Ray and Belinda. . . ." He, too, could say no more, but supported Laura into the hospital. Chris took my arm and we followed. It was Chris who remembered to say to Joe Duncombe : "Tell that young woman in my car that we'll join her in a moment."

7

It was bad, but it might have been worse. Mell had told us nothing of what to expect, and it would not have surprised me to find two corpses. What we found was Belinda, conscious, in the women's ward, and Ray, unconscious, in the men's. Belinda was lying on her back, evidently in great pain, and after we had exchanged a few words with her we were hustled out into a corridor where we were told that a surgeon would have to see her right leg, which was broken in two places : one just below the thigh and one in the lower leg. She had been given a sedative, and we must let her sleep.

Then we were taken to the men's ward, and Chris held me up when we looked down at Ray on the bed. His head was swathed in bandages and we should not have known who he was. Only the eyes were visible. We were allowed no more than a look at him, and were once more hustled out.

My mind was full of apprehension. It might be anything. It might be a fractured skull. But I was reassured. They were only cuts that had not reached the skull. But they were deep, on top of the head and on the face. He must be left alone till he came to himself.

Outside the hospital we found Joe Duncombe consoling Rosy. She was awake now and out of the car, clutching her umbrella. She ran to me at once and buried her head, which just reached my chest. She was weeping. " And only the other day," she was saying, between her sobs, " he was tellin' me all about trees and flowers."

It was Mell who remained in command of the situation. He was as moved as any of us, but he knew there were decisions to be made, and he made them.

" You can do nothing here for the moment," he said to Laura. " Joe had better run you and Chris back to Dros-y-Mor. You can take this young woman with you. Alice and I will find a hotel, so that we can see how things go here when the surgeons have done their work. We'll telephone you now and then."

And this was done. We watched them go, with Rosy and Laura clutching one another in the back seat, and then Mell said in his solemn definitive way : " Now we'd better find a hotel."

We found the Red Lion, put my car in the garage there, and settled down to wait. " You'd better have some tea," Mell said, and we did so in the dark comfortable lounge, and when that was over, Mell asked : " Will you be all right for a bit by yourself? I ought to find out what happened. I suppose the police will know."

It was simple enough, as I learned when he came back. After all, it's the sort of thing that happens on the roads every day and no one bothers much about it. Ray and Belinda were approaching Truro, with Ray driving. They came to a blind corner, and round the corner, on the wrong side of the road, came a lorry. There was nothing for it but a head-on collision or an effort to squeeze through the small opening that the lorry left between its side and the hedge. Ray took the chance, collided with the hedge, and overturned. The lorry went on and had not been identified. An A.A. patrol man had found them, Ray unconscious, Belinda, despite her pain, able to give Mell's telephone number and his name, with some account of what had happened. The A.A. man went to the nearest telephone and got into touch with the hospital, and then returned to await the coming of the ambulance. The hospital communicated with Mell.

That was the bones of the story that Mell told me, and there was nothing to do now but wait.

8

I think Mell's long sojourn among the ancient Romans had given him a stoicism that was denied to me. In the lovely spring weather that continued to bless us he did his best to keep my mind off the reason for our being in Truro. He walked me round the cathedral, discoursed on its architectural qualities, took me into the country thereabouts, talked of old days in Cardiff and at Oxford, and generally was the perfect cicerone. I knew that he was suffering as much as I was, and so I did my best to be interested in all he had to say ; but I wouldn't have cared if Truro cathedral had been sunk in the sea provided that Ray and Belinda had escaped the misfortune that had overtaken them.

We rang up Dros-y-Mor daily, and I had painful talks with Chris and Laura ; and Mell and I went at appropriate hours to the hospital. Ray's scalp and face had been stitched and Belinda's leg had been set The sight of both of them never failed to send me out, weeping, on Mell's arm, and it was vain for him to assure me that, seeing how much worse things might have been, they were doing splendidly.

My dream of bearing them both in triumph to Dros-y-Mor was ended when I was told that Ray could go home on the morrow but that, for a time, Belinda must stay where she was. Chris brought Laura over to Truro, for she insisted on being with Mell and seeing Belinda. Chris and I then drove Ray home, and it was anything but the fore-gathering that we had expected not long before. I needed all Mell's stoicism now. Chris sat at the wheel, driving slowly, and I sat behind with an arm round my son. But so different a son from the more cheerful being he had become when, having left Mapson, he had been with us at the Rowans. He was more conscious than I was of the change in his appearance. Gone now was the handsome, if at times sulky, boy that I had known. He would always bear the marks of that disaster in his face. It was seamed with scars that would be for ever there. Down both his cheeks deep grooves ran, and, diagonally across his forehead was a weal that might perhaps lose something of its livid look but that seemed to cut his forehead in two. And he would talk of nothing but Belinda. She seemed to obsess his mind, and a deep sense that his own faulty driving had laid upon her a lifetime of misery ate him up.

Joe Duncombe was waiting at the garage, and Ray, Chris and I walked along the path through the wood. At that time of year it was enchanting : the trees and shrubs at their best, the stream singing, the air a-flutter with birds at their springtime business. But, for all the lift of the heart he got out of it, Ray might have been walking along a platform in a provincial railway station. His thoughts were all backward. When we came to a spot whence we could see his hut, he paused for a moment and looked at it through the trees, and then said : " Old Sandy and I had some good times in that hut."

" You'll have some good times in it yet," Chris said reassuringly. " You're not dead, you know."

" No," he said, " not like Sandy."

On the quarter-deck Em Pritt—I could never think of her as Mrs. Joe Duncombe—was waiting with Rosy. She kissed Ray, whom she had known as a child, and Rosy, with a fist clutching a bundle of twigs said : " I've found all the ones we picked that day when we had a long walk."

She presented her little bouquet to Ray as shyly as a small child presenting a bouquet to the speaker who had opened a country show. I guessed that she and Em had discussed their first move : no reference whatever to Ray's accident or his changed appearance of which Laura had warned them.

Ray took the bouquet, and for the first time smiled. And who could forbear to smile at that mite with anxiety to do the right thing written all over her face ? " Thank you, Rosy," he said. He handed her back the small bunch of twigs. " Put them in a vase on the table in my hut," he said. " That's where I shall be sleeping."

" You'll find it all in order," Em Pritt said, anxious to be in a picture which was becoming a little brighter. " I've given everything a real polish every week, and your mattress has been out in the sun."

" Thank you, Em," he said. " Now let's have a sit down. I've got to get used to this place all over again. It's a long time since I've seen it."

Deck-chairs were set out on the lawn, and as Rosy bustled off on her small commission, as proud as someone who has been given the portfolio of a Ministry, we let ourselves down and Em Pritt went into the house to get coffee.

It was a long time since I had seen it, too, and I was glad that I was seeing it now in sunshine. The tide was up, and the dinghy was bobbing on the water looking, under Joe's ministrations, as bright as ever. The swans were there along the water's edge and the trees were bursting with new leaf, and the sky was blue over it all. The Mapsons of the world might elsewhere be transforming the England we had known, country and cities alike, but they had not touched us here. I watched a few swallows overhead, and sighed with content. Then Ray's hand reached out and touched mine. " A good place to find one's feet again," he said. " You and Chris leave me now to have a sleep. I wasn't sleeping well in that hospital."

We left him there and went into the house.

9

Every day we rang up Mell and Laura in Truro, and at last Belinda was allowed to travel home. Her two fractures had healed, and she had hopped about a bit in the hospital on crutches. Now she needed nothing but a walking-stick, and she hoped soon to put that aside too.

In the time that passed until she arrived a great change had taken place in Ray's appearance and manners. Days of sitting in the sun had worked wonders with his wounds. They were apparent as scars, but they had contracted to streaks across his forehead and down his cheeks. " I can soon deal with these," he said. " When I was in the Mediterranean I grew a beard, so why not now ? "

There was a reception committee outside the garage when

Joe Duncombe, bringing home Laura, Belinda and Mell, came to a stand there. Chris and I were with this Ray who looked as though he hadn't shaved for a week, as indeed he hadn't. (Chris called him Captain Kettle, after a by now ancient character of romance.) And there were Rosy and Em Pritt. So, on that very spot where once there had been only trees, and where I had fainted into Ben Davies's arms, we awaited we hardly knew what. They came at last, and we all rushed forward to have the honour of opening the car door and helping Belinda to alight. But Mell was before us all. He fairly leapt from the car then turned to give Belinda a hand. And the first thing she did was to laugh. Her face was untouched. It was the face we had always known, a little paler, perhaps ; and as she leaned on her stick, with Laura getting out behind her, she caught sight of Ray, brown with the sun, bearded, and she laughed. " Oh, Ray," she said, " come here and let me kiss you. I've never kissed a bearded man in my life."

Ray rather sheepishly allowed himself to be kissed, but the laugh had done it. He had come out prepared to find goodness knows what—pain, anxiety, all the things that he had been telling himself had flowed from his own carelessness and incompetence. But when Belinda laughed his face cleared. He was forgiven, if there had ever been anything to forgive. Belinda, with a stick in her right hand and her left arm tucked through his, began the slow walk through the woods to the house. Em and Rosy had run before us, to see that all was in order for so royal a reception. Belinda, though not a chatterer, chattered now in her anxiety to let Ray know that she was feeling better than in fact she was. It made him happy, and I, following behind with Mell, Laura and Chris, was moved to see how tenderly he treated her, stroking the hand that was laid upon his arm.

So we came to the old seat, and there she said : " I think I'll rest a bit now," and he let her gently down. There was not much room on the seat, so Mell and Laura and Chris went ahead to the house, and I was about to take my place with Belinda and Ray when Ray gave me a glance which I could not misunderstand, and I hurried after the other three. I do not know what passed between them, what words of sorrow and pardon, but when half-an-hour later, Mell, as anxious as an old hen, went to see how they were getting on, he met them making slowly for the house, he laughing at her stick, she laughing at his beard.

It was a happy holiday after all. Rosy had the spare bedroom in the Duncombes' house. Ray slept in his shed, which Rosy took as her own province, keeping it neat and renewing from time to time the leafing twigs upon the table. Mell and Laura had one of the bedrooms up aloft, Chris and I the other. Belinda slept in the small room in which I had done so much typing for Frank, and this made it unnecessary for her to climb stairs. Old Dr. Nancarrow had long been dead, and a young doctor named Sturgis had now taken over his practice. He looked in now and then to see how Belinda was getting on, and, as likely as not, would stay to smoke a pipe with Chris on the quarter-deck, Belinda being out. For she had taken to long expeditions with Ray in the dinghy. It was like seeing a queen embark. They would start when the tide was well up, and we were all there to see that she was comfortably installed, with cushions and blankets in the boat and provision for lunch. Mell and myself, Chris and Laura, and, as often as not, Joe Duncombe. Em would be at her work in the house, Rosy busy in Ray's shed. I often wondered about Rosy and these embarcations for Cythera. She always kept out of the way, fussing over her twigs, and remembering, I imagined that late winter's day when Ray and she had gathered twigs together.

Be that as it may, off they would go, Ray rowing gently through the continuing spring weather; and when they were out of sight round the bend Mell would return to his scattered proofs in the big library, and Laura and I would sit for a while on deck-chairs on the lawn, wondering a lot, but saying nothing.

10

Our minds were now at rest. Ray and Belinda were improving daily, though Dr. Sturgis warned us that Belinda would always find a stick necessary. There was a slight shortening of her leg. We had been expecting such disasters that this was almost good news, and in a happier moment I wrote to Bernard Mapson.

" Dear Mr. Mapson.—You probably do not know that Ray had an accident on his way down here to join us in a holiday. The papers are so full of accidents on the roads that one more or less seems to make no difference and, if this one was reported at all, you may well have overlooked it. Ray was bringing his friend Belinda Conybeare, whom I think you have met, to join me and her father and mother when the collision occurred, upsetting them in a ditch outside Truro. The lorry, which was the other party concerned, went on and has not been discovered, but that, too, is becoming so usual as to need no comment. Both the young people were badly cut about though, so unpardonably late am I in letting you know about this, Ray's wounds are now healing and are concealed for the most part behind a beard. Miss Conybeare, however, came off more badly, and the doctor thinks that one of her legs is permanently shortened, and that she will always have to use a stick. However, they get about and are enjoying the wonderful spell of weather we are having here. I don't think Ray or anybody else has let you know about this, though Miss Conybeare has, of course, written to the Foreign Office, where she is employed, and got her holiday extended. All our good wishes. Sincerely, Alice Harris."

I did not think it necessary to tell anybody about this letter, and did not myself expect more than an acknowledgment of its receipt, if that. To my surprise a letter came, in Mapson's own rather flamboyant writing.

" Dear Mrs. Harris.—No. I had not heard or read a word about the accident, and am more pleased than I can say that things have not turned out worse. However, I'm coming to see for myself. It so happens that I've promised myself a look at one or two towns in the West Country that were knocked about a lot during the war and may need some building up again. Towns in Devonshire I'm particularly thinking about, but Devonshire is no distance from you in a good car, so I'll be able to look over. Please don't make any special arrangements for me, because for one thing I don't know when I shall come, and for another I'll look after myself and probably stay in Falmouth, which the map tells me is no distance from you. My good wishes to you all. Bernard Mapson."

Ray and Belinda had been out in the dinghy as usual that

day, and I kept Mapson's letter to read to everybody when we were assembled for dinner. Ray was sitting next to Belinda, and he took her hand and said : " We've got more exciting news than that. Belinda and I are engaged to be married."

He was rather excited, rather defiant, but Belinda was, as they say, cool and collected. She smiled at us all and said : " Yes, we should like to be married. That is, if our parents consent."

I think we had been expecting it, all of us. Even Mell, who was not given to emotion, rose and came round the table and kissed the pair of them. " Now," he said, with one of his rare smiles, " I shall be able to get on with my work without wondering when we should be permitted to know the news. Needless to say, this one parent gives his consent."

There was not much left for any of us to do but follow Mell's example. It became a merry party. Chris went out to the kitchen and returned with a cork-screw and a bottle of Burgundy. He filled my glass and Laura's, Mell's and his own. We drank their healths and our tongues were loosed and everybody declared that we had been expecting this, that it was only a matter of time. Joe Duncombe and Em Pritt were called in, and they, too, drinking a toast, said it was only a matter of time. Belinda alone declared that it wasn't, at any rate, to her. " I was never so excited, or so surprised," she said, " as when Ray proposed to me."

Be that as it may, it was a happy evening, and it was only broken up when Ray said that he and Belinda were going for a bit of a walk together. They had forgotten us all, and went arm-in-arm through the woods towards Joe's cottage. The rest of us went in the dying light to sit for awhile in chairs on the quarter-deck. Rosy was in the dinghy, collecting the rugs and cushions that she would air and warm for the morrow, when, she had no doubt, they would be wanted again. It was Mell who called her and told her of the engagement. She said nothing, but carried her armful up to the house. And she carried them down in the morning.

It was two days later, when our excitement had a little subsided and Ray and Belinda had gone away in the boat as usual, that Mell came barging through the woods where he knew that at that hour of the morning he would find me, sitting on my bench. The London newspaper, which was late in reaching us, was clutched in his hand. He let himself down beside me and said : " We shall not be seeing Mr. Mapson after all."

He gave me the newspaper, his finger pointing to the news. Unlike Ray and Belinda, whose smash had been reported only in our Cornish newspapers, Mapson was national news. He had set out from Exeter, driving westward, on the day before this. There was no one else in the car. It had been found at the roadside, with Mapson dead in it. A doctor who had been called, had certified that the death was caused by a cerebral hemorrhage. There was much else. There was a photograph of Mapson and there was the story of his spectacular rise to wealth from nothing. I sat there thinking of the days of nothing, of the little room in Pimlico and the youth so full of dreams. He had stood for many things that I disliked, but I had liked Mapson. He had been faithful, after his manner, to Ray, and faithfulness is not common. I read the last line of his obituary : " Mr. Mapson had recently sold his house Whitecotes at Chorley Wood and had bought an estate, with a Georgian house, in Sussex. He leaves a widow."

Chapter XIV

By the end of that year we were all situated thus. Mell's book had been published in the autumn and, as the author had expected, was not selling well. A few libraries, a few scholars, had bought copies, but it was dragging out a feeble existence. Mell was unperturbed, and was assembling notes for a further book on the same subject. He was doing this in a flat at Chelsea, and was happy in his way. He had little money; he had married a wife who had none; and his profession had not brought him much. But he didn't want much, and his aunt, Poor Judith, had left him what she had, which didn't amount to a great deal. Now that Belinda was married, he had enough to go on with, and that was all he asked. A friend of his had rashly bought the Chelsea house, and was glad when Mell and Laura offered to take the first floor off his hands. Mell wanted to be nearer to the British Museum. So there they were, with a window that gave a view of the river, content with their life.

Chris and I were now installed at Dros-y-Mor. We were concerned about Em Pritt and Joe, for Chris had said that he could look after the car himself and get a man in now and then to do what was necessary in the woods. Em had been with me and Mell now for a long time, but fortunately, and rightly, she thought more of Joe than of either of us, and Joe, without any rancour, found a way out. He had always been a cautious and saving man, and when a roadside garage, about a mile removed from us, came into the market, he bought it, and we allowed them to keep their old cottage for a peppercorn rent. So we were left with only Rosy Midge at Dros-y-Mor. And she was all we needed, for I did the cooking and typing myself.

I had expected that I should never look at a typewriter again, but one late autumn night Chris surprised me by producing some pages in his atrocious hand and saying, " Have a look at this, Mrs. Harris." It was his mode of address when he was pleased with himself or with me. We had finished our evening meal and there was a good fire burning. Chris was not only pleased but diffident, so he took himself off to my old room along the passage and left me to my reading.

I must say here a word about Chris. He had in his time written a play or two, but long ago had found his true calling in turning the novels of other people into plays. He had been successful in this, but the theatre was changing its habits, and the sort of plays he liked to write were going out of favour. He had no sympathy at all with the plays that were being demanded by both the theatre and television; and the consequence was a sense of frustration. At first he tried to write the sort of novels that Frank had written, but he never got beyond a chapter or two. They were not his thing, and he could not do them, as Frank so blessedly could. It was a long time now since he had done anything at all. He had said nothing to me, but I was aware of his growing sense that he was no good—a misfit in a world that was changing. But there was one world that did not change, that went gaily on side by side with the new methods. And this was the world of the " romance " and the detective novel.

This was the world Chris now endeavoured to come to terms with. He had not been gone for long that night before I realised that he had the trick of it. It was a great change from working for Frank ; but the tale was successful in its own way. I dared even to put in a line or two, a word here and there, which I would never have had the hardihood to do with anything that Frank wrote. But here the intention was different : not a searching of the heart and of manners, but simply a mounting tension that was released in the last page. It was what they call " bunk ", about a detective of supernatural insight, a fumbling local inspector of police, a murder at the manor house during a house-party, and the squire unexpectedly, but at last obviously, the guilty man. It was a short story of a few thousand words, wasted, I thought, because it could easily be extended by an incident or two, a character or two, into sixty thousand words—all, I admitted to myself, nonsensical, but not seeming so when read quickly, as these things were read.

I was just finishing my reading when Chris came back, rather sheepishly. I put down the manuscript and kissed him. "Between us," I said, " we can make something of this."

He began to laugh. " Between us ! You've never written a word in your life ! "

" I know all about that. Now listen to me."

I told him how and where his story could be lengthened, how new people and new incidents could be brought into it, and, remembering Frank, I was waiting for the moment when he would tell me to go to the devil. But he listened patiently and at last said : " I think you're right. Let's collaborate on it."

" If collaboration means giving a hint here and there, we'll collaborate on it. But don't expect me to write. And to begin with, you'll have to give your detective a new name."

I felt rather like the wife in Barrie's *What Every Woman Knows*, giving hints for her husband's political speeches, but never letting him think she was doing it. " Ralph Roberts is a rotten name for a detective. If he were James Slim, known to all as Slim Jim, you'd be fixing him in people's minds."

We talked it over. Henceforth we always talked over Chris's successive novels about Slim Jim, who became almost as well-known as Maigret or Poirot.

" It's not what I *want* to do," Chris declared that night, " but it's something. I must do *something* or bust. Perhaps it'll keep the pot boiling."

It did, handsomely. But we didn't expect that as we sat over the fire that night and I put my ideas about Slim Jim into Chris's mind. I wanted only to keep him happy and occupied. A man with nothing to do but mooch about the house was not likely to be either. Even Sergeant Beasley, who shared Slim Jim's glory in many an encounter with crime, was born that night with all his quirks and idiosyncrasies, and so was Herman Herries, which was the name with which Chris signed the Slim saga.

Thus it came about that my old routine began again. Chris never went into the hut in the woods to write. I think he felt, like me, that this was not the sort of stuff to trouble Frank's ghost with. He wrote in the library, not caring if anyone disturbed him, in his large almost indecipherable hand. As for me, I took my daily instalment into my typing room, and, saying nothing to Chris, altered and added as I saw fit. Whenever he spotted these alterations and additions he said nothing, and so, at last, Slim Jim was launched. He kept us in a modest affluence for many a year, and I never felt so proud of having a hand in his creation as I did of my simple routine work as the typist of Frank's books.

2

Ray had had a salutary jolt. His marriage to Belinda and Bernard Mapson's death, leaving him dependent on himself alone, seemed to snap the thread of his lethargy. For one thing, he found that he had been leaning on a support not too reliable. Mapson had shot up too high too quick. Mapson Enterprises were by no means bankrupt ; but, when an investigation was made into them, it was found that they were not so sound as all that. The young woman who had been Miss Rosamund Hornbrook, and who had become Mrs. Bernard Mapson, was glad to dispose of the mansion and estate that she had too soon induced him to buy, and to regret that so early she had persuaded him to sell Whitecotes. Given a year or two more, Mapson would either have come out on top or been listed among the men who had ended like Ronald Lilywhite. As it was, his death had come when he was deeply committed but when it was still possible for his estate to break even. There was enough for his widow, his only beneficiary, to stand on her feet. The " Enterprises " themselves were absorbed into an even bigger enterprise which continues to this day to rear and to delve up and down wherever there is a tree left standing or a building remains to remind us of what England once was.

We gave the Rowans to Ray and Belinda as a wedding present, and Mell and Laura, as their gift, added two acres of land which adjoined it. I had been up with Chris to see the young people and had taken Ray for a walk. They had just returned from their honeymoon, and as we leaned over a gate in the wintry weather I said to Ray, hardly daring to trust myself on such a topic, " Now you'll have to think about ways and means of keeping Belinda."

" That's all settled," he said. " We are going to be market-gardeners, with flowers as a side-line."

If he had said they were going to be Hottentots I could not have been more surprised. But Ray was very serious. " I was never cut out," he said, " for office work. The very thought of it bores me stiff, and Belinda, as you know, has thrown up her job in the Foreign Office. She'd rather be in the country than in London, and she says she was getting nowhere anyway—little more than a high-class typist. We've talked over this gardening business day after day. We were set on it at Dros-y-Mor. The trouble was where we were to get the money from to make a beginning. When you gave us the Rowans and those two acres adjoining it were in the market, we began to see a bit of light. That was when Belinda persuaded her father to buy the extra land. He was baffled as to why two young bankrupts like us wanted anything more than the bit of garden. We were going to get things under weigh before we said anything to anyone, and now you've jumped it all out of me."

I was overjoyed, and I let him go on. For a long time I hadn't seen Ray enthusiastic about anything, but I had released some springs of enthusiasm now. He talked about the little brook that Poor Judith and I had often sat beside, while she pondered on Bryan and I dreamed my vague dreams. But there was nothing vague about Ray. He spoke of the importance of water, London as a handy market, even of old Dr. Nancarrow who had helped to bring him into the world.

"D'you remember that old doctor at Dros-y-Mor? I used to wander up to his place now and then, and there he'd be, cutting up his delphinium roots as happy as a lark. He was always after new varieties and new colours. Well, there's always that, for one thing. It'll have to be cabbages, I suppose, to begin with, and the more obvious sort of flowers. But there's no reason why we shouldn't develop into our own specialities in time. Then there's fruit. Pears and apple trees, gooseberries, strawberries. We'll have to employ a hand, I suppose. . . ."

I saw the two acres blossoming like Eden, with the apples doing a bit of good, not the damage they had done elsewhere. "You'd better take me and Chris round your place and show us on the spot what you have in mind."

"Would you be interested?" Ray asked. "I could show you to-night a set of plans we've worked out."

"Do that, there's a dear boy. Let's get back now to tea."

That night, when we had cleared dinner away, Ray and Belinda produced their plans. "It's fortunate for us," Belinda said, "that this bit of a stream flows right through the middle of our two acres. We'll never be without water."

"'And a river went out of Eden to water the garden '," I thought, and let them go on.

"Just a pipe here and there to draw it off," Ray said. "We can lead it where we like."

"There'll have to be greenhouses, of course." This was Belinda. "Tomatoes and all that sort of thing. And there'll be the young stuff to bring on. Fortunately, I've never been extravagant. I've saved up, and I think I can buy greenhouses cheap. I've heard of a building development not far away. It'll take in a market garden, and the greenhouses are going for much less than I would otherwise have to pay."

"You'll need labour," Chris warned them. "At the beginning specially. Two acres of pasture land aren't turned into a market garden without work."

"There's old Jimmy Napier," Ray said. They had thought of everything. "You don't know Jimmy, do you? He was in much the same boat as I was. R.N.V.R. all through the war, and never settled down to anything since. I ran across him once or twice when I was trying to settle down myself, and I've kept in touch with him."

"He was out here last week," Belinda said. "You wouldn't believe the luck we had to find him. He was working in the very place that's being taken over for development. He's picked up a thing or two there, and he's as keen as we are on what we're going to do here."

We left them poring over their plans when we went to bed that night. But it was a long time before we went to sleep. "What do you think of my son now?" I asked.

"Well, he's enthusiastic. I suppose even on sites that have been developed people have to eat, and Ray's got as much chance as the next man to be one of the feeders. We'd better wait and see. Anyway, they want to do it, and that's a change in this world where the only idea of government is to tell people what they've got to do, whether they want to or not."

3

We walked over the two acres the next day, and James Napier joined us. I liked James Napier. He was rather cocky, a bit younger than Ray, and I guessed that the peace hadn't been all that good to him. He had tried one thing after another and hadn't been happy with any of it till he struck the market garden which stood on a site now to be "developed". Thus, with a number of other people, he was thrown out once more. This was particularly unfortunate for him, because at last, though, as he put it, "there weren't so many bawbees in it," he was happy. Happy to be out in the open air, happy to be with growing things, happy to be away from glass and cement with which, apparently, he had been much acquainted. He was a garrulous person, given to larding his conversation with quotations that everyone knew. " And now here we are again," he said, " and once more God's in his heaven and all's right with the world, as old R. L. S. said." R. L. S. was the only writing person he seemed ever to have heard of, and " old R. L. S." had to bear the brunt of all Jimmy's quotations, which were many and various.

Chris and I were out of it. We just tagged along with the three young people and listened to their lives unfolding. Greenhouses, furrows, compost heaps, flowers, fruit and vegetables were deployed before us, and Jimmy was appealed to again and again as the final authority. And he seemed to know what he was talking about. It was lunch-time before we had finished the perambulation and Eden had been mapped. " Well," said Jimmy as we went back to the house for a cold lunch, " bliss was it in that dawn to be alive, as old R. L. S. says."

We could only hope. We had seen dawns before.

Before going back to Dros-y-Mor, we called on Mell and Laura. Seeing that the Rowans now belonged to Ray and Belinda and that they had plenty to be going on with, we left them to it and settled for a few days into a hotel in London. The flat that Mell and Laura had in Chelsea was wise enough not to be big enough to put up visitors. We had not announced our coming and found that Mell was out for the day. He had gone to the British Museum, where, heaven knows why, he was accumulating facts about agriculture in the days before the Romans went from Britain. This left Laura with time on her hands, and we settled down to a discussion of more modern agriculture at the Rowans. She and Mell knew no more than we did ourselves. They had seen the plans, they had heard them expounded as they walked over the two acres ; " and now," said Laura, " I suppose we shall just have to leave them to it. After all, planning out one's life doesn't always work. You certainly didn't, Alice, and yet here you are. That poor fellow Mapson did, and other people's lives, too, and we know where he ended. Mell and I have talked it over, and we've decided to leave them to make what they can of it."

There didn't seem much else to do. We looked out of the

window at the river, where Mell's Romans had sailed up to Londinium, and a great many people had sailed since. Ebb and flow, coming and going, for time out of mind. Failures and successes, and millions of little lives that were neither the one nor the other, but just existed, and passed, and were heard of no more. The fortunes of two acres seemed a small thing, but, as Chris took my arm and we strolled together along the Embankment on leaving Laura, he said : " Well, we could let them stew in their own juice, as Mell and Laura seem to have resolved to do, but I think, as old R. L. S. says, that we'll fight and we'll conquer again and again. Somehow, I feel involved."

" And so do I," I declared. " Those two acres have got to blossom as the rose."

" As old R. L. S. doubtless said."

" Give R. L. S. a rest, and turn your thoughts to Slim Jim," I advised Chris. " If I'm a prophet, we shall make something out of him, and we might as well plough him back where he'll be doing someone a bit of good."

4

Joe Duncombe and Em Pritt occasionally looked in at Dros-y-Mor, and as that winter was turning to spring Chris said to Joe : " Do you think you could buy me a serviceable run-about truck, Joe ? "

Joe said he'd look about, and a week later reported that he had " the very job " in the garage if Chris cared to look at it.

Chris was as unlike Frank as any man could be. Joe had strolled along with this message as a morning's work was in progress, and I could well imagine what that would have meant in Frank's day. But Chris dropped his pen at once, asked Joe to stop and have a cup of coffee, and, when that was done with, all three of us walked through the woods to the garage. " The very job " was soon brought out on to the road. Chris approved the look of it, and said : " What about a bit of a run ? "

They both climbed into the truck, with Chris at the wheel. " See you at lunch-time," he said to me, and the truck started off with a professional roar. It was soon out of sight round a bend.

At lunch, Chris told me that he had decided to buy it. " It's done only a year's work," he said, " and I think it's just what we want."

" For ' us ' read ' Ray '," I suggested.

" Well, that was the idea. He's got a birthday coming soon. I thought it could be a joint present. From what his letters tell us, he's not sending much into Covent Garden at the moment —just a few spring flowers and so forth—and what goes is put on the railway. That chap of his, James Napier, could take this truck into town in no time, and it'd be a saving in the long run. The cost of petrol and wear-and-tear of the truck wouldn't cost as much as the railway freights. There's not any profit, so far as I can see, till now."

" You know very well that there's not. I don't know what Ray and Belinda would have done without a Dutch uncle like you."

It had been one expense after another. The cost of tearing up two acres of pasture and turning it into a workable garden. There had been a hired plough and a hired ploughman for that. The cost of the greenhouses on the land that was to be "developed" had not been negligible. The cost of plants. The cost of transport. Jimmy Napier's wages. One thing after another.

Chris was cheerful about it all. He had by now published the first of the Slim Jim series, and this had succeeded so well that he had been asked to turn it into a television play. This was the work he had been doing on that morning when Joe called about the truck. Slim Jim became a television character. Not only, as the books piled up, were they televised, but a series of short episodes in Jim's life were written especially for the screen and became popular there. As the thing developed, I used to rough out the ideas, whether for books or screen, and Chris would do the rest. We saw Jim on the screen, (for we hadn't a television set), only on rare occasions when we were at someone else's house. We kept the secret of his authorship to ourselves, and even Ray and Belinda never knew about it. However, it was out of Slim Jim that we bought the truck, and, till Ray was standing on his own feet, much else. " Standing on his own feet " are the important words. He would never have done this with Mapson. But from the first at the Rowans it was clear that an outdoor life, a life in which he made his own decisions, suited him best. He made mistakes and learned from them. He did the right thing and profited. He didn't care now if buildings reached as high as the Tower of Babel, so long as he could remain on the ground.

5

Rosy Midge was giving us trouble, and trouble was the last thing you would associate with Rosy. She was as short as ever, but life in the country had agreed with her, put a bit of bloom into her cheeks and flesh on to her bones. She even had a word to say for herself now and then, and had ceased to be the timorous mouse that we had found in Mamie James-Villiers's flat and that I had dressed in Kensington. She had never forgotten the long walk with Ray when they had gathered the twigs and he had talked to her about birds and growing things.

For memory's sake, and the sake of my own life's blooming, I paid a visit every week to Frank's writing hut, kept it in order, and saw that any damage was repaired. His old ink-bottle and a few sheets of quarto paper were kept as he had left them, and I had gone so far as to have the electricity carried out there, so that once a week, with an electric fire, the place could be warmed. That was the only change I had made in the hut as Frank knew it.

Ray's hut was another matter. He would never want it again, I was sure. Well, I argued with myself, neither would Frank want his. And this was the moment when I came face-to-face with the fact that the memory of Frank outbore all other memories, that neither Ray nor Chris would ever have the place in my heart that he had held. Chris, I think, knew this. He said nothing but was always especially tender with me when I had come up from my weekly visit to the old hut.

Ray's hut had not been well sited. It cloaked the view of a fine camellia, and the weather had made it a bit of an eyesore. It was falling to pieces, and I thought the woods at that spot would be all the better if it were taken down. Once a year we had a man in, lopping and trimming and pruning, and, going through the woods with him one day, deciding what should be done, I told him that the hut might as well go. I had written to Ray and he had agreed to this. There was plenty to be going on with at the Rowans, he said, without bothering about a ramshackle hut a few hundred miles away. " Especially," he wrote, " now that I shall not be able much longer to count on help from Belinda."

This was the first hint that Mell, Laura and I were to be promoted to grandparenthood.

The hut didn't need much shifting. It was demolished in an hour or so, and Chris and I, wandering down there, were agreed that the woods were the better for its clearance. But we had counted without Rosy. We were free and easy in our treatment of her. There was no " day off " once a week, but she was at liberty to come and go as she pleased. She had told us the day before that she intended on the morrow to walk into Helston " to see to a few things ". Chris had offered to drive her in and to pick her up later in the day, but since the accident to Ray and Belinda, Rosy had a fear of cars. Moreover, she liked walking. We watched her go that morning with a stick in one hand and a basket in the other.

" Rosy is becoming quite a person," Chris said, but we did not know till later in the day how much of a person she had become.

It was late in the afternoon that we walked down to see how the woodman was getting on. Ray's hut, a pile of planks and beams, was already lying on the path, and the camellia which it had hidden was splendidly in view. " I'd better burn all that," the woodman said, stirring the old planks with his toe, " but what about all this other stuff, Mr. Harris ? "

The other stuff lay in a heap to one side : old plasticine models, beginning to disintegrate and run about like hot fat in a frying-pan, glass jars containing a few fresh leaves, a map of the world that had been pinned to the wall, the old truckle bed, odds and ends of this and the other.

" Take it all away and burn it," I said, and Chris and I began to walk towards the house.

We had not gone far when Rosy, returned from Helston, overtook us in a state of great agitation. " What's that man doing with Mr. Ray's hut ? " she demanded.

We explained that we had decided to take down the hut and that " that man " was only carrying out orders. But Rosy's agitation remained and suddenly I thought of the fresh leaves in the glass jars. I had not put them there, nor had Chris.

In a moment, my mind was back to a scene that had been enacted years before. Ben Davies was outside his cottage watching the trees go down so that the garage could be built. He loved his trees. He disliked change. He was as adamant as an ancient Briton watching the Romans with their new-fangled ways spreading across the country. Roads, forts, walls. All that sort of thing. It had not occurred to me or to Chris that, in the same way, Rosy had loved the old hut, that she was keeping its altars clean with new leaves, that she was remembering Ray and the long walk she had taken with him. It was a moment of solidity in her young life which had been till then a ramshackle chivvying affair. She did not want to change it, or anything that reminded her of it. It was the more precious because it had been a secret. And now it lay in ruins, and " that man " had the impiety to propose burning the lot.

It was the more unbearable because Rosy had been saving up to buy presents for me and Chris. There was no occasion, no celebration. It had just entered her head. The " few things " she had brought back from Helston included a cheap gun-metal cigarette case for him and an " art-jewellery " brooch for me. She said nothing more about the abominable work that the woodman was engaged in, but she was still agitated as we all three took tea in the library. She shyly presented her small gifts, which I think she saw as some return for that day in the shop at Kensington, and we told her that Ray himself had given permission for the hut to be removed. We said that it was unlikely that he would ever want it again. But all made no impression on her, and she went early to bed. She had left on the floor of the library her basket containing " the few things " that she had bought in Helston. These were spilling out, and we saw that they included a few bright vases. They were only tin, but they had been given a meretricious shine, so that those who didn't know might think they were silver. They were evidently intended to replace the old glass jars in the hut, to be seemly vessels for the altar. We looked at them, and we looked at one another, knowing that we were faced with a more subtle problem than Slim Jim had ever been called upon to solve. In bed that night Chris said : " If there's to be an infant at the Rowans, they'll want more help than they've got, I think. I'd better write to Ray and Belinda in the morning."

I read the letter before he sent it. " Dear Belinda and Ray. —Ray says in his letter that he can't expect much longer to count on help from Belinda. Reading between these subtle lines, I have come to the conclusion that I shall soon be thanking the pair of you for leaving me here, married to a grandmother. Oddly enough, neither the grandmother nor myself can gratify you by feeling as old as the hills. We should like to, but we can't. We are, as the newspapers always say of a prince returned from some foreign tour, " bronzed and well," full of beans, in fact. We are wondering about you, rather than about ourselves. Won't you need, at any rate till this agreeable crisis is past, some help indoors rather than out ? I don't think that young woman, Rosy Midge, is altogether happy with us. Might we sound her about the Rowans ? She was with us there, and was happy enough. I think, if she were put in charge of an infant's early days, she might bloom again, and it would be that much off Belinda's shoulders. Rosy, of course, may not want to come, but shall we speak to her about it ? After all, she is town-bred and may relish an occasional run up to London. We can offer her nothing but Helston, which as you know, is a quaint old Cornish town where they dance annually, bedecked in lilies of the valley, usually accompanied by rain. You can possibly do better. Anyway, think about it, and meantime accept our congratulations on being about to make Alice a grandmother. She has reminded me that she was just about Rosy's age when she first set eyes on the Rowans, in the days of Mr. and Mrs. Bryan Graves. All our love. Chris, a grandfather of sorts."

The answer came from Belinda, who confirmed our guess and went on : " I am writing for Ray, because he is very busy, what with the garden and the legal work concerned in turning this place into a company. The only shareholders will be Ray and James Napier, unless, for form's sake, you care to take a few shares, as Daddy is doing. So it will remain a family business. You, no doubt, are wondering how this all comes about, so I'd better say a few words about James Napier. He has for a long time been on his own, with both parents dead, and no brothers or sisters. He is reticent about his parents, but I gather that they were not much good to him, and that he grew up how and where he liked. The war came, and it was not till after the war that he discovered that he was an orphan. He fiddled about with one thing and another, and finally settled down, as you know, in a market garden. This suited him down to the ground, and it was of a piece with all the bad luck he had before, that the advance of science once more threw him out to look after himself. Then he joined us, with lodgings not far away, and he has worked like a black, and been well worth his salary.

"He came to us not long ago in a state of great excitement, and assured us that ' as old R. L. S. says, everything comes to him who waits.' When he had calmed down a bit, he explained that for a long time he had been an addict of ' the pools ', and now, of all the strange things on this earth, he had, as he put it, ' struck a bonanza '. In short, he had won some thousands of pounds. And that, we thought, is the end of Jimmy. He continued to work as well and as hard as ever, but we were pretty miserable, expecting him to hand in his notice every day, and to have to look round for a man half as good. Then, to our surprise, and I may say to our joy, came this utterly unexpected proposal of forming a company. ' You put in the value of the land,' he said, ' and I put in the cash.' To say it all very briefly, that is what we are doing now, and, though Jimmy will work as always, we shall be able, too, to get an extra man, which will make all the difference. ' And when we are a company,' says Jimmy, ' we'll get a good tax man, and think what we can do with expenses ! '

"Well, I suppose there is that, too. But you'll be wanting to know what I think of this Rosy Midge proposal. It could not have come at a better time. Once this company is established, book-keeping will be a more important matter than it is now, and I am cast for the part of secretary. What with that, and an infant to look after, I shall certainly need some help about the house. Rosy and I are no strangers to each other. As you know, I came across her when I used to call on old Miss James-Villiers, and I expect, under Alice's tuition, she is not quite such a mouse

as she was then. You can tell her that I *must* have someone, and
I'd rather have her than anyone else. I have talked the matter
over with Ray, and he is of this opinion, too.

" But what about you ? This seems very mean and cadging
of me . . ." and so forth.

But we didn't bother about that. There wasn't much to do
at Dros-y-Mor, and I could do it myself. On those days when
Rosy chose to be absent, Chris had shown himself to be a useful
man in a kitchen. Without benefit of washing-up machines and
all the other " amenities " of modern life, we could whack through
the lot in a few moments, and we were never happier than when
alone in the house. It had been different in Em Pritt's time
with Ray growing up, but once he had gone away to school I
was not sorry when Joe Duncombe took Em off my hands.

So we called in Rosy, and with a discreet avoidance of the
subject of Ray's hut, we put the matter to her. Belinda was
asking for her, and so, we made clear, was Ray. And there
would be a baby. Rosy didn't take long to make up her mind.
There were a few days during which she " considered " the
matter, but we knew it was only a question of waiting, and
were not surprised when she opted for the grandson or grand-
daughter, whichever it proved to be, and left the grandmother
in the lurch.

Chapter XV

It was a grandson—Roger Melvill. Chris and I had been up to
the christening, had given the child a silver mug, and had spent
a few days in London, which we hadn't seen for a long time and
were glad to get out of. We were frightened by what the Mapsons
were doing, and were looking forward to being by ourselves in
Dros-y-Mor. But before going home we accepted an invitation
to have lunch with Peter Sissons.

Sissons was the publisher of the Slim Jim books. There had, so far, been only two of them, as well as the bits written especially for television. He was anxious to meet his author whom he had known only by correspondence, and was surprised when Chris introduced me as his fellow-writer. Even Sissons had not known till then that the books were not altogether a one-man affair. My part in their writing was explained to him ; I rose in his estimation, and did not fall when he was told that I had once been married to Frank Melvill. He was a rather young man, not long started on his own, aware of strong competition, and glad to meet an author who had become at his first stroke a " cert ". He promised to keep our secret to himself, and the next day we set out for home.

It was good to be back. The summer had fully come and Dros-y-Mor was very lovely. We had seen Rosy Midge happy in her new work, an atmosphere of go-aheadness and confidence at the Rowans, and there was nothing left for us now save to get on with our own things in our own way with one another for company. We got into a routine of work. Every morning I would go into my room and sketch an outline of the next incident in the book we were working on. Chris would take the one I had prepared the day before, and work at it in the library. Sometimes he would build his writing round it, sometimes he wouldn't. In the afternoons we would go for a walk, or row from the creek to the river, or merely sun ourselves on the quarter-deck. In the evenings after dinner we would discuss the work we had in hand, and Chris was apt to be like the elder Dumas giving instructions to one of his many ghosts. It was all very different from what it had been in Frank's day, when the work was locked in his own mind and I was the humble slave of the typewriter. But I was happier to be now giving a hand, and day by day the conviction grew on me that, despite Chris's masterful ways, he was tagging along on a track that I had laid down.

I remember only one quarrel in the course of our married lives. If you can call it a quarrel. It was rather a dispute in which each was determined to have his own way. I had written my outline for Chris's day's work, and he had gone off at quite a different angle. I objected when the writing was handed to me for approval. " But, Chris, this will cut right across my next bit of stuff. It will make complete nonsense of it."

It was the first time I had made any sort of claim to be a collaborator. Chris asked, still half-laughing : " Who's writing this book—you or I ? "

" We're both having a hand in it, I hope."

" Well, let's leave it to stew for a bit. Let's get out and take a breath of air."

We went out, but we were not at ease with one another. Presently I broke out again : " As I see it . . ."

" Yes, but you don't see it far enough. Now sit down for a moment and let me tell you how it goes."

We sat on a bank by the roadside, as solemn as if we had been Erckmann and Chatrian, or Besant and Rice, and Chris began his exposition.

" But that just won't do," I cried when he had finished.

" Well, think it over," he said. " Let's get on with our walk. We'll discuss it to-night."

We didn't discuss it, for all Chris said that night was : " Well, I'll have another go at your stuff to-morrow. Perhaps you've got something."

I could have crowed, but I was wise enough not to. I contented myself with the feeling that at last I was in the fullest sense a collaborator.

2

Mell and Laura proposed themselves for a visit towards the end of the summer. We had finished the book and had been looking forward to seeing Ray and Belinda with the infant Roger, and perhaps Rosy ; but an atmosphere of stern endeavour seemed to have settled on the Rowans. All we got was a brochure setting out what was for sale there, and a letter from Belinda. When she had done justice to the excellences of Roger, she went on : " You will see that we have rather changed our line. We no longer go in for cabbages and that sort of thing, but we are doing all we can to make ourselves known for first rate flowering shrubs and plants. Though we are still in an experimental stage, we have not regretted the change and have a few evidences that we have at last got on to the right lines. Our two acres are now four, and Ray and Jimmy Napier are working like blacks. I'm taking entire charge of Roger, and Rosy is deep in the technique of packing. She is good at it, and seems quite a new and confident person. Anyhow, all I want to tell you is that we are on the eve of considerable developments, that we are full of hope, and that it would be as much as my life is worth to suggest a holiday to Ray at the moment."

The summer was reaching towards autumn as we sat beside our quay wall and read this letter together. The air was very still and a yellow leaf or two fluttered down. The day was warm, but Chris had put a blanket over his knees and shifted his chair farther into the sunlight. "That's the best letter we have had from the Rowans for a long time," I said. "It's grand to know that Ray thinks his work more important than a holiday."

Chris agreed and said it had been time Ray got out from under Mapson. "He was being cosseted," he said, "and knew it, and hated himself for it."

"It's a good day for good news. We shall be in September in a day or two, and it's as warm as midsummer. Why don't you take that old blanket off your knees ? "

"It's not so warm as all that," he said. "I thought it rather cold." And began sneezing.

I don't know why, but I was back in a moment to that wretched little house in Openshaw where I had been a child with a lovely mother and a dreary father. I heard my father sneeze and saw my mother wrapping up a warmed brick to put in his bed.

I was alarmed at once. "You'd better get to bed," I said ; and he laughed at that. "For a bit of a sneeze ? " he asked.

I insisted on getting him indoors and putting him to bed at once. There was not such a thing as a hot-water bottle in the house, so I remembered my mother, found an old brick in the garden and warmed it. I took it upstairs, wrapped in flannel, and put it at his feet. He laughed, glad to be made a fuss of, and snuggled down into the bed. "Don't be too long coming up," he said. "You're as good as three bricks, with your red hair and all. Don't bring me any dinner. I'm going to sleep."

I didn't make any dinner for myself, either. I wandered for a while in the darkening woods, feeling lonely and apprehensive. A bit of wind shook the trees, and I felt the leaves falling about me with an extraordinary sense of finality. I almost ran back, and by eight o'clock I was in bed, hugging Chris to my side. He gave a grunt and put his arms about me.

When I awoke in the morning, he was standing at the bedside with a tray that carried our customary tea and biscuits. " Get this into you," he said. " You've been sleeping like a log."

So I had—a sleep of utter exhaustion, mental and physical.

I wanted to weep, but all I could say was : " Oh, you old fraud ! "

He was as well as ever, and as we drank our tea I told him about my father and the hot brick.

" I wondered," he said, " from what depths of atavism that brick had been resurrected."

We were gay with one another, but I had learned a lot about my feeling for Chris.

" Now, out of bed with you," he said. " We've got a morning's work before us."

" What we've got before us," I assured him, " is a good day in the open air."

And that is what we had. The autumn had never seemed lovelier, and the falling of the leaves was without premonition.

3

When, a few days later, Mell and Laura arrived, Laura seemed older than I was. She *was* older, but only by a few years, and this difference in age had not struck me before. We were both grandmothers—a daunting thought—but she looked one, and I didn't. Her hair was white, which could well have been an asset, but it was accompanied by a brow that was furrowed and a mouth that was sad. I longed to say to her " Cheer up ", but I didn't dare. It would be like cracking a joke with a vestal virgin. I thought of the day when Frank and I, to our surprise and amusement, had come upon her leaning on the Embankment in London, and Mell, stealing a kiss, had knocked her hat sideways. It seemed a long time ago.

I considered Mell, too. It was a considering kind of holiday. There had been a time when Mell was most worshipful to me, and I remembered him still as the youth who had set my feet on the way they had gone ever since. But I was glad now that he had never been more in my life than that. I had hoped at one time that he might be. But it had been Frank, and then Chris, both careless men. Where his work was concerned, Frank had been as solid and immovable as a rock, but once his work was done " Let's " had been his key-note. Let's do this and Let's do that. And they had always been sprightly and sudden notions that had joy in them, and in which I had been glad to share, whether it had been merely a walk to some neighbouring sea-coast or a sudden unpremeditated journey to another land.

So far as Chris went, work itself never stood very high in his regard, which is a dreadful thing to say in these days when nations are taught that to be great they must be full of hardworking types who have forgotten all about Keats's " leaving great verse unto a little clan." Chris, I admit, had just enough to live on, but I would rather have shared a crust with him than eat caviare daily with the sort who now proliferate, and are admired. I had only to suggest leaving work for a morning, or even for a day, to have Chris all with me, ready for any nonsense. " D'you know we've never been on Goonhilly Downs ? " or " D'you know we've never climbed Brown Willy ? " was quite enough to jerk an answer out of him. " Well, let's do it now."

Mell had never been a go-getter either on a national or a personal scale. He had had his ambitions, but they had been disappointed, and he seemed to be not unduly set back by that. But one remark of Laura's stuck in my mind out of the many she made during that holiday. " I wish he'd come shopping with me now and then." It suggested at once two worlds existing side by side, not one world which was shared by two people. Laura had little interest in what went on day after day in the British Museum, and Mell had little enough in how she spent her lonely days. He was as courteous as any " gentil parfait knight ", and was always ready to offer an arm to Laura as he had done to me when we walked through the Llandaff Fields, so long ago, after I had been ill and he had introduced me to Tennyson.

Chris and I did our best to rouse him during that holiday, for he had brought work with him even to Dros-y-Mor. But he might as well have been counted out. " Do, please, excuse me this morning. There are one or two points I want to clear up if I can." "I hope you won't mind if I don't make one of the party to Land's End to-day. I must put a few ideas down while they are in my head."

I remember one day when it was especially fine. It was a warm autumn day with a full tide in the morning. "There won't be many days like this before it's too cold for bathing," Chris said at breakfast. "What about a swimming party just before our eleven o'clock coffee ? "

" Oh, I haven't swum for years," Mell said. "You'd find me a bit stiff in the joints."

I did my best to drag him out of this mood. "D'you remember, Mell," I said, "how we taught Belinda to swim ? She was a tiny thing then, and you were a great hand at it. I was with Belinda in the dinghy, and you were in the water. ' Throw her in ! ' you said. And we had to throw her, too. You insisted. We ended by dropping her on to your shoulders, and she clung to your hair, and you swam ashore with her. After that one try, we had to do it again and again, and soon she was swimming on her own."

But Mell could not remember the incident, or would not, and he did not come with us that day. Once his mind was made up, that was that. What distressed me was that Laura did not join us in urging him. I suppose by that time she knew him too well ; but she came with me and Chris, and we made it as merry a morning as we could, for they were going on the next day.

Mell packed his papers with neat care into his despatch-case and took his seat at the wheel. We had walked through the woods to the garage to see them off. They went, at a solemn pace.

"I wonder," said Chris, "what Mell would think of Slim Jim, or of us if he knew that we had created him ? "

" I refuse," I said, " to consider any more academic questions. Let's go for a walk."

And we did, just as we were. The hedges were full of bryony, scarlet with fruit, and the yews with berries on which the thrushes were gorging themselves. We returned late in the evening, and found that Mell, remembering his manners to the last, had left a note in his bedroom, thanking us for a jolly holiday.

4

We spent the winter concocting between us another Slim Jim novel. Young Peter Sissons, our publisher, could not have enough of him, for Jim was well on his way to being not tolerated but asked for. However, " concocting " was still the word for those books, and I don't know what Mell, or for that matter Frank, would have thought of a book put together in that way. They tell us that the silliest trash has to be believed in by its author if it is to succeed. I can only say that we must have been exceptions to this doubtless golden rule, and that, confronted in fact with a problem that Jim solved with ease and suavity, we should have been as baffled as the local police whose wrong conclusions it was Jim's business to put right.

However, he was done with for the moment, and was making far more money than I could have hoped for from the reprint now and then of a novel by Frank. " I think," I said, " that we'd better go and see how those children are getting on at the Rowans."

I never could remember that " those children " were now getting on for middle-age and that Chris and I were rather battered wrecks of an older generation. When we got to the Rowans, there was little for us to do save watch other people making their lives. Everything was changed from the simple place at which I had arrived from Cardiff so many years ago. The bit of lawn where I had been accustomed to sit with Judith was still there, but the view from it was no longer of open fields on which cows grazed. A thick-set hedge enclosed the acres ; greenhouses twinkled in the sun ; a packing-house had been built ; and every bit of land was rich with plants. In a new wooden building which was known as the office Ray spent hours of every day, and Rosy Midge, wearing a kind of land-girl's uniform, was to be found in the packing-shed, where she had an assistant, and exercised her authority with a new sense of being at last a person and not a bit of flotsam drifting wherever the wind pushed it.

Chris and I looked into Ray's office one morning and found him filing orders. There was on a table a pile of the company's notepaper, and Chris was entranced to find listed among the directors the name of Rose Midgley. There were two others : James Napier's and Ray's. " Ray, who is this Miss Rose Midgley ? " he asked with a grin, knowing well enough.

Ray said very seriously : " Oh, that's the girl you used to call Rosy Midge. It was Napier's idea. She's such a whale for work and knows the name of every plant. She's put her back into the thing, and Napier thought we ought to give her some recognition. That's why her name's there, and Rosy Midge didn't look very well on paper. So she's always known now as Miss Midgley. Napier thinks she's a great acquisition. I shouldn't be surprised if he marries her some day."

" What ? Our Rosy Midge ? "

" Miss Midgley, please," said Ray. " Now, if you'll excuse me . . ."

We left the office in a holy awe and proceeded on our perambulation of the estate. We found James Napier superintending the digging of some trenches. " We've got to put out a lot of stuff we've been bringing on under glass all the winter," he said. " Primulas and what not."

He looked fondly about the slopes of the land and said : " Well, there it is. It's returning money at last. We're not millionaires, but as old R. L. S. says, everything comes to him who waits."

He seemed as anxious as Ray had been to get on with his work, so we left him to it and joined Belinda, who was walking now without a stick. She was waiting for us outside the house, with young Roger in his perambulator. Chris took the handles and addressed himself to the donkey-work.

5

We had arranged before we left Dros-y-Mor for a woman to come in now and then and give the place a look over. A letter, readdressed in her large sprawling hand, came for Chris while we were at the Rowans. We had arranged that day to go for a long walk together. The beeches were entrancing with their new leaves, and everywhere about us the woods, fields and roadside hedges were waking to the mild sunshine. We put a

few sandwiches in our pockets and Chris shoved the letter after
them into his. " Looks like old Uccles's writing," he said. " I
wonder what he wants ? Haven't heard of him or seen him
for years."

I had never heard of old Uccles, and thought no more about
him. Nor did Chris until at midday we sat by the roadside and
dived into our pockets for our sandwiches. Uccles's letter
fluttered down into the dust, and Chris, between his munches,
said : " I used to know this chap years ago. I was rather given
to literary parties at that time, and wherever I went I met Uccles.
A rather tall, dark chap, beautifully dressed. He seemed to
know everybody, and the joke was that nobody knew him.
I remember one night when someone said to me : ' Who is that
dark chap over there ? ' ' Oh, that's Uccles,' I told him. ' Yes,
I know it's Uccles,' he said. ' But who *is* Uccles ? ' He didn't
know him from Adam. Neither, for that matter, did I. But
everybody seemed to want to keep on the right side of him.
He knew everything that was happening, and everybody who
was writing anything, and when it would appear, and who was
publishing it. If a chap had a new book about to come out, he'd
say : ' I suppose I'd better ask Uccles to lunch.' Well, that's
Uccles."

I laughed heartily at mysterious Uccles. " Just a voice
whispering in every ear and listening to every tongue," I said.

" Yes. You'd run on him in the most exclusive restaurants,
eating the most exclusive dinners, with the most exclusive
authors, who were about to publish most exclusive books. The
sort of books that excluded all readers."

" He must have got a hint," I said, " that you're the author
of the Slim Jim stories. Well, nearly. For goodness' sake open
the letter. It may not be from him at all. In any case, I'm dying
to hear it."

" Yes," said Chris, tearing open the letter. "It's from
Uccles, though I've only once heard from him before. But the
handwriting is unmistakable."

He read it aloud.

" Dear Christopher Harris.—You'll think it odd of me to be
writing to you after so many years, but I expect you'll remember
me. We used to meet fairly often here and there. I wonder

whether you are ever in town these days ? There's a matter which I should like very much to discuss with you, though it's hardly a thing to put on paper. If you are likely to be up soon, do drop me a line. Till then, ever, Matthew Uccles."

"Yes," said Chris. "Mysterious Uccles. As usual, giving nothing away. At any rate, he has materialised behind an address. West End, too. Well, what do we do now ? "

"You write and tell him that you are married to a peerless woman, and that you and she will be delighted to take lunch with him. I can hardly wait to see him."

The mysterious Uccles—how I longed to give that title to a Slim Jim novel !—was as Chris had said, tall, dark and thin. He was also handsome and well-dressed. He wore his things with an air, all the more impressive because he seemed unaware of it, as though he could buy his clothes off the hook and still look as if he had used a first-rate tailor. I remember a cantaloup melon and Uccles's long tampering fingers passing me the sugar. Not much more of the lunch, because Uccles talked of everything except why he had asked us. We learned what editor of a popular magazine was soon to be sacked, and what first novel was to be a great success, and how old So-and-So was really beyond it and his latest effort would probably be his last. "He's bobbing about from one publisher to another—always a bad sign, you know."

A young man with a couple of beatnik-looking girls came in. He waved towards our table as he went by. "Young Rogerson," Uccles said. "I give him a year or two at most. He can't take it. Owes hundreds in income-tax."

All very well, I thought, and all very amusing, and a nice change after being buried for a long time at Dros-y-Mor. But I wished Uccles would come to the point. He did in his own good time by calling for the bill and signing it with a flourish. Then he said : "I think we'll take coffee and a cigar at my club, Harris. Sorry, Mrs. Harris, but it's one of those male haunts— you know, the head waiter, who's been there for fifty years, would fall dead at sight of a woman."

I said I could amuse myself for an hour or so, and arranged where I should meet Chris at tea. "You couldn't do better than one of Dingley's places—excellent éclairs—say the one in

Bond Street," said Uccles. He saw me to the door, shook hands and bore Chris away.

It was not till nearly five o'clock that Chris joined me at Dingley's. "Havanas," he said. "*And* brandy with our coffee. What d'you think of him ? "

"What does the waitress think of me ? I've been gorging éclair after éclair. I expected you about four o'clock."

He had evidently had an exciting hour or two. "He's rumbled us," he said. " Rumbled me, anyway. The first thing he said when we settled down in his club was : ' Well, I want to talk about this Slim Jim stuff you're doing.' You could have knocked me down with a feather."

" Yes, as old R. L. S. doubtless said at one time or another. Well ? "

" I think Sissons must have let it slip in an unguarded moment," Chris said. " You know how these things happen. There's more than one first-rate writer," he added with some pride, " doing this sort of thing."

" Well, there's more than one writer, first-rate or otherwise, concerned with Slim Jim. What about it ? "

I have told before how Chris himself had turned several novels into plays, a novel by Frank among them. He had also written a play or two himself, with moderate success, but that was in times when plays were not what they are to-day. Chris was lost in the modern world of the theatre. Slim Jim had been a godsend to him, if only to keep him out of mischief. Now, it seems, Uccles had the notion that Slim Jim could be the leading figure in that kind of entertainment called a musical.

" All I ask," he had said to Chris, " is that you should leave it to me. I know the sort of people who do that sort of thing, songs and all the rest of it. You can take it from me that *Hugger-Mugger* isn't going to last much longer. They'll be looking round for a new piece for that theatre, and I think Slim Jim could hit the mark."

It seems that mysterious Uccles had already been busy, had approached song-writers and dialogue-writers, to say nothing of financiers, and was awaiting only Chris's consent before, as he put it, setting the ball rolling.

" Well, what do you say about it all ? " Chris asked.

"I say, let's go while the going's good. If you can keep in the background—if you want to keep in the background—all right. No one need know that Herman Herries is Christopher Harris."

"Well, I can tell Uccles to go ahead?"

"You can tell Uccles to have a go. I'm still doubtful about the whole thing."

6

We spent that summer at Dros-y-Mor, busy at our own work and not hearing much from Uccles. Now and then he would make a laconic "progress report" which told us little except that the matter was still in hand. We went up to town in June to attend Rose Midgley's marriage to James Napier. At any rate, that was our ostensible reason. In fact, we wanted to see Uccles again. The financial side of the affair had been left unsettled, and Chris was anxious to know where we stood. If we stood anywhere. If the matter was going on as we hoped it was. The "ifs" were accumulating and we were getting restless.

This was the first time I remember that we were in London without seeing Mell and Laura, and the reason was, I think, too much preoccupation with our own affairs. I could not help recalling the days of Frank, when my part was a secretary's duties, and nothing else. We were not so well off. No novel that Frank wrote ever brought in what we could count on now from a single book; but my mind was not as tranquil as it was then. I began to wish that Uccles had never come into our lives. We had plenty to live on. Why were we bothering about more?

However, Chris wanted to see Uccles again, and so one morning I mooned about London by myself, while he went, as he put it, to "have it out" with him. "There ought by now," he said, "to be some hints in the papers about it." He was in a rather peppery mood, and as I strolled along the Embankment, always my solace in a difficult moment if I chanced to be in town, I could not help contrasting this with Frank's mood. In his own words he "didn't care a damn" what he made by his writing. The writing was the thing, and if I misplaced a comma in his typescript he was likely to be more annoyed than if a pack of reviewers had been at his heels.

Chris didn't see Uccles after all. The porter in the block of flats where Uccles lived said the man was on holiday. Somewhere in the Greek Islands, he believed. There were orders that letters were not to be forwarded. Mr. Uccles was " moving about ". He had left no precise time of his return.

I was sick of London, which was changing before my eyes into a town I neither knew nor liked, but one thing we did before returning to Cornwall was to attend a cocktail party. " It'll be something for you to laugh about during the long winter evenings," Chris said grimly. He had been alone to call on his publisher, Peter Sissons, who greeted him as one does greet the goose that lays the golden eggs. Sissons had no idea that he was in London, and invited him to the party. " I knew you wouldn't come up especially for a thing like this," he said disparagingly, " but now that you *are* here, if you're doing nothing better to-night . . . ? "

Chris said that he would be there and bring me with him.

Sissons's party was not, like some of these jamborees, in a spacious room at a hotel. He had collected his guests round him in his own offices which occupied one floor of a house in a Bloomsbury square. They drifted in like bees swarming. Before the evening was over, they were standing back to back, and front to front, and neck to neck, shouting into one another's faces, bawling at the tops of their voices, so that one heard no words but a confused vibrant hum, couldn't move an inch, and didn't know who the Bobbie was or the Charlie, or the Maisie or the Virginia, to whom from time to time Sissons, barging his way with someone in tow, made a casual introduction. The room was full of this sustained hum, and the air was full of waving curtains of cigarette smoke and the stink thereof, and my head was aching, and someone's elbow was pressing into my back, and I went on talking to a face that I didn't know about an inch from mine. Altogether, it was, I suppose, a typical and topping party, and, at last, by the luck of the draw, as it were, coming face-to-face with Chris, I begged him to take me home.

To thank Sissons for a lovely party was out of the question. We couldn't get near him. Nobody was aware of our going as we prized ourselves out of the pack, went down into the air, comparatively fresh, of the square, and leaned for a moment on the railings.

" Thank God you came in time," I said.

" Yes," said Chris, " you might have been dead. If you had been, there wasn't room to fall down."

And that was when I thought of the next Slim Jim book, called *Party Matters*.

7

We were back at Dros-y-Mor with a winter's work before us when it seemed to me that it would be an agreeable thing to give Chris a surprise. Hitherto, we had roughed out an idea between us, and my contribution had been a daily sketch of the way we were to go. Chris would elaborate this into something readable, though now and then he might reject it for an idea of his own.

We had talked of one thing and another, but had decided nothing, when I sat down to the first chapter of *Party Matters*. I had been greatly impressed, in more ways than one, by the gathering at Sissons's office. I had been to few parties in my life, and never to one so asinine as this. Frank had fled the things like the Devil, and so, in the main, had Chris. Perhaps it was my very innocence, or ignorance, that stamped the occasion into my mind. What had struck me was the ease with which I had got into the room and with which I had got out of it. I might have given any name to the man at the door. He would have announced it and no one would have taken any notice of it. I could have smuggled myself out in the same way.

Before I knew where I was, I was writing not an outline but a full-length picture of that parrot-house full of squawking shouting creatures, and among them, with his elbows firmly pressed into my back, was a Ruritanian ambassador who was as dead as a door-nail, but no one knew it until the crowd began to thin and he slumped to the floor. What easier for the man who wished to kill him than to give him, in such circumstances, a jab in the back with a hypodermic needle filled with the most deadly poison ? He would take it for a lady's brooch or goodness knows what. Slim Jim himself would have his work cut out to discover who had been the killer in a mob like that. Anyway, I was so filled with the pride of authorship, of doing on my own what, till now, I had only suggested that someone else should do, that I scribbled away happily and had just brought my party to its consternated and fatal end, when Chris put his head round the door and said : " What about lunch, eh ? "

I did not tell him. This was not the moment. The time for that was to-night, when we would light the log-fire in the big library-cum-sitting room and settle down to a discussion of our day's doings. It would be, I told myself, a great surprise for him. He would find that his wife was a writer !

So I knocked together a cold lunch and told him that he should have a hot dinner. He was very kind and understanding about such matters. " Been up to the eyes in letters ? " he asked.

I said without a blush that I had, and he was well content.

<h1 style="text-align:center">8</h1>

There's no need to pretend that I was not in a mood of great excitement. I was ready for the medals to be pinned on. We had washed up together. We had lit the fire and drawn the curtains in the library. Chris filled his pipe and sprawled in his chair, ready for the evening's talk. " Uccles is out," he said. " I didn't want to worry you about it, but I had a letter from him to-day. That's a chancey world, you know, where he was venturing, and the whole thing's fallen through. Ah, well, I suppose it's better to dress up the work of an author who's been dead for the statutory time. You don't have to pay him any royalties then."

" Never mind Uccles," I said. " Just you listen to this."

Like a conjuror producing something out of a hat, I produced the first chapter of *Party Matters*. I hadn't been reading long before I became aware that Chris was listening with a strange attention. However, he let me go on. When I had finished, he knocked out his pipe on the fire-bars and asked : " Who's writing these novels—me or you ? "

I was astonished and hurt. I had hoped so much to please him, to be told that I had done a good job, had had a bright idea ; and very foolishly in my surprise and confusion I brought

319

in Frank's name. " I wouldn't have dared," I said, " to do a thing like this to Frank. His books were another matter. I did what I was told and typed them. But this is something else, isn't it, darling ? I thought this rather a good idea, and I wanted to take some of the fag off your shoulders."

I couldn't have chosen a worse moment for saying anything of the sort. I didn't know it, but he had been worrying all the day about Uccles. He had pretended that he didn't care, but now I saw how much he did care. He had been expecting more than I had ever done from Uccles. I had never liked the man, never hoped for much, if anything, to come from his odd underground ways. But Chris, optimistically, had been in a golden dream, and now he had wakened.

This was bad enough, but I had told him in so many words that Frank and I had dwelt in a different world from his—a world whose product was spikenard and myrrh, not ragged robin to be pulled out of any wayside hedge.

If he had raved at me, I should not have been surprised. I had touched him in a spot whence jealousy might easily spring. All he said was : " I should expect you to be a great admirer of Frank's work. Let me say once for all that your admiration could not be greater than mine."

I got up then and kissed him. He looked so desolated. " Don't worry about Uccles," I said. " We got on very well before he came upon us, and we shall do very well now that he is gone."

" I'm not worrying about Uccles," he untruthfully said, " but it *is* a little worrying to find you dashing into a thing like this. I'll take it and have a look at it, but I shall have to re-write it."

He was so determined to be the master-mind of Slim Jim ! Well, so was I ; but I saw clearly enough in that moment that the master-mind had better keep in the background and work only by suggestion.

" Now what's your idea about how this book should go ? "

I told him, and he said : " Well, I'll chew it over."

His first bit of chewing was done the next morning on the chapter I had written, and I couldn't see that he had made much change in it. But I took care to keep in the background of that book, as I had done heretofore.

Chapter XVI

The last thing I had expected from Rosy Midge—Miss Rose Midgley, Mrs. James Napier—was energy. There had been nothing much in her life to bring energy out. She had been booted here and there. In this rough world she had become like a football attacked by twenty-two feet. She had settled down a bit when she met Mamie James-Villiers, and she had settled down more after Chris and I had taken her in hand. But though a certain tranquillity had come to her, she remained a mouse. She was not like Mapson, who, I suspected, had been booted about in his time and had fought tooth and nail to be one of the booters.

Her marriage, combined with something to do, and something she found she wanted to do and could do, and worked hard at doing, soon made her a governing spirit in her small world ; and governing spirits are rare whether in a big world or a little one.

Chris and I went two or three times a year to London, and on these visits we always took in what was now called the Rowans Plant Farm. There was no longer any question of supplying a few things to Covent Garden. There were no more vegetables, and fruit only insofar as it was represented by young trees. There was a lot of experiment going on, and we found Rose proud to be associated with a new delphinium, named the Rose Napier. This had been shown at Chelsea, where the Rowans Plant Farm had made its first appearance. It was not to be long before its stands were appearing at all the great shows of the country—at Shrewsbury, Southport and many another. It was still, Ray assured me, a thin living. There was more labour to be employed, there was more land to be bought, and the original couple of acres seemed nothing but a small patch devoted to young trees.

" But we're all happy," Ray said. " That's the great thing. Salaries are small, even for me and Jimmy Napier, because at the moment we're putting most of it back into the land. But we'll come through."

He was tall and bearded, and I thought of the small fair boy that we had handed over to another Jimmy—James Sanderson—when first we took him to school. "What about Roger? Seen him yet?" he asked, and I realised with something of a pang, that there was a generation between the small boy that Frank and I had parted with and this bronzed bearded man who now casually asked whether we had seen his son.

2

How do you know that a place is going well? This was the first time I was strongly aware of it at the Rowans. There was no need to make an accountant's examination of the books, which Belinda was most accurately keeping. It was in the air. We found Mrs. Napier giving instructions about the thinning out of beds. She was no longer a packer. She was a general overseer. She was glad to meet us, and said she was just finishing what she had to do. She would run us up to her " little house " if we had a moment to spare.

Chris and I looked at one another in what can only be called " a wild surmise ". Rosy Midge behind the wheel of a motor-car was something we had never, in our maddest dreams, thought of. Ever since the moment when Belinda and Ray had smashed outside Truro she had feared the things and could be persuaded only with difficulty to enter one. Yet here she was embarking us in a small car that was parked near the Rowans and herself sitting most professionally in the driver's seat.

" It's no distance," she explained, " but I can spare only a moment, so we might as well ride."

I think, despite her explanations, Rosy wanted to show us her car. She certainly wanted to show us her house. It was, as she said, no distance away. It was, indeed, that very house, a little farther along the ridge, to which Poor Judith had taken me and Frank years ago to meet her newest friend. But now there was no Victorian knicknackery about it, but every evidence of a hard slog to " make do ". I said nothing to either Rosy or Chris about having been there before, but wandered through the rooms as Mrs. Napier proudly displayed them. It was this pride that came out in everything she showed us. " I made them," she would explain as she handled the curtains or the cushions, the rag mats or the bedspreads. It was this sense of being I, Mrs. James Napier, after so long a time being merely Rosy Midge, that made her at last a woman.

" Of course," she said with a touch of her old ingenuous frankness, " we're buying it through a building society."

Of course. But there was no doubt in my mind that the building society would be paid to the last penny. Rosy and James Napier were not the sort of people to bite off more than they could chew.

" Now, just time for a cup of coffee, and then I must be back to work," she said.

We did not see James Napier during that visit. He was away on the business of the Plant Farm. But Chris and I returned to London satisfied for the first time that Ray and Belinda were on the right track.

3

Chris and I never heard from Uccles again. But that did not worry us. Slim Jim from the first had taken the imagination of the people who read that sort of book ; but, if anything can be said to have established him, it was *Party Matters*. And Chris knew, as well as I knew myself, that that was my book. My instalment of morning scribble had dictated every twist and turn of it, and Chris had done nothing but what I might have done myself. When I had so proudly read my first instalment, he had asked " Who's writing these novels ? " It had been a red light to me, and I had slipped quickly back to my place, with a sense of having averted a danger. But now that the book was finished and roaring to a great financial success I knew that the danger had been only averted, not overcome.

We were back at Dros-y-Mor, taking our ease before another spell of work, and I was aware of an increasing restlessness in Chris. We had gone in the car for a drive, had garaged the thing, and had taken to our feet on the wild moors that lead to Land's End. We walked for a time in the lovely day over the springing heather and the great boulders that were lively with lichens of green and orange and red. It was a day to cheer the heart and the larks were singing. The summer rush had not begun, and, save for an isolated walker here and there, we were alone.

So we came to the edge, to the place where you are indeed at the land's end, and below you is nothing to be seen but the restless surging of the water, and the rocks that go down and down into its coldness in fantastic shapes.

I loathe heights. Even on a cliff of no great height at all I wonder when I shall cast myself down, and instinctively move inland. But Chris had found a niche between two granite rocks where the ling was soft and tender and a little grass grew, and there he let himself down. I sat beside him.

For a time we said nothing. The tide had reached that moment between ebb and flow when the water that can pound and hammer and seem as though intent to undermine the world is sleepy and tranquil, kissing the rocks on which the gulls take their ease. But I was nervy at the height, ready at any moment to rise and move inland. Chris had his back against a warm rock and his fingers were playing with the sea-pinks. Out of the blue—and it was indeed a blue and white day—he said : " I suppose you'll have to be getting on with a new book soon."

" There's no hurry," I said. " Let them wait. We can take a few weeks off. A few months, come to that. We can do as we've always done—enjoy ourselves in the summer and begin to think of work when the autumn is drawing in."

" Just as you like," he said indifferently.

" Why raise the matter now, anyway ? I know what Frank would have said about a day like this. It's a day for soaking things in, not giving them out."

" I know, or can guess, what Frank would have said. But Frank and I are two different matters."

I had been uneasy about Chris for some time. Now I cursed myself for a fool for having said the wrong thing. I should not have mentioned Frank's name. My concern should have been all for Chris, who was talking in a dead, flat voice, lying upon the ground, not looking at me. I began to think of the words he had used. " *You*'ll have to be getting on with a new book."

"Just as *you* like." Not *we*. He was creating a gap between us. The cliffs seemed suddenly dizzying, terrifying. I got up and pulled him to his feet. " I loathe being so near the edge," I said. " Let's get a bit inland."

He came willingly enough, but walking as it were with weighted feet. We sat down where we could not see the water save as a distant sparkle and the heather was all about us. " Now, tell me, Chris. What's the matter ? What has come over you ? "

" There's nothing the matter with me," he said doggedly in the same flat voice.

There was no gain in letting this thing stay underground. I knew what it was. First there was Uccles and all the disappointment he had brought about. Chris, I was sure, was not thinking of the money. We had money enough if we never wrote another word. But Chris had been disappointed at not getting back where his heart always was, and that was in the theatre. He would have had nothing to do with it. The songs, the scenes would all have been by another hand than his ; but he would have been back in the theatre. He would have sat and gloated at the applause, the laughter, assuming that Uccles and his men had been able to call these forth. As if underlining my own thoughts, he said : " I'm not even a novelist."

I could have killed myself then for the pride with which I had knocked off the first chapter of *Party Matters* and for the concision of the outlines I had given him each morning thereafter.

" But Chris," I said, " there are plenty of novelists, believe me, who would give their ears for your circulation. Every word you write is serialised, and then there are the books . . ."

But he broke in with the same dull voice that was getting on my nerves : "You know, as well as I do, that the books are yours. They owe everything to what you give me each morning. I do nothing but write them. Even so, you are apt to quibble about what I have written, and I write it over again."

" Well," I said, determined to keep the moment light, " call me your collaborator. I'll bet that even Gilbert and Sullivan had moments when they didn't see eye to eye. We've got along very well so far by the method we've hit on. We can go on in that way, if you like, or I'll stand down and be what I was used to being. I'll just type what you write."

But nothing would please him that day. " Far more sense," he said, " in typing what *you* write. There's only one name put to the blasted books, and you can have it, for me, and welcome. And now," he said, getting to his feet, " we've given enough out this morning, and, as Frank would have said, this is a day for taking things in. So let's get about a bit and take things in."

4

Chris was himself when we began a new book later in that year. But I had " taken in " two things that day at Land's End. The first was to keep Frank out of all save my secret life. He was there as much as ever, but I did not mention him again. The bitterness with which Chris had thrown back his words at me was a warning. He admired Frank's work ; he had liked Frank as a man ; but there was a rankling in his mind at the thought that I believed what Frank had done to be more important than what he was doing. The second thing was to obliterate so far as possible my own part in the work we were at together. I never questioned again anything that he had written, and more than once he began his morning's work with no " outline " to go on. He knew, as well as I did, I would tell him, how the point in question was to be solved, and I became more and more the dutiful secretary unless asked for an opinion.

There was one matter in which this edifice of pretence nearly tumbled about us. " I think," Chris said one day at breakfast, " that I'll take my morning's work down to Frank's old hut. Humanise the place a bit. Give it some reason for existence."

My first instinct was to say : No.

I thought of my first intrusion into the hut so many years ago when, a girl new to Frank and all his ways, I had arrived from London, full of enthusiasm, thinking the most important thing in the world was to announce my coming and to let Frank know that his loneliness was ended. I had been coldly received, had been rebuffed, and had gone out to the seat in the woods and wept.

That and innumerable other things rushed to my mind, things that had made the hut almost a sacred place which to this day I swept and tended.

And then I looked at Chris, and the denial of this sanctuary became impossible. It was his attempt to get nearer to me, to create again conditions which once had existed, and I could not bear the thoughts that would have sprung to his mind. " So the sort of stuff I write mustn't be written where Frank's holy books first saw the light." That would be the least part of his bitterness.

" Why, yes, Chris," I said, " I'll bring you out some coffee at eleven o'clock. After all, the hut was built for writing. Why shouldn't you write in it ? "

He looked like a boy who has been praised. " I'm glad you don't mind," he said. " Perhaps I'll do better there."

5

Frank had been in his way a stoic when he was at work. An old rug thrown over his knees, and maybe a pair of mittens on his wrists were enough for him in even the coldest weather. Hidden as it was by trees, the hut had tended to be damp, and that was why I had had an electric fire put in, so that once a week I could give the hut an airing. Now that Chris had taken it for a workplace this fire was always switched on when he was there. During my expeditions with the morning drink I noticed that small evidences of comfort were changing the old place into something I had not known. A print of Degas dancing girls appeared on the wall and the trestle table was dismantled and put to one side. A firm table had taken its place, and there Chris would be installed in a comfortable chair instead of the rickety kitchen chair that Frank had used. The warmth in so small a place was often oppressive, and, worst of all, I felt at liberty to speak ! This was something new. It had been my custom to put the coffee at Frank's elbow, kiss the back of his neck, and withdraw like a shadow. Sometimes a grunt would acknowledge my presence ; more often there was not even that.

But Chris was always ready for a talk. Indeed, he seemed to expect it. " Take a chair," he would say ; and I would get Frank's old kitchen chair out of a corner, sit upon it, and listen to all that Chris had to tell me about the work he was engaged upon.

"I like a morning break," he said one day. "Bring the coffee-pot out here with you, and we can have a drink and a chat together."

It was towards the end of that winter that the gale came upon us. It had been a cold still day, but as we sat by the fire after dinner the wind began to whimper. Soon you could hear the trees rustling uneasily, and an hour later they were creaking as the wind in ever-increasing force rushed through them. Now and then we heard a branch crash down, but islanded as we were, safe from the weather, we enjoyed the tumult without, drew our chairs closer to the fire and, as men will when hearing of afflictions that do not concern them, took comfort from our own security. But even here, with a roof over our heads and a fire at our feet, we felt at last how frail was any place when elemental forces were unleashed and rampaging. For the wind increased as the night wore on, and as bedtime drew near there was such a sobbing and crying of wind as I had not heard in our woods throughout the many years I had spent at Dros-y-Mor.

"It's a lucky thing," Chris said, "that the lopping-man will be coming over to-morrow afternoon from Helston. I'll have to go round with him and see what there is to do. Plenty, I should think, after this lot."

We always called him the lopping-man—the man who came every year to tidy up the woods. It certainly sounded as though he would have plenty to do. As we climbed the stairs we could hear no diminution of the cries, the crashes, that seemed everywhere to be gaining in fury as the wind rushed through the night like an express train through a tunnel. Now the noise was down to a whimper, but no sooner were we comforting ourselves with the thought that the worst was over than with a renewed shriek the tempest was roaring upon us again. Within the very house doors creaked; and the carpet stirred on the floor. I remember thinking how "the long carpets rose along the gusty floor" on the Eve of St. Agnes, as I took Chris by the arm and listened to a pelt of rain on the roof.

We slept uneasily. We had passed the moment when we could take comfort in our own security. I awoke from time to time from dreams of Ray in such a night on his destroyer, of poor Mapson heaving and tossing in his battleship. And then I awoke again, found Chris asleep at my side, and saw a pale light against the window-pane. The cry of a bird fell on my ear. It was an owl, and it was to me as welcome as the dove to Noah, for I realised that it was crying through a great silence. The wind was gone. Sanity had followed the madness of the storm, and I slept again, now dreamless, till I was waked by the sound of Chris padding about the bedroom. He was shaved and dressed. " I was up before you," he announced triumphantly. " I've been down and got the breakfast ready. Just throw a rag on and come and eat."

He had lit the fire. My rusks and a coffee percolator were on the table. He was a heartier eater than I, and went to the kitchen for his fried bread and bacon, his toast and his marmalade.

" Well, it's over," he announced, smacking them down on the table. " I can do a morning's work after all."

It was indeed a heartening morning. Through the great window I could see the creek, all muddy at low tide, and the rain-spangles hanging on the trees. It was as still as though the night had not known its madness, and a wintry sun was filling the sky with pale light.

" Well, mind you're warm in that hut," I said. " The woods will be damp after such a night."

" I'll look after myself," he promised. " I won't come back with a cold and want one of your warmed bricks at my feet. I've got a pair of carpet slippers down there, and I'll wear my gum-boots for splashing through the woods."

" Off you go then," I said, like a mother sending her child to school. " I'll see you at eleven o'clock with a hot drink."

" Wasn't I a good boy, getting the breakfast ? "

He had never done such a thing before, and his bacon had been rather burnt. " You'll do," I said, " to be getting on with."

He pulled on his gum-boots, kissed me, and went.

When he was gone I pulled on gum-boots myself and went out on to the quarter-deck to look at the day. The dinghy, which in all these years had served us faithfully, was gone. Half-way between me and the bend in the creek I could see it thrown up on the slope of a field. Near it was a group of elms, and I had often wondered how, year after year, the rooks' nests built there withstood our winter winds and, with a little patching in the spring, served as the nurseries of another brood. The nests were gone now. A few twigs, like blackened hay, were all that I could see, hanging forlorn and bedraggled against the winter sky. One of the elms was down. It lay in the creek, and all the rubbish that a low tide brings to light was tangled, a dirty mess, in its branches. The roots lay just beyond the upturned dinghy, a fantastic picture of wood and earth, still weeping the rain that had fallen upon them.

They had grown into my life, that group of trees, and I was mourning the loss of the old elm when a farmer whose fields these were came running past the trees, shouting indistinguishable words. He continued to run, pointing to the woods behind me, and turning to look, I saw smoke rising there, and then a flare, and then a flame. He had waded across the mud at our end of the creek, rushed up the landing-steps, and was almost at my side as I began to run. "A fire! A fire in your woods," he shouted.

In five minutes we were there, at the hut, too late. It was all reconstructed, very reasonably, at the inquest. Chris had lit the electric fire and settled down to work. A moment later, a tree, whose roots had been loosened by the storm, fell upon the hut. A beam in the roof went down at the blow, upset the fire and struck Chris upon the head. In his unconsciousness he was not aware that the electric fire was still burning, though overset, putting a flame to a paper here and to this there. The place was alight when we reached it, and with great gallantry the farmer rushed into it and pulled out the body. All too late. Chris was clutching a pen as we laid him on the path and I knelt beside him and wept.

Chapter XVII

The papers announced Chris's death rather because of the circumstances in which it had happened than because of Chris himself. The author of a few plays now out of date, the adaptor of other men's books for stage purposes, did not amount to much, and it was not known that Christopher Harris who did these things was also the Herman Herries whose name appeared on the Slim Jim novels. His family, too, was extinct. He and Mamie James-Villiers had been the last of them, and, what with one thing and another, there was no assembly when we laid him in the churchyard within a stone's-throw of the place where Frank, by no more than the blink of an eye-lid as these things go, had preceded him.

Ray and Belinda alone stood at my side. James Napier and his wife had moved for a few days into the Rowans to look after the young Roger, and Mell, who, I had hoped, would be with me for this ending as he had been almost at the beginning, was laid up with a heavy cold. Laura had stayed at home to nurse him.

It was one of those heart-breaking days that come sometimes in mid-winter. All thoughts of stress were gone. There might never have been a cloud in the sky or a wind in the woods. The sun shone out of a pure pale blue, and the graveyard was fragrant with the scent of winter heliotrope. The trees were tranced in the stillness, and the birds were stirring as though with thoughts of nesting and new young life. Then it was over, and even as the grave-diggers were throwing in their clods, Ray moved over the few yards of grass and stood looking down at the place where his father was buried. I felt it in my heart like a reproach, and Belinda, who was still a little lame but moved now without a stick, took my arm and led me out of the graveyard.

331

In the earliest spring of the next year I said good-bye to Dros-y-Mor. It had been sold by an agent, I scarcely know to whom, for I could not bear to have anything to do with it. The place had meant too much. It had meant Frank and Chris, the young Ray and his friend James Sanderson, Em Pritt and fun in the boat, and tossing Belinda overboard on to Mell's shoulders, Rosy Midge and Poor Judith and Mamie James-Villiers, Dr. Nancarrow and Joe who had become Em's husband and who was now thriving and on the County Council, and ever urging better and wider roads for Cornwall ; even Ronald Lilywhite, who went back further than any of them, ignominiously falling into the water in his fine yachting clothes as Frank casually pushed him.

All these things and people were in the back of my mind as I made my lonely pilgrimage of farewell. Here was the bank on which, so long ago, I had lain down to sleep. It was just such a day as this : a day of bird-song and opening flowers, leaves as new as brides with all life before them, not even a summer storm in sight. I had awakened to find Ben Davies lifting me in strong arms, and there was the cottage to which he had carried me and where his rosy wife had put me to bed and old Dr. Nancarrow had come fussing in and out. They were all dead now —Ben and his wife had gone the way of their old lady over to Gweek, and Dr. Nancarrow had for ever said good-bye to his delphiniums.

I moved along the path through the woods and sat down on the seat where first I had set eyes on Frank. It had been patched, the old seat, times out of mind. The stream was at my feet, bordered still with kingcups and primulas that Jane had planted. The woods were full of the glad crying of the birds ; camellias bloomed in red and white and magnolias added their lordly opulence to a scene that nevertheless was all sadness now. From here it should have been possible to see Ray's hut where Rosy had made her genuflexions before the altar which she had kept adorned with young leaves. It had long been gone. A forsythia where it had stood was already a golden fountain, but the small wistful figure of Rosy, so grown-up now and business-like, seemed to flit before me in the wood, hastening to the house lest anyone should discover her mind's preoccupation.

I got up from the seat and hastened to the end of my pilgrimage. Here was the spot where, morning after morning, I had left the path from the quarter-deck and turned into the woods with my morning drink. The moss of the track to the hut was still beaten down where day upon day feet had trodden it. But the hut was gone. The track ended in nothing. They had made a clean job—the men I had ordered to take away the rubbish and leave not a trace. It ended in nothing, but to me in so much that I hastened on with eyes blinded by tears.

3

I spent the night in Falmouth, and was in London by the evening of next day, in a small hotel I had often gone to with Frank. Mell joined me at dinner, so solicitous that I almost expected him to send me to bed after the meal and to say that he would be up in half-an-hour to read to me about Guinevere. Strange that I had not perceived in those far-off days what an old owl he was—an owl I was very fond of, but an old owl none the less. However, in the working out of time—swifter than I had believed time to be—we had at any rate arrived at this situation : that he was the grandfather and I the grandmother of the same boy, young Roger Melvill. But it was not of Roger he wanted to talk, or of Chris. He talked about Frank. He had just finished a book—I think it was his third—on the Romans in Britain, and he asked my permission to dedicate it " To the memory of my uncle, Frank Melvill."

" I'm afraid," he said apologetically, " that it won't sell widely, but it will sell well—to the right people, I mean."

It was the only consolation left now to poor Mell—that his books found their way into the hands of people as dull as himself. I said that he could use the dedication he wished, and that I was sure that Frank himself would have felt honoured ; but I could think only of the night when Frank and I had found him leaning on the wall of the river up which the Romans had come, himself for once forgetting the Romans and engaged with Laura in one of his rare personal and emotional moments.

333

" How is Laura ? " I asked him.

" Oh, she is more and more out at the Rowans, deeply concerned with Belinda and young Roger," he said. " But I get on very well at our place at Chelsea."

I could not help wondering how well " very well " might be, and after dinner, this being a fine night of spring, I took him out to walk on that very route which we had followed so long ago when, I being a red-headed slip of a thing, he had first brought me from Cardiff to London and we had stayed there for an evening before going on to the Rowans. I found that I could recall every moment of that evening—how the lights had fallen on the leaves of the plane trees and how the towers of the House of Commons had stood against the darkening but still flushed western sky and he had discoursed to me of the labours of Bryan Graves being conducted within. Life could never be to me again quite the romantic thing that it was that night, but the detail of it, the thrill that had been in my young heart, could be recalled in all its essence. But Mell, that time, had been on his way back to Oxford, and doubtless other matters had called to him and filled his mind. At any rate, he said nothing of the moment, and when he shook my hand and said he would walk on to Chelsea I hoped that Laura would be there to welcome him. " Oh, no," he said. " She's staying at the Rowans overnight. She sometimes does, you know. It makes a change for her."

4

Peter Sissons had done me the honour of calling upon me. Chris and I had known him for a long time before Chris died, and had had our share in turning him from a young man wondering how to pay the rent into a thriving publisher. He and Uccles, who knew everything, were the only people who knew that Christopher Harris and Herman Herries were the same person, and he alone knew of my part in making Herman Herries what he was. As for Uccles, I never heard of his giving away a secret and this one proved as safe with him as many others that he carried in his strange head. Peter Sissons had written to me when Chris died, and when, in reply, I had said that I should leave Dros-y-Mor and live somewhere near London, he had proposed this meeting which took place in the early summer of that year.

Chris had never said anything to me, or I to him, about his income, but I now found myself a fairly well-to-do woman. Mrs. Mapson had long ago sold the house called Whitecotes, and now it was in the market again. I bought it in a sentimental moment from a colonel's widow, and took over with it a handyman named Doidge, who lived in a cottage not far away, and a woman, as old as myself, named Mrs. Oscott. Her husband had been the colonel's batman in India, in what already seemed the distant days when we had troops there, and, the husband being now dead, the colonel's widow was gone to end her life with a daughter. In the only conversation I had with the old lady, I gathered that this daughter was married to a man who was all for giving back any part of the world to anyone who wanted it at any time they wanted it. I hoped they would all be happy together, but I never heard from her again.

I was glad to have Mrs. Oscott and she to have me, for she had nowhere to go, no relatives that she knew of in England. We divided the work between us. I did the cooking ; she did all else ; and Doidge, who was younger than either of us, did everything out of doors.

It was here, then, that I awaited Peter Sissons on a morning of late May, just as, long before, Mapson had waited for me and Frank to see his new house, hung with hunting-horns over the Vlaminck. Though I had seen it so rarely, it was a reminiscent sort of place, even with my own stuff and Frank's about me. One room in which I worked I had given over to his books, which reached, as they had done at Dros-y-Mor, from floor to ceiling. I devoted one shelf to books that he had written himself, which, with their many translations, made an imposing show. I was humble enough to put the Slim Jim books, which had no translations at all, though they had American editions, on a lower shelf. These books, with my typing table and a writing table and a comfortable chair by the fireside, were about all that the room contained.

In this room, whose windows looked upon the garden which still had white cotes with a few pigeons tumbling about them, Peter Sissons and I took coffee after we had lunched. What we talked about does not matter until he said : " We've been in the habit of publishing a new Slim Jim novel in time for Christmas. That has happened for some years now. What do we do this Christmas ? Do we have one ? "

" Slim Jim," I said, " is as dead as a door-nail. You can make it clear if you like that Christopher Harris who died lately, was the Herman Herries who wrote the books, and that therefore there'll be no more of them."

" That would be a pity," he said, " for both of us."

He was a slow-spoken man, and when he had said this he said nothing more until I had thought it over. Then he added : " There are two things I wanted to remind you of. When you and Chris brought along the first book, you were kind enough to take me into your confidence about the way you worked together. Wasn't there something about a sketch that you gave him every morning—a kind of indication of the way the chapter was to go ? "

I could only say that that was so. " But I had given up doing that," I added.

This was indeed true, for I had felt in Chris more and more the desire, even the need, to say " All my own work."

" The second thing is that you were his typist, too, I suppose? "

I admitted that I was, and he said with a smile : " Having known you and Chris for a number of years now, it wouldn't surprise me if you slipped in a phrase here and there."

I recalled one of those phrases. I remembered how Chris, who never read the typescript, was cock-a-hoop at the breakfast table one day when a new Slim Jim book had arrived. " Good, don't you think ? " he said, reading the words aloud. " And I haven't the least recollection of writing that. One gets into the way of doing these things, I suppose, and then they go right out of one's mind."

I didn't disillusion him, and I said nothing to Sissons now. We talked for an hour about indifferent matters, and then he rose to go. " We should have to draw up a new contract," he said, as he was shaking hands. " The old one was between me and Chris. The new one will have to be between you and me." He added with the smile that I liked so much : " Contracts are sacred. Nothing about them leaks out. Unless the authors talk."

" Well, we'll see," I said. " You are a very persistent man, Peter."

" Very well, then, Alice. In a few months ? "

" We'll see," I repeated.

" Good. That's all I ask."

5

My life now became a routine. Every morning I wrote ; every afternoon, whatever the weather, I walked ; and every evening I read. So it was from Monday to Friday. At the week-ends I went sometimes to see Ray, Belinda and Roger ; sometimes to see Laura and Mell.

I was rather afraid of Ray. He was not as Frank had been, or Chris either. He never said " Let's . . .", and dropped everything, and did what was new and surprising. It was as though he were making up for the years after the war, the years when he had loafed about making a pretence of working for Mapson. It was difficult to recognise in this tall, broad-shouldered, bearded man either the youth who then had been peevish, having a hundred quarrels with life, or the eager boy who worked in his hut at plasticine models and went off on " digs " with James Sanderson. It happened that, in bringing a new bit of land into cultivation, the men he employed had come on some ancient bricks which were undoubtedly Roman, and had reported the find to him. Even James Napier had been more excited than Ray. I was at the Rowans when the find was made, and Jimmy, as everyone called him, walked me along to have a look at it. " Takes you right away," he said, " into the backward and abysm of time, as old R. L. S. put it."

He stood pondering on the bricks, with Mrs. Napier, our old Rosy Midge, at his side. She said : " You've got to dig pretty deep before you come on that stuff. Mr. Melvill says they'd better be covered up and things grown over them before people hear of them and a lot of busy-bodies come poking about."

Ray was Mr. Melvill to everyone, as surely as James Napier was Jimmy. He gave the bricks a casual look-over, confirmed that they were Roman, and that was that. They were now to be buried again. I would have liked to see him more inquisitive, more eager, stirred now and then by something outside his daily preoccupations, even interested in his plants as more than commercial articles. But nowadays he didn't even read except such things as bore on his job. Frank's books stood on his shelves, a neat row, dusted now and then but unopened. Roger was approaching the age at which Ray had been when he went to his first school, and I ventured diffidently to ask what arrangements had been made about the boy. " We'll make him, I hope," he answered, " a good market gardener, and all he'll want for that he can learn here. There'll be no need to send him away to school."

I took what comfort I could from the evident prosperity of the place and from the growing display of cups won at the great shows. This was the autumn time, with a book behind me, the first Slim Jim that I had turned out on my own. Much as I had laughed with Chris about all Slim Jim's works and ways, there was a sense of possession, a pride in having done something for myself, a knowledge that it had, in its way, saved me from brooding over-much on what Peter Sissons called my troubles. Certainly I should have been desolate without something to do, and Peter was kind enough to say that this was the best of the series.

I had arrived for that visit to the Rowans on a Friday afternoon. On the Saturday morning I took young Roger for a walk. Belinda was very anxious that I should. " It's going to be a busy morning for me," she explained. " Saturday morning always is. I go through the books on a Saturday, send out our accounts and write the cheques. If you could take him off my hands. . . ."

So I took him off her hands. He was a leggy little boy who was attending a day school in Harpenden. One of the men drove him in every morning in a Land-Rover and picked him up in the evening. He ate his mid-day meal at the school.

He told me these things when we set out, as Poor Judith and I had done long ago; on a blackberrying expedition, furnished with walking-sticks for hooking down high branches. But it wasn't such an expedition as Judith and I had known that day. The road was no longer dusty but solid tarmac ; houses had sprung up here and there ; motor-cars were plentiful, and, I thought with a grim smile, women had the vote, which would

338

have pleased Bryan Graves immensely. He would have seen a new world at once, but all I could see was the multiplicity of the little houses and the absence of blackberry bushes. I couldn't see the absence of warfare, which Bryan had assured me would be an almost instant consequence ; I could see only women in the armed forces everywhere.

But I said nothing of this to Roger, who was growing up in a world where such things were accustomed. He asked me from time to time when were we going to find the blackberries.

We came to some at last, but they were nasty roadside things, smothered in fumes. We picked what we could, but there was no overflowing crop that day, so we climbed through a hedge and sat in the sun, which was not yet controlled by some international body. We had a prospect of the wide valley and we ate our lunch. I put all the usual questions to Roger and found that he was bored to tears by school and was an indifferent scholar. " But that'll all be over one of these days," I said. " And what then ? What do you want to do with yourself ? "

" I want to do something hazardous," he said, bringing out the grand word with difficulty. " I want to swim in a submarine right under the polar ice-cap. Something like that. Or climb some high mountain like Sir Edmund Hillary. Or travel somewhere like David Livingstone. It would be great fun if someone found me in a tent years later with all my black servants and said ' Mr. Melvill, I presume ? ' "

" But David Livingstone found all sorts of new things," I pointed out. " There's not so much to find nowadays, is there? "

His answer pleased and rather surprised me. " There's plenty to be found by those who want to find it."

" What does your father say to all this ? " I asked. " Do you ever talk to him about it ? "

" He's very pleased," he said, " when I'm packed off to school in the morning and he can get on with his primulas and delphiniums. I loathe the sight of them."

We munched away at the sandwiches we had brought and swigged coffee out of a Thermos flask, but I never felt Roger was much with me.

" Your husband—all your husbands," he amended, as though

I had a new one every week, " wrote books, didn't they ? My mother talks to me sometimes about them."

I admitted the shameful fact that my husbands had written books, and Roger said, rather morosely : " Now my grandfather's at it. I loathe books."

So he loathed books and he loathed plants, and no one was doing anything about the things he didn't loathe.

" Well," he said, " I suppose it'll have to be a submarine. Sir Edmund Hillary's about cleared up the mountains, and, as you say, explorers have about cleaned up the land. There's not much left except the sea."

So that was that. The sea had it. Under the sea. I thought of Ray's old friend James Sanderson who was under the sea for good ; and we took up our basket of rather dusty blackberries and started for home. Roger consented to carry them. " Not that they're much good," he said. " A pretty dusty lot. Still," he magnanimously conceded, " thanks for having me and letting me run on. I'm generally turned over at week-ends to Mrs. Napier. She's trying to teach me packing of all things ! "

6

It was tea-time when Roger and I got back to the Rowans, and our small gift was not received with much enthusiasm. It was rather a gloomy meal anyway. I was looking forward to a talk with Ray about Roger's future, but he was not there. Roger scrambled through the meal, asked permission to go, and went.

" Where's Ray ? " I asked Belinda.

" I don't know," she said. " There's some new machine wanted on the place, and Mrs. Napier has got wind of one going second-hand. She and Ray are off somewhere in the car to have a look at it."

I thought of the time when Chris and I had made them a marriage present of the Rowans. We had all four walked over the garden, and the young people were full of enthusiasm. The stream that would furnish endless water. The hedges that would cut out the wind. Every yard, every inch, almost, of the place was to have its usefulness. Already it had its attractions. They were up in the air about it. They were full of go. All the dreams had now come true, insofar as dreams can ever become practical things. The place was bigger. There were machines for doing this, that, and the other thing. They were prosperous. For the first time they had gone so far as to have a catalogue, a delightful thing illustrated with photographs in colour and with drawings. There was a picture of a bench-full of cups that had been won.

But I wasn't happy. For the first time I felt a discord in the air. I noted that Ray and Mrs. Napier had " gone off somewhere in the car ". To everyone but Belinda she was Rose. She had been so to Belinda for a long time. Now she was " Mrs. Napier". When Chris and I were doing what we could to wean Ray from Mapson he had stayed with us here, and he had taken Rosy Midge, as she then was, for a walk and had introduced her to a few plants. And after that she had kept his hut tidy at Dros-y-Mor and had made her shy offerings. She was the only person who seemed to care when his hut was torn down, to give a better sight of a camellia. And now she was a different person : a self-assured person who had found what she wanted to do, and was doing it well, and she had become Mrs. Napier to Belinda, and she was gone off somewhere in a car with Ray.

After tea, Belinda said that she must get on with her weekly accounts, so I left her and wandered unhappily about the grounds. It was a busy time at the nurseries because hundreds of rose plants had to be grafted, and I found James Napier superintending the job. He was in gay spirits and took a moment to explain to me what they were doing and how they did it. " It all comes rather dear," he said. " These chaps have to be paid double for working on a Saturday afternoon when they're normally off. Still, the customer pays in the long run and we're doing very well."

" I suppose," I said, " that this new machine that Ray's gone to see with Mrs. Napier will be a great help ? "

" Oh, those two. They're always out after something. Ah, well. On with the dance. I've got plenty to do here, without chin-wagging."

I left him untroubled by any of my own dark thoughts, and went up to the house. " Tell Ray," I said to Belinda, " that I've had to dash off home. I'm not feeling too good. I think that long walk with Roger was a bit much."

She was at once all solicitude, but I was resolved to go, and I went. Whitecotes seemed very peaceful when I got there, and I settled down to have a good long abstinence from interfering with other people's lives.

7

On a morning in the winter that followed the postman brought me a packet done up in brown paper and addressed to me in Mell's writing. It was rarely now that either Mell or Laura wrote to me, for we were seeing one another fairly regularly. Or rather I was seeing Laura, for, most times when I called at the Chelsea flat, Mell was out on his frequent visitations to the British Museum.

I had just finished breakfast and was about to take myself off for a morning's work in the cosy room that had become my study. It was my custom never to open a letter or to do anything that might, as I rather grandly put it, " let the world in," till my work was done, and I could not believe that Mell had anything important to say to me or to send me. But something tingled through the paper and I found myself a moment later sitting in my room before the fire which had just been lit, snipping the sealed string with a scissors. Inside the parcel was another parcel, tied round like the first, portentously sealed with wax. On top of this was a letter addressed to me. I opened it and read.

" Dear Alice.—I have written a novel, or rather a yarn for children."

I could have dropped off my chair with laughter. The idea of Mell—sober, solemn, serious Mell—writing a yarn for children! But then I thought of Lewis Carroll, a serious, solemn don, who had written *Alice in Wonderland*, and of Kingsley, a sober parson, who had written *The Water Babies*, and I read on :

" When you have read this letter, please yourself about opening the parcel which is enclosed with it. Nobody has read it yet except me—not even Laura who thinks I have been doing another of my books for dons. I have not entrusted it to her for typing, which is why I hesitate to send it to you, because it is in my handwriting, which isn't easy to read. But I should dearly love to write a book which isn't read only by scholastics, and this is my effort to do so."

Dear Mell ! How he had tried always to conceal that feeling, always to pretend that he didn't care so long as one or two men, here and there, thought his work good. I was flattered by his confession.

" So if you *do* open the inner parcel," he went on, " you will know what to expect, and you will know that I value your opinion. After all, you have been married to two men who were better writers than I can hope to be. If, after this explanation, you decide not to be bored by the thing, I shall quite understand. In that case, please send back the inner parcel, which you will see is addressed to me and stamped, and I shall not be offended. Ever yours, with love, Mell."

He was so meticulous. Addressed. Stamped. Everything according to protocol and precedent. Dear Mell !

I hesitated for a long time to open that inner parcel. I had worked for Frank. I feared what I might find. I recall the moment clearly : the wintry sunshine, the frost crackling on the lawn without. To my amazement, these were the first words I read : " The sunshine was heartening though it had little warmth. The frost crackled on the grass."

This coincidence of what I was seeing and feeling with what I had read seemed to me so odd, and the beginning was so un-Mell-like, that I read on, and was soon convinced that Mell had done it. He had set his tale in a place and period that he knew —Roman Britain—and round a Roman farmer in the Sussex country and the English boy who worked on the farm. He had vividly brought to life all the probable happenings of a distant day. The boy's father, who loathed the Romans as invaders, the farmer himself, who had become half a Briton, the boy who had become half a Roman and would continue the Roman tradition after the legions were withdrawn, all was there, put down with a simplicity and yet with a truthfulness that kept me reading on and on, for Mell, by luck or a subtle skill, had tumbled on the first secret of a good novelist—the ability to keep the reader agog to know what happens next.

It was a short novel. It took me two hours to read it, and I had just put the manuscript aside with both satisfaction and surprise when Mrs. Oscott came in with my eleven o'clock coffee. She put it down, made up the fire, and announced : " There's a man wants to see you. I told him you never see nobody in the morning, but he won't go. He says perhaps you'll make an exception in his case. He's waiting now. A man named Conybeare."

" Show him in," I said, " and bring another cup."

It was Mell, hot on the footsteps of his manuscript. I hugged him and kissed him, and he said, looking at the litter on my table : " You've opened it ! I came to take it away ! "

He was full of apologies. It was just an impulse. He was sorry he had bothered me with it. He would take it away. Please don't think any more about it.

I filled his coffee cup, put some coal on the fire, and said : "Sit down. If it was an impulse I suppose it was the first in your life. It's time you had an impulse or two. You've been all buttoned up since I first knew you."

He sat down, stirring his coffee, looking as though he had committed a sin. I began to understand why he had not succeeded in his career. He was thoroughly reliable, the man who never made a mistake, but he must always have authority, the already done, behind him. He was without impulse, incapable of a brilliant improvisation. I found myself talking to him as if to a child.

" I've not only opened your manuscript," I said, " I've read it—every word of it. I know what's come over you. You want to take it away, verify all the incidents, touch it up, make it a proper studio photograph."

" Well, there are one or two things——" he began, but I broke in again. " Well, I prefer it as it is—just as you imagined it might be, not as some stuffy old historian might back you up about this point or that. Don't you see, Mell, that the thing's *alive*. For goodness' sake, don't put in a lot that will make it as dead as a pancake."

" You've really read it ? " he asked.

" It's read itself *to me*," I amended. " I've read every word you've written, Mell, in all your books. I suppose that surprises you. Well, I have ; and what's more, I've forgotten all of it. There was nothing to make it stick. But I shall never, as long

WINDS OF THE DAY

as I live, forget this little English boy, going out on frosty English grass in an English winter morning, with the sun coming up, red and solid. You *saw* that, didn't you ? You didn't find it in some old—well, what I suppose you would call authority."

" So you've really read it ? " he repeated.

" I've really read it, and you're not going to take it away. I'm a good typist."

" I couldn't do that," he said. " Laura does my typing, but I wanted this to be a secret from her. I could send it out to someone, and then, if any publisher wants it, we could put a false name on it."

" You're ashamed for Laura to read it," I teased him, knowing I was near the truth. " Well, I've spent a lot of my life typing other people's books, and I'll do this one. And, what's more, Mell, I shall be proud to do it. And, what's more still, you'll put your own name to it and go on putting your name to more like it."

He went at last, in his rusty old car, a bit enheartened, I think, but dubious still. However, there was no doubt in my own mind. I sat down at once, put Slim Jim into a drawer, and began to type Mell's book.

A few days later I rang up Peter Sissons and asked him to give me lunch. We went to the Café Royal. He was becoming a bit stout, very prosperous-looking, and had an enviable reputation as a publisher of " winners ". He was also becoming a gourmand and ordered me such a lunch as I should not have dreamed of ordering for myself. We had reached the coffee and Armagnac stage, and I had declined the Armagnac, when I said: " You've heard, I expect, of my fellow grandparent, Melvill Conybeare ? "

" I've heard of him—yes. But I had no idea he was related to you."

" Well, he has the honour of being the grandfather of my grandson."

" One of these learned old cocks, isn't he ? Sells five thousand copies with luck. More like two or three thousand, I should say."

Then I went in like any bagman with a washing-machine to sell at the door. I " plugged " Mell's so-far unnamed book. I produced my typescript and handed it over to Sissons. " Take it and read it," I said, " and ring me up at Whitecotes when you've done it. Forget all that Mr. Conybeare has written. Not that you've read any of it, I imagine. But forget his reputation. And when you want to see him, as you will, let me know, and I'll bring him around to your office."

" You seem pretty sure that it's in my line."

" I am sure it will make you money. When you sign a contract with him I'll be there to read it."

" By the way," he said, " your own contract for the Slim Jim books is due for renewal."

" Yes. That's what I was thinking of."

" Blackmailer," he said. " All right. I'll take it and read it."

You can still read this book of Mell's. A new printing comes out every Christmas-time. But he will never read it, never read the one thing he wrote that thousands of boys and girls, and their parents, too, read in edition after edition. He died that day when I took lunch with Peter Sissons. Having nothing else to do, my day being disrupted, I went from the Café Royal to call on him and Laura. There was no answer to my ringing at the door of the house in Chelsea. Deciding that they were both out, I returned to Whitecotes, I would like to say with a heart full of premonition. But there was nothing of the sort. All I felt was gladness at having been able at last to do Mell a good turn : he who, picking me up from a broken pavement in Cardiff, had set my feet on the way they had gone ever since. Perhaps they would have found that way anyhow, but it was Mell who set them there, and now, for the first time, I was able to do something for him.

That morning Laura had gone off to the Rowans to see Belinda. Mell had said that he would stay at home to go through a note or two. When she returned in the evening he was dead in his chair. A seizure of some sort. It was as simple and straightforward as that. Was it before or after I had rung at the bell ? I never knew, but I knew in the core of me that Mell had been the first man who had treated me as a gentleman treats a lady. Does that sound old-fashioned ? Very well then. It is old-fashioned. I have lived long enough to dislike many new fashions. Now I should never be able to do anything for Mell. For his memory—yes. But not for him. I sat down and wept for him as I had not wept for Frank or Chris. It was an older woman who had met them, and for Chris, at least, I had felt some pity as well as some love. But neither of them had picked up a small servant-girl from a pavement in Cardiff and shown her that she was a human being with aspirations. I know that Mell would have done what he did for a cat or a dog, but, as it happened, it was for me. Perhaps it was of me that I was thinking —of me and years long gone, when Tennyson seemed the last word in poetry and the Llandaff Fields were paradisal with the Cathedral spire standing up against a sky that never was, and life all new and radiant. I don't know. But I know that I wept for Mell as I had never wept before, that the last thing was now gone that had been there when I banged the door on the Lilywhites and faced alone the winds of the day.

Chapter XVIII

In *The Times* there were a few lines about Mell and one or two papers of the more learned sort gave some space to what he had done to increase knowledge of the Romans in England, particularly in the years just before the legions went. None of them knew, Laura herself did not know, what he had been doing in the British Museum for a year before he died. I left it to Sissons to explain all that. It was early in the year that I saw Mell for the last time, and it was not until Christmas that the book was published and young Roger read it. He was then living with me at Whitecotes, for, in all our lives, there had been great changes.

It was by Belinda's wish that Laura had given up the flat at Chelsea soon after Mell's death, and had gone to live with the young people at the Rowans. Well, comparatively young. Their days were busy. They were prospering, and they had little time to spare for her. The consequence was that she spent all the time she could with Roger. Nothing more disastrous could have happened to the boy. Laura had been a school-mistress, and she was a school-mistress still. It did not take her

long to discover that Roger had been allowed to grow up more
or less as he liked, his parents thoughts about him on nothing
much save that one of these days he would enter the family's
business. It had taken me one day's walk with him to find out
that this was far from his intentions, and that, indeed, his own
intentions had never been considered or inquired into. Laura
hitherto had known him only when he was on his best visiting
behaviour, and she was shocked now to discover that beneath this
lay some rebellious inclinations that she made it her business to
correct.

With no Mell to look after, no home to keep or typing to do,
she had plenty of time for her fell purpose. She nourished a
school-mistress's belief in the virtue of examinations, in taking
each hop at a given time. With our Rosy Midge, who had been
an awkward and insignificant child, and who had, when the right
moment called, seized it and become a person—with this under
her eyes, she nevertheless set to work in her old style on Roger.

My own visits to the Rowans were now few, but I remember
going over there when the summer holidays came on. I was
wandering in the gardens, which seemed very extensive to me,
remembering them as they had been in Poor Judith's day, and
in the distance I saw Roger and his grandmother walking together.
I, too, was his grandmother, but never in these days did I get
a chance of one of those long walks and talks with him that I once
enjoyed. James Napier joined me, and gesturing with his head
towards the distant figures, he grinned and said : " Well, Mrs.
Harris. As old R. L. S. used to say ' Bring up a child in the
way it should go.' I shouldn't be surprised if she's talking to
him now about something—well, cosmic."

That was a pretty important word for Jimmy, but I didn't
want to hear any of Jimmy's words just then. I was aware only
of those two distant figures. Laura knew a wife's duties to her
husband even when he was dead. She was one of the last women
I have come across who took " going into mourning " seriously.
She was still in a widow's black, a strange apparition to me who
had not " gone into black " for either Frank or Chris. Roger,
at her side, was wearing nothing but plimsolls and a pair of khaki
shorts, evidently anxious to be off on his own concerns, and having
the look of a wild young thing who has been corralled and is

being trained for his own good. I don't know what cosmic things Laura was talking about to him, if any, but I know that she was always aware of Mell, and of how his whole career had been a taking of one premeditated step after another, and of how only the malice of men, jealous of his brilliance, had prevented her from being an ambassador's lady. It was a comforting thought which could be divorced from Mell's own inefficiencies, as I saw them now.

Slowly, and without any obvious intention, I made my way towards them, and when I was some distance off Roger detached himself from Laura and came to me with an eager step. " Let's go and pick blackberries," he said. He put a brown and rather dirty paw in mine, and began to draw me away.

" But blackberries are not ready for picking in the beginning of the summer holidays," I said.

"Well, I know *that much*," he answered with an unmistakable look towards Laura. " I mean let's go for a walk somewhere and do anything."

The whole of Frank—the whole of Roger's grandfather—was upon me in a moment. " Let's go somewhere. Let's do anything." That was Frank all over in one of his slacker moods. It might land us in some foreign place ; it might end in a day's loafing on a neighbouring cliff ; but he would stuff a few things into a rucksack and off we would go. Somewhere. Anywhere.

Laura said : " I happened to meet one of the mistresses from Roger's school the other day. Naturally, we got to talking about Roger and the progress he is making. She tells me his French pronunciation is atrocious. We've been trying to correct that. We've been taking the flowers and hedges and anything we came across. Still—if Roger would prefer a walk——"

" I would," said Roger, rudely and emphatically.

He and I took our walk.

2

After that, it was an understood thing that, whenever I visited the Rowans, Roger and I walked together. I don't suppose I was there more than once a fortnight, so that Laura had plenty of time for his company. She and I had a talk about him, and I found her genuinely concerned with the way he was growing up and what she called his low scholastic standards. She had had a talk with Ray and Belinda, too, leaving them in no doubt that her wishes for the boy were different from theirs. They would have liked nothing better than that he should leave school at the earliest possible moment and devote himself to the gardens ; but in her mind was a vision of Roger following in Mell's footsteps and becoming all that Mell had somehow failed to become. That Mell had chosen his own path, and that Roger showed no inclination to follow it, did not, to her, enter into the matter. Busy as they were, with the growing scope of their work to occupy their attention, Ray and Belinda saw no reason why Laura should not gratify herself for the moment, confident that, when the time came, Roger would fall in with their plans.

I suppose a sub-conscious knowledge that he was a matter of contention must have made my visits something that the boy looked forward to. As a rule, I reached the Rowans in time to take lunch with all of them ; then Roger and I would get away for the afternoon, and after tea I would set off for Whitecotes again to eat my solitary dinner. The thought that he could talk about anything he liked, that he could go where he liked, was obviously precious to him. On most of these rambles he would begin : " Let's go to our secret place."

The secret place was nothing much. It was just a gap where you scrambled through a hedge, sat down on a cushion of ripening bracken, and had an immense unspoiled view of the countryside falling before you into the valley. But it was, for Roger, his own, a place that no one came to unless he were there to guide them, a place where, as likely as not, I would fall asleep in the sun. As I saw it, the virtue consisted in its being a secret place where no one could get at him to talk about things he didn't want to discuss.

When the summer holidays were drawing to a close we had been there as usual and I had brought Roger back to tea at the Rowans. I went straight upstairs, as I always did, to make myself presentable for the meal, and when I came down Ray, Belinda and Laura were seated at the table. As Ray got up to draw out a chair for me, he asked : " Where's Roger ? "

" He came back with me," I answered. " I expect he's gone to wash his hands. Let's begin. I'm rather in a hurry to-day."

We began our meal, but Roger did not appear. Ray went to the foot of the stairs and called him. There was no answer. He looked into this room and that; he shouted in the garden; but there was no Roger.

The party disintegrated. We looked here and there; but Roger did not call and was not in sight. Then we formed two search-parties. Laura and I went one way, Belinda and Ray another. We met at a given point, but neither party had seen anything of Roger.

"I can't understand it," Laura said. "We had a definite arrangement. We were to get down to some French irregular verbs after tea."

We looked at one another, and I think in that moment Laura and I came as near as we ever were to hating one another.

"Well," said Ray, addressing me, "you'd better be off. Another of his tricks, I suppose. He'll turn up in his own good time. We'll give you a ring at Whitecotes to-night."

There seemed, indeed, nothing else to be done. I got into my car and drove towards home, feeling as miserable as I had been in my life. I had no fears for Roger. He was somewhere about, and would, as Ray had said, turn up in his own good time. But what would happen then? It was this that set my nerves on edge, and I wished that Laura were not living at the Rowans.

While he was at it, Mapson, during his brief occupation of Whitecotes, had been rather stylishly at work and had built a garage that would hold three cars. The words "status symbol" were beginning to be bandied about, and I suppose a person with only one car was a pariah. However, the doors were open and I took my dusty two-seater, and it lay there like a very small child put to sleep in the great Bed of Ware. I was looking about at the rather hopeless mess the place was in, for the lawn-mower was housed there now, with spades and forks and all Doidge's odds-and-ends, when I heard a thumping on the door of my car's boot. Then there was a barely audible voice. "Let me out."

I knew at once that this was Roger and opened the door. He had coiled himself up like a bit of rope in the small space, and rolled out—dirty, brown as a berry, and wearing nothing but the sandals and khaki slacks which were all he had on when he accompanied me that afternoon to the secret place.

351

I was trembling with emotion, lit up by joy that it was with me that he had run away; but I felt that at all costs I must keep the moment easy, for I could see that he was both fearing a rebuke and half-deadened by his crazy adventure. " Dr. Livingstone, I presume ? " I said.

At that, he rolled into my arms and I could feel that he could hardly stand upright. Holding him up, I took him into the house, where Mrs. Oscott said accusingly : " You're late. Dinner's spoiled."

" In a moment," I said irritably. " Get me a cup of tea and some biscuits."

While she went off to do this, I half-carried, half-led Roger upstairs and put him into the visitor's bed, pulling off his sandals and leaving him unwashed and tousled. " You'll have a cup of tea in a moment," I assured him. " Then go to sleep." The rest could wait.

When I came back five minutes later he was already asleep. I left him, and sat down with little appetite to my dinner. I lingered over it, but at last faced the task before me. I rang up the Rowans. Fortunately it was Ray, not Laura, who spoke to me.

" Roger is quite safe," I said. " I found him hidden in my car. He was pretty exhausted, so I've put him to bed."

" Well, of all the young fools ! " said Ray, but I could sense the relief behind his tone. " What will you do with him ? Can you spare time to bring him back in the morning, or shall I come for him ? "

" To-morrow's Sunday," I hedged. " Why not let him stay here for the day ? "

" Well, Monday will be an awkward day for me. What about Laura ? She could come over any time. I'll ask her when she comes in. She's still out with Belinda looking for him. I'm standing by the telephone in case there's any news."

Everybody was indeed out. As I learned later there had been, as Roger would have said, a " regular schemozzle ". Mr. and Mrs. Napier were tramping the countryside ; Belinda and Laura were trying to pick up a trail ; Laura had informed the police. It was a proper hue and cry, and I felt a most unrighteous satisfaction that all the time Roger was asleep under my roof.

" Well, let's leave it that I'll bring him back in a day or so. After all, school doesn't begin again for another week, and he might as well finish the holiday with me. You can tell all the searchers that he's quite safe. And, at this moment, sound asleep."

" That's all right by me," Ray said. " And thanks for looking after him. But we'll have to see what Laura says about it all."

I hung up the telephone, thinking that Laura had already said and done too much. I wanted to be fair to Laura. I remembered that it was she who had inserted me into Madame Coignet's establishment, and thereby into many things that had followed.

The late summer evening, merging on autumn, had turned a little cold, and when, as fussy as a bird with a new chick, I had been up and had a look at Roger and pulled the bedclothes about him and found him sleeping like a log, I went down to my room, lit the fire, and thought of Laura.

She had been a long time in my life now, and she had never shown me anything but kindness. During the first war, when I had returned from Paris, she had taken me into her house, and though, out of the Government's meagre wage, I had somehow managed to pay for my keep, I had done little else but give her my company and help her now and then with her never-ending work of correcting French exercises.

Yes ; I tried very hard to be fair to Laura that night as I sat in silent session over my fire. But again and again, thinking of her camped now at the Rowans, the notion recurred that she had everything and I had nothing. She had lost a husband, but so had I. She had my son, she had my daughter-in-law, she had my grandson. I felt left out, and I was convinced that she was bad for Roger.

My fire burned out. I went up to bed, and gave a last look at Roger. He had just awakened and seized my hand as I tried the temperature of his forehead. " This is a good bed," he said, and wriggled like a sybarite deeper into the sheets. " How long shall I stay ? "

" As long as you like," I answered.

3

Mell's book, which we called *Turns Again Home*, was coming out in the late autumn. Peter Sissons had sent me a proof copy. I tore off the covers and the title-page, so that there would be no indication of authorship, and in the morning, making sure that Roger was still asleep, I left the remains casually on his counterpane. Then I had my bath and breakfast and carried up his breakfast on a tray. He was sitting in bed, without a shirt to his back, for he had come to me all but nude, and was reading.

" This is a good yarn," he said. " You can fair wallop through it from the word go."

It was all I wanted to know, and I said nothing more about it.

He put the book aside and laid into his breakfast. He seemed quite recovered from the exhaustion of the day before, and symptoms of repentance began to appear. I sat at his bedside and left the talking to him.

" I suppose," he said ruefully, " I'll have to go back. Running away is all very well. Going back is not such fun."

My mind went through the years to the far-off night in Cardiff when I had run away from the Lilywhites. The man who had written this book, which you could " fair wallop through from the word go ", had picked me up and set my feet on the path which they had erratically followed ever since. Running away was not so simple as I had thought. It's as well to have someone by to ask where you were running to. Who was going to do it now for Roger ? Would he have to go back ?

The telephone rang at that moment downstairs, and I hurried to answer. It was Laura. " You've taken such a weight off all our minds," she said. " I don't know what came over the boy. Ray talked some nonsense about your keeping him to-day and my coming over to see you to-morrow. But there's no need for that surely ? I'll come over to-day. Could you spare me a bit of lunch ? Then I could take him back with me. A thousand apologies for all the trouble you've been put to."

She sounded rather breathless, and I tried hard to keep calm. " He's an early bird," I lied. " He was up and about before I was myself, and he's gone off now to explore, as he calls it, all this new country. Goodness knows when we'll see him again. He's taken a few sandwiches with him for lunch. Fortunately it looks like being a fine day."

She was taken aback. "You haven't let him out of your sight again ? "

The thought of being always in someone's sight annoyed me. " Perhaps," I said, " he *wants* to be out of sight for a bit. Anyway, he's gone."

There was a pause ; then Laura said : "Well, may I look in about lunch-time ? He'll probably drift in some time during the afternoon. Then he'll be back here by bed-time."

" Well, let's leave it like that," I said, hung up the receiver, and hastened back to the bedroom, feeling like a gypsy who abducts orphans.

Roger had finished breakfast and was again laying into Mell's book.

" Would you like to stay in bed reading for a bit ? " I asked.

" I'd like it very much," he grinned, " so long as you don't come along later and ask me to parse the sentences. How can you read when you're thinking all the time of parsing the sentences ? "

It was a revealing question—revealing of much that had been happening in his young life—and I agreed that that was no way to read. "You want to wallop through a book first and then think about it afterwards," he said.

" Very well," I said. " Go on walloping, but stay here till I come for you."

I went down to the kitchen and told Mrs. Oscott that Laura would be coming to lunch. " But there'll be only the two of us," I said. " My grandson will be out all day."

" Well, that's a good thing," she said. " We've got nothing much in the 'ouse. It might go round one visitor, but not round two. Especially if I know anything about the way boys eat. Proper 'eathens they are for golloping food."

" You won't have any heathens to-day," I promised her, " so just try and knock up something for two."

I wandered out into the morning. Mrs. Oscott was convinced that I lived on scraps. Nothing would shake her on that, not even a sight of the household bills. But I knew that, despite her grumbling ways, she was fond of me enough, and that whatever she " knocked up " would go round two and leave something to spare.

They were a proper pair of old grumblers, Mrs. Oscott and Doidge, and now I had him to deal with. He lived all by himself in a cottage about a mile away, and I found him in his garden, which was incredibly neat, forking up potatoes. " Oh, it's you again, is it ? " he asked, not bothering to take the pipe out of his mouth, and looking at me as though I were the plague of his existence. " What's it now ? "

" D'you know anything about boys ? " I asked.

He leaned on his fork and gave the matter deep consideration. " Well," he said at last, as though revealing a secret I would find it hard to believe. " I suppose I was a boy myself once."

He thought over the matter as though himself surprised at the conclusion he had come to. " Not that I like boys," he said, examining the bowl of his pipe. " I expect I was a proper young devil."

The thought that old Doidge, standing there among his potatoes, had once been a proper young devil, was indeed a fairly deep one.

" Aye, that's what boys are—young devils every one. They all ought to be bundled orf like me. That's what I was—bundled orf."

Who did the bundling, and where the proper young devil had been bundled off to, did not appear, and I hoped it would not. We were already in sufficiently deep water.

" Well, there's a boy staying with me at the moment," I said.

" Aye, I know all about 'im. The one as arrived last night in your motor-car without a mortal stitch on 'is body. I 'eard all about 'im from Mrs. Oscott when I took 'er a few taters up to the 'ouse—before you was out of your bed, I bet. A proper young devil, 'e sounds like."

I explained that, young devil or not, the boy was my grandson and that he would be staying with me for some time. " Do you think," I asked, " that you could put up with him for a day ? I'll come over for him late this afternoon."

He considered the matter. Doidge had a way of considering

everything. He might at this moment, be a Prime Minister considering the destiny of a nation. " Well," he said at last, " there's them old dropping-boards."

I had never kept hens and I didn't rightly know what dropping-boards were. " Come an' 'ave a look at 'em," he invited.

He had rigged up a hen-run along one side of his garden wall, and now he led me towards it. He explained what dropping-boards were, and certainly they were in a deplorable state. " All them, for one thing," he said, " 'ave got to be cleaned, an' while he's doing that I can give a look to them ole bees."

" Well, so long as you keep him busy," I said.

" Oh, I'll keep 'im busy," he promised with relish. " There'll be no time for devilry while I'm about. You pack his rations an' bring 'im over."

I murmured my thanks and set off for home, glad that Doidge's cottage and garden were in a " secret place ", at the end of an inconsiderable lane.

I found the boy in a flutter of white pigeons on the lawn. They were on his head and on his shoulders and on his out-stretched hands that were full of biscuit crumbs. When he saw me, he threw what was left in a wide arc, and the greedy lovely birds flew from him and began scrambling on the grass. He came slowly towards me, looking sad. " Well, that's that," he said, brushing his hands together. "I suppose someone is coming for me to-day ? "

" To-day," I said, " you are going to see an old friend of mine, a gardener called Doidge. He's a queer old cuss and I expect he'll find you plenty to do. Would you like that ? "

" Are you coming with me ? " he asked suspiciously.

" I'm coming over with you, and you'll take your lunch with you. Then I'll come for you late this afternoon. I'll be very busy most of the day. I'm expecting visitors."

" Shall I stay with you to-night ? "

" I hope so. I expect so."

I got Mrs. Oscott to pack him a mighty lunch, and we at once set out. At the end of Doidge's lane I left him to himself. I dared not face Doidge again. " Just go and ask for Mr. Doidge," I said. " Say you are the boy Mrs. Harris talked about. I'll come for you this afternoon."

I watched him go with some apprehension. I wished I had a shirt to offer him. It would make him look less like a young devil. But I hadn't.

4

Laura arrived at about eleven o'clock. She was in a solemn mood, as of one who has an important task to do and is determined to do it well. She gave me a peck of a kiss and settled down to business straight away. " I'm surprised at you, Alice," she said. " To-day of all days you should have kept Roger at home. There's so much I wanted to talk to him about. He's scared his parents out of their wits."

I very much doubted it, and above all, I did not want this to be an indoors affair, sitting face to face, with a desk between, like delegates at a conference. I had carried a few deck-chairs on to the lawn where we could see the blue sky and the white pigeons. There was a coffee-pot on the table between us. " Have some coffee," I invited her.

" I couldn't drink a drop," she replied. " I hardly touched my breakfast. I was so anxious to come and see that the child was safe. And now I find him off again, as free as ever to be up to some mad trick."

" You are making a mistake about Roger," I said. " He isn't a child, and his coming away in my car wasn't a mad trick. It was a rather surprising one, but it wasn't mad. It was well thought out."

" Why on earth should he have wanted to do it ? "

" Why does anyone want to run away ? " I asked. " Don't forget that I'm a bit of an expert on running away. I was on the run when I first met Mell."

" I don't see," she said, " that that has anything to do with it. I've heard that story often enough from both you and Mell. You had good reason to run away because I suppose you were utterly miserable and hadn't a friend in the world. But here was Roger surrounded by everything that love and thoughtfulness could do."

" And yet he ran away."

" Yes. And yet he ran away. I don't understand it. It's not

as though he had severe parents. They are so busy building up their business that they have hardly any time for him. They're at it all day, and sometimes half the night, too. There was no one to give him any orders or put any regularity into his life until I took him in hand myself."

"Took him in hand" made me think of Dickens, and young Pip, and Joe Gargery's wife who brought Pip up "by hand". But I said nothing of that. Laura would have wondered what I was talking about.

I filled her cup, whether she wanted it or not, and took a sip at my own. "What are your schemes for him?" I asked.

"Well, to begin with, he'll have to pass the G.C.E."

How Bryan Graves would have loved those three letters! Anything that could be said in letters instead of words had an almost mystical significance for him.

"I've known plenty of children with the General Certificate of Education," I said, "who are as dull as ditch-water and as uneducated as anything between here and Timbuktu. What on earth do you mean by education? When is education going to fit in with children instead of children fitting in with education? Do you want to turn them all out like sausage-rolls in a baker's shop?"

"There must be standards," said Laura with dignity.

"But, bless my soul," I cried, "children don't all reach the same standards at the same time. What do you do with those who don't reach your precious G.C.E. at the precise moment when you think they should? Are they to be the new proletariat, emptying the dust-bins for all the privileged others?"

"I'm afraid," she said wearily, "we are getting a long way from Roger."

We got no nearer to him. I didn't want her to. I wanted to wear her out and send her away, and I did so after a long talk on the lawn among the pigeons and another over lunch. I saw her into the car and promised that the "long talk" would be with Ray and Belinda. But I was in no hurry for it, and even rang up Ray while Laura was on her homeward journey and got his consent to Roger's staying with me for a day or two. Then, feeling less as though I had abducted the child, I had a needed sleep before setting out to salve what was left when

359

Doidge had done with him. To my dismay, I found nothing but a square of cardboard hanging on the garden gate. In Roger's unmistakable writing, it informed anyone who cared to know that " Mr. Doidge will be back in half-an-hour." As no time was stated for Mr. Doidge's setting out, this wasn't very enlightening, so I sat down to wait, having first assured myself that the dropping-boards were in a state of cleanliness that would have delighted the heart of any member of the Egg Marketing Board. The hens needed only to be put in a battery to be perfect, all guaranteed to be holders of the G.C.E. of egg production.

They returned in an hour's time, looking pleased with one another and with themselves. " We been up in the woods," was all that Doidge had to say for himself, and then he went into the cottage, unlocking the door with a vast key which looked as though it gave entrance to nothing less than the treasures of the Bank of England, or of Christie's on a day that was to precede a sale of old masters at new prices.

Presently, he came out with a large brown tea-pot full of a lethal brew, and placed this on a garden table before us. " You get the cups, mate," he said ; and Roger, who evidently by this time knew the house inside out, went in and produced these, saucerless. There were also some biscuits, guaranteed to fall to dust when handled, and with these ingredients, and a Sunday newspaper of the more scandalous sort spread as a table-cloth, we sat down to it. I gazed at a girl, all legs and bosom, who would have driven a dress-maker out of work in a week, concealing her as well as I could beneath a hail of biscuit crumbs.

" So you've been off for a walk ? " I asked, sipping something that tasted as though it had come from an eruption of Vesuvius.

" Ay, an' if you'll take 'im 'ome, I'm now going to 'ave a smoke an' a bit of a read. I'll wash up later."

Old Doidge charged his pipe, twitched my girl from beneath my cup, and settled down, with an antiquated pair of spectacles on his nose, to the Sunday afternoon enjoyment of the masses.

Roger rose with me. " Thank you, Mr. Doidge," he said. " I'll come again some time."

Doidge waved him away. " Don't mention it, mate," he said. " Any time you like."

Roger was full of chat on the way home. Doidge had been giving him much information about India : for example, that widows were burnt on funeral pyres and that Thugs were rampant. " But all that," he said, " was a long time ago, and I had to put him right." Doidge had admitted that it was indeed a long time ago and that he had only been " trying it on ".

" But he *does* know about badgers," Roger said, with admiration.

They had been in the woods, and Doidge had pointed out where the badgers lived. " You come up 'ere with me," he said, " on a moonlight night, an' I'll show 'em to you. I know 'em every one, and they know me."

There had been much talk of badgers, and sitting on the edge of the woods, where Doidge, whistling a series of calls, had brought down various birds to feed on biscuits crumbs. " I think we could have some good times together," he said. As to foxes, he was not certain. " I likes 'em, mind you, but proper ole devils they are, an' I got to shut up my 'ens pretty safe to get the better of 'em. Now you'd never find a badger doin' that. Except now an' then an old rogue. But they're rare, they are. Give me a badger every time. You can trust 'em better than most Christians."

All in all, I gathered from the boy's chatter that he had had a better day than he would have had among French irregular verbs. Mrs. Oscott had cooked a good dinner for him, and he thanked her nicely. " You're a better cook than Mr. Doidge," he said.

" I should think I am," she said with some asperity. " But there's one thing I will say for the ole rascal. He do bring his vegetables clean to the kitchen."

" Well now," said Roger. " I'll help you with the washing up."

" Well, you couldn't be much worse than them old washing machines," said Mrs. Oscott ; and she permitted his sortie upon the scullery : " and not a plate chipped," she said to me afterwards with satisfaction, " an' every bit of grease scrubbed off."

I sent him to bed soon after that, and he went readily enough, worn out by the experiences of a most unusual day. Worn out ;

361

but, I was glad to think, very happy. " It was a good idea, diving into your old car," he said with a grin, tugging the clothes about him. And he was asleep in no time.

5

It was all very well to reflect sagely that Roger had had a better day than he would have had among French irregular verbs. But there *are* French irregular verbs and they had better be learned about. There were, after all, such things as discipline, application, and a decent foundation. The trouble with Roger was that he was getting nothing else. I remembered Ray's school, and how the head-master had been keen on otters, and how he had encouraged the boys in their " digs " if anything worth digging for were found in the neighbourhood. Roger was getting none of that. He was getting nothing but what was deemed good for him, but was, in fact, bad, calculated to turn out just another of those little official bureaucrats that I detested.

It was not till the next day that I learned about Mulligan. So far as I knew he didn't have a Christian name. He was just Mulligan. Roger told me about him as we were having breakfast. " And now," he said, " I can't even go about with Mulligan."

I let him chatter about Mulligan, who was a boy at his school and his particular friend. If anyone deserved Doidge's name of a " proper young devil ", it was Mulligan. He was a small blue-eyed Irish boy who had no father. I guessed that he was, like my own mother, illegitimate. There was a factory of sorts not far from the school, and Mulligan's mother worked in it. She did not get home by the time school ended, and Mulligan was at liberty to find his own amusements. Roger, who was fascinated by Mulligan's independence of speech and habits, sometimes accompanied him on those excursions, which could be as mildly harmless as raiding a turnip-field and slicing up the booty with a pen-knife. A feast under a hedge would follow, and Roger's late arrival home would have to be explained away. Laura had now got into the habit of driving in to meet him every day and transporting him to an orthodox meal.

From Roger's rather rambling story, I gathered that one of the teachers had warned Laura that Roger was seeing too much of Mulligan, and the consequence was that the only boy Roger had ever become friendly with was now absolutely taboo.

That might have been the end of the episode if Mulligan, returning to his home one afternoon, had not found his mother absent as usual. He roamed about the town and was allured by the lavish display on open stalls in a multiple store. He wandered among these, and found it the easiest thing in the world to slip cubes of dye, and carpenter's tools, and electric light bulbs, and goodness knows what, in the loose top of his trousers. He was leaving the store, congratulating himself like a tycoon on the ease with which riches could be secured, when he was tapped on the shoulder.

Mulligan was up at a children's court, and as this, so far as anyone knew, was his first offence, he was severely warned and his explanation accepted that he " never took nothing " that wouldn't be useful to his mother. Unfortunately, Laura learned of this escapade, the Riot Act was read, and any commerce with Mulligan was forbidden. It was small consolation to Laura that Roger had chosen me as a substitute for Mulligan, but that was how I saw it : for Mulligan and all the other boys and girls he ought to be associating with. As it was, there was no-one but hard-working parents and a grandmother with nothing to do.

I could not blame Laura. She was doing what she thought to be the right thing ; but I did blame a system by which children like Mulligan were left with no parental love and oversight. What I was concerned with now was the way all this had recoiled upon Roger, who had now recoiled upon me. He had read in the local newspaper, as Laura had done, what had happened to Mulligan, and his admiration for that blue-eyed child had not been lessened. There was, indeed, more than a hint that it had been fortified and increased.

" Not," he said, " that Granny Laura "—as he always called her—" need worry about me. Mulligan's gone now."

How he had picked up the ins and outs of the Mulligan affair I don't know ; but it was from him that I gathered the threads of that story. Mrs. Mulligan had a childless sister, married to a boiler-maker, and these two worthy folk, by some family arrangement, had removed the child from Mrs. Mulligan's hands.

So now there would be an aunt to greet him when he returned to school, and Mrs. Mulligan would be left undisturbed with the right to earn her own living and come home when she liked.

6

I took Roger to the Rowans the next morning and left him there, and then drove into London. Peter Sissons had asked me to lunch. Peter had not forgotten what he owed to me and Chris who had entrusted him with our first novel, or of what he still owed to Slim Jim. But Jim was now little more than one of his side-lines, a tale that had gone on and on, and which he could count on profitably each year for his Christmas list. But he had launched into many new directions, and it was concerning one of these that he now wished to talk with me. His office, in an old Georgian house, was no distance from the restaurant, and we walked back together. We were no sooner seated in his comfortable room than he said : " I'm looking for a good French editor and translator. I thought you might like the job."

There was a history in several volumes by a French writer, called " Les Anglais ". Peter had acquired the English rights of it, and wanted a translator. " I've heard that you once did a lot of translation from the French. What do you say to taking on the job ? "

" And who's going to write your Slim Jim books ? "

" Oh, you do that on your head," he said airily. " Don't tell me that that's more than a part-time occupation. Besides, I want an editor, a full-time editor, who will supervise the work of other people. I'm going in for a lot of stuff from the French. This history is just the beginning of it."

As usual, when he had a new idea, Peter was full of go and enthusiasm. He would do this, with me or without me. That was clear ; and it was also clear to me that this was a thing I didn't want. I thought of the long hours I had spent as a translator, and, no, I didn't want it.

It was then that the idea of Laura first came to me. I suppose my mind was still full of Roger whom I had dumped that very morning, in a mood far from buoyant, at the Rowans. If there was one thing more than another that delivered Roger into

Laura's hands it was that she had nothing to do. If I could remove that obstacle, my work was half done.

Shamelessly, I called Laura to Peter's notice now. I "plugged" her, as they say, for all I was worth. I spoke of her long residence in France, of her years as a French teacher, of her travels with Mell, of her abilities as his secretary.

" Sounds like an angel dropped straight from Heaven," Peter said drily. " Well, I don't say we won't give her a chance to try her wings with us. I suppose, if I write to her, I can mention your name ? "

" Do anything but that ! " I cried in alarm.

He looked at me quizzically. " Well, there are ways of getting round that, too," he said ; and I left it to him.

A week after this I received one of Peter's laconic letters. He never wasted words. " The day after to-morrow someone you know will be leaving my office at 12.30 sharp. I will see that this time is observed. It might interest you to be casually strolling by."

I was strolling by as casually as I knew how, and almost collided with Laura. " I've got a job," she said.

I had not seen her so animated since Mell's death. She had fallen beneath that blow in a way that distressed me who had never considered that anyone's death was the end of my own life. Now I put an arm through hers and felt her squeeze it. " After all this time ! " she said. " To have something to do ! "

" It's nearly lunch-time," I said. " Come and have lunch with me. You can tell me all about it."

We found a quiet table, and she poured out her story. " I don't know," she said, " how Mr. Sissons ever heard of me ! "

" Well, he's heard of you now. What does he want you to do?"

" There's the translation of this history to begin with. Of course, I can do that on my head."

I didn't want to discourage her, but I reminded her that a good translation was more than a word-for-word rendering from an original. But nothing could discourage Laura that day. She was to do the work, she said, at home, and she had no doubt that she could make a good job of it. And if she did, anything might follow. Mr. Sissons was going in for a lot of translation, and she might be appointed as editor-in-chief, with translators working under her.

I let her run on, pleased that here at last was something that would relieve her loneliness, something which, if it didn't do much else, would give her the feeling that she was wanted, that she had a job, that there was someone who relied on her.

7

Laura spent one day a week in Sissons's office. For the rest of the time she worked at home. She was now much too busy to bother with Roger. He had not been too well received by his parents when I returned him to the Rowans. He was given to understand that he had caused a good deal of anxiety and had more or less upset the whole neighbourhood. What stuck in his head was that the police had joined in the search. This gave him a sense of importance, and what was perhaps worse was that now he had a feeling of being under constant surveillance. Nothing pleased him more than getting out of sight for an hour or two, with a notion that at any moment some wandering bobbie would touch him on the shoulder. It would be very much like Stanley finding Livingstone.

It was not too difficult in these circumstances for me to raise the question of his coming to live with me at Whitecotes. Rather to my surprise, I now found an ally in Laura. I had come over for my week-end visit, and we had seen Roger safely into bed when six of us sat down to a late dinner. We had asked James Napier and Rosy Midge, James's wife, to join us, and it was Rosy who asked me : " Who's is this Doidge that Roger keeps on about ? "

" He's an old soldier who works in my garden," I said. " Roger took quite a fancy to him when he came over with me."

" Fancy ! I should say he did," Rosy exclaimed. " Whenever I meet him in the gardens he talks about nothing else. It's Mr. Doidge's badgers and Mr. Doidge's birds all the time."

" Sounds rather like our old head-master at school," Ray said. " He was mad on otters. Many a day I've spent with him, lying down by a stream in Devonshire watching the otters. I believe he knew them all one from another. Otters could do no wrong. Anybody who killed an otter because it was after the salmon was in his black books for ever. I believe he wrote what he called a monograph about them. Otter hunts were his abomination."

" And badger-digs are mine," said Napier. " Not that there's so much of it as there used to be. But there's too much. What with all these new houses and one thing and another there'll soon be no wild animal left in the country. We'll be too antiseptic for words."

" Well, it's all these new houses, with their new bits of garden, that bring you half your orders for plants," Rosy reminded him practically.

" Ay, that's all right so long as new houses come," Jimmy grumbled. " But soon we'll all be living in flats in what they call ' density areas ', and then there'll be nothing but house-plants and window boxes."

" I remember," I said, " when crowded places were called congested areas. They were called that in Bryan Graves's time, and the reformers were all for cleaning them up and giving people a bit of space to live in. Now a congested area is a density area, and the reformers are all for them."

" Ay," said Jimmy, " it reminds me of something that old R. L. S. once said. . . ."

I let them go on for a bit before I brought the conversation back to Doidge. I spoke to them about Doidge as enthusiastically as I had spoken to Peter Sissons about Laura. The old villain would himself have been surprised to hear what a paragon he was, and how he had enlightened Roger's short stay with me.

Rosy and her husband went as soon as the meal was done, and we four sat over our coffee for a long time. " I've been wondering," said Belinda, " who's going to take Roger in to school when the new term begins, and fetch him back when classes are over. It's hardly fair on you, Mother, now that you've got all this new work on hand."

Laura was glad to be seen as a worker, and no longer as someone who just mooched about the house looking for something to do.

" I'd go on doing it, and think it my duty to do it, if I could," she said. " But this job of mine *is* rather a drag, and I know that

Ray is off to his work as soon as he's finished breakfast. Before breakfast, too, often enough."

"And that leaves me," Belinda said with a smile. "Well, you can count me out. I haven't said a word yet even to Ray, but there are reasons why I'll soon be finding plenty to do here. I'm going to have another baby, and in the meantime I sha'n't feel like jogging about on the roads."

"Why jog? Aren't there such things as school buses?" I asked. "I thought it was a sin against society nowadays for a child to walk a mile?"

But my poor little bit of irony was ill-timed and lost. Ray and Laura were all over Belinda. One would have thought she had declared herself to be in the last stages of an awful and fatal disease, instead of in the first stages of a disease that had been going on, with more or less success, since Adam delved and Eve span. There was more concern over this embryo than over the living boy who was causing me so much anxiety. I left them to it and went to bed, with Laura declaring: "No. I'll do the washing-up. You must take care of yourself."

8

Laura had her own car now. Everybody had an "own car" now, even I, who hated the things and thought them little better than a mine laid under such civilisation as we had achieved. I saw her off to London the next morning and then got into my Morris ready to go back to Whitecotes. Ray had spared a moment to wish me good-bye, and Roger was mooning about, saying as plainly as he could that he wanted to come with me. Belinda called him into the house, and when he was gone Ray said: "The young beggar seems genuinely fond of you."

The note, almost of surprise, in his voice, did not please me, but I let that go and said: "Perhaps that's because I'm fond of him. Any time you find him too much of a handful you can bring him over to spend a day or two with me. It might," I added quickly, putting the car into gear, "be a good solution of the problem we were talking about last night if he made a really long stay with me—say till Belinda's got over this new baby."

I waved and was off before he could make any answer.

I suppose they talked it over when Laura returned from London that night. At any rate, Ray rang me up the next day and said : " Could you give me lunch on Sunday ? We've been having a bit of a pow-wow about what you suggested when you were over at the week-end."

" Yes. How many of you will be coming ? "

I hoped desperately that Roger would be of the party.

" Oh, just me," said Ray. " Till Sunday then. I must go now. A bit of trouble in the gardens."

He rang off, but now I didn't care. I felt sure that I had won, that Roger would be mine. I had left my work to answer the telephone, but I was too disturbed to go on with it. I went into my room, swept Slim Jim into a drawer, and went out to meditate. The lawn was newly cut. The smell of it rose all about me. Old Doidge was leaning on the handle of the lawn-mower, throwing crumbs to the white pigeons who were strutting round him. Seeing his employer at so unaccustomed a moment, the old villain trundled the machine into the garage where he kept it, emerged with a rake, and made some pretence of raking the gravel. " That'll soon be off your hands, Doidge," I said. " It's one of the jobs I've got in mind for my grandson."

" Is that young devil comin' again ? "

" Yes. For a long stay this time, I expect. I'm looking round for a few jobs to keep him occupied."

" We'll be able to go out some night and see my old badgers? "

" I shouldn't be surprised."

" It'll take the edge like off my loneliness."

It was a new thought to me—the thought that old Doidge might be lonely in his cottage at the end of the lane.

" It's what we want around here—a bit of young life," he said, spat on his hands, and went on with his raking.

It was on a Tuesday morning that Ray rang me up, and he would not be coming till Sunday. So sure was I, however, that he would bring what, to me, would be good news, that I began at once to prepare for Roger. What I should do about his schooling I did not know, but I was determined that he should not grind along on the conventional track, stopping where everybody else stopped, then going on to a new and pre-destined termination. All that would have to solve itself. After all, I kept on reminding myself, Roger was Frank's grandson, and Frank had gone about gaining his knowledge of the world by living in it.

I busied myself for days over Roger's room. A fanatical believer in privacy, which the boy had lacked, I set about preparing a bed-sitting room. His bed, his bookcase, a table to write on if he felt like writing, an easy-chair to read in : all was tucked into this little room which had a window looking upon the lawn and the dovecotes. He could choose his own books. We would spend a day in town, and come back loaded with books and all sorts of other things which would suggest themselves when we saw them. So that the bookshelves should not look too bleak, I stuffed in a few that had come down from Frank's own childhood. He could never part with a book, and these, unread and unlooked-at for years, had been on a shelf at Dros-y-Mor and had come to me with all the other books by Ballantyne and Michael Scott, Henty and Manville Fenn. *With Clive in India*, *Nick o' the Fens*—oh, no end to them, and they all went in.

Mrs. Oscott, who at times didn't know her place, stood at the door as I was giving the finishing touches to the room. " You expecting a baby or something ? " she asked with a grin.

Well, I was, in a way. And when she turned and went, I sat down in the easy-chair that was to be Roger's and suddenly felt very lonely. I wondered how much this was to be for him, how much for me ? Doidge had said : " It'll take the edge off my loneliness." He wasn't the only one.

I sat down in the easy chair I had provided for Roger and looked the truth in the face. I had provided it for myself. I had not so much wanted to help the boy as I had wanted the boy to help me. More than a hint of Frank had come to him through Ray : in his looks, in his determination to go where he wanted to go, to know whom he pleased. All these old books of Frank's childhood, spotted with mildew, the covers falling from the pages ! They had been among the things I first thought of. It was Frank I had had in mind, young or old.

The world was changing about me, as fast as it could change. Even Doidge had been asking for a motor-mower in place of the antiquated machine that he said made his back ache. And Mrs. Oscott thought that " telly " in her sitting-room would make the evenings not so long. Who was I to bring Roger up on Frank's old books and my own old notions ?

I had intended that afternoon to go in to town. I thought it possible that Bumpus's would have a book on the habits of badgers. But I didn't go after all. I took some old gardening papers on to the lawn and went through them with Doidge. From among the many best grass-cutters on the market he chose one that pleased him, and I went in and sent a letter ordering it.

9

Once or twice Ray had been up to his old school in Devonshire, just, as he said, " for old time's sake ". He had played for the " old boys " in the annual cricket match against the present youngsters, and, so affluent did he feel in these days, he had even made a contribution to a new laboratory. " We just used to make do with a few stinks," he explained when he called for lunch on the following Sunday. I had hoped Roger would be with him, but he wasn't. " They're having a fine new building," he explained. " Something in touch with modern trends."

I reminded him how Frank and I had taken him for his first term there, and how proud Frank had been of the new motor-car. It was then that he had met James Sanderson with whom he became so friendly.

" Yes," he said. " And there was another chap that you didn't hear so much about. He was a few years younger than me and Sandy and we didn't get to know him very well, but we liked him. And, of all things, he's become the head-master there now. I've seen him the last few times I've been up, and we get on all right."

I knew what was coming, and it came. " It seemed to me," he said, " that it would be a good place, after all, to send Roger to. I wrote a long letter to this man Hanger, and he can luckily fit him in if he's the right sort of boy. Roger and I are going down there in a day or two, and, if everything turns out satisfactorily, he'll start there when the new term begins."

" You might as well get used to being without him," I said, and I felt as though I were talking to myself rather than to Ray.

371

" Well, there'll be that. He's a ticklish little beggar to handle, but we've got used to having him about. We shall miss him, but, with this Mulligan affair and one thing and another, we feel that he wants a bit more oversight than we can give him. Especially now that Laura's got this job that takes so much of her time."

" Yes. I suppose Laura's job has made all the difference."

" Well, it did when we talked the matter over seriously. You see, he was getting nowhere. She pulled him up a good deal. But now this has suddenly landed on her plate. She's so dead serious about doing the thing well. It's made a new woman of her. I will say that. She used to moon about the house, but now she's lively as a cricket. What with her work for Mr. Sissons and now this new baby of Belinda's, she's at something or other all day long. And we really think taking Roger in hand as well would be asking too much."

" It looks as though this Mr. Hanger stepped on to the scene just in time."

" Yes. And we'll soon have to get someone to do all the book-work, I suppose. Certainly, Belinda won't be able to carry on with it much longer. One problem after another. You're lucky to be out of it. A snug little place and no problems at all."

I congratulated him on having settled the matter so satisfactorily. I sent my love and best wishes for his future to Roger, and I settled down to enjoy my snug little place with no problems at all.

Chapter XIX

Since leaving Dros-y-Mor, which now seemed a long time ago, I hadn't kept in touch with anybody in that part of England. I had sold the house, and that was that. I was always a one for clean breaks since the day when I had banged the front door in Cathedral Road. Cornwall and all that it had meant to me were matters of the past. I had no wish or intention to haunt the place, a returning ghost with no-one but ghosts to meet me. Suddenly, my life there irrupted about me.

It was in the autumn of that same year, and I had spent the morning saying good-bye to Slim Jim. I had had enough of him. He had been a good friend to me and Chris, to say nothing of Peter Sissons, and had feathered our nests for a long time. But that morning I had packed off my last manuscript to Peter, with a letter saying simply : " Nay, I have done. You get no more of me." There would be arguments and persuasions ; but I meant it. I had warned Peter that I was on the last of the books.

I motored to the nearest post office, posted my parcel, and ate a solitary lunch. Then I sat on a deck-chair on the edge of the lawn and watched Doidge cutting the grass in about twice the time it had taken him with his old handmower. He was for ever stopping, and kicking the starter, and muttering about " them ole plugs. Fair devils they be."

I let him have his grouse out, for I knew what was the matter with him. He had that morning found one of " his " badgers laid out flat and dead by a motor-car. It was the sound of a motor-car stopping at the front gate which took me gladly away from a sight of his rheumy old eyes which had been liable all day long to fill with tears, not only at the thought of his badger, but at the thought of all wild things disappearing as inevitably as bears and dinosaurs had done.

I didn't know the two people, a man and a woman, who were coming down the path. They were middle-aged, prosperous and well-dressed. They had stepped out of a Daimler, and, as I got near the gate, they advanced upon me with every sign that I would know them and be glad to see them.

Suddenly I knew why I had not recognised them. Em Pritt was plastered with paint and powder and Joe Duncombe had grown a luxuriant moustache. Em threw her arms round me and kissed me. Joe said : " Well, here we are ! "

I was overwhelmed with emotion, for here indeed I stood at the parting of the ways. I remembered Joe as a young man in a Truro garage on that far-off morning when Frank and I had taken Ray for the first time to his school in Devonshire, and

Frank had been shyly proud of his car. He had not yet learned to drive and Joe had driven us, and, when the boy had been delivered, had taken us right back to Dros-y-Mor. All seemed to have followed from that moment : the coming of the garages to Dros-y-Mor, the departure of Ben Davies who had loved his trees, the installing of Joe in his place, and Joe's marriage to Em Pritt.

Since I had sold Dros-y-Mor and left the region I had not kept in touch with them. I knew that Joe had bought a road-side service and filling station, that he had made it prosperous, and that he had been elected a member of the Cornwall County Council. They unfolded their tale as they sat with me over a cup of tea on the lawn. Joe still owned the garage, though an underling now ran it.

" I've blossomed out a bit," Joe said, and indeed he looked it. He was now the owner of a fleet of motor-buses that took profitable loads of people here and there about the county and about Devonshire and Somerset as well. " Ah," he said with satisfaction. " West Country Buses are something—no expense spared to make 'em the most up-to-date and comfortable things on the road."

He was, too, the founder and managing director of a firm called West Country Transport whose motor-lorries would carry anything from a pig to a piano anywhere at any time. All in all, he had, as they say, done well for himself and for Em, too, who was a good example of a middle-aged middle-class sort of woman. I remembered the time when Ben Davies had accused her of hanging about the garage whenever Joe Duncombe was there. Well, she had hung to some purpose, and had her reward. She had little to say and left it all to her lord and master who had enough to say for two, and had become, I thought, rather self-consciously a successful man of business. He was now, he said, an alderman.

It was with difficulty that I edged a word into Joe's saga of a life on the up-and-up ; but at last I asked : " And how is Dros-y-Mor getting on ? I've never had a word from the people I sold it to."

" Now, that's just why we called on you," Joe said. " The place is ours."

It was his trump card, and he played it with obvious satisfaction. I congratulated them both and hoped they would be as happy there as I had been myself.

"Ay, I think we shall," Joe said. "We've had it now all this year, and we haven't gone into it yet. There were inconveniences, but I managed to iron them all out, and now we've shifted in our own furniture. When this holiday is over we're going back there and I think we shall be comfortable enough."

"We've never been abroad," said Em, speaking for almost the first time.

"I thought it was time Em went abroad," Joe said. "I've plotted out a route that'll give her something to talk about when all them other people are talking about their foreign holidays. Everybody's at it now, and all them travel agencies are doing well. I might start one myself one of these days."

I thought of all the travel agency posters I had seen : never a car in sight—nothing but a solitary girl in a bikini lolling on golden sands. Perhaps an old salt or two mending nets. Sun all the time. A ruined tower here and there and a few donkeys driven by lovely if rather ragged girls.

"The point is this," Joe said. "I've come to London on Council business, but I needn't go into that. When it's settled, Em and I are on the wing. Now we had a talk about it in our hotel last night, and we looked you up in the telephone directory, and here we are. Because it just occurred to us that, while we're away, you might care to have a look at Dros-y-Mor. As I said, we've had all the furniture shifted in, and we've installed a good woman who'll look after you, Mrs. Trenance. Just a line from me to her when I get back to London to-night, and you'll be treated like a princess."

Alderman Duncombe leaned back in his chair, and lit a cigar, obviously confident that human generosity could go no further. I was deeply disturbed. I knew, if he didn't, that all I was asked to do was to go and have a look for myself at the pinnacle which he and Em Pritt had at last reached, and all that was in me said No to that. At the same time a sudden stirring of desire to see once more the tracks that I had trodden as a girl, the place where I had met Frank, the place where my son was born, where Chris had first come into my life : all this said Yes.

375

" It's very good of you, Alderman Duncombe," I said ; but he interrupted me. " Joe to you."

" It's very good of you, Joe, and of Em, too, to think of me. I shall be glad to see the place again. As it happens, I have time on my hands at the moment."

" Well, go down now while the autumn's coming on," Joe said. " We're taking a month's holiday for the first time in our lives. We've had to put up with a week now and then till now. I'll write to Mrs. Trenance when I get back to London to-night, and we'll be on our way abroad in a few days. And tell that chap not to kick his starter so much. The plugs want cleaning, that's all. I hate to see a motor misused. He looks as though he ought to be using a scythe."

They got up to go, and I walked as far as the gate with them. They climbed into the Daimler, and I wished them a happy holiday. " We'll have that all right," Joe said. " And I'll keep my eyes open on this tourist business while I'm about it. There's money in that, you know."

They moved off. The car was purring like a contented cat. Em was, too.

2

I took the 10.30 to Falmouth and arrived there in the late afternoon. I put up at a hotel and spent the evening dutifully seeing the sights : the fortress that Henry VIII had built on the headland at Pendennis, the place in the town where a sailor had first come ashore with news that Trafalgar was won and Nelson was dead ; the tall plinth of granite overlooking the sea which now was inscribed with the names of the dead in two wars. The surest way to get a monument seemed to be to have had something to do with war in one way or another. I could find no monument to Humphrey Davy, though he was born thereabouts in Cornwall, or to Trevithick, another Cornishman, who was left to die penniless at Dartford, or to Opie, or to Joseph Conrad who wandered these streets on the eve of the great adventure described in *Youth*. I went to bed disconsolate, fearing what I should find in the morning.

It was a lovely day, but it was a day of late autumn. I had

first come into Cornwall, a girl with a rucksack on her back, on a day of spring, rejoicing that the war to end wars was behind me, and before me I knew not and cared not what. There was not much before me now. I got into the 'bus that was to take me to Helford Passage, and we went with the quiet blue sea always on our left hand. The hedges were ripe with autumn berries and old man's beard and there was a great stillness in the air, with no birds singing. Those that were going were gone—the swallows and all the birds that follow the sun.

Where the road narrowed, we rustled downhill, almost touching the trees on either hand, lit with sepia and yellow and gold. And there the great river was at our feet, the river that now I must cross in a boat to come to the creek which, on the opposite shore, wandered through fields to Dros-y-Mor.

The tide was on the flow, and I had no difficulty in getting a boatman to put me across. I could have come by car, and, fetching through the country, have arrived at the place where the Dros-y-Mor garages stood at the entrance to the woods— that spot where, so long ago, I had sat down to rest and Ben Davies had found me and carried me into his cottage. But I had always thought that the best way to arrive at Dros-y-Mor was by the creek, with that last twist in it that brought the house suddenly and dramatically into view. There it would be, white and shining in the autumn light, with the quarterdeck before it, and all about it the hydrangeas still in bloom—blue and white and red and all you can imagine of these colours rioting one into another.

So that was the way I went, through the quiet fields, and as the rowlocks creaked and the water fell in sparkling drops from the oars, I found my heart besieged by memories. I thought of the quiet evening when a posh dinghy from a yacht in the river had pulled towards the quarter-deck, and how, a moment later, I had looked my last on Ronald Lilywhite, soaked to the skin and climbing back into his boat to go the way he had come. I thought of the quarter-deck spotted with coloured deck-chairs and young voices calling on the water as I placed the small Belinda on to Mell's back and of him swimming ashore with her crying excitedly " Do it again, Daddy ! " I thought of night after night when I sat there, doing nothing but hold Frank's hand, and he with little to say but letting his own power flow into me. And I thought of nights when Chris and I had sat there discussing the idiotic adventures of Slim Jim. There was plenty to think of as we moved slowly over the water with the autumn trees motionless, the wind asleep ; and most of all I was thinking how these things would always be there without benefit of any substantial house, or water, or fields, to call them back. I wondered, and not for the first time, whether I ought to have come, an ageing ghost, revisiting the glimpses of the moon.

I knew this old boatman who was sitting at my side, and he knew me, but he was a glum and silent sort who had not much to say for himself. At last, however, he broke upon my meditations. " You'll find the ole place changed a lot, my dear, since Alderman Duncombe started work on it. A go-ahead sort he be. None of this comin' by water for him. Never out of a car that chap. No waitin' for tides. He'll get there, day or night. Well, there it be. There be the ole 'ouse."

He had pulled round the last bend, and there it was—Dros-y-Mor. The place was on the telephone now, and I had rung up Mrs. Trenance from Falmouth the night before to say that I was coming by water. She was on the quarter-deck to meet me. Behind her, like scratches on the sky, was the aerial of a television set, and there was no such quarter-deck as I had known, no hydrangeas. The quarter-deck was paved in Delabole slate, and where the hydrangeas had grown was a new building of concrete blocks roofed with corrugated iron. The door of this building was painted a bright magenta, and so was every inch of the façade of dear Dros-y-Mor, that had been so white ; and all the wood-work, the window-frames and the door, was a bilious yellow.

Mrs. Trenance had gone into the house. " I've had a letter from Alderman Duncombe," she said, " and you're to make yourself quite at home. Any time you like I'll show you over the house and where your bedroom is." Then she had picked up my bags and gone. He was gone, too, the boatman, giving me a wave as he rounded the bend. I was left alone with Dros-y-Mor.

It was not a Dros-y-Mor that I had ever known. I sat with my back to it, looking at the water, lapping at full tide on the steps. The sound of the water was the only sound in the quiet of the autumn morning. I loved the sound, and the water, and

378

the trees growing along the bank. All else was inimical to me and I kept my back to it. It would not be inimical to Joe Duncombe and Em Pritt. It would be a sign of their emergence into the " higher income brackets ", a sign that they had done what they set out to do.

Mrs. Trenance was, as they say, kindness itself. She brought me out a cup of coffee and placed it on a table at my side. " Now have a good time while you're here," she said. " Alderman Duncombe said in his letter you're to go everywhere and see everything. He said you used to live here yourself. You'll be surprised at the improvements he's made."

I thanked her, and said I'd see the improvements in due time. For the moment, I'd just sit where I was. I felt rather tired.

" Well," she said, " there'll be a good lunch for you at one o'clock. I've managed to get a bit of veal. I'll have to go in now and make the stuffing."

She went, but was back in no time. " I forgot to tell you," she said. " Alderman Duncombe says if you want to get about a bit there's a car at your disposal. I've only got to ring up one of his men, and the car'll be here. No walking through the woods now. The car can come right up to the front door."

No walking through the woods now. I sat there when I had finished my coffee, and surging through my head was an old jingle I had learned in my time at Madame Coignet's. " Nous n'irons plus aux bois. Les lauriers sont coupés."

Well, we had begun the intrusion on the woods ourselves. I had been lying on a bank, and there Ben Davies had picked me up, and his wife had tended me ; and at that very spot the trees had come down, and our own garage had appeared, and Ben Davies and his wife went to look after the old lady over to Gweek. Whatever Alderman Duncombe had done, he had but continued our own efforts. But what had he done ? I got up to see, and the first thing I saw was that the path through the woods was gone. Now there was a hard road that led, as Mrs. Trenance had said, right up to the front door. And it was a wide road, wide enough for the most stylish car. So wide, indeed, that the stream was no longer there. It was confined in a culvert over which the road passed. No more was there a rippling sound to fall on the ear. All the primulas that Jane had planted along that sparkling edge, all the water buttercups and waving weeds, were battened down, and the seat was gone. The seat on which, after my illness, I had fallen asleep with Philippe Frémont's book in my hand, and, waking, had looked up to find Frank's tall grey figure before me. We had patched the old seat, we had renewed it, but always it had been there, somewhere to sit, to listen to the stream's music, to the bird-song, the conglomerate voice of the woods. The woods had never been much : just a planting of trees, some that we loved for the beauty of their flowers, some that lived in their own tall green right, thrashing in the winter winds and making a high canopy in summer. It was a fairly narrow strip that had stood between us on the path and the fields beyond them. But we called them the woods, because they seemed to shut us in, to hide what lay beyond, to give a secrecy to our rutty path, to enclose us in beauty and a green gloom.

I suppose it was the gloom that was not to Alderman Duncombe's taste. So he had thinned the woods by the simple means of cutting down and uprooting the tall trees and taking out a shrub here and there. Now you could look from the beautifully macadamed path right through them and see the fields beyond. The mystery of the place was gone. All that remained was a wide well-lighted way right up to the front door.

At the end of the path, where you came on the woods hard by what had once been Ben Davies's cottage, the way had been open. You just walked through a gap in the hedge and there you were. But there you were no longer. Alderman Duncombe was aware of what belonged to the entrance of a gentleman's domain. A stout brick pillar had been built on either side of the gap, and between these pillars was hung a gate, and upon one of the pillars was a board on which was painted : " Dros-y-Mor. Private."

I wandered back, I cannot say disheartened and disconsolate, but feeling a stranger, ungreeted by so much as a ghost. There was nothing to remind me that this place had once been mine : no singing water, no seat to loll upon, no tall trees, no pathway full of roots and ruts—nothing but a straight road from one place to another : from the gate that told me that this road was private, straight to the front door.

And so I was delivered to the front door like a parcel by the postman, and Mrs. Trenance was waiting to regale me with veal. "You can have the telly on while you eat, if you like," she said. "Alderman Duncombe always has it on while he eats." "Well, what do you say to a glass of stout ? " she asked. "Mrs. Duncombe always has a glass of stout."

But I declined both the telly and the glass of stout, and I pleased her by praising her veal and stuffing. She left me after looking anxiously at me for a while, as though I were not quite all that Joe Duncombe's letter had promised. I ate my veal and roast potatoes and cabbage and looked about me in a room to which I was a stranger. Books and books and books, I had thought when, as a girl rather shaky on her legs, I had first beheld it. Shelves stretching from floor to ceiling all about me, promising endless exploration. They were all gone, those shelves, with their friendly beckoning into the realms of gold. The walls had been papered, and were hung upon by pictures of triumphant ones at Monte Carlo rallies, and Isle of Man Tourist events, and even of motorboats speeding across the quiet—the once quiet—waters of the Lakes. The pictures seemed to drum in my ears—these pictures of the new bulwarks of Britain's supremacy abroad.

My eye wandered to the fireplace over which Jane's photograph had kept an eternal vigilance. It had been a rough and ready thing of bricks, where we lit our fire of logs on winter nights. It was gone, with so much else, to make room for an electric fire of up-to-date design. Em Pritt, sitting before it, must often have thought of the old days when all that charred ash had daily to be cleared away. Now the touch of a switch did all that was necessary.

"You'll find great changes, Mrs. Harris. Wander about the house and see anything you like. Them's Alderman Duncombe's orders. I'm going to wash up."

I went first to what had been my own office. The window had looked on the hydrangeas—a circle of them round an old well-head. They were gone, flowers and well-head alike. There was nothing to see now but this new building of concrete blocks, roofed with corrugated iron. A green wash had been spread upon the blocks. The roof was painted red. This little room which had been mine, which no one had entered without my permission, housed a large roll-top desk, with a chair before it. Nothing else. It was evidently Joe's office. More pictures of the great ones of the earth, in the moments of their high exaltation, adorned the walls. Goggled eyes, helmeted heads, motor bikes, motor-cars. One picture of an almighty crash, with a car over-turned, its wheels spinning in the air. And, among it all, a picture that was not of a car but of a launch in America. A space-ship of some sort, just setting off on its celestial business. Were we all, I wondered, so fed up with the mess we were making on earth that we must now leave it to stew in the juice we had created, while we tried our luck in messing up some other planet? I could allow myself a smile at the thought that Joe's travel agency, if and when he established it, would be among the first to advertise trips to the moon, made more desirable perhaps by pictures of female Selenites, in bikinis, lolling on a lunar beach, strumming at guitars. Or perhaps the future would not be so idyllic.

I wandered back along the short passage to what had been our dining-room and lounge. "You'll find great changes, Mrs. Harris." Yes, indeed. It had evidently been all wrong for me and Frank and Chris to clatter up those bare lovely stairs to bed. The stairway had been boxed. A stairway shouldn't rise straight out of a room that was lived in. So I opened the door at the bottom, pressed a switch for some light, and ascended stairs carpeted and mossy. Mrs. Trenance, hearing me, bobbed her head round the doorway to announce : " Your bedroom, if you want a sleep now, is the last one along the corridor, I've put in your things and made the bed."

It was the room that Poor Judith and Mamie James-Villiers had shared. It had, even in their day, been a poorish place, rather bleakly furnished, with one window that gave a view along the path through the woods. Well, now the path was gone, and there was this view of the new stylish road that " led up to the front door." But if the view was to me not what it had been, especially when the primulas were blooming, the room itself was something to write home about. Joe had evidently given Em a free hand, and she had let herself go. She had realised her dream of a film-star's bedroom, and God knows I was no film-star. I was ashamed to tread in my old shoes upon the magenta carpet.

I would not have disturbed the magnificent curtains and pelmets even to see a Rolls-Royce, which had come through the gates marked " Private ", proceeding in state over the impeccable road to the front door. I pushed off my shoes, lay down on the bed, and was soon asleep, more exhausted than I had been for many a day.

There was a postcard from Joe in the morning. " Just off. Shall call at Monte Carlo. Em very anxious to see it."

Well, I wasn't. For all I cared, Monte Carlo could be sunk to the bottom of the sea. But Joe's postcard made to-day better than yesterday had been. It brought me to my senses. After all, this was Em's and Joe's holiday, not mine, and this was Em's and Joe's house, not mine. The place I had existed in with Frank and Chris remained only in my memory. And so did the world. It was their turn now to make what they could of it—the world and the house. It would have been false in me to pretend that I did not think my house and my world to be better than any they would ever know, but now I found that I could look more calmly on the one and the other. For me, the rutty path and the singing stream, the broken-down seat and the sagging huts. For them, the well-made road that led straight to the front door, the stream battened down, the old mementoes put aside as so much cumbering rubbish. The sooner I was back in Whitecotes the better, but there were Em and Joe to think of, and I could not rush away in too much of a hurry. I owed it to them to stay awhile, to leave a letter of thanks, and I could be brazen enough to say in it many things I did not mean.

And here was Mrs. Trenance, putting her head round the door to promise me more of those " great changes " which she seemed to think would interest me so much. So I went with her into the kitchen. Everything in it, she assured me with ecstasy, had " come from London ". There was a cake-mixing machine, and a washing-up machine, and a drying-cupboard and much else, and at the touch of a few switches the whole place roared and vibrated like the boiler-room of a warship.

I expressed my false admiration for all of it, and I hope I was hearty enough, and that I made her feel that all great changes were great improvements. But I didn't believe it and I never would.

I went and sat on the quarter-deck. The tide was out and the creek was little more than an expansive mud-flat with a stream running through it. I noted how my own dear stream, having been hidden underland for so long, here leapt into freedom through a wide pipe that jutted over the creek. It made but a little runnel of water, awaiting the coming of the greater water which would embrace it and make it one with all the water of the world, rising and falling eternally. Box it in as you would, that was its destiny, and, sitting there in the mild autumn sunlight, it seemed to me that, whether boxed in with " great changes ", or running free among the ferns and the flowers, it was very much like the lives of us all, adding a spoonful at last to the sea's insatiable abundance.

I waited till the tide had turned, taking the waters of Dros-y-Mor into its mighty embrace, and it pleased me to think that this would go on happening when fields and woods were gone, when our roofs had reached the sky, and Alderman and Mrs. Duncombe had reached the moon. I wrapped the past about me like a cloak, and fell asleep.

Falmouth:
January 10, 1963
February 8, 1964